Sheila O'Flanagan is the author of many No. 1 best-selling novels, including *How Will I Know?*, *Anyone But Him* and *Too Good To Be True*, as well as the short story collections *Destinations* and *Connections*.

Sheila pursued a very successful career in banking, becoming Ireland's first woman Chief Dealer, before she decided to become a full-time writer. She has a weekly column in the *Irish Times*, and she also plays badminton at competition level.

Suddenly Single

Sheila O'Flanagan

headline
review

First published in Great Britain in 1999
by HEADLINE BOOK PUBLISHING

First published in paperback in 1999
by HEADLINE BOOK PUBLISHING

This edition published in paperback in 2006
by HEADLINE REVIEW
An imprint of HEADLINE BOOK PUBLISHING

A HEADLINE REVIEW paperback

37

ISBN 978-0-7472-6236-7

Typeset in Galliard by Palimpsest Book Production Limited,
Polmont, Stirlingshire
Printed and bound in Great Britain by
Clays Ltd, St Ives plc

Headline's policy is to use papers that are natural, renewable and
recyclable products and made from wood grown in
sustainable forests. The logging and manufacturing processes
are expected to conform to the environmental
regulations of the country of origin.

HEADLINE BOOK PUBLISHING
A division of Hodder Headline
338 Euston Road
London NW1 3BH

www.reviewbooks.co.uk
www.hodderheadline.com

To: Carole Blake for her support and friendship through thick, thicker and thickest. I could not have found a better agent.

Anne Williams – ever patient, always encouraging.

The Survivors' Group – especially Patricia – for everything!

Damien O'Gorman of BRC Shooting Club for his advice.

My family once again – every one of you.

Colm. As always.

Chapter 1

Alix Callaghan stood up and snagged her tights on the corner of her desk.

'Shit!' She examined the run which was progressing down the side of her leg. 'I just took these out of the packet this morning! Why does this always happen when I'm about to go to a meeting?'

'It's one of those laws of nature things,' Jenny Smith told her. 'Whenever a woman has something important to do, her tights let her down.'

Alix grinned and opened the desk drawer. 'And the other law is, be prepared,' she told Jenny as she rummaged through the drawer and fished out another pair. 'Especially if you work in Europa Bank and you know that the managing director calls meetings at every available opportunity. If he's looking for me, tell him I'll see him downstairs in five minutes.' She picked up her bag and the tights and opened the door of the dealing room. 'He probably *will* ring. You know how much he enjoys cracking the whip. Oops!' She nearly collided with Dave Bryant, the senior dealer, as he walked in carrying a brown paper bag with his lunch for the day – two filled baguettes, a slice of banoffi cake and a tin of Diet Coke.

'I'm off to the management meeting,' she told him. 'There's

1

no change in our positions. We're holding some dollars but not much and I think we should stay that way. I don't think I'll be too long, I can't imagine that our glorious leader has anything new to tell us.'

'OK,' said Dave. 'Are Marks and Spencer up for discussion?'

Alix stared at him. 'What are you talking about?'

'Why are you bringing tights along to the management meeting?'

She looked at the packet in her hand. 'These are my emergency pair,' she told him sternly. 'And they are *not* Marks and Spencer. They're a ridiculously expensive pair of Donna Karan which I bought in the duty free last time I came back from Paris.'

Dave laughed. 'I obviously don't know as much as I thought about women's lingerie.'

'Just as well,' said Alix. 'Otherwise I'd be worried about you.'

'Oh, I'm good on stockings,' Dave told her. 'I'm an expert on stockings – it's tights I can't stand. I'm against them on principle.'

'Stockings have their place,' Alix agreed. 'But not during office hours. Not for me, anyway.' She grinned at him. 'See you later.'

She was the last to arrive in the boardroom. She apologised for delaying them and sat down in her usual seat opposite Des Coyle, the managing director of Europa Bank Dublin.

'I thought we'd discuss profitability,' said Des. 'I know that Pat has a few things he'd like to bring up.'

Pat Enright, the bank's chief accountant, began his presentation. Alix half listened to him. Although she was obviously concerned about the bank's overall profitability, her priority was the profitability of the dealing room. She'd been Europa's head of treasury in Dublin for the past few years, and each year, she had exceeded her targets. She had a reputation for spotting trouble, for finding new ways of making money and for concluding deals that no one else managed to complete. While Pat talked about the profitability of the credit department (down because of a problem with a syndicated loan), Alix was planning a strategy for a customer to borrow yen and switch the proceeds into euros.

'And the dealing room?' Des broke into her thoughts. 'Another good month last month, Alix.'

'Yes,' she said. 'We did a couple of nice trades for Inico and Constant Images. We stayed long of US dollars and US bonds, both of which have performed well for us.'

'Excellent.' Des smiled at her. 'Keep up the good work.'

She nodded. Nobody ever made comments about the dealing room and what the team of four traders did. Nobody understood enough about it and, anyway, every one of the five men around the table was slightly in awe of Alix Callaghan and didn't want to ask her a question that might appear stupid. Alix had a habit of exposing someone's lack of knowledge – something that nobody at Europa Bank could afford to have happen to them. Least of all at a management meeting.

When the meeting was finally over, Alix ran back upstairs to the dealing room. Dave hurriedly closed the sports page of the *Irish Times* as she opened the door.

'How's it going?' she asked.

'Boring,' said Dave. 'We bought a few more dollars but the rate hasn't changed. It's a dull, dull day.'

'Never say that!' She slid into her seat. 'It's tempting fate. And we've had a good week this week so let's not mess things up.' She looked around. 'Where's Gavin?' Gavin Donnelly was the newest and youngest member of the dealing team.

'He's at lunch with Alfonso in Banco Andalucia,' Jenny told her. 'You know how much he loves lunching with the opposition.'

Alix laughed. 'He keeps trying to find out who's earning more than him. He's obsessed with status.'

'I know,' said Jenny. 'Who are you telling?'

'Oh, don't worry about him,' said Dave. 'It's just youth and exuberance.'

'I'll give him youth and exuberance,' said Alix. 'He knows perfectly well he should be back by now.'

⌇

Gavin arrived back from lunch at four o'clock. Alix looked pointedly at her watch when he walked in the door.

'I know it's Friday,' she said. 'And I know that it hasn't been a particularly busy day. But *you* know that you're meant to be back here by two thirty, Gavin. Where the hell were you?' She didn't really need to ask. It was obvious that Gavin and Alfonso had decided to go for a liquid lunch. Gavin's eyes were bleary.

'I was with Alfonso Moya. We were talking,' he said defensively. 'It's good to know what our opposition are doing. They gave the five-year sterling swap this week.'

'That's fascinating information,' said Alix dryly. 'In how much?'

Gavin burped gently. 'I didn't ask. It's not the sort of question you ask, Alix. You should know that.'

'You're so right,' she said sweetly. 'So they're making money in five-year sterling, are they?'

4

'Yes,' said Gavin.

'The same position that you lost six thousand on last week?'

Gavin stared at her. Jenny busied herself with the phones and Dave immersed himself in the paper again.

'Gavin, it's time for you to grow up,' said Alix. 'Don't believe everything that everyone tells you. Don't ever spend four hours at lunch without my permission again and do your trousers up properly. They're a dead giveaway on the alcoholic lunch.' She got up and walked out of the room.

Dave and Jenny tried to smother their grins.

'She's a bitch!' Gavin tugged at his flies. 'She thinks she's so fucking high and mighty. Well, she's not! There are plenty of people out there better than she is. I suppose she thinks she's smart and witty! Well, one day I'll pay her back.'

'You *were* rather late,' said Jenny mildly.

'Oh, I might have known you'd stick up for her,' said Gavin. 'Well, you won't get very far, Jenny Smith. She won't do another woman any favours, you know. She likes to be in control. But one day she won't be and I'll be right there laughing at her!'

Alix went downstairs to Dermot Cullen's office. She couldn't have stayed in the dealing room because she would have laughed out loud at the injured look on Gavin's face when she told him to do up his trousers. Gavin Donnelly had lots of potential, Alix thought, but he had to channel it properly. And four-hour lunches in the pub were not the best way.

She knocked on Dermot's door and walked in. He was the

head of settlements and a settlement problem earlier in the week had cost them money.

She sat down opposite him. 'Was it a simple mistake or is there something wrong with our system?' she asked.

'It was a mistake,' said Dermot. There was no point in bullshitting her. 'Noleen should have caught it. She's very apologetic.'

'It was an expensive mistake. Someone should have spotted it.' Her eyes glittered green.

Not a good sign, thought Dermot. It was common knowledge in the bank that Alix's eyes appeared grey when she was relaxed but green when she was angry or excited. He didn't want her to get really angry. Dealers were notoriously temperamental. And, thought Dermot, women dealers were worse than men.

'It'll be sorted,' he told her. 'It shouldn't happen again.'

'I hope not,' said Alix. 'It's hard enough making money without someone else pissing it away.'

'I appreciate that,' said Dermot. 'But you have to acknowledge the fact that Noleen is still relatively new at the job and things were very pressurised last week.'

Alix grimaced then smiled. 'You're right,' she said. 'But you know how it is, Dermot, we're all under pressure.'

'Who are you telling?' Dermot sighed. 'I need more staff. But the budget doesn't allow it.'

'I know.' Alix got up and walked to the door. 'How are things otherwise?'

'Oh, fine.'

'Good.' She smiled at him and her eyes were grey again. 'I'd better get back upstairs.'

'See you, Alix,' said Dermot. He sighed with relief when

she'd gone. It annoyed him whenever she interfered in the settlements area but she was right. They should have spotted the mistake.

'Any change?' asked Alix as she walked back into the dealing room.

'No.' Jenny shook her head. 'It's quiet. Wyn rang to remind you about baby-sitting for her. It's not for a while but she wanted to be sure it was in your diary. She said, "My sister forgets family duties if I don't remind her."' Jenny grinned as Alix made a face. 'And your friend Sophia phoned. She wanted to know if you were going to the forex seminar in London next month.'

'I've better things to do,' said Alix as she picked up the phone and hit the speed-dial button. 'The last one I went to was such a waste of time! I could have given the course myself.'

'This is Sophia Redmond,' said a voice. 'I'm not at my desk at the moment but if you'd like to leave your name and number I'll call you back as soon as I can.'

'Bloody voice-mail,' muttered Alix. 'Hi, Soph! It's me, returning your call. I'm not going to the London seminar but I might just go over to do some shopping. Talk to you soon.' She hung up and looked at her watch. 'I think I'll head off early,' she told Jenny. 'Give Paul a shock!'

'You haven't forgotten about Eimear's drinks, have you?' Dave looked at her in surprise.

'Oh, God!' Her hand flew to her mouth. 'I had forgotten. How could I? Especially since I've just been talking to Dermot Cullen.'

'A much more exciting weekend in prospect?' asked Dave wickedly.

'I wish!' Alix laughed.

7

'So you'll come to the pub?'

'Of course I will. I can't let our only decent settlements person leave without saying goodbye. If she'd been around on Tuesday there wouldn't have been a problem on the dollar account.'

Alix dialled her home phone number but there was no answer. Paul was obviously out but why, she thought crossly, doesn't he ever switch on the bloody answering machine? She tried his mobile, but that was switched off too. Oh well, tough, she muttered. Just because he couldn't be bothered to stay in touch. She knew Paul, though. He'd be pissed off with her for being late home.

⟨~

Eimear Flaherty, the girl who was leaving, was having her booze-up in O'Reilly's bar. The dealing-room staff arrived together and Eimear ordered a round of drinks.

'You look as though you've been here a while.' Dave grinned at Eimear who blinked at him.

'I can hardly stand up,' she confessed.

'A few drinks at lunchtime?' asked Alix unsympathetically.

'Afraid so.' Eimear's eyes were glazed. 'But fun.'

'You didn't bump into Gavin Donnelly, did you?'

'Gavin? No. Why?'

'He also had a liquid lunch,' Alix told her. 'Staggered back into the dealing room at four with his flies undone!'

Eimear laughed. 'Poor Gavin.'

'What do you mean, poor Gavin?' demanded Alix.

'I bet you chewed him up and spat him out,' said Eimear.

'No I didn't,' said Alix. 'I was very moderate.'

8

Eimear was still laughing when Jenny joined them.

'So, Flaherty, what are you going to do with your life?' asked Jenny.

'I am going to devote myself to my children,' replied Eimear. 'Although they'll never appreciate the sacrifice I'm making, giving up the glory that is working for Des Coyle and Europa Bank!'

The girls laughed.

'I think you're lucky,' said Jenny. 'It must be wonderful to chuck in your job.'

'I'm not sure.' Eimear took a mouthful from her bottle of Budweiser. 'It's such hard going rushing out and back and trying to be there at the right time and everything. And I know I'm wracked with guilt every time I kiss Tom goodbye at kindergarten. And even more wracked with guilt when I leave Cliona at the crèche. But I'm afraid my mind will go.'

'Go where?' asked Alix.

'Just go. That all I'll want to talk about is nappies and playschool and shit like that.'

'I'm sure they'll be the last things you want to talk about,' said Jenny.

'Maybe.' Eimear looked worried. 'But perhaps they'll be the only things I *can* talk about.'

'Oh, I don't know.' Alix laughed. 'You can chat about FedWire and Euroclear and Cedel to all the other parents.'

Eimear grinned at her. 'That'll wow them at the PTA meetings, I'm sure. I need to be able to chat about Barney and Postman Pat, not the best way to send a million dollars to the States.'

'You are so lucky, Eimear Flaherty.' Linda Crossan, one of the bank's accountants, waltzed over to them. 'Not having to get out of bed at the crack of dawn every morning. Not having to stay in the bank until all hours at night. I tell you, one day I'm going to chuck it in myself.'

'You'll have to have a nice doctor husband like Eimear has before you can afford it,' said Jenny sternly.

'I supported him through college,' said Eimear. 'It's the least he can do now.'

Alix was starving. There had been delicately cut sandwiches at the lunchtime meeting but she hadn't bothered to eat any. Now there was a guy standing in front of her with a tray of cocktail sausages and she speared three of them at once.

'Ow!' she cried. 'They're bloody hot.'

'They're meant to be.' Dave Bryant took four. 'I love them.'

'I'll have blisters on my tongue,' complained Alix.

'Might shut you up for a few minutes.'

'Very bloody funny.' Alix gulped some beer to cool her mouth.

'Any better?'

'A bit.'

'We had a good week this week,' said Dave.

'Not bad.' Alix blew on a sausage before biting into it. 'It's just as well. Pat was going on about overall profitability at lunchtime.'

'Not good?' asked Dave.

'Could be better,' said Alix.

'At least we're making money,' Dave told her.

'I know,' said Alix. 'That's what we're paid for.'

'What are you paid for?' asked Des Coyle, the managing director.

'Making you money,' replied Alix.

'Absolutely,' said Des. 'And you do it so well!'

She grinned at him and he ruffled her hair. He had to reach up to do it because Alix, in her low shoes, was still taller than he was.

'Cigarette?' Jenny's eyes were unfocused.

'No thanks,' said Alix automatically. 'I've given them up.'

'No, I meant d'you have a cigarette?'

'I told you, I've given them up.'

'Don't give me that guff,' said Jenny. 'I've seen the packet in your desk drawer.'

'They're only for emergencies,' said Alix. 'And I really and truly don't have them with me.'

Alix looked at her watch. Almost ten o'clock. She supposed she should leave. She'd tried to ring Paul at six to tell him that she'd be a bit late and to go ahead and have something to eat without her. But he still wasn't in and he still had his mobile switched off. So she didn't give a toss any more about Paul. Even though she knew he'd be annoyed at her for getting drunk. Paul didn't drink, which was one of the things about him that both appealed to her and appalled her. It was great having someone who could drive everywhere and on whom she could depend. It was awful having someone who looked disapprovingly at her when she wobbled her way up the stairs.

'Eimear!' She waved at the settlements clerk. 'I gotta go. Things to do, people to see, all that sort of stuff.'

'OK, Alix. I'll be in to see you all, I'm sure.'

'Have a great life,' said Alix. 'Don't miss us too much.'

'I won't.'

Alix walked unsteadily down the stairs. She'd drunk much more than she meant to and it was stupid because she actually

11

didn't like getting drunk. She enjoyed having a few drinks, but usually stopped at three or four bottles of beer. She'd had a lot more than that tonight.

The night air made her feel dizzy. She waved at a taxi and got in. Lucky to find one free, she thought, as she closed her eyes. Although it was late the city was crowded with people. All the tourists in T-shirts and shorts because the weather was exceptionally mild made Alix feel overdressed in her coffee-coloured business suit and brown court shoes. In her last job the dealers had worn jeans and casual tops. But not T-shirts. She wished it was the same in Europa Bank.

The taxi edged its way through traffic that was almost as busy as during the day. It was blocked solid at St Stephen's Green.

She leaned forward to the driver. 'You can let me out here. I'll walk the rest of the way.'

'If you like,' he said.

Baggot Street was quieter. She yawned as she walked past the Georgian houses and wondered, as she always did, what it must have been like when the owners had lived on the street and it had been residential. Wonderful to have all that space, she thought. The apartment on Percy Place – despite its duplex status and the fulsome praise of the estate agent who had sold it – was sadly lacking in space by comparison.

She walked up the steps and rummaged in her bag for her keys. She wished she didn't always carry a bag so jam-packed with stuff that it was impossible to find anything. She shook it a couple of times to make the keys rattle but she couldn't hear them.

'Oh, bugger,' she muttered and pressed the bell.

'Hello,' said Paul.

'Hi! Sorry I'm late,' she called. 'I can't find my keys.'

She heard the buzzer and the door to the block opened. She took off her shoes and walked along the corridor in her stockinged feet.

Paul had already opened the door to their apartment.

'Hello, Alexandra.'

'Mrs Hunter.' Alix blinked at the sight of Paul's mother. 'How are you?'

'I'm fine,' she said. 'And how are you?'

'I'm fine too,' said Alix. 'I didn't know you were calling around tonight.'

'Of course you did,' said Paul grimly. 'I told you about it on Wednesday. You said you'd nothing planned.'

'Well, I hadn't really.' Alix looked embarrassed. 'I'm very sorry. One of the girls left the office today and there was a bit of a booze-up for her. I tried to ring you earlier, Paul, but you were out and the machine was off.'

'I was collecting Mum,' he said.

'I realise that now,' Alix said contritely. 'I'm sorry.'

'It doesn't matter.' Mrs Hunter's smile didn't reach her eyes. 'I understand you had better things to do.'

'I didn't have better things to do,' said Alix. 'Honestly. If I'd remembered . . .' She didn't say anything else. Paul's eyes warned her to be quiet.

'Would you like a coffee?' he asked.

'Not unless you're having one.'

'We've just finished,' said Mrs Hunter. 'But I'm sure Paul won't mind making some more.'

'It's OK,' said Alix hastily. 'Don't worry about it, Paul.'

But he was already rinsing the percolator.

Alix was beginning to get a headache. Bloody hell, she thought. How could I have forgotten about the battleaxe?

Paul's mother didn't like her. Had never liked her although Alix wasn't sure why. Maybe it was because Paul was her only child – she'd disapproved of all his girlfriends. Maybe it was her job – Mrs Hunter had seen *Wall Street* and *Other People's Money* and strongly disapproved. Or maybe it was simply the fact that Alix and Paul had never quite got around to actually getting married despite having lived together for the past three years. Whatever the reason, the antipathy was, by now, mutual.

'Here you are.' Paul handed her a mug of barely filtered coffee.

'Thanks.'

'How was your day?' he asked.

'Busy. Yours?'

'Equally busy,' he said dryly.

Paul was a freelance journalist. She'd met him when he interviewed her for a piece entitled 'Career Girls – on the up and up'. It was, as she admitted to him later, lust at first sight. They'd moved in together a couple of weeks later and she still thought he was the sexiest man she'd ever known. Pity about his mother though.

She drained her mug and smiled at him. 'Thanks, Paul. I'll just head off to bed.'

'OK,' he said shortly.

'Goodnight, Mrs Hunter.'

'Goodnight, Alexandra.'

I really hate that woman, she thought as she opened the bedroom door. She knows my name is Alix. Plain and simple. Not short for anything. Just Alix.

She closed the door sharply behind her.

Chapter 2

It was three o'clock in the morning when she woke up. The bedroom was hot and stifling and her mouth was dry. She hadn't heard Paul come to bed, but he lay beside her, sleeping soundly, his arm flung across the duvet.

Alix slid gently out of the bed and padded down to the kitchen. She poured herself an orange juice and opened the balcony doors.

The night air was pleasantly warm. She stepped out onto the balcony and leaned over the rail. Beneath her, the water of the canal was dark and murky. She could never understand how people could swim there in the summer, but they often did. The canal had been another one of the estate agent's selling points. He'd waxed lyrical about sitting beside the water while the sun sparkled off the surface. He hadn't mentioned the water rats which she sometimes saw scurrying along the banks.

Alix sat on the wicker patio chair and sipped her orange juice.

She wished she'd remembered about Paul's mother. She knew that Paul was furious with her and she didn't blame him. She was furious with herself. She hated the idea that smug Mrs Hunter would go home to her empty house on the Stillorgan Road and sigh deeply over the fact that her beloved only son was living with someone like Alix Callaghan. Deirdre Hunter wanted someone better for Paul. Someone who would support him and look after him and look up to him.

Alix drained her glass. Well, she did support Paul. Not in the way his mother would have wanted, of course, not by being there every minute of the day and sympathising with him when he was stuck in the middle of a piece with no idea where it was going. Alix supported him by earning four times as much as he did. By walking into the office most days so that he could use the BMW if he wanted. By not hassling him when he was working. And she looked after him. She went shopping with him and made him buy decent clothes instead of chain-store jeans and sweatshirts. She didn't cook for him because she was a rotten cook and he was much better at it than she was. Besides which, he enjoyed cooking, whereas she'd be lost without Marks and Spencer and a microwave oven. So that didn't count. And she looked up to him. Despite what Mrs Hunter might think. She was in awe of his ability to make the most uninteresting subjects sound interesting or to find a new way of looking at an old subject.

Alix loved Paul. But she wished he had a different mother.

◡

'Alix?'

She opened her eyes at the sound of his voice and blinked a couple of times in the dawn light.

'Alix. Are you OK?'

'Yes. I – ouch!' She rubbed her neck which hurt badly. She couldn't believe that she'd fallen asleep on the patio, wearing nothing more than the silk top of her pyjamas.

16

'What on earth are you doing out here?' Paul looked at her in amazement.

'I woke up and I was hot. So I came out for a breath of fresh air.'

'Honestly, Alix!' He raised his eyebrow. 'Dressed like this?'

'It was darker when I came out,' she said. 'Anyway, nobody can see me up here.'

'I wouldn't be so sure of that. Any old busybody could be looking out.'

'At four in the morning?'

'You never know.' He stood at the balcony rail and peered across the canal.

'Paul, I'm sorry about being late.'

'I said it didn't matter,' he told her tightly.

'I know what you said. But you didn't mean it, did you?'

He was silent.

'I really do try to get on with your mother,' continued Alix. 'It's just that she doesn't like me. She doesn't understand me.'

'My mother is OK,' said Paul. 'Maybe she's old-fashioned.'

'I can't be the sort of person she wants me to be.' Alix got up from the chair and stood beside him. 'I can only be the sort of person I am.'

'And what sort of person is that?'

'Oh, I don't know.' She slid her hand under his T-shirt. 'Wicked, wanton, sexy?'

'Not now, Alix,' he said.

'Oh, fine!' She withdrew her hand. 'Fine. Your mother's thoughts about me are more important to you. Great. Be like that!'

'It's not that at all,' said Paul.

17

'Of course it bloody is! You dance attendance on the old bat as though she was the only woman in your life. It's time for you to grow up, Paul!'

'Really?' His voice was cold. 'I don't think I'm the one who needs to grow up. I'm not the one who drinks myself stupid and loses my house keys, am I?'

'I wasn't drunk,' protested Alix. 'And I didn't lose my keys. They were at the bottom of my bag.'

'You were pissed as a newt,' snapped Paul. 'And you can't find anything in that bag.'

'Why are we arguing?' she asked. 'This is silly.'

'Yes,' said Paul, 'it is.' He turned round and walked back into the apartment. Alix stayed where she was and clenched her fists.

~

He'd left a note to say he'd gone to Carlow to do an interview. Alix had gone back to bed and was still asleep when he left. It was nearly eleven by the time she woke and she couldn't be certain whether she'd really spent half the night on the balcony or whether it was part of a fuzzy dream. But she knew that the bit where she'd arrived home, fairly drunk, to find Paul's disapproving mother sitting in the apartment had been real. She groaned. That woman was a real pain. If there was one good reason for not marrying Paul, it was his damned mother!

To make up for her forgetfulness the previous evening, she booked a table at Dobbins for dinner. Paul liked Dobbins and they hadn't eaten out in ages. It would cheer him up, she thought. No man could resist being stuffed with food.

It was nearly eight by the time he arrived home.

18

'Hard day among the celebrities?' asked Alix brightly.

'Yes,' said Paul.

'I've booked Dobbins for half eight,' she told him. 'You'll just have time to hop under the shower.'

He stared at her. 'Why did you do that?'

'I thought you might like to go out. We haven't been out to dinner in such a long time. Save you having to cook or me having to pretend!'

'I don't want to go out,' said Paul.

Alix smiled at him. 'Of course you do. You're just tired and . . .' Her voice faltered as she looked at him. He was still angry, she realised. Far too angry to simply forget about it. 'Look, I'm really sorry about your mother,' she said. 'I've said it about a hundred times already and I mean it. I won't do it again. But there's no point in smouldering with anger about it, Paul. That doesn't help.'

'I know,' he said.

'Well, then.' She smiled at him. 'Let's forget about last night and go out to dinner.'

He pushed his fingers through his jet-black hair. 'No,' he said.

She shrugged. 'If you don't want to, that's fine. I'm sorry. I should have asked you first. I thought it was a good idea.' She turned away from him.

'Alix, it's not that.' He reached out and touched her shoulder. 'It's nothing to do with last night. Not really. Well,' he sighed, 'maybe it is, partly.'

She turned to him. His blue eyes were troubled. 'What's the matter?' she asked.

'We need to talk,' said Paul.

Alix was astonished. Paul wasn't one of life's talkers. Paul did

19

things or wrote about doing things. Alix had never sat down with Paul and had a meaning-of-life conversation. She wasn't sure she wanted to now.

'OK,' she said finally. 'What do you want to talk about?'

'Us,' said Paul and she nearly choked.

'What about us?'

'It's not really easy to say this,' said Paul. 'I've thought about it a lot, but saying it is something quite different.'

'Say what?' Alix didn't like the tone of his voice.

'I care about you a lot, Alix. I know you've been good to me. In the way that you know best – materially – but there's more to it than that.'

'I know there's more to it than that!' Alix stared at him. 'And I don't just look after you in a material way. That's a horrible thing to say.'

'I know. It came out all wrong. That's what I mean about this being difficult to say.'

'Look, Paul, are you trying to tell me it's over or something?'

'I . . .' He looked uncomfortable.

Alix couldn't think of anything to say. She loved Paul. She'd thought he loved her. She couldn't believe that he was just going to walk out on her.

'But why?' she asked.

'We've been together for three years,' said Paul. 'And we haven't really gone anywhere, have we?'

'Where did you plan on us going?' she asked tartly.

'You know what I mean.' His voice was harder. 'We're still living here. You're still doing the same thing. We're getting older but not behaving any differently.'

'How do you want to behave?' Alix was truly surprised. She couldn't understand what was troubling Paul.

'I want to get married and have a family,' he said. 'I want to change jobs. I want to settle down.'

'Settle down?' She looked at him in astonishment. 'You're the most settled person I know. You're not like the stereotypical journalist who spends his time in pubs. You work all day and you come home and write all night – how much more settled can you be?'

'I likc doing it,' said Paul. 'But it's not my whole life. Not the same way as the bank is yours. I'm not a career person, Alix. I enjoy the work and I enjoy writing but I don't have this great ambition to win Pulitzer prizes or be a media mogul. Which is what you'd be like if you were a journalist!'

Alix looked sheepish. He was probably right. 'So what do you want to do?' she asked.

'I've accepted a job offer from RTÉ,' said Paul. 'It's a salaried job – no more freelancing.'

'But that's great!' She smiled at him. 'Really great. Although you could've told me you'd applied.'

'I didn't want to. In case I didn't get it.'

'But you have.' She kissed him lightly on the cheek.

'Yes,' he said. 'And it's the start of a new way of life for me.'

'Is this where all the family thinking is coming from?'

'Maybe.'

'So what do you want?' she asked. 'For us to get married? For me to get pregnant? To leave work? We couldn't afford this place if I left work. Not unless they're paying you an absolute fortune in RTÉ!'

'It's your apartment, not mine,' said Paul. 'I have the house near Malahide. But you wouldn't live that far out of town.'

'It's not that I wouldn't,' said Alix. 'It just seemed silly when I already had this place.'

21

'You see,' said Paul. 'We always do things your way, Alix. You never think about what I want or what I'd like.'

'But it doesn't matter where you live!' she cried. 'It's just as easy for you to live here! Plus it's quicker for you to get into town.'

'This is silly,' said Paul. 'Arguing about who should live where.'

'If you want to get married and start a family then we should sit down and talk about it properly,' said Alix. 'Not have a silly row like two teenagers.'

'That's the whole point,' said Paul. 'Sometimes you act as though you were still twenty-two. Alix, you're thirty-two years old. I'm thirty-four. We can't go on living our lives like twentysomethings.'

She sighed. 'I don't live my life like a twentysomething.'

'Yes, you do,' said Paul. 'You do this crazy job that has you high as a kite most evenings. You enjoy going to the pub on a Friday night – Friday being the one evening I like to be at home – and you spend half your life trotting off to London or Paris for meetings. It's not the lifestyle of someone who's ready to settle down.'

'We *are* settled,' said Alix tightly. 'And I go to London and Paris on business. I don't spend the time out on the piss, you know. Of course I go for a drink on Fridays. But it's usually only one drink. And I didn't know that you missed me. You're usually locked away with the computer. Which I bought, by the way.'

'I knew it would come down to this at some stage,' said Paul. 'That you'd throw your superior earning power at me.'

'Don't be absolutely ridiculous,' snapped Alix. 'We have a joint account, for goodness' sake.'

'You don't put everything into it,' said Paul.

She stared at him. 'I'm going to forget you said that.'

'Yes, do.' He sighed. 'I'm sorry. I didn't mean it.'

She walked to the sofa and sat down. She hoped that by sitting she would diffuse some of the tension in the room. She couldn't understand Paul tonight. His sudden desire to 'settle down'. His totally unexpected need to have children. It was extraordinary.

'So how come you've decided all this?' she asked.

'I've been thinking about it for a long time,' said Paul.

'And you haven't said anything?'

'There never seemed to be a good time.'

'Paul.' Alix smiled at him. 'We've gone through the odd bumpy patch before. We can work this one out. Can't we?'

He was silent.

'We can work it out, Paul.' She watched him carefully.

'I don't think so,' he said finally.

'Why not?'

He looked uncomfortable and Alix felt a cold band suddenly wrap itself round her heart.

'Why not?'

'Because I'm not sure about us,' said Paul.

'Why?' asked Alix dangerously.

'I – might have met someone.'

'You might have met someone?'

'I've met someone and I like her a lot.'

Alix swallowed. 'And do you love her?'

'I don't know. How can I know?'

'So you've met someone and because of that you don't want to give us a chance, is that what you're saying?'

'No, it's not.' Paul glared at her. 'Don't twist things around,

23

Alix. I've met this person and she's the sort of person I'd like to spend more time with.'

'What's her name, this person?' asked Alix.

'Sabine.'

'Sabine?'

'Sabine Brassaert.'

'Sounds French to me.' Alix wrinkled her nose.

'She is French,' said Paul.

'Where did you meet her?'

Paul exhaled slowly. 'In Paris.'

'In Paris?' echoed Alix. 'When did you meet her in Paris?'

'When do you think?'

Alix stood up. 'You mean you met this Sabine person when we were on that trip to Europa Bank for the opening of their new office? You met her there?'

Paul looked uncomfortable. 'Yes.'

'I don't believe you.' Alix stared at him. 'I brought you on that trip. And you got a great lifestyle piece out of it too!'

'I know,' said Paul.

'And you met a French woman with whom you now want to set up a love nest and make babies.'

'Alix, it's not like that.'

'Well, what's it like?' she demanded.

'I met her. I talked to her. I got on with her. Being with her made me look at you and me in a different light. That's all.'

'Being with her,' repeated Alix. 'How long were you with her? Who was she? I don't remember her. Was she one of the dealers? One of the dealers' wives, maybe? It was Paris, after all.'

'Alix, stop it.' Paul's voice was harsh. 'She wasn't a dealer. She was a designer.'

'A designer!'

'Yes,' said Paul. 'The colour schemes, that sort of stuff. And she did the quotations.'

Alix remembered the quotations. They were painted on the walls of the dealing room and she couldn't make up her mind whether they were clever or simply pretentious. Certainly *De l'audace, encore de l'audace, et toujours de l'audace!* (boldness, and again boldness, and always boldness) was apt, although Alix wasn't sure that dealers needed much urging towards boldness. A bit more caution might be more appropriate, she thought.

'How on earth did you manage to chat up the designer?' she asked.

'I didn't chat her up,' said Paul. 'I went outside for a breath of air and she was there too. We got talking.'

'And on the strength of a fifteen-minute conversation with this Sabine person you've decided that our relationship is over and you want to marry her and have babies. Is that it?' Alix's eyes glittered. 'Or have I missed something along the way?'

'It wasn't just a fifteen-minute conversation,' said Paul.

'Well, what then?' Alix demanded. 'When else could you have spoken to . . .' Her voice trailed off. 'The next morning,' she said slowly. 'That's it, isn't it? When you allegedly went jogging. While I was in bed. You met her.'

Paul looked uncomfortable. 'Yes.'

'You bastard!' Alix could hardly speak but she managed to get the words out. 'You complete bastard! While I was asleep you were shagging Miss Parisienne.'

'Alix, don't be ridiculous,' said Paul. 'I certainly wasn't shagging her, as you so delicately put it. We met, we chatted, that's all.'

'And what happened? Did she say to you that she wanted

25

to have babies and suddenly that was it, you fell for her? Is that it?'

'No,' said Paul.

'Then what?' cried Alix. 'Because I can't believe this situation, Paul. Honestly I can't. Last night you're mad with me because I'm not home in time to meet your awful mother who absolutely hates me and tonight you're telling me that actually you want to leave me and marry a girl you've known for a few hours and have babies with her.'

'Alix, you're twisting it all around.'

'I don't think so.'

'Yes, you are,' said Paul. 'I don't know whether I want to marry Sabine or not. I hardly know her. But I do know that our relationship isn't working and I need to get my life together.'

'Oh, good for you,' snapped Alix.

'You don't want to get married and have babies, do you?' asked Paul. 'I mean, it's not exactly on the great Alix Callaghan five-year plan, is it?'

'I don't have a five-year plan,' said Alix.

'Don't you? What about your comments that very night to Guy whatsisname, the French treasury bloke? I want to be a director before I'm thirty-five? That doesn't exactly fit in with marriage and babies, does it?'

'Guy Decourcelle is thirty-six. He's married. He has two daughters. It hasn't been a problem for him,' said Alix grimly.

'Oh, come on, Alix. You know it's different for you.'

'Why?'

'Because you'd have to take time out to have kids. And you're not ready to take time out. You don't hear your biological clock ticking, but it is! And so is mine. I want to have kids now, when I can enjoy being with them and play with them and have a good time with them. I don't want them to be a carefully crafted part of my executive lifestyle, thank you very much.'

'Paul, I do want to have kids. Some time. Not exactly now, I'll admit. That's a choice I have to make. I thought that when the time came I'd be having them with you. I love you, Paul.' Suddenly Alix's eyes were full of tears which she did her best to hold back. Alix prided herself on not being the sort of woman who cried during an argument. She hated crying women.

'Maybe we will,' said Paul. 'Alix, don't you see? I just don't know any more. That's why I need some time to think about things. That's why I have to move out for a while.'

'And where are you going to move to?' she asked bitterly. 'Paris?'

'No.' Paul sighed. 'The lease on the Malahide house runs out next month. I'm going to move back there.'

'And in the meantime?'

'I'll stay with my mother.'

Alix stared at him. 'Was that why she was here last night? Were you both going to spring this on me then?'

Paul shook his head. 'No. I'd already asked her over, remember? But we talked about it – when you didn't come home and she started to ask me what I saw in you.'

'And you told her nothing much and that you were thinking of shacking up with some French tart instead.'

'Alix! Sabine is not a French tart. I'm not going to shack up with her. She was just the catalyst.'

'So have you seen her since the reception?' asked Alix. 'That was – how long? Two months ago?'

'I've spoken to her on the phone,' said Paul.

'And when is she coming to Dublin?' asked Alix.

'Not yet,' said Paul. 'We haven't decided. I haven't decided. It's not about you or Sabine, Alix. It's about the future.'

'It's a crock of shit,' said Alix and walked out of the room.

Chapter 3

S he hadn't expected him to be still there but he was. She'd stalked out of the apartment, got into the BMW and driven across the toll bridge and along the coast road to Dollymount. She parked the car and walked along the old wooden bridge of the Bull Wall until she was sitting beneath the huge and ugly statue of Our Lady Queen of the Seas. Alix liked it out here. It helped her to think.

She couldn't believe the scene that had just taken place. It was as though it had happened to someone else. She hadn't known about the job, hadn't known about Sabine, hadn't known that Paul suddenly wanted to join the ranks of people whose weekends were spent in Mothercare and DIY stores. It wasn't what they had planned when they moved in together. Then, it had been strawberries and cream in bed. Brunch in Café Java on Sunday mornings. Weekends in Cork or Galway, or London or Paris.

It had been wonderful then.

Alix wrinkled her nose as she thought of morning sickness, smelly nappies and sleepless nights. It was a phase he was going through, she decided. He'd change his mind quickly enough.

'I didn't want to walk out without saying goodbye,' he told her when she got back.

She looked at the suitcases and the plastic bags beside him. 'This is absolutely ridiculous,' she said. 'I can't believe you won't sit down and talk about it properly. I thought you loved me, Paul.'

'I thought I did too.' He looked puzzled. 'But now I don't know, Alix.'

She grimaced. 'Cuttingly honest. Journalistically honest, in fact.'

'I'm sorry.'

'Yes, well.' She had decided to be practical. So that he could see that she wasn't the sort of woman to crumple and cry and fawn over him. 'If that's the way it has to be. You're going back to Stillorgan then?'

'For a few weeks.'

'I'm sure your mother is delighted.'

He smiled faintly. 'Pleased, I guess.'

'She never liked me, did she?'

'No.' He smiled again.

'Have you ordered a taxi?'

'I was waiting until you got back.'

'I'll drive you,' said Alix.

'Really, Alix—'

'Come on. It won't take long.'

'But—'

'Oh, for God's sake, Paul. There's no point in arguing with me now, is there?'

He shrugged and lifted the cases. Alix grabbed the plastic bags.

They were silent during the ten-minute drive.

Alix pulled up outside the house. 'Give me a call sometime,' she said.

'Oh, Alix—'

'I'd better rush. There's a programme on Channel Four I want to see. About the UK and the euro. Starts in half an hour.'

His eyes caught hers and she hated the fact that there was sympathy in them.

'See you,' she said quickly and rammed the car into gear.

~

She was sitting on the balcony staring unseeingly over the canal when she remembered the photographs. The night that they'd gone to the reception in Paris for the opening of Europa's new headquarters had been one when numerous photographs were taken. She remembered posing with Paul as they'd entered the building. And more photos in the marble and glass foyer. And still more in the state-of-the art dealing room. The one where Sabine Brassaert's selection of quotations adorned the walls. She'd been given some of the photos and she'd shoved them into a folder somewhere.

She pulled a box from the wall unit and rummaged through it. Photographs spilled out onto the floor.

She bit her lip as she looked at them. They were mainly photos of herself and Paul the first time they'd gone to Paris together, a month after he'd moved into the apartment. She was standing outside a patisserie, looking wide-eyed at the cakes. And standing beside the Seine trying to look graceful but, in reality, looking big and healthy. And sitting in the gardens at Versailles, still looking big and healthy but surrounded by its manicured beauty. The kind of photos you take on your first romantic weekend in Paris.

31

Eventually she found the ones she was looking for. There was the photo of herself and Paul as they entered the building. There was a group photo of everyone in the dealing room, with herself standing beside Guy Decourcelle and smiling broadly. And there was a photograph of the crowded room.

Alix picked up the one of the crowded room and looked at it closely. In the top right-hand corner was a splash of red. Almost everyone had worn black that night. She'd worn black herself, a stunning silk dress by Jasper Conran. Everyone had remarked how lovely she'd looked in it. But the designer had worn red. She remembered someone pointing her out. So that must be her, fuzzy and out of focus, but in red all the same, with cropped blonde hair.

Alix could remember her more clearly now. Guy had introduced them and she'd smiled – smiled – at the bitch and told her that the quotations were great. *'De l'audace, encore de l'audace, et toujours de l'audace!'* she thought again.

Sabine had shown boldness, though. Alix sighed as she turned the photograph over. Sabine had been bold enough to whip Paul from under her nose and she hadn't even noticed it being done.

She stared at the photograph. Even out of focus Sabine Brassaert looked very pretty and terribly young. 'Bloody French women,' she said out loud. 'Bloody, bloody French women.'

❧

She was first into the dealing room on Monday morning. She called a trader in London and sold ten million dollars. Then she checked her appointments for the week. Although Alix liked trading more than she liked anything else, her diary was full of meetings with clients and prospective clients. Some weeks she was lucky and could spend the week at the desk. This wasn't one of those weeks. She was going to be out of the office for most of it.

'Good weekend?' asked Jenny as she hung her jacket over the back of her chair.

'OK,' replied Alix. She wasn't going to talk about Paul. She didn't talk about her personal life in the office very much anyway.

'You look tired.' Jenny switched on the terminals in front of her. 'Hard night last night?'

Alix had gone to bed early but hadn't slept much. She'd kept rolling into the space where Paul's body should have been.

'No,' she said. 'Jenny, will you get some background on the next G7 meeting for me?'

Jenny looked at her in surprise. 'What sort of background?'

'Background,' snapped her boss. 'Just background.'

⌐

'Alix, I need to buy twenty million dollars,' said Charlie Mulholland. 'For settlement next week. Against euros. And, Alix, I need a good rate.'

'You always need a good rate,' Alix laughed as she checked her screens. 'And don't I always get you one?'

'You usually beat the competition,' admitted Charlie. 'But that could just mean that the competition is lousy.'

'What a thing to say!' Alix pressed the mute button on her phone so that Charlie couldn't hear her next words. 'Gavin, get Don Jones, will you? I think they're long dollars, they might show us a good price. Jenny, will you get a price from Nikki Brown? She was a seller earlier this morning.'

'In the full amount?' asked Gavin.

'Yes,' said Alix. 'We're short ourselves or hadn't you noticed?' She wasn't making any money on the ten million she'd sold an hour earlier. The price hadn't moved at all.

'Alix, what's keeping you?' asked Charlie plaintively. 'You know I have to get two quotes. The other guy is showing me a price already. Where's yours?'

'Just a second, Charlie.' She clicked out of the line again. 'Come on, guys, what's happening?'

'Slow at making the price,' said Gavin.

'Nikki wasn't there,' said Jenny. 'Her sidekick's quoting me.'

'Oh, bloody hell.' Alix glanced at the screen. She clicked into the line again. 'Charlie? I can offer them to you at eighty.'

'Eighty!' Charlie sounded disgusted. 'I can get them better than that.'

'How much better?' asked Alix.

'Much,' said Charlie.

She looked at the screen again. Dougherty Brewing, the company for which Charlie worked, was a good client. Twenty million dollars was a big trade to lose. She thought about improving the price for a moment but rejected the idea. She was already short dollars, the market wasn't moving in her direction and she really couldn't afford to throw money down the drain.

'Sorry, Charlie,' she said firmly. 'Eighty's the best I can do.'

'Forget it,' he said.

She put the phone down. 'He got better away from us.'

'You could've stalled him,' said Gavin. 'I had two ticks better.'

'I don't think so,' said Alix. 'And I didn't like how long it took to get those prices. The market hasn't been doing anything. They should've been quicker.'

'Being short ourselves didn't help,' said Gavin.

'I know,' said Alix.

Gavin made a face. 'Why did you sell first thing?' he asked. 'You didn't want to stay short more than five million over the weekend. The rate has barely changed. Why bother?'

'I thought it was a good idea at the time,' said Alix tiredly.

Gavin looked at her in surprise. Normally, she'd have chewed him out for asking questions that made her look stupid.

Dave answered the phone. 'It's for you,' he said. 'It's Charlie Mulholland again.'

Alix clicked into the line. 'Hi, Charlie. Need to do some more?'

'No.' Charlie sounded annoyed. 'The other guy dropped me. When I went back he pulled the price.'

'Oh?' Alix raised her eyebrows. 'So you didn't deal?' Gavin and Jenny stopped talking about the missed trade and looked at her. 'What price had he shown you?'

'Eighty-five,' said Charlie.

'Charlie, I'd love to help but I'm not going to be able to show you anything better than eighty.' She gesticulated to Gavin and Jenny who both got on the phones again while Alix called up a dealing screen.

'If you can show me the twenty at that I'll do it.' Charlie sounded resigned.

The screen prices were changing but Alix was confident that she'd be able to buy the dollars she didn't have back at at least the same price as she was selling them to Charlie. And, if she was lucky and the price was right, she'd buy back the ones she'd sold earlier, as well as the five million they'd stayed short over the weekend. She'd lost her belief in this position.

'OK, Charlie. That's done.'

'Great. Thanks, Alix. Gotta rush.'

'No problem. Anytime.'

'I can get ten at eighty-one,' said Jenny.

Alix nodded at her as she cancelled Charlie's line. 'Take them.'

'Eighty is my best,' said Gavin. 'No, sorry, change – eighty-three for ten, Alix!' His voice rose, knowing that the price was moving in their direction.

'Do it,' said Alix. 'And ask for a price in another fifteen.'

'Where are you left?' Gavin nodded that the deal was done.

'Alix, Nikki Brown is on,' Jenny cut across the conversation. 'She has up to twenty to go at eighty-six!'

'Done in fifteen,' said Alix. 'Gavin, we're off that!'

'OK,' he said.

'Yes, thanks, Nikki.' Jenny tapped the trade into her computer. 'That's great. You too.' Jenny smiled. 'OK. We're all done.'

They sat back in their seats.

'Well done, everyone,' said Alix. 'Good work.'

Jenny and Gavin grinned.

'Just as well.' Dave Bryant, who'd been talking to a customer about the current situation in Australia, hung up the phone and pointed at the screen. 'Look where the price is now!'

Alix had sold dollars to Charlie at a rate of 1.2280. That meant for every million euros Charlie gave her, she gave him one million, two hundred and twenty-eight thousand dollars.

They'd bought the dollars in the market themselves at a higher price, which meant that they received more dollars per euro. But, as quickly as it had gone up, the price had gone down again. Right now, it was 1.2270.

'Timing is everything,' said Alix as she picked up the phone to answer the next call. 'Always remember that, Jenny. Timing is bloody everything.'

Alix's first meeting was at ten o'clock. It was with the financial controller of a large supermarket chain which had recently started doing business with Europa Bank. She didn't really need to go to the meeting – James Clark, their business development manager, had organised it – but she was going in case treasury business was discussed.

'Keep as flat as you can in the dollar,' she told Dave before she left. 'I was very bearish on it, now I'm not sure.'

'OK,' he said. 'Are you all right, Alix? You look tired.'

'Anyone would be tired in this madhouse,' she said. 'I'll see you later.'

'She looks awful,' said Gavin. 'I bet it's because of the dollar position. We were bloody lucky to get out of that! It's higher than where she sold it this morning. If Mulholland hadn't come in she probably wouldn't have covered them back and we'd be offside now and––'

'Give it a rest,' said Jenny. 'You never shut up, do you?'

'I'm just pointing out that––'

'Gavin!' Dave's tone was dangerous. 'Leave it, will you.'

'But you're right about her looking awful,' said Jenny after a couple of seconds. 'She was white as a sheet earlier.'

'She isn't pregnant, is she?' Gavin's eyes lit up. 'Maybe she's up the pole and she'll have to take three months off!'

'Gavin!'

'Well, she will if she's pregnant,' he said stubbornly.

⤳

William Taylor, the financial controller of the supermarket chain, had the most boring voice that Alix had ever heard. She couldn't concentrate on what he was saying and it wasn't very relevant to her anyway. She really didn't care about the shelf life of whole-wheat products.

She was thinking about the dollar/euro. It had been a mistake to sell this morning. One which she'd just managed to get out of, but a horrible mistake all the same. Given that the dollar hadn't weakened in New York on Friday, she should have reappraised things when she'd come in this morning. But no, she'd just barged in and sold them without thinking about it. And it could have been a disaster. Gavin had been right.

She rubbed the back of her neck. She had a headache. She was tired. She didn't want to be at this meeting. And she couldn't stop thinking about Paul.

It was ridiculous. The man had made it perfectly clear that he didn't see a future for them together. But she couldn't accept that. She couldn't simply let him walk away and into the arms of that blonde bimbo from France. She'd invested in him, for God's sake. She'd invested three years of her life and she'd told him that she loved him. He'd told her that he loved her. And now, because of some kind of male midlife crisis (he was too young to have a midlife crisis surely!), he'd decided that he was walking out.

Well, she wasn't going to give in. She'd been too shocked to think things through properly when he'd first told her. But what she needed to do now was to sort out her priorities, think about her life and work out how to get Paul back. Because that was what she was going to do. She wasn't going to let him waltz off into the sunset with this designer woman who, let's face it, was hardly going to start giving him babies straightaway. A woman who wore a red dress to a reception where everyone else was in black was hardly home-baking and baby material. It wasn't a settling down thing at all. That was just an excuse. It was probably sex.

She gritted her teeth at the thought of Paul having sex with Sabine. He'd denied it, but then he'd hardly admit it, would he? And Paul was good at sex. She bit her lip. Very good at sex. She remembered—

'What do you think, Alix?'

She flushed as she looked up at William Taylor. She'd heard that men thought about sex on average every six seconds. She wondered if it was true. She hauled her mind back from her first night with Paul and smiled at William. She'd been listening to the conversation in the background and it took a second for her to replay his question in her mind.

'It shouldn't be a problem,' she said, hoping she was answering the right one.

'Excellent.' He smiled broadly at her.

'OK, then, William. We'd better be off.' James stood up.

'Nice to see you,' said William. 'And you, Alix.' He leaned across the desk and shook her hand. He had a dead-fish handshake. She immediately allocated his account to Gavin.

'Went well,' said James as they got back into the car.

'Good,' said Alix.

'Are you OK?' he asked. 'You were unusually quiet, I thought.'

'Busy,' she said.

He glanced at her but she was looking out of the car window. He made a face and drove back to the office.

She had another meeting, this time with a dealer from Dresdner Bank, who called in to her office. They discussed limits for dealing with each other and looked through some outstanding trades. She couldn't keep her mind on the conversation. She kept seeing Paul and Sabine in bed together. She kept thinking about strawberries and cream. She thought she was going mad. When the dealer from Dresdner Bank left, she opened her desk drawer and rummaged around. Then she stepped out into the dealing room.

'Who took my cigarettes?' she asked sharply.

'No one.' Dave looked up from the article he was reading on the likelihood of a sharp fall in the Dow Jones Index.

'Someone must have. They were here last week.'

'I thought you'd given them up,' said Jenny. 'You told me you'd given them up!'

'I have,' snapped Alix. 'I just wanted to know where they were, that's all.'

'Why should you care?' asked Dave.

'Look, quit hassling me and just tell me where they are.'

'Honestly, Alix, I haven't seen them,' Jenny told her. 'I've got some chewing gum if you like.'

'No thanks.' Alix stalked towards the door. 'I'll be back in a few minutes.'

'Oh, Alix, don't give in!' Gavin joined the conversation. 'If you can't stay off them, who can?'

'Shut up, you little runt,' said Alix and walked out of the room.

The other dealers stared at each other.

'What the fuck's wrong with her?' Gavin asked.

Dave shrugged. 'Time of the month.'

'Oh, Dave!' Jenny made a face at him.

'Or else Gavin's right and she's pregnant.' Dave grinned at her.

'Either way it's hormonal,' said Gavin. 'And she needn't think she can talk to me like that.'

'Let's leave it.' Dave picked up the phone. 'We've other things to worry about. Come on, let's see how things are in the FRA market.'

Alix took the lift down to the ground floor and walked out of the Europa Bank building. She squinted in the bright light of the sun which reflected off the white flagstones outside the door. Then she walked the few yards to the small newsagent's.

'Hi, Marty, twenty of the usual, please.'

'Alix!' Marty Stephens, the manager of the shop, looked surprised. 'I thought you'd given them up.'

'I have,' she said. 'But I need one now.'

'That's not the way to go about it,' he told her. 'Look, why don't you have some chewing gum instead?'

Alix gritted her teeth. 'If I wanted chewing gum I'd have asked for chewing gum. I want a cigarette, Marty, and I want it now.'

'OK.' He sighed and reached for the packet. 'But it's a shame to go back. What's the matter, markets giving you a hard time?'

She shook her head, suddenly close to tears. 'No. Nothing like that.'

'You OK, Alix?'

'I'm fine.' She handed him the money and walked out of the shop. She wasn't going to burst into tears in a newsagent's store.

There was a no-smoking policy in the office building. Alix sat on the steps outside and inhaled deeply. She felt the soothing sensation of the smoke hit her and almost instantly relax her. She was annoyed at herself for giving in to the urge, but she couldn't help it. She'd almost lost it in the dealing room earlier. Both dealing with Charlie Mulholland – the deal had been OK but she'd handled it badly, she thought – and then later with Gavin. She felt uncomfortable, lacking in the authority she normally had. It was as though being without Paul had somehow lessened her belief in herself. And she couldn't understand why that should be the case because she'd had buckets of self-belief before she'd ever known him. So why should she feel vulnerable now?

'You should give them up, you know.' The man approaching the building grinned at her as she finished the cigarette and ground it out under her heel.

'I *have* given them up,' she told him.

'That was the last?' he asked. 'I've witnessed someone actually putting out their last cigarette?'

'Perhaps,' she said. She wasn't in the humour for this kind of chitchat and, although he was obviously a customer of the bank, she didn't feel like being nice.

'Don't you feel totally marginalised having to smoke outdoors?'

'I don't have to smoke at all. And it's a nice break from inside.'

'Why? Difficult day?'

'Look,' Alix smoothed her skirt, 'I'm really not in the mood for this kind of thing. I know that smoking might kill me. I know I'm totally anti-social. But I don't want to talk about it. OK?'

'OK,' he said.

'Fine.' She pushed open the glass door and walked back into the building.

He went to the reception desk. 'Matt Connery of Anatronics to see Alix Callaghan.' His voice carried across the foyer to where she waited for the lift to arrive.

She groaned. It was turning into another bad day.

Chapter 4

A lix walked back over to the reception desk.
    'I'm Alix Callaghan,' she said, extending her hand. 'I'm sorry, I didn't realise who you were.'

Matt Connery grinned at her. 'No problem. I'm a bit early. I'm afraid I caught you off guard.'

'Not at all,' said Alix briskly. 'Just taking some time out.'

'Busy day?' he asked sympathetically as he followed her to the lifts.

'As usual.' She pressed the button for the third floor.

She said nothing as the lift moved upwards. She was furious that a client had seen her sitting on the steps like some careless clerk with nothing better to do. She was also annoyed with herself for getting into a tit-for-tat spat with him. She was supposed to be a professional person and she knew that she hadn't acted in a professional way. But he'd arrived just as she was imagining Paul and Sabine's hurried meeting in Paris while she had been asleep in bed after the Europa Bank reception. She'd been visualising them running towards each other, holding each other, Sabine asking if he was sure it was OK to meet and Paul telling her yes, absolutely, Alix was safely sleeping in the luxury of the Georges V and there was no chance of her waking before noon.

She hadn't guessed, that was what hurt her the most. She hadn't thought that Paul had any doubts about their relationship. She knew that she was sometimes impatient and often self-centred about how she lived her life, but she'd honestly believed that Paul was happy about things. How could she have been so stupid?

The lift sighed to a stop.

'This way,' said Alix shortly. She led Matt past the dealing room and into the small meeting room on the corner of the building with its views over the Liffey and back towards the city.

'So what did you want to discuss?' She was brusque to the point of rudeness. Usually when she met a new client she was courteous and helpful. She'd try to find out a little about them, their likes and dislikes. She'd engage in some meaningless conversation just to get the measure of them. But she didn't feel like that right now.

Matt Connery opened his briefcase and took out a sheaf of documents which he passed across the table to her. 'This is some background on the company. This shows growth projections. These are our receivables – as you can see they're mainly in dollars but we have payments in a variety of other currencies, including the Far East. I want to streamline the way we look after things. I've also been talking to your credit guy, John Collins. We should have a facility in place soon.' He smiled at her. His eyes were blue but not the same deep blue as Paul's. Matt Connery's eyes were a lighter blue, a product of what seemed to Alix to be Scandinavian ancestry, because his hair was wheat-coloured and his skin was golden brown.

She skimmed through the papers. Anatronics was a computer

animation company and, if the figures were to be believed, it was growing very quickly. It could be an interesting account.

'OK,' she said. 'Here's the way I think you should play it.'

She talked for ten minutes, going through a range of products, becoming more and more confident as she spoke. She forgot about the less than fortunate meeting with him on the steps of the building. She forgot about the fact that she thought her heart was broken. She talked about spot rates and forward rates and futures and options while he listened carefully, stopping her once or twice for clarification.

'Thank you,' he said when she'd finished. 'Obviously we've thought about some of this already. I need to chat to my people back at the office and talk through these scenarios with them.'

'That's fine,' said Alix. 'If you need anything else or if you want me to come and give a presentation to your board, just give me a call.'

'I will.' He smiled and looked at his watch. 'If you're not busy would you like to join me for lunch?'

'Lunch?' She looked at him in surprise.

'It's after one,' he said. 'And I'm hungry!'

'Thank you, but I'm busy.'

'That's a shame.'

'I've been out of the office a lot this morning,' she said. 'I need to get back to the desk for a while.'

'I see.' He smiled at her. 'Some other time, perhaps?'

'Well, yes. Maybe. Let's see how you get on with your people. Perhaps we could all meet up, have lunch here.'

Matt sighed. 'Perhaps.'

She looked at him quizzically. 'Did you intend to see John Collins or anyone else while you were here?'

He shook his head. 'Only you. And I'm delighted to have met you at last.'

'At last?'

'Oh, I mentioned to a guy I met at a corporate treasurers' dinner that I was meeting you today. He was full of praise. Charlie Mulholland.'

She smiled. 'Charlie's a good customer.'

'He told me you were the nicest trader he ever dealt with.'

'Did he really!' She smiled, remembering Charlie's abruptness earlier in the day.

'Anyway, I'd better get going. Let you get on with the churning and burning or whatever it is you do.'

'Thank you,' she said. 'I'll see you out.'

∽

Gavin was shouting 'Done, done!' when she walked back into the dealing room.

'What's going on?' she asked Dave.

'I know you said to stay flat in dollars,' he said, 'but Gavin heard of a couple of buyers coming out of New York. So we picked up a few and we're just squaring the position now.'

She glanced at the price. The dollar had strengthened considerably since the morning. Thank God she'd covered back the ten million she'd sold earlier. Otherwise she'd be licking her wounds by now.

'How'd you do, Gavin?' asked Dave.

'Out at fifty.' Gavin grinned, pleased with himself.

'What did you make?' asked Alix.

'Ten grand,' replied Gavin.

'Well done,' she said.

47

'Thanks.' He grinned again. 'Took your advice, Alix. I didn't get too greedy. Though it'll probably strengthen a bit more. There's talk that Soros is buying.'

'Oh, really?'

If George Soros, one of the world's biggest investors, was buying dollars, then Gavin was probably right. But deep down Alix still thought that dollar rates would fall and so would the value of the currency. The Federal Reserve Bank in the US was having its monthly meeting on Thursday and an announcement about rates could be made afterwards. Alix thought they might cut because one of the members of the board, who'd always been against a fall in rates, had recently resigned. But Janis Kerrigan was only one member of the board and George Soros had much better contacts than Alix Callaghan! Soros was more likely to be right.

'You should go to meetings more often,' said Gavin. 'I do better when you're not here!'

'I'll bear that in mind,' said Alix dryly and picked up the phone.

∽

There was a different feeling in the apartment. When Paul had lived with her she never really felt lonely, even when he wasn't there. In fact she liked being alone. But this wasn't the same at all. This was knowing he wasn't coming back this evening. This was loneliness. She took a bottle of Miller out of the fridge and walked into the second bedroom, the one where Paul had done so much of his work.

It was almost frighteningly tidy. Paul was a neat and tidy person when he worked, there were never huge mounds of paper scattered around the place, but there had always been lots of it – newspapers neatly stacked by the desk, back copies of magazines in which he'd had articles published, reference books piled against the wall. He'd taken almost everything.

She gulped some of the beer and placed the bottle on the desk. Then she switched on the computer.

Although Paul had used it a lot, the computer was actually connected to her terminal at work. She couldn't execute trades from home, but she could monitor prices. The dollar was even stronger. Once again she breathed a sigh of relief that luck had been on her side today.

The phone rang and startled her so much that she knocked over the beer. She swore as it formed a golden puddle in the middle of the desk.

'Hello,' she said.

'Hi, Alix. It's me.'

'Paul.' They'd only been apart a couple of days and yet it seemed like forever. 'How are things?'

'Not bad,' he said. 'And you?'

'Fine.'

He cleared his throat. 'I rang because I left some stuff in the apartment.'

'Really?' She looked around. It didn't seem like there was much left to her.

'Yes. In the filing cabinet. Some papers and some disks. Remember that series on Georgian houses that I did? Also, the CD-ROM set. Sorry about this but I wondered, could I come and collect them sometime?'

'When did you have in mind?'

'Some afternoon.'

'I won't be here in the afternoon,' said Alix.

'I know.'

'How will you get in?'

'I have keys. I left mine there but I forgot about the ones we left with Mum. I'll leave them behind.'

'Why don't you come over now?' asked Alix.

'Can't,' said Paul.

'Why not?'

'Just can't.'

'Whenever,' said Alix. 'I don't care.'

'Alix?'

'What?'

'Look – I'm sorry.'

'Oh, sod off,' she said and hung up.

She got a cloth and wiped up the beer. He wouldn't call now because he was afraid of seeing her. Afraid that he'd suddenly realise that he'd treated her badly. And she knew that, even if he didn't think he loved her, he still did. They worked together. She knew it.

She went into the living room and curled up on the sofa. What would it be like to have children? she wondered. It wasn't something she'd thought about before now. Not since she'd been at school, anyway, and they'd played at being parents. Children were something that grown-up people had, that demanded time and attention. Children went with houses and gardens, not apartments along the canal. Children were other people. Messy people. Noisy people. People with their own agendas.

What would their children be like? Would they be dark and have navy-blue eyes like Paul's? Or would they look like her? She got up and stared at herself in the wall mirror. Grey-green eyes in an oval face. Dark brown hair with glints of red, pulled back, as she always wore it. Generous lips. Kissable lips, as Paul had once told her.

She leaned closer to the mirror and gasped. She couldn't believe it. She undid the tortoiseshell clip that held her hair and pushed her fingers through the strands. But she hadn't been mistaken.

Clumps of grey! Not just the occasional grey that had amused her in the past. Not the solitary silver thread running through dark tresses. These were real grey hairs and there were at least half a dozen. She pushed her hands through her hair again. There were more. Not clumped together now, more occasional, but still more.

She had grey hair. She was getting old. Paul was right. There must have been something wrong with her when she hadn't heard the ticking of her biological clock before now. The alarm bell was about to go off! You are a woman in your thirties, she told herself. You are getting too old to have your first child. You have grey hair!

Was this why Paul had left her? Had he noticed the grey and decided that she, Alix, was getting too old for him? Was that why he'd lusted after the Lolita-like Sabine? She shook her head. She was being paranoid now. Paul had the odd grey strand in his thick black hair. Although on men grey looked distinguished. On women it just looked old.

She pulled her hair back from her face again. You didn't really notice the grey unless you were actually looking for it. You'd have to be staring at her to be certain it was there.

She'd get it coloured as soon as she could, all the same.

Chapter 5

G avin yawned and leaned back in his chair. It was Thursday,
the day of the Fed meeting, but the markets were quiet.
There wouldn't be any news from the States until later and
nobody in Europe was trying to move bonds or currencies
dramatically one way or another. Alix was meeting a client for
lunch, Jenny had gone for a walk, and only Gavin and Dave
were in the dealing room.

'Peaceful,' said Gavin.

Dave glanced up from the copy of *The Phoenix* he was
reading. 'What?'

'Peaceful. Here. Without Alix ranting and raving and without
Jenny backing her up.'

Dave closed the magazine. 'You really hate her, don't you?'

'No,' said Gavin. 'But she's such a fucking prima donna. And
I hate it when she starts snapping.'

Dave laughed. 'Snapping?'

'Reminds me of one of the teachers in school,' said Gavin.
'Always nagging, nothing ever done right.'

'You're being a bit unfair,' Dave said. 'She actually gets a
lot right.'

'Not this week.' Gavin tapped on the computer keyboard

and called up the profit and loss account. 'She's done some shitty trades this week.'

'It hasn't been one of her best,' admitted Dave. 'Although Monday was OK.'

'That was me,' retorted Gavin. 'My call on the Soros buying. We made money on my trade and then she called a couple of clients and we made money on the back of their trades. But it was me that set the whole thing going. Left to her, we'd still be short dollars with our arses hanging out the window!'

Dave laughed. 'So what do you want me to say? Well done, Gavin?'

'No,' said Gavin. 'I just think you should back me up a bit more. I can't understand how you can side with that woman when she's probably taking home twice as much money as you although you're easily as good as her. You're so passive about it!'

'She'll burn herself out,' said Dave. 'I know I'm not a knife-in-the-back type of operator – not like you'll be! But she's getting on a bit now and I'll bet you anything you like she'll get married to her boyfriend and start producing babies by next year.'

'You think?'

'Absolutely. I met Paul a couple of months ago. He was muttering about settling down and families and all that sort of stuff. So she might be throwing her weight around a bit now but it'll be a different story in a few months.'

'Make me a price,' said Gavin.

Dave grinned. 'In what?'

'Weeks before she gets engaged.'

Dave considered for a moment. 'Ten/fifteen. A fiver a week.'

'You're reading me,' Gavin complained. 'And you could drive a bus through that price.'

'It's not an easy market to read.'

'I thought you were convinced.'

'I know what I think.' Dave grinned at him. 'What do you think?'

'Oh, all right, you're done at fifteen,' said Gavin. 'If she gets engaged before fifteen weeks are up, you win. After, I collect.'

'Done. But you'll be paying me, Gavin.'

'It's worth it,' he said. 'If some bloke takes her off our hands before fifteen weeks are up, I'll pay gladly.'

Dave laughed. 'She might get engaged. But she won't leave.'

'If she gets engaged she'll get married soon afterwards. Why wait? And if she gets married then it's lots and lots of lovely snotty-nosed kids! I can almost believe it myself.'

'Believe what?' Jenny walked into the room and draped her jacket over her chair.

'Nothing,' said Gavin.

'Nothing,' said Dave.

Jenny looked from one to the other. 'It's a man thing, is it?'

The two guys laughed.

'Hopefully,' said Gavin. 'Hopefully.'

⤙

It was nearly three o'clock by the time Alix got back. She went directly to her small office in the corner of the room and took some paracetamol from a packet in the desk. She had a raging headache. Lunch had taken longer than she'd expected and

Fergus Reilly, the client she'd met, had insisted on ordering a second bottle of wine and telling her not to worry, he was picking up the tab. Fergus was a good client and normally she enjoyed a boozy lunch with him. But she hadn't been in the humour today, she'd found it difficult to laugh at the off-colour jokes he told, which normally amused her, and she couldn't help wondering why she was there in the first place.

If I was married with children, she'd thought as the wine waiter topped her glass with Pinot Noir, I'd be sitting in the garden playing with them right now. I'd be laughing and having real fun instead of pretending to laugh at jokes that aren't even halfway funny.

Are you mad? she asked herself as she thought about it again. She sat up straight and flexed her hands behind her head. You'd hate to be sitting in the garden with a brace of children.

'Line four, Alix!' Dave's voice carried through. 'It's Christie Reardon.'

'I'll take it out there,' she replied.

Christie, a treasurer in a manufacturing company, wanted to talk about interest rates. While Alix chatted to her she massaged the back of her neck and wished she'd kept off the red wine.

'What do you want to do about this evening?' asked Dave when she finally hung up.

'What do you mean?'

'Our positions. We're flat on the currency book but we're holding some treasuries. Do you want to leave it like that?'

Alix rubbed the bridge of her nose. She still had a sneaking feeling about rates. And the dollar. But she wasn't as convinced as she'd been before she'd heard about Soros.

'What do you think?' she asked.

Dave leaned back in his chair. 'Stay flat currencies. Lose the treasuries. It doesn't look like the Fed'll do anything, despite Kerrigan. I know you think they'll cut but they might not want to do it straightaway.'

Alix sighed. 'Whatever you think, Dave. I'm heading off now anyway.'

'Now?' Dave glanced at his watch. It was only four o'clock. Alix rarely left the office before five.

'Yes, now. I have a headache.'

Jenny looked at Alix in surprise. A headache had never sent Alix home before.

'Gavin, even if you have some good information from your US friends, stick to whatever Dave says, will you?' Alix pulled on her Mondi jacket and picked up her bag. 'Don't go trying to be a hero. OK?'

'OK,' said Gavin. 'But someone might have—'

'Gavin!' warned Alix.

He sighed.

'See you guys tomorrow,' said Alix and walked out of the room.

The three remaining dealers stared at each other.

'I'm telling you,' said Gavin, 'she's up the pole.'

'Gavin!' Jenny looked angrily at him.

'She must be,' he said, unabashed.

'I doubt it very much,' said Jenny dryly. 'Alix wouldn't drink or swallow paracetamol if she was pregnant. You know her, everything by the book.'

Gavin looked disappointed. 'You might be right. But there's something wrong and that spells opportunity for all of us.'

'You make me sick,' said Jenny. 'You're like a vulture. And you,' she turned to Dave, 'you're not much better.'

'I haven't said a word.' Dave looked at her innocently.

'You don't need to,' she snapped.

~

Paul's compact discs were still on the table where she'd left them. Alix was pretty sure he'd arrive today – his Thursday schedule was usually light. She hadn't set out with the intention of being in the apartment when he arrived, but she'd suddenly thought about it as she was talking to Christie Reardon. And from that moment she'd wanted to be back in the apartment, to see him.

She rubbed her eyes. She was tired. She hadn't slept properly since he'd left and she was annoyed with herself for caring so much.

Her feelings about Paul fluctuated wildly from one moment to the next. Sometimes she thought that it was a good thing he was gone – he could be demanding, fussy, disapproving and make her feel like an irresponsible adolescent. Other times she missed him so much it physically hurt her. But she needed to see him. If she saw him face to face she might be able to decide how she really felt.

It was almost five o'clock when she heard the key in the door. Her heart beat faster and she could feel adrenaline coursing through her body. He walked into the living room and looked at her in surprise.

'What are you doing here at this hour?'

'Headache,' she said. 'I had lunch with a client, drank too much wine, couldn't concentrate.' Almost immediately she wished she hadn't mentioned the wine. He disapproved strongly of her drinking at lunchtime.

'I've never known you to come home before,' said Paul.

'The screens were making it worse,' she told him. 'And I need to be OK for tomorrow. There's the bank reception tomorrow night.'

'Oh, yes.' Paul made a face. 'I'd forgotten about that.'

'Why should you remember?' asked Alix. 'You're not going now, are you?'

'Are you serious?' asked Paul.

'No,' she said. 'Despite the fact that your name is on the guest list.'

The reception, to be held in the bank the following night, was to celebrate its ten years in Dublin. All bank employees and their partners, together with a select client list, were to attend.

'Haven't you told them I won't be there?' asked Paul.

She shrugged. 'It doesn't make any difference. It's a buffet and I expect half the people who said they'll turn up probably won't. They won't miss you.'

'Thanks,' he said wryly.

She smiled slightly at him. 'Sorry, that sounded worse than I meant.'

'Doesn't matter.' Paul gestured to the table where the CDs were stacked. 'Is this all of them?'

She nodded, even though it made her headache worse.

'I thought I'd packed them all,' he said as he put them into a box he'd brought with him. 'I completely forgot about these.'

'Doesn't matter.' She watched him. He looked well, she thought. He didn't look as though he'd spent an almost sleepless week. He was clean-shaven and his eyes were clear. He was wearing a denim shirt and jeans and he looked fit and healthy.

Alix had changed into a pair of figure-hugging blue trousers and a white lycra sports top when she'd come home because she knew he liked them. But she regretted it now, not wanting him to think she'd made an effort.

'Have you been talking to Sabine?' The words were out of her mouth before she could stop them.

'Yesterday,' he said. 'Just for a couple of minutes.'

'And has she decided if she's coming over?'

'Why?' asked Paul.

'I just wanted to know.' She shrugged. 'I'm sorry, it's none of my business.'

'Not yet,' said Paul shortly.

Alix bit her lip. 'Would you like a drink?'

'No, thanks.' He shook his head. 'I'm in a hurry.'

'Anything important?'

'This and that.'

'I see,' said Alix.

'I'd better be off,' he said uncomfortably. 'I've a few other things to do.'

'Sure.' She stood up.

Paul held out his hand. 'The keys to the apartment,' he said. 'Better not take them away with me.'

'Better not.' She smiled at him.

'Alix – you've been great about this,' he said as he picked up the box of CDs. 'And I am sorry if I've hurt you.'

'If?' she said.

He grimaced. 'OK, I've hurt you. And I'm sorry.'

'Oh, I'll get over it,' she said. 'You know me.'

'It's one of the things I admire about you,' said Paul. 'You're a strong woman, Alix. You don't let things defeat you.'

'But you don't want a strong woman,' she said. 'You want a feeble little one around the house having babies.'

'That's not true,' he said sharply. 'Just because a woman is at

59

home it doesn't make her feeble! My God, Alix, if your female friends heard that they'd lynch you.'

'I didn't say women who stayed at home were feeble,' said Alix. 'I just said *you* wanted a feeble one.'

'Alix, we're having a row,' said Paul. 'And we don't need to have a row, do we?'

'No,' she said. 'I just wanted to clarify things in my mind.'

'Look, Alix.' He reached out and took her hands in his. 'It's not that I don't care about you, I do. It's not that I think you're too strong and too self-sufficient. It's just that I want someone who depends on *me*. And you don't depend on anyone!'

'But what if I did?' she asked. 'What if I gave up my job and depended on you? What then?'

'Then you wouldn't be Alix Callaghan,' said Paul.

'But I'd be someone you'd settle down with.'

'You'd be a different person.'

She smiled. 'I can be a lot of different people – you should see me at work.'

'I'd better go.' He let go of her hands.

'Yes, sure,' she said. She leaned towards him and kissed him lightly on the cheek. 'I'll look out for your articles.'

'I'll look out for you,' he said. 'See you, Alix.'

'Goodbye, Paul.'

～

She walked into town. It was warm and the evening sun reflected off the pavement and hurt her eyes. Her headache still nagged at her just behind her right eye.

The city was crowded. Mainly, she noticed, with couples.

Grafton Street was infested with men and women holding hands, gazing at each other, whispering to each other.

She walked into Break for the Border and ordered a bottle of beer. She'd chosen it because it wasn't really a couples sort of place, but there were lots of couples there all the same. And a group of girls, laughing hysterically as they fitted a mock veil to one of their number and hung a sash round her which said 'Official Hen Night'.

'It'll be you next, Lisa!' cried the bride-to-be. 'I'll throw the bouquet at you for extra special luck.'

Lisa laughed and kissed her friend but Alix thought that the girl had actually looked despairing.

It was a whole different world, she thought. You belong when you're part of a couple. It doesn't matter how great your job is or how well you cope with your life or how much money you earn. When you're a woman, people expect you to be part of a couple. And when you're part of a couple, they expect you to be a family. She sighed. The idea of starting all over again was horrible. She didn't want to spend nights in bars looking over the available talent. She didn't want to look at each new man she met and wonder if he was the one. She didn't want to be single. She wanted Paul.

She finished the bottle of beer and caught a cab back to the apartment. Her headache was still there and she knew that she shouldn't have drunk any alcohol.

She opened the fridge door. There was a large carton of Häagen-Dazs ice cream in the freezer. Cookies and cream, one of her favourites. She took a spoon from the drawer and then walked out onto the balcony with the ice cream.

She ate it all and felt marginally better. Then she went back inside, lay on the sofa and closed her eyes.

It was nearly ten o'clock when she woke. With a shock, she realised that she'd forgotten all about the Fed meeting. Dave was probably right though, she thought as she logged on to her computer. The Fed wouldn't cut rates so soon after Kerrigan's announcement.

'Oh, shit!' She looked at the headline on the screen. 'Shit, shit, shit!'

The Fed had cut rates by twenty-five basis points. She should have stuck with her instincts. The dollar had fallen just as she thought it would.

Chapter 6

She was at her desk by seven the following morning. The dollar was still weak. She checked their position to see if Dave had sold the bonds. Naturally, he had. Because of the rate cut, bonds had increased in value. Dave had sold them at a price which was fair for yesterday but which was way below the price she would have got today.

Alix sighed. It could have been worse, they could have been holding dollars and be sitting on a huge loss this morning, but she absolutely hated the idea that she could have made money if she'd stuck with her gut feeling. In the end, though, she'd bottled out. Why? Because she was tired, because her mind was on Paul and not on her job.

Did this happen to blokes? she wondered. If she'd dumped Paul, would he sit at his computer, a blank screen in front of him, and struggle to find the words for an article? Would he miss deadlines, not concentrate and turn in a piece that was absolute rubbish? Or would he be able to push his misery to the back of his mind while he was working so that he could write just as well as he ever did?

Somehow she didn't really want to know the answer.

Dave's hurried entry into the office made her shelve her thoughts.

'Bloody hell,' he said. 'I didn't think they'd do it.'

Alix grimaced. 'I suppose I didn't either. Otherwise I'd have told you to short the dollars and hang on to the bonds.'

'It was the right decision,' said Dave. 'Odds were in favour of them doing nothing. It would have been risky to run both positions.'

'I should have taken the risk on one of them,' said Alix. 'I was so certain when I heard the news about Kerrigan. It was stupid not to.'

'But if they hadn't done anything the dollar would probably have strengthened and the bonds would have fallen and you'd have been losing money. As it is, we haven't lost. We just haven't made anything.'

'I know,' said Alix. 'But I hate making nothing. It's nearly as bad as losing.'

She lost again that afternoon. She sold sterling to one of her retail customers, thought that the currency would weaken, and then realised that it was going stronger. She lost two thousand pounds on the deal and she was furious with herself.

Gavin, on the other hand, had made five thousand dollars on a swap deal with a new customer and had celebrated his second good trade of the day by exchanging high-fives with Dave and generally exuding a sense of confidence which Alix didn't feel.

By five o'clock their overall profit for the day was around ten thousand dollars, not a particularly good day, but good enough.

'I'm heading off now,' said Alix. 'I'll see you guys back here at seven for the reception. Don't be late – you know how Des is if we're late.'

'We're going to the pub for a couple and coming straight back,' said Dave.

'All of you?' Alix looked around at them.

'I'm having a quick one and then off home to change,' said Jenny.

'Oh. OK.' She picked up her bag. 'See you later then. Don't be absolutely plastered by seven.'

They watched her as she walked out of the room.

'She's not happy about us going for a drink without her,' said Jenny.

'She's been a pain in the neck all day,' said Dave. 'Sulking over the rate cut. It's much better that she goes home and gets over it.'

'What she needs is a good seeing-to from that boyfriend of hers,' said Gavin.

'Oh, Gavin, that's a revolting thing to say.' Jenny made a face at him.

'That's her problem,' said Gavin. 'She's not getting it enough.'

'I thought you decided the other day that she was pregnant.'

'I did. But I bow to your superior knowledge on that issue.' Gavin grinned at her. 'You're probably right. She wouldn't be downing Pinot Noir and Hedex in equal measures if she was up the spout.'

'She shouldn't be doing that anyway,' said Jenny.

'Why don't you have a nice little girlie lunch with her and find out what's wrong?' suggested Dave. 'We can't operate in this room without all the facts. And Alix is certainly keeping something from us.'

'Maybe the bloke has dumped her,' said Gavin. 'That's what happens to you women when you're dumped, isn't it, Jen? You get all mopey and wistful and you can't concentrate.'

'I wouldn't know,' said Jenny acerbically. 'I'm always the

one that does the dumping. Why don't you use your own experiences, Gavin? How did you feel when that girl you were hanging around with left you for someone else?'

'She was a stupid cow,' said Gavin. 'And I went out, got pissed and met someone much, much nicer.'

Jenny laughed. 'There's no putting you down, is there, Donnelly?'

'Nope.' He laughed too.

'Come on,' said Dave, 'let's hit O'Reilly's.'

⌒

Alix sat in the hairdresser's and explained that she wanted a colour to hide the grey.

'It's not that bad.' Tina examined her client's hair.

'It's bad enough,' said Alix. 'And I need it to look good tonight, we have a reception in the bank. I don't want to be some dowdy middle-aged crone in the corner.'

'Alix, you could never be dowdy,' said Tina. 'You're getting this out of proportion, don't you think?'

'No,' said Alix. 'I can't afford grey hairs. Dealing is a young person's game. I start turning up looking like someone's grandmother and I'm toast.'

Tina laughed. 'Well, why don't you do something else?'

'Like what?' asked Alix.

'I don't know,' said Tina. 'Surely you should be in charge of something that doesn't depend on the colour of your hair! You're not a bloody supermodel, after all.'

'You can say that again.' Alix peered at her reflection. 'I look like shit, Tina.'

'You'll look great after this,' the stylist promised. 'I'll stick close to your natural colour and then lift it with some red tones. It'll be lovely.'

'Thanks.' Alix sat back in the chair and waited to be transformed.

It looked perfect, she decided later as she stood in front of her bedroom mirror. Tina had delivered on her promises and now Alix's hair glinted reds and russets in the evening sunlight. Because of the reception tonight she'd asked Tina to put it up, which immediately made her look even taller and more elegant. If only my eyes didn't match the red, she said to herself, I'd actually look OK.

The redness in her eyes was due to both a lack of sleep and looking at the screens all day.

She went into the bathroom and put some Optrex drops into them. She blinked a couple of times. At least she looked less exhausted now. It took her ten minutes to do her make-up. Alix wasn't the sort of person who spent a lot of time on cosmetics, and mostly she didn't need to. She slid her emerald earrings into her ears and hung her matching gold necklace with emerald stone round her neck. She'd bought the jewellery with her last year's bonus.

She took her black silk Jasper Conran out of the wardrobe. The same dress she'd been wearing the night Paul had met Sabine. That had been the first time she'd worn it. Some women she knew would probably never wear it again. But she liked it and it was just right for tonight. All the same, she felt a surge of rage as she zipped it up. Paul had zipped it up the last time. She gritted her teeth. It's only a bloody dress, she told herself. It doesn't mean anything.

∽

The reception area of the bank was already quite full by the time she arrived. Des Coyle kissed her on the cheek and looked around.

'Where's Paul?'

'Couldn't make it, unfortunately,' said Alix. 'He sends his regards.'

'Right.' Des steered her through the crowds. 'Have a word with Norman Keogh, will you? He's on his own and I don't think he knows anyone.'

'OK.' Alix grabbed a glass of wine from a passing wine waiter and walked over to the customer. 'Norman!' she exclaimed. 'I haven't seen you in ages. How are you keeping?'

She drifted from customer to customer, always saying how pleased she was to see them, exchanging a few words about the markets and asking about their families. Alix knew that she was good with the clients. They liked her and the majority of them trusted her. Usually, at functions like this she'd be aware of Paul's slightly condescending presence. Paul wasn't a crusading journalist, nor did he have vehemently socialist beliefs, but he would always have a gently mocking word for the business functions she dragged him along to.

'It's all a sham,' he'd say. 'You pretend you like these guys and they pretend they like you and everyone is wondering if they're making more than everyone else. It's sad really.'

'You talk such bullshit.' She'd snuggle up to him and kiss him on the cheek. 'You know that we're keeping the wheels of commerce turning.'

'And you're all trying to outdo each other and make more money than each other.'

'Give it a rest, Paul.' And then he'd kiss her on the lips

and sometimes they'd end up late for whatever the function was.

She missed him tonight. She'd hardly spoken to him on the night of the Europa Bank reception in Paris but she'd been glad that he was there. Glad that when Rolf Schwimmer of the Swiss office had sidled up to her and asked her where she was staying the night, she was able to point to Paul and tell Rolf that she was staying with that man over there. And she was pleased that Paul was in the traditional tall, dark and handsome mould whereas Rolf Schwimmer was short and pudgy and had beads of perspiration on his brow.

'Hi, Alix.'

She turned round, the voice vaguely familiar. Matt Connery grinned at her. 'How are you?'

'I'm fine,' she said. 'And you?'

'Great.'

'It's a good evening, isn't it?'

'Absolutely. You guys certainly pushed the boat out. Imagine importing the Eiffel Tower!'

Alix smiled. The centrepiece of the buffet table was a huge ice carving of the Eiffel Tower which had drawn admiring gasps from everyone.

'It does a special party trick,' she said solemnly.

'Oh?'

'Turns into the River Seine at midnight.'

Matt laughed. 'It's beginning to lose its shape a bit.'

'It's hot in here.'

Alix was right. There were nearly two hundred people swarming around the reception area and it was becoming increasingly difficult to move.

'It's warm outside too,' said Matt.

Alix nodded but she'd been distracted by the sight of Gavin Donnelly deep in conversation with Des Coyle. Both of them were laughing. Alix didn't like to see someone as keen and aggressive as Gavin hobnobbing with the managing director. It sent a frisson of worry through her. She looked around to see if she could spot either Dave or Jenny but it was impossible to identify them in the crowd.

'I'm sorry?' She looked at Matt. 'I didn't catch what you said.'

'I asked if you'd eaten yet.'

Alix shook her head. 'To be honest I'm not hungry. Never am at these sort of events.'

'That's a shame,' said Matt. 'I thought it might be nice to sit outside with a plate of something.'

'Feel free,' Alix told him. 'Eat as much as you like!'

'With you, I meant.'

She looked at him. 'I think I'm supposed to circulate,' she told him.

'Not attend to the every whim of your clients?'

'Certainly not.' But she smiled to show him that she hadn't taken offence.

'I spoke to our managing director,' said Matt. 'We were wondering if you'd be free either next week or the week after to call in to the company and go through some of your proposals.'

'Sure.' She smiled brilliantly at him and he realised that her eyes were an amazing shade of green. 'Give me a call on Monday and we'll fix it up. Can you excuse me a moment? There's someone I need to talk to.' She moved away from him and tapped Jenny on the shoulder. 'Hi.'

'Oh, Alix, isn't it just the pits in here – so bloody crowded.'

'Yes.'

'You look great,' Jenny told her. 'How is it you can look so wrecked at five and so sophisticated now?'

'Probably because I didn't spend a couple of hours in O'Reilly's.'

'I wasn't there long,' said Jenny. 'Just had one and left.'

'And what was going on while I wasn't there?' asked Alix. 'What are the two boys hatching?'

'Hatching?' Jenny raised an eyebrow.

'Don't look at me like that,' said Alix. 'I've seen the two of them huddled together. They're up to something and I want to know what it is.'

'They're not up to anything,' said Jenny. 'Nothing.'

'You sure?' asked Alix.

'Certain. You know them, they're probably just putting bets on horses or something.'

'You think so?' Alix wasn't sure, Jenny could see that.

'Yes,' said Jenny as convincingly as she could.

'Alix! Hi, haven't seen you in ages!'

Jenny breathed a sigh of relief as Stuart Phillips, a client, waved at Alix. Another second and she'd have told Alix about Dave and Gavin's dreams of changing the dealing room. Jenny felt uncomfortable about the situation. Alix had given her the opportunity of a dealing career. She didn't like to think of her being stabbed in the back by the other dealers. But if she was, maybe there'd be greater opportunities in store. You couldn't be grateful forever.

Jenny waited until her boss was talking to Stuart and then made her way over to the bar area where Dave was chatting to one of the girls who worked in the settlements department.

'Got to talk to you for a minute, Dave,' she said, hauling him away. 'Sorry, Jackie, you can have him back shortly.'

'What?' asked Dave. 'I was getting somewhere with her.'

'Don't be ridiculous,' said Jenny briskly. 'Jackie Walshe has no interest in you whatsoever.'

'How do you know that?' he demanded.

'Because she's going out with Richard Cornwell in Chase.'

'Well, she may be going out with Richard but she was having second thoughts while she was talking to me,' Dave told her. 'We'd just got onto our favourite pub.'

'Oh, forget about her,' said Jenny impatiently. 'I was talking to Alix. She wants to know what you and Gavin are up to.'

'Up to? We're not up to anything,' said Dave.

'Oh, come on, Dave. After all the conversations we've had this week? You know perfectly well that you're up to grabbing her job.'

'Only if she makes a complete tit of it,' said Dave. 'Let's face it, Jen, so long as she's making money, there's nothing we can do.'

'But she knows you have something in mind,' said Jenny. 'She knows—'

'She knows nothing,' said Dave. 'Because there's nothing for her to know. If she trades well then there's no hope of either me or Gavin managing to dislodge her. But if she has another week like this week . . . We're paid to make money and she didn't do it.'

'She would have if she'd shorted dollars last night,' said Jenny.

'It was her call. She could have opened a position and made the money. But she didn't.' Dave shrugged.

'You were the one to suggest selling the bonds.'

'She asked my opinion and I gave it. Look, you can't blame me because I told her to stay out of the market.'

'No,' said Jenny, 'but would you have stayed out if it had been your own decision?'

Dave sighed. 'Maybe. Maybe not. It was a messy week. It could have been a lot messier. And she wasn't a bit confident about her call. So I gave her a conservative opinion.'

Jenny looked at him uncomfortably. 'I like Alix,' she said.

'So do I,' said Dave. 'And I'm not going to hang her, Jenny. But if she hangs herself then I'll step into her spot. And I don't have a problem doing that.'

⌒

Alix wandered up to the dealing room. She liked being there on her own. She turned on the monitor to see how markets were trading in Tokyo time. The dollar was still falling. She'd been such a fool not to go with her gut instinct. Just because she'd felt tired and headachy and not in form for making constructive decisions. She'd never felt like that before and it was stupid. Really stupid.

She sat down in her high-backed chair and closed her eyes. Everything had been so right until Paul dropped his bombshell. Now she felt as though her life was disintegrating and she couldn't understand why. She'd been ambitious before she met him. She'd been successful before he'd moved in with her. So why did she suddenly feel scared when she looked at the screens? Where had the confidence gone?

She looked at her watch. Almost midnight. The crowd downstairs would be thinning out.

A sudden shadow across the flickering screen made her look

up. Matt Connery was standing outside the glass wall of the dealing room and looking in at her. She got up and opened the door.

'I know it sounds like a bad spy movie to say this,' she told him, 'but this is a restricted area. You shouldn't be here.'

'I know,' he said. 'But I was heading home and I wanted to say goodbye. One of your colleagues said you'd probably be up here.'

'Really?' She smiled slightly. 'I didn't realise I was that predictable.'

'Why are you sitting in the dark?' he asked.

'No need for the lights.'

'How are the markets?'

'Dollar is down again,' she told him. 'The yen is staging quite a good rally in Tokyo.'

'Do you love it?' he asked curiously. 'All this?'

'It's all I've ever wanted to do,' said Alix. 'When I was in college everyone talked about banking and finance as though it was some sort of huge mysterious subculture. I always wanted to be involved. And when I studied finance I just loved the idea of capital markets, moving money around the globe, financing trade deals – all of it.'

Matt smiled at her. 'And have you burned out yet?'

'Do I look burned out?' she laughed.

'No,' said Matt. 'You look lovely.'

Alix hadn't blushed in years but she felt the sudden surge of colour in her cheeks and was grateful for the semi-light of the room.

'Flattering the dealer is not necessarily going to make the pricing of your trades any better,' she told him.

He smiled. 'Shame, and I thought I was so irresistible.'

'I can resist everything except chocolate,' she told him as she switched off the monitor again. 'Come on, I'd better go down. If people are leaving I suppose the least I should do is say goodbye.' She waited for him to leave the room first and followed him to the lifts.

'What do you do when you're not working?' asked Matt.

'I go to the gym a couple of times a week,' she said. 'I know that sounds terribly boring. And I shoot.'

'You what?'

'Shoot,' she said.

'You mean hunt? Foxes and rabbits, that sort of thing?'

She grinned. 'No. Target shooting.'

'What sort of targets?'

'Ordinary ones – rings. And silhouettes.'

'Silhouettes?'

'It sounds awful. But little shapes. Like chickens and rabbits and rams. They're at different distances. And you get points for shooting them.'

'My God.' He stared at her. 'Are you good at this?'

'Not bad,' she said. 'I've won a couple of competitions.'

He looked at her with a new respect. 'I guess I'd better not get on the wrong side of you.'

'I guess you'd better not.' She smiled at him and stepped into the lift.

◡ə

Dave, Gavin and Jenny plus a handful of the settlements staff were going to the Riverside Club.

'Are you coming, Alix?' asked Jenny.

'Why not?' she said. She noticed that Dave and Gavin had

75

exchanged glances. Those two bastards were up to something, she knew they were, no matter what Jenny might say.

She looked around to say goodbye to Matt Connery but he was nowhere to be seen. Probably giving her a wide berth after her revelations about the shooting club. She smiled to herself. She'd call out there tomorrow, she hadn't been shooting in nearly a month. And it relaxed her.

The nightclub was crowded and the music was loud. Alix bought two bottles of wine and poured for everyone. Dave and Jackie disappeared into the crowd. Gavin Donnelly and Peter Strong, one of the settlements people, began chatting up a couple of extraordinarily attractive girls who were standing at the bar.

It reminded her of her life before Paul, when she'd gone to nightclubs almost every night and wondered (without really believing) whether that night she'd meet the man who would change her life completely.

Why did I do this? she wondered as she looked around her. I don't really want to be here.

'You OK?' asked Jenny.

'Fine,' said Alix. She smiled half-heartedly at Jenny. 'I'm beginning to think I'm a bit old for this, that's all.'

'Not at all,' said Jenny.

'I'm glad you think so.' Alix sipped her wine. 'I just sometimes wonder about it, Jen. Whether or not it's worth the struggle.'

'What d'you mean?'

'Look at them.' Alix nodded at Dave and Gavin. '*They're* my struggle. Wondering if they're about to shaft me.'

Jenny took a gulp of wine. Not again, she thought. Alix was far too good at spotting trouble.

'You'd tell me, Jenny, wouldn't you?' said Alix. 'If they were plotting anything.'

'I – well, sure.' Jenny looked at Alix uneasily.

Alix gazed at her younger colleague. Jenny's face was flushed.

'They're up to something, aren't they?' she demanded. 'Those fucking bastards are up to something.'

'Not really,' said Jenny. 'Honestly, Alix. Not really.'

'Then what?' asked Alix. 'Don't lie to me, Jenny.'

'It's just that – that they think there's something wrong with you and they're wondering if it might be to their advantage.'

'Something wrong with me?' Alix stared at her.

'You've been acting funny all week. They thought you were pregnant.'

'What!' Suddenly Alix began to laugh, the first time she'd really laughed since the previous week. Jenny grinned uncertainly. 'I'm not pregnant,' said Alix. 'Not at all.'

'Good,' said Jenny.

'Why?'

'Gavin made me a price. I dealt. He owes me twenty quid.'

Alix laughed again. 'You see, young Jenny,' she said. 'Stick with me and I'll make us both money.'

⌒

It was two o'clock by the time she got home. The apartment was deadly quiet. No Paul to nag at her for drinking all night. No Paul to shove her out of her spot in the bed.

She poured herself a glass of orange juice and drank it. She'd never liked going to bed on her own.

Chapter 7

Alix adjusted her position and looked through the gun scope. She breathed slowly and easily, allowing herself to fall into a gentle rhythm so that she knew exactly when the sight would be perfectly aligned on the target. She squeezed the trigger gently and was pleased when she saw the bullet hit the ring nearest the bull. You had to be relaxed when you were shooting which was why she enjoyed it so much. She wasn't very good at sitting around doing nothing, but forced relaxation was something else altogether. She squeezed the trigger again.

'How'd you do?' asked Niall Rourke, the chairman of the club, when she'd collected the target.

'Hundred and eighty seven,' she said.

'You should come more often.' Niall grinned at her. 'We could make you two hundred out of two hundred.'

'I like to think I'm not perfect.' She smiled. 'I'm going to have a go at the rams.'

She moved to the silhouette area and took aim at one of the small metal rams two hundred metres away. The bullet hit it and sent it spinning off its stand.

'Poor innocent creature,' whispered Niall in her ear. 'You looked positively malevolent that time.'

'Me?' she murmured. 'Never.'

She hit nineteen of the twenty rams. 'You're right,' she told Niall. 'I need more practice. I was slow.'

'You're shooting well,' he said. 'Are you going to enter the next competition?'

'Perhaps.' She slid the scope from the rifle. 'I don't have much time, Niall. I'm supposed to go to Paris for a meeting and I'll be in London soon too.'

'Oh, for the life of executive stress,' he said.

'I bet you have a much nicer life than me,' she told him. 'London and Paris are very dull when you're at meetings all the time.'

'Paris could never be dull,' said Niall. 'I haven't been there in years and I'd love to go back.'

'I'll send you instead of me the next time.' She looked at her watch and gasped in dismay. 'Is that the time? I'd better dash, I'm supposed to be baby-sitting for my sister tonight.' She kissed him on the cheek. 'I'll be out again soon.'

'Bring the boyfriend the next time,' said Niall. 'I thought he was keen to join.'

'Oh, you know these journalist types,' she said lightly. 'They'll say anything and all they want is a good story.'

'I hope not,' said Niall. 'I'd be completely disillusioned if that was the case.'

Alix got into the BMW and drove off. She didn't want to talk to Niall Rourke about Paul who'd been flattering and charming when he'd been at the club and told Alix afterwards that he thought that target shooting was for weirdos. 'So I'm a weirdo?' she'd asked and he'd smiled and told her that she was the best sort.

When she got home she changed into another pair of jeans and sweatshirt and grabbed some earplugs to take to her nieces. Nessa, who was eight, and Aoife, aged four, loved the brightly coloured squashy earplugs and always demanded some when Alix turned up.

❧

Wyn's house was in a small terrace of three near the Merrion Gates. It had spectacular views of Dublin Bay from the upstairs bedrooms and Wyn had said that it was the views which had clinched it for them, outweighing the fact that the garden wasn't as big as they would have liked. 'Although,' she told Alix wryly one day, 'I don't get any time to sit in the bedroom and look at the view any more. I'm too busy running after my lunatic children.'

The lunatic children were watching a cartoon video when Alix arrived and looking the picture of innocence.

'Have you got anything for us?' demanded Nessa.

'No,' said Alix.

'You must have, Alix. You always have.' Aoife looked distraught.

'You should be glad just to see your aunt,' said Wyn, 'and not always expect her to be bringing you things.'

'But she always does,' Nessa said firmly. 'Always.'

'Oh, here!' Alix laughed and handed her the earplugs. 'And these are for you and Aoife too.' She gave her niece a bag of jelly sweets.

'You spoil them rotten,' said Wyn as her daughters flopped in front of the TV and began doling out the sweets. 'They only associate you with someone who brings them garbage!'

'I like indulging them,' Alix smiled. 'And I don't always bring rubbish.'

'Wait until you have your own.' Wyn led the way into the kitchen. 'You won't be indulging them!'

'I don't think I'll ever have kids,' said Alix. 'It isn't me, somehow.'

'But what about Paul?' asked Wyn. 'Doesn't he want them?'

Alix said nothing.

'Why didn't he come with you tonight anyway?' asked Wyn. 'Is he working?'

Alix pushed her hair out of her eyes. 'I don't know.'

Wyn, who had been rummaging through her handbag looking for a lipstick, paused and looked at her sister. 'Why don't you know?'

Alix sighed. 'Paul and I have – aren't living together at the moment.'

'Alix!' Wyn stared at her. 'Why? What happened?'

'Oh, this and that.'

'Alix!'

It was harder to tell Wyn than she'd thought. She'd imagined mentioning it casually to her sister, saying that it was temporary and that they were just working things out, but now that it came to saying the words her throat was dry and she was afraid that she'd burst into tears.

'When did it happen?' asked Wyn.

'Last week.'

'And was it his decision or your decision?'

Alix shrugged. She didn't trust herself to speak.

'Hi, Alix!' Terry, Wyn's husband, barged into the room.

'Hi, Terry.' She smiled faintly at him.

'We're talking,' said Wyn. 'I'll be with you in a minute.'

Terry looked at both of them and joined his daughters in the living-room.

81

'So, are you going to tell me about it?' demanded Wyn.

'There's nothing much to tell,' said Alix quickly. 'We weren't going anywhere. We weren't sure what we wanted. So we're giving each other a bit of space, that's all.'

'Spare me this "space" nonsense!' Wyn made a face at her sister. 'You've split up, haven't you?'

'For the time being,' admitted Alix.

'So he's left the apartment?'

'That's usually what happens when you split up. One of you leaves. And it *is* my apartment.'

'And is it over for good or is it really just a "space" thing?'

'I don't know,' said Alix. 'I think we'll get back together again. He loves me. He's just having a bit of a midlife crisis, that's all.'

'You sure?'

'Pretty sure,' she said.

'Is there someone else?'

The image of Paul and Sabine together almost made her throw up.

'No,' she said, deliberately misinterpreting Wyn's question, 'although there's a corporate client who keeps asking me out.'

Wyn looked at her shrewdly. 'I meant has Paul got someone else?'

Alix shrugged. 'I knew what you meant. Not really. He met this French girl in Paris and I think meeting her made him question what he wanted out of life, all that sort of stuff. But he's not living with her or anything.'

'Hardly, if she's in Paris,' said Wyn dryly.

'Anyway,' Alix smiled brightly at her, 'it's no hassle. We'll work something out.'

'Are you sure?' asked Wyn. 'And are you OK? If it only happened last week—'

'I'm fine,' interrupted Alix. 'Honestly, Wyn, it's no big deal. We'll probably be back together next month.' She opened the kitchen door. 'Come on, you'll be late.'

When Terry and Wyn had left, Alix sat down beside the two girls.

'Can we play doctors and nurses?' asked Aoife. 'I like being a nurse.'

'And I'm the doctor,' said Nessa bossily. 'You're sick, Alix, you have a pain in your head.'

'I certainly have!' exclaimed Alix as Nessa pulled at her hair. 'Let go, you little horror!'

⌒

'It sounds serious to me,' said Wyn as Terry turned the car onto the Strand Road. 'She didn't want to talk about it.'

'Who does, if they've split up with a partner?' asked Terry. 'She probably still feels upset.'

'But you know Alix.' Wyn shook her head. 'She never gets upset.'

'This is bound to upset her.'

'With a normal person, yes. But Alix isn't normal, Terry. She doesn't let things upset her. She seems to shrug it off and then she does some brilliant deal in the office and everything's OK.'

'I've never seen her upset,' admitted Terry. 'But that doesn't mean she doesn't get upset.'

'Not when it comes to boyfriends,' said Wyn.

'Well, maybe not now,' said Terry. 'She probably feels that she's too old to start sobbing in our kitchen.'

'She was never upset about boyfriends,' said Wyn. 'Never. When we were teenagers and going out with blokes I was always distraught if someone dumped me. But she just shrugged it off. Used to say that she needed to study more and it had come at a good time. Not that she cared much about guys anyhow. If they asked her out, fine. If not, it didn't seem to bother her.'

'I thought you told me she had loads of boyfriends.'

'Loads of blokes asked her out,' said Wyn, 'but she was very choosy about the ones she actually went out with.'

'She *is* very picky, your sister,' said Terry. 'You can see it in everything she does. It has to be the way she wants it all the time. I suppose she couldn't stand chopping and changing boyfriends and having to get used to different people all the time.'

'I never thought about it like that.'

'She's a control freak.' Terry slowed down as they came to the booth on the toll bridge. 'She's a nice girl, Wyn, and good fun. But only on her terms.'

'You're not being very fair,' said Wyn. 'She lived on her own for a long time. She got used to doing things her own way.'

'I'll tell you something about Alix.' Terry glanced at his wife. 'Remember ages ago she gave me a lift out to the airport?'

'When you were going to Scotland?'

'Yes,' he said. 'On the way I asked her to switch on the radio. So she switched on a CD.'

'And? What was wrong with it?'

'There was nothing wrong with the CD. But when I asked her what radio stations she listened to, she told me that she never listened to the radio in the car except Radio Four for the business news.'

'So?'

'I asked her why she didn't listen to FM104 or 98FM or something a bit more cheerful than Radio Four or the Patsy Cline stuff she was listening to. She said that she preferred listening to CDs because that way she knew what track followed what. She said that she didn't like listening to a mixture of stuff and that's what you got on FM104. She said that she preferred to control her own listening.'

'Well, that's fair enough,' said Wyn defensively.

'Come on, Wyn!' Terry turned into the Point Depot car park. 'Imagine not listening to the radio because you want to listen to songs in sequence. Patsy Cline at that! There's something seriously wrong with your sister.'

Wyn sighed. 'I think it was because of Dad. I think '

'Don't let's worry about Alix now.' Terry reversed the car into the nearest space. 'She's got her own life to lead. And we've got a night out together. Don't let's spoil it by talking about your father.'

'OK.' Wyn smiled at him.

'That's my girl.' Terry leaned towards her and kissed her gently on the cheek. 'Come on, let's get a drink before the concert starts.'

⌒

Alix would have liked a drink herself. It wasn't that the girls were particularly difficult or disobedient, but they were full of high spirits and insisted on her sharing all their games, most of which involved chasing around the house. Alix often wondered if Terry and Wyn's other baby-sitter, a girl who lived in Blackrock, ever spent as much time playing with Nessa and Aoife as she did. Because she didn't enjoy the games very much,

Alix tried doubly hard to get involved and usually ended up either injured, when one of the children accidentally poked her eye or tripped her up, or covered in paint or crayon or glue if they were going through one of their creative phases. Tonight they played hospitals (Alix suffered a number of painful injections administered by Wyn's basting syringe), followed by jewellery making (hoist by her own petard, Alix told herself, since she'd given Nessa the kit the previous Christmas).

An hour after she first proposed it, the girls were finally bathed and in bed, and looking angelic. She read them a couple of stories and – amazingly, given their excitement of earlier – the two of them had fallen asleep before she finished an instalment from *The Secret Seven*.

She tiptoed downstairs and poured herself a gin and tonic. She honestly didn't know how Wyn coped with two children. She knew that they were in school during the day and that Wyn didn't spend every waking moment with them, but they seemed to take up so much effort. Nessa went to ballet classes and music lessons twice a week. Both girls went swimming. And Wyn had to be there to take them wherever they needed to go. She had to organise her life around them.

Alix never ceased to be amazed at how Wyn had adapted so easily to the role of wife and mother, happily abandoning her career to do so. And Wyn had been the really clever one, Alix thought as she sipped her drink, Wyn had been the one with the string of As in her Leaving Certificate, including higher-grade maths. Alix had only got a B in maths, yet she was the one shifting money around the world while Wyn had given up her actuarial job with one of the country's most prestigious life assurance companies. Wyn could have had a really good career. Alix stretched her legs out in front of her.

She wondered if her sister thought that the sacrifice had been worth it.

She checked on the children an hour later. They were both sleeping peacefully. She felt a surge of affection for them. How much would it change her life? One baby, one child?

She walked quietly out of their bedroom and into the spare room. She stood in front of the wall mirror and looked at her figure sideways on. She leaned back as pregnant women did. It was amazing how different it made you look. Then she picked up a cushion from the cane chair in the corner and shoved it under her sweatshirt.

The effect was frightening. Alix stared at her reflection in horror. She actually looked pregnant! Not like a woman with a cushion at all – a real, live, pregnant woman.

She whipped the cushion out from under her sweatshirt and threw it back onto the chair. If only the rest of it was that easy.

The final credits for *Terminator 2* were rolling up the TV screen when Alix heard the car pull into the driveway. She went into the kitchen and switched on the coffee filter.

'We're home.' Wyn pushed open the kitchen door. 'How were the girls?'

'Fine.' Alix took some cups from the cupboard. 'They were very good. We played hospitals.'

Wyn sighed. 'Ever since Nessa cut her arm and we had to bring her to casualty they've been playing hospitals.'

'But that was over six months ago!'

'I know,' said Wyn. 'But they don't forget. Things that mean absolutely nothing to me get stored in their brains and regurgitated when I'm least expecting it.'

'But you love them all the same.' Alix's tone was light-hearted.

'I can't imagine life without them,' said Wyn. 'I'm not exactly sure it's the same thing.'

Alix loaded up the tray and carried the coffee into the living room where Terry was stretched out on the sofa.

'Coffee?' she asked.

He nodded. 'So what's all this Wyn tells me about you and Paul?' he asked, ignoring Wyn's glare. 'That's a bit of a surprise, Alix.'

'I guess so.' Alix sat down beside him. 'I don't know whether it's for good or not yet, Terry.'

'He's probably not good enough for you anyway,' said Wyn loyally.

Terry snorted. 'He's a decent bloke!'

'I know.' Alix smiled at him. 'We're just working things out, Terry. That's all.'

'What happened?' he asked. 'Did he fall at the commitment hurdle?'

Alix raised an eyebrow.

'Did you want to get married and have kids?' asked Terry. 'I know a lot of men get cold feet about marrying and having kids.'

'As it happens,' said Alix calmly, 'it was him that wanted the kids. I wasn't sure about it.'

There was a taut silence.

'Oh,' said Terry.

'Do you want more coffee?' asked Wyn.

～

Even though it was nearly one o'clock in the morning, Alix drove home with the sunroof open to let in the air. It was oppressively hot and her sweatshirt was sticking to her back.

She thought about babies again. She kept seeing herself standing in front of the mirror with the pillow stuffed under her top. It was a freaky kind of picture and it terrified her. But she couldn't let it go. The same way she couldn't let Paul go. She wanted to let him go but she couldn't stop thinking about him and it frightened her.

Surely the Sabine thing was a symptom, nothing more. He wouldn't actually be happy living with a Parisienne who floated around doing arty kinds of things with swathes of muslin and pots of paints. Paul was a practical sort of person. That's why he did journalism and not creative writing. He couldn't see the sense of made-up stories when there were so many real ones to be told. Besides, Sabine was a child. She'd probably just graduated and was barely out of her teens. She'd got the design job for Europa because she knew somebody, Alix was sure of that.

Did Sabine love Paul? Did Paul love Sabine?

Alix ground her teeth as she listened to Patsy Cline tell her she was crazy.

Chapter 8

A lix flew to Paris on Tuesday morning for a meeting with
Guy Decourcelle and the treasury managers of some of the
other Europa Bank branches. It was one of the regular quarterly
meetings when everyone talked about their perspective on
markets and which trading strategies they currently preferred.

'The problem with Canada is the lack of confidence in the
government,' said Jaques Martin. 'Nobody can believe a word
they say. They've had more fiscal reform packages than they
know what to do with – and they don't know what to do with
them most of the time anyway.'

'It's like Japan a few years ago,' Remy de Valmy agreed with
him. 'Too little, too late.'

'It's a market I want us to stay out of,' Guy told them. 'Concentrate on what we know best. What do you think, Alix?'

She looked at him. She knew he didn't think she'd been
listening, but she had.

'I have never traded Canada as a market, as you should know,
Guy,' she told him. 'We've occasionally transacted Canadian
dollar foreign exchange for our clients, but we've never run any
positions ourselves. We've always passed them on to Remy.' She
smiled at the tall, muscular Canadian trader. 'And I'm sure you
did very well out of them too.'

He grinned at her. 'Never well enough.'

'Oh, come on! What about the time I sold you Canadian dollars just as the market went up?'

'What about the time you bought them from me and the market went even higher?'

'What about—'

'OK, OK.' Guy looked at them both irritably. 'Come on. Lunch is no doubt waiting for us.'

The dining room of the bank's headquarters was on the tenth floor of the building and had wonderful views over the city. Alix chose a seat where she could look at the Eiffel Tower. She remembered standing at the top with Paul, holding him tightly, afraid to look down.

'Are you going back to Dublin tonight?' Guy sat down beside her.

'Yes,' she replied.

'Why don't you ever stay?'

'What for?' she asked.

'Why does anyone stay in Paris? The food, the nightlife – whatever!'

She smiled and delicately attacked a shrimp. 'I don't like rich food. I'm quite happy with a burger and chips. As for the nightlife, I get that at home.'

'How is your partner?' asked Guy.

'Fine,' replied Alix.

'Don't you ever tire of him?'

She turned to look at Guy. 'No, I don't.'

'Are you always faithful to him? You are not married, are you?'

'Guy!' She glared at him. 'It's really none of your business. Are you always faithful to your wife?'

Guy took a sip of Chablis. 'Not always. But it doesn't mean I do not love her.'

'I'd forgotten,' said Alix sourly, 'about the French way of doing things.'

'It's often the best way,' said Guy.

'Well, it's not my way,' Alix snapped.

'Such a shame,' Guy murmured. 'You miss out on so much.'

Alix swallowed a whole cherry tomato and almost choked. By the time she'd regained her composure, Guy had turned to the trader from the Madrid branch and was ignoring her completely.

⌒

She'd forgotten to buy milk. She was dying for a cup of coffee, there was no milk in the fridge and it was almost midnight. If she'd stayed in Paris she could have gone to a fashionable restaurant, drunk fine wine courtesy of Guy Decourcelle's expense account and then had brilliant and wonderful sex with him. Well, maybe not the brilliant and wonderful sex, although he'd given her the distinct impression that it was a possibility. It was flattering to think that he might be interested, all the same. She needed to think like that right now. If I was any good at being single, she thought, I'd have stayed in Paris and flirted madly with Guy. It might have even been good for my career! Instead of which I'm in this bloody apartment drinking black coffee which I absolutely hate and I'll be sleeping on my own which I don't much like either.

Tomorrow, she promised herself, as she slid between the sheets, I'll get my act in gear tomorrow.

But she woke up late the following morning. She blinked

sleepily in the morning light and realised that it was already eight o'clock. She swore softly, hopped out of bed and under the shower.

She walked to work. It was infinitely quicker than driving through the rush-hour traffic although by the time she'd reached the office she had a blister on her heel and felt hot and bothered.

'YO! SUSHI!' Gavin was standing on his chair exchanging high-fives with Dave while Jenny sat on the edge of her desk and laughed at them.

'What on earth is going on?' demanded Alix.

'Oh, hi.' Gavin beamed at her and jumped from the chair. 'How was Paris?'

'Fine,' said Alix. 'What were you doing just now?'

'Trading,' Gavin replied. 'What do you think I was doing?'

'It looked like you were standing on your chair to me,' she said.

'Celebrating,' said Dave. 'As we've every right to.'

'Oh?'

'Gavin landed a new account,' Dave told her. 'We did their first trade this morning and we've just bagged a few grand.'

'What's the account?' Alix took off her chocolate-brown Jil Sander jacket and hung it over the back of her chair.

'A crowd called Anatronics,' said Gavin. 'He was selling yen.'

'Matt Connery?' Alix looked at him. 'Was it Matt Connery that called?'

'Yes,' answered Dave. 'D'you know him?'

'Don't be bloody stupid, Dave. I had a meeting with him about ten days ago! And he was at the reception on Friday. It's hardly a new account.'

'We haven't dealt with them before,' Gavin pointed out. 'That makes it a new account.'

'It's an account I was handling,' said Alix. 'I'm supposed to be making a presentation to them next week.'

'They obviously don't need you to do anything,' said Gavin. 'And Matt whateverhisname was perfectly happy to deal with me. So I'd call it a new account and I'd call it my account. Anyway,' he added, 'wouldn't have done much good if he had asked for you because you weren't here.'

Alix could feel the acid churn in her stomach. Because she'd been in a bad mood when Matt had called she hadn't bothered to set up Anatronics as an account on their internal system. Usually she would have entered all the relevant details on the computer and assigned someone to look after the account. Anatronics, with its base of business both in the Far East and the States, looked very interesting and profitable and she had wanted to look after it herself.

But they had an unwritten code in the dealing room that if someone did a deal for an unallocated account, they were given the job of looking after the client. It was her own fault that Gavin was trying to pinch the Anatronics account.

'I'll talk it through with them at the meeting,' she said finally. 'They might have other ideas about their account manager. *Did* Matt Connery ask for me?'

'No,' said Gavin rudely. 'Why should he? I told you he was perfectly happy with the pricing of the deal.'

'Good,' said Alix and stalked into her office without even checking the screens.

Gavin and Dave exchanged glances. Dave shrugged and Gavin grinned. Jenny sat down in her chair and picked up the telephone.

Alix opened her copy of the *Financial Times* and stared at the top story without seeing it. Her heart was pounding and now she had a pain in her stomach. That bloody pup, Donnelly, she thought furiously. He's so fucking pleased that he's pinched a deal from under my nose. 'You weren't here,' he'd gloated. The little shit. And Dave Bryant had said nothing, just looked faintly pleased with himself.

Well, she thought, if I somehow end up leaving this place, Dave won't last very long. Not with Gavin breathing down his neck. Gavin is the kind of bloke who wants to go straight to the top. And he'll probably do just that. But not, she muttered, without a lot of work. And not over me.

She walked back into the room, sat down at her desk and started calling clients. But business was slow and she hadn't done a single trade by lunchtime.

'Want to join me for a sandwich?' she asked Jenny at midday.

Jenny glanced anxiously at Dave who studiously ignored her look.

'Well, OK.'

'You don't have to if you don't want to,' said Alix. 'If you've something planned—'

'No, nothing,' said Jenny hastily. 'I'd love to have a sandwich with you.'

'Great,' said Alix. 'I've got to pop down to settlements for a couple of minutes. Meet you in reception at a quarter past?'

'Fine,' said Jenny.

Gavin stuck out his tongue at Jenny and licked the air as Alix left the room.

'Oh, give it a rest,' Jenny snapped at him.

'Have a sandwich with me!' said Gavin in a falsetto voice.

'And tell me what those nasty boys in the dealing room are up to.'

'Stop it.' But Jenny giggled.

'You better come back with more information than you impart,' said Dave. 'Because we'll be quizzing you in the pub afterwards.'

'Not tonight you won't,' smirked Jenny. 'I've got a date!'

'Don't forget he'll definitely respect you in the morning,' Dave said.

'Thanks for the advice.' Jenny got up from the desk. 'I'm off to meet the boss for lunch. See you later!'

She stood in the reception area and waited for Alix to arrive. Part of her felt sorry for Alix who was obviously going through some kind of crisis these last few days. Jenny had never seen her boss look uncertain, or go home early, or arrive at the office late. And she couldn't believe that Alix hadn't already set up an account for Anatronics! What had she been thinking of?

She smiled as Alix strode through the swing doors.

'O'Reilly's?' asked Alix.

'Fine,' said Jenny.

It was another glorious day. The sky was clear blue and the sun was hot. The smell of the city's traffic hung in the air and mingled with the odour of the Liffey as it wound its way to the sea.

'I hope it's like this for Anna's wedding,' said Jenny brightly as they walked along the quays. 'She needs it to be warm because she's wearing a dress that's almost indecent it's so low cut.'

'What date?' asked Alix.

'Next month,' said Jenny. 'The eighteenth.'

The eighteenth. Paul's birthday. Last year they'd gone to

Paris for his birthday. Absolutely nothing to do with work, she hadn't gone near the Europa Bank building. They'd stayed in a small but elegant hotel near Montmartre and they'd had a loving and romantic weekend. Alix had bought a bottle of Dom Perignon and a huge punnet of strawberries and they'd brought them back to the bedroom and—

'Are you OK, Alix?' Jenny looked at her curiously.

'I'm fine,' Alix replied. 'Come on, there's a break in the traffic!'

They ran across the busy road to the pub and sat down at one of the outside tables.

'At the reception the other night I got the impression from you that Dave and Gavin were out to get me,' said Alix after they'd ordered baguettes and beer. 'How badly are they out to get me?'

'It's not that bad at all.' Jenny shifted uneasily in her seat. 'I told you. They thought you were pregnant. I told them you weren't – I had to so's I could collect on my bet.'

'And why did they think I might be pregnant?'

'You've been acting strangely. Going home early. Missing trades. Being in late this morning. Not setting up the Anatronics account – Alix, why on earth didn't you set it up?'

Alix shrugged.

'But it could be worth a lot of money,' said Jenny.

'I'm the boss,' said Alix. 'I allocate the accounts. And even if I let Gavin keep it, that doesn't mean all the profit will be matched against his name.'

'But that's not fair,' protested Jenny. 'Matt Connery wasn't going to deal until Gavin persuaded him that we could show him the best price.'

'And why wasn't Matt Connery going to deal?'

97

'Because—' Jenny sighed and shifted in her chair again. 'Because he told Gavin he didn't know him.'

'And Gavin said?'

Jenny fiddled with a paper napkin.

'Jenny?'

'Gavin said that he looked after your accounts while you were away and that since you'd been in Paris he wasn't expecting you back until tomorrow at the earliest and he wouldn't advise Connery to wait in case the rate went against him.' Jenny's words tumbled out in a rush.

Alix said nothing. She knew that if she'd been Gavin she would have done exactly the same thing. She could hardly fault him for enthusiasm and for hanging on to the client. Matt Connery might have tried a different bank if Gavin hadn't been so pushy. But, she thought, Gavin had lied when he said Matt hadn't asked to talk to her. She would never have lied about that. Never.

'Alix?' Jenny spoke tentatively. 'Alix, what's the matter?'

Quite suddenly, Alix wanted to cry. She wanted to put her head on the table and sob her heart out and tell Jenny that Paul had dumped her for some French nymphet who was dying to have his babies. She wanted someone to put their arms round her and tell her that it didn't matter, that Paul was a shit and that there were other fish in the sea. She sat up straight in her seat.

'Nothing's the matter.'

'But it's not like you,' protested Jenny. 'Being late, or being caught out – any of it.'

'I've just had a rough week or so,' said Alix. 'I am entitled to the occasional off week, don't you think?'

'Of course you are.' Jenny smiled at her. 'But it's unsettling,

Alix. And I hate it when I think the guys are ganging up on you.'

Alix laughed. 'You sound like my big sister when you say that.'

'I didn't mean it like that. It's just that there are so few women doing really well in this profession. I'm really proud that I work with you and that you're so good at the job. I hate to think that you'd let someone get the better of you.'

I've been dumped by my boyfriend, I'm making a mess of my career and I'm still a role model for Jenny Smith. Alix sighed. Some bloody role model.

'I won't let anyone get the better of me,' Alix promised. 'And when they debrief you on the result of lunch with me, you can tell them that I'm not pregnant and that I'm entitled to be late occasionally and that I haven't got any dreadful disease. You can tell them that I'm perfectly in control.'

'Great!' Jenny beamed at her although she still wasn't convinced that everything was OK.

'So, come on,' Alix pulled her chair closer to Jenny, 'tell me all about Anna's wedding. What are you going to wear?'

Chapter 9

The letter in the postbox was addressed to Paul. Alix could see at once that it wasn't an official letter that could be thrown in the wastepaper basket and ignored. This was a bulky letter, but it was personal. The envelope was pale blue and Paul's name and address had been handwritten. It wasn't a woman's writing, though, she decided. And it wasn't from Sabine Brassaert because the letter had been posted in Cork. Alix turned the envelope over and over in her hand. There was no return address. Whoever had sent it obviously didn't know Paul well enough to know he wasn't living in the apartment any more.

She picked up the phone and dialled the number for RTÉ. It just might be important for Paul to know about the letter – it could be information for a piece he was working on and he might need it urgently.

'I'm sorry,' said the guy who answered the phone. 'Paul isn't available right now.'

Alix glanced at her watch. After six. 'When will he be available?'

'He's working on something. I guess he'll be finished in about an hour.'

'Thanks,' said Alix.

She hung up and stared into space. There had been countless times when Paul had been waiting impatiently for original documents or certain correspondence to arrive by post – he'd always grabbed the envelope immediately and spilled its contents onto the table. He'd want this letter right away no matter what else he was working on.

She went into the bedroom and opened the wardrobe door. The one good thing about Paul's departure, she thought bitterly as she looked through the rails, was that she finally had enough room to hang up all her clothes.

She selected a wraparound skirt in vivid purple and a shocking pink T-shirt. She undid her hair from its clip and shook it loose around her head. Without her hair tied back and wearing the clashing T-shirt and skirt, she looked infinitely younger. Could almost pass for early twenties, she said to herself as she leaned towards the mirror to check for more grey hairs. As long as you didn't get too close.

She sprayed herself liberally with Escada Sport and slung her canvas bag over her shoulder.

The traffic through Donnybrook was terrible. She tapped the steering wheel impatiently as the Fiesta in front of her stalled on Morehampton Road. Oh, for God's sake, she muttered as the hapless driver failed to restart the engine, what the hell are you doing on the road if you can't drive? She glanced in her mirror, flicked the indicator and roared past the Fiesta.

Alix had been in the RTÉ complex a couple of times before. Once she'd been on a radio programme talking about interest rates and the need for a tighter fiscal policy. She'd been the only woman on the panel and the presenter had discriminated very positively in her favour so that she'd received loads of airtime while the men around the table glared furiously at her.

The second time she'd appeared on a television current affairs broadcast, talking about the impact of a change in China's foreign policy on European markets. Everyone in Europa Bank had watched the TV interview and had told her that she looked great. Feminine, Des Coyle had told her, but professional. And she'd made it sound interesting. Alix had laughed and told him that Chinese foreign policy could never compete with *Coronation Street* but she'd done her best.

Alix parked her car and walked up the steps to the radio studio.

'I'm looking for Paul Hunter,' she told the receptionist.

'Who shall I say?'

'Alix Callaghan.'

The receptionist dialled a number.

'He's in a meeting,' she told Alix. 'He might be a while.'

'Can you make sure he's told I'm here and waiting for him? It's urgent.'

'Sure. Would you like to take a seat?'

Alix nodded and sat down.

'. . . and now for financial news. Currency markets were quiet today with little activity. The US dollar . . .'

Alix didn't want to listen to RTÉ's financial report. She picked up a magazine and tried to ignore the radio broadcast.

'Alix! What's the matter?' Paul hurried into the reception area looking hassled.

'Hi.' She smiled at him. 'How are you?'

'I'm OK,' he said. 'But busy. What's the problem?'

'There's no problem,' said Alix.

'But they told me it was urgent.' Paul stared at her. 'I've just come out of a very important meeting because I thought there might be something wrong.'

'How sweet.' She smiled again. 'It might be urgent but I don't think there's anything wrong.' She took the envelope out of her bag. 'This arrived for you today. I know how you always have to rip your letters open so I thought—'

'But you dragged me out of a meeting!'

'How was I to know which was more important, your letter or your meeting? I just went on past experience. I'm sorry if I've upset you.'

'No.' Paul shook his head. 'You didn't upset me. Just surprised me.'

'You'd better get back to your meeting,' she said.

'Oh, it can wait a moment now,' said Paul. 'How are you, Alix?'

'Me? I'm fine.'

'You look great.'

'Thank you.' She smiled at him. 'I'd say the same but you look tired, Paul.'

'Oh, busy day, that's all.'

'I can imagine,' she said sympathetically. She ran her fingers through her hair. 'We've been pretty busy ourselves lately.'

'And how are things in the dealing room?'

'Not so bad,' she told him. 'That little shit Gavin Donnelly is getting a bit too big for his boots.'

'I'm sure you'll find a way to stamp him down,' Paul laughed. 'You generally do.'

'I'm much more mellow these days,' said Alix.

'Don't try to fool me,' said Paul. 'Mellow is something you'll never be.'

'Maybe not mellow,' she conceded. 'But I do my best. Anyway, I'd better go. I simply thought I should give you this in case it was something vital.'

'Thanks,' he said. 'It was thoughtful of you.'

'Anytime. Well, not anytime, I can't spend my life hurtling out here. Traffic was awful.' She pushed her hair back from her face again.

'Why are you wearing it like that?' asked Paul.

'Sorry?'

'Your hair? You usually tie it back.'

'A change,' she said. 'I told you, I'm trying to be mellow.'

'Oh, I see.'

'I bet you don't!' She grinned. 'Look, Paul, water under the bridge and all that – why don't we go for a drink?'

'I can't,' he said. 'I told you, I'm in a meeting.'

'I didn't mean straightaway.' She grimaced. 'You don't have to take me so literally. I meant some evening. You and me.'

'I'm pretty busy most evenings,' he said. 'As you can see.'

'Indeed.'

He met her eyes. 'But you're right. Water under the bridge, as you said.'

'How about tomorrow?'

'Tomorrow?'

'Why not?' She shrugged. 'It doesn't matter. Forget it. Maybe it's not a good idea.'

'No, Alix, wait. It is a good idea. I think we need to have a civilised drink together.'

'You sound like your mother.' She smiled wryly at him. 'A civilised drink. Like we were going to have two glasses of sweet sherry!'

'God forbid I should sound like my mother,' he laughed. 'OK, tomorrow.'

'Seven o'clock?' she suggested. 'Kiely's?'

'That would be great.'

'Absolutely,' she said. 'I'll see you then.'

'OK,' said Paul. ''Bye, Alix.'

She strolled down the stairs of the radio centre. He still fancied her. At least that was something!

❦

For the first time since Paul had left, Alix didn't wake up heart thumping and throat dry in the middle of the night. She went to bed at eleven and woke, refreshed, at six o'clock, just before the alarm went off.

She was at her desk by seven, flicked through news reports on overnight trading and had just completed a study of the last fortnight's profit and loss account for the dealing room when Dave Bryant walked in. He was surprised to see her.

'Morning,' he said as he dumped a bundle of newspapers on the desk. 'You're early.'

'Thought I'd make a head start.' She grimaced. 'I've been a little later than usual these last couple of weeks so I decided I'd better get myself back on track.'

'Everything OK?' asked Dave.

'Not a bother,' she told him. 'What on earth were we doing when I was in Paris? We seem to have been churning the sterling/euro book.'

'Just trading it,' said Dave.

'But so many trades.' Alix scratched her head. 'I know we ended up in profit at the end of the day, but you must have had a few dodgy exposures in the meantime.'

'We had some interests—'

'But these are all professional trades,' Alix interrupted him.

105

'None of them are on the back of corporate interests. You didn't have any customers calling, only other banks.'

'It was very volatile,' Dave said. 'And we thought we should take advantage of it.'

'I see.' She gazed at him for a moment and eventually he looked away.

Jenny arrived with some hot croissants from the shop across the road and prevented further discussion.

'Good morning!' She beamed at them. 'How are you all this morning?'

'Wonderful,' said Alix. 'Is one of those for me?'

'Of course, my leader!' Jenny smiled at her. 'You're looking very chirpy this morning.'

Alix knew that she looked good. She'd brushed her face with Christian Dior, her eyelids with Estée Lauder and her lips with Chanel. Despite her lack of interest in make-up she was forever buying it in the duty free and she normally wore it to work. But since Paul's departure she hadn't bothered. Now she was pleased she'd made the effort again.

She took a croissant from Jenny and poured some coffee from the pot. Everything was getting back to normal, she thought to herself. She felt OK again.

Gavin burst into the room. 'Sorry I'm late, Dave! I got stuck in – oh, Alix, hello.'

'Good morning,' she said. 'It doesn't matter that you're late. We hadn't started the morning meeting yet.'

Gavin flushed to the roots of his hair. Alix smiled at him. 'But now you're here, let's start.'

She outlined the strategy for the day, listened as Jenny gave a rundown on some interests their customers had, and reminded them that a guy from the New York office was

106

dropping by that afternoon. 'So I want us to look smart and efficient and at least make him think we know what we're doing!'

It was a busy morning. Alix talked to her customers, completed a few trades, felt good about things. At eleven o'clock she answered one of the flashing lines.

'Alix?'

'Yes,' she said. 'This is Alix Callaghan.'

'How are you? It's Matt Connery.'

'Hi, Matt. Sorry, I didn't recognise your voice.'

'That does my ego a lot of good,' he laughed. 'You're still meeting us here on Friday?'

'Absolutely,' she said. 'Eleven o'clock.'

'Looking forward to it,' he said. 'In the meantime, it's just small, but I have a quarter bar euros to put on deposit for a month. What can you pay me?'

A quarter of a million euros was a small amount in terms of interbank dealing.

'Three per cent,' she told him.

'OK, that's fine. Deutsche Bank will be paying them.'

'Great,' she said. 'Thanks for the call. And I believe we did a foreign exchange trade for you while I was away.'

'Yes,' he said. 'I was sorry to miss you. But the guy told me you were in Paris and mightn't be back this week.'

'I was in Paris all right, but I was back the next day.' She laughed although her eyes glittered green as she looked at Gavin.

'I'm glad I caught you this time,' said Matt. 'Though Gavin was very efficient.'

'All my team are efficient,' said Alix, 'especially Gavin.'

'I've got to go,' said Matt. 'My other line is ringing. One

day I'm just going to pull the plug on the phone! I'll see you Friday.'

'See you.' Alix clicked out of the line. 'Gavin?'

He met her eyes. 'What?'

'Why did you tell Matt Connery I'd be away this week?'

'I didn't,' said Gavin. 'He's getting it wrong.'

'I see.' Alix nodded. 'Thank goodness the customer isn't always right.'

She was pleased to see Gavin's face turn an interesting shade of red.

∽

'Alix, it's Paul for you. Line two.'

'Hi, Paul.' She sounded bright, breezy, confident.

'Alix, it's about tonight.'

'Oh?'

'I'm not sure I can make it. I'm really busy.'

'It's four o'clock,' she told him. 'Surely you'll be free by seven?'

'I hope so,' he said. 'It's just that I have a deadline of ten tomorrow morning for the piece I'm working on, and I'm nowhere near finished.'

'Ten in the morning is hours away!'

'Look, my work isn't like yours. I have to spend a lot of time thinking. I can't just write something straightaway.'

'I can't just execute a trade straightaway either,' she said. 'Not always.'

'You know what I mean,' he said. 'Anyway, I just thought it might be a good idea to leave it tonight. We can meet another time.'

'When?' asked Alix.

'Next week?' he suggested.

'OK.' She called up her electronic calendar. 'How about next Wednesday?'

'It looks OK,' said Paul. 'But it'll depend on how things are.'

'Paul, have you taken a job that allows you no social life whatsoever?' demanded Alix. 'Because it seems to me—'

'Wednesday's fine,' said Paul hastily. 'Sorry about this, Alix. If I'd been here longer maybe I wouldn't worry about it so much. But I want to get everything just right. Surely you, of all people, understand that? You're such a perfectionist yourself.'

'I'm not a perfectionist,' she said.

He laughed, a genuine laugh. 'Don't be utterly ridiculous. Of course you are.'

'Maybe,' she conceded. 'Thanks for ringing.'

'See you next week.'

She walked out of the dealing room and into the toilets. He was backing out of the deal, she thought with rage. He'd said he'd meet her and now he was backing out because – because why? He was afraid of her? That didn't make sense, he couldn't be afraid of her. Because he was afraid of himself? Because he knew that if he saw her again he'd want to move back in with her and have everything the same as it was before? Or was it simply that he didn't want to see her at all? But he'd been nice yesterday, she thought, they'd behaved in quite an adult way.

She leaned her head against the frosted glass window and sighed.

She wished she knew what she wanted from her life. At the moment, all she knew was that she didn't want it to be like this.

~

The light on the answering machine was blinking at her when she got home. Maybe Paul had rung, she thought, maybe he'd changed his mind and wanted to meet her after all. She kicked off her Bruno Magli slingback shoes and padded across the room.

'Alix? I suppose you're not there. I didn't want to ring you in the office. It's Carrie. What's all this about you and Paul? Ring me as soon as you get in.'

Alix groaned. She really didn't feel like having a long and involved conversation with her mother about her relationship with Paul. And any conversation with Carrie Callaghan became long and involved because Carrie had an opinion on everything and insisted on sharing it with whoever she was talking to.

I'll get changed, then call, Alix decided. She picked up her shoes and went into the bedroom. She took off her suit and hung it in the wardrobe, all the time wondering what Wyn had told their mother about her split with Paul.

Because the only way that Carrie knew was from Wyn. The two of them had always been close, much closer than Carrie and herself. Wyn and Carrie enjoyed long and intimate heart-to-heart discussions with each other, eagerly sharing the latest gossip about national and international movers and shakers. And Carrie was perfectly placed to find out lots of things about people. She ran a small but very exclusive beauty salon at the Grafton Street end of Chatham Lane and she also had a stake in a health farm just outside Wexford town. Her clients were rich and successful women and the wives of rich and successful men. Carrie never talked to anyone other than Wyn about them, but she had to talk to someone. And Wyn enjoyed being part of it all.

Alix knew that she had inherited her mother's business sense while Wyn had inherited her love of people. She often wondered what either of them had inherited from the father who had walked out on them when she was three years old. His academic skills was the obvious answer, yet Alix didn't want to think that her brains were the gift of someone who'd abandoned her.

She remembered her mother holding Wyn and herself closely to her and promising that she'd never leave, they were all strong women in this together.

It was after John Callaghan walked out that the two girls started to call their mother by her name. Neither of them ever referred to her as Mum again.

Alix pulled on a loose T-shirt and a pair of Levi's. She walked into the bathroom and sprayed Evian water onto her face. Then she went into the kitchen and took a bottle of Miller from the fridge.

She was just about to pick up the receiver when the phone rang.

'Hello,' she answered.

'Alix! It's me.'

'Hi, Carrie.'

'Did you get my message? I rang earlier.'

'Of course I got your message. I was just about to call you back.'

'Huh.' Carrie sounded disbelieving. 'I bet you didn't want to call! Have to tell me all about your love life.'

'I don't mind telling you.' Alix sat in her favourite armchair and tucked her legs beneath her. 'Paul and I are spending some time apart.'

'Why?' asked Carrie.

'I'm sure Wyn has already told you why,' said Alix acidly.

'Come on, Alix. Don't be like that. She's your sister. She's worried about you.'

'Oh, for heaven's sake! If she's all that worried she should have called me.'

'She just wanted to let me know.'

'So that you could spend ages talking about me behind my back.' Alix's voice trembled.

'Alix, darling, don't be ridiculous,' said Carrie gently. 'We just want to be sure you're OK. That's all.'

'I'm sorry,' said Alix. 'I didn't mean to get ratty. Sure, I'm OK.'

'You don't usually get ratty,' Carrie pointed out. 'So it's obviously having some effect.'

Alix sighed. 'I'm still upset, of course. I'm not sure how things are going to work out.'

'Do you want to get back together? Is there someone else?'

'No,' said Alix cautiously.

'How do you know?'

'I – it's – Paul is having a bit of a midlife crisis,' she told her mother. 'He wants to settle down and have kids.'

'Actually, a midlife crisis is usually where the man thinks having a wife and kids was a mistake,' said Carrie. 'And he has a messy affair with a girl who usually looks like a younger version of his wife.'

They were both silent for a moment.

'Did Dad have a midlife crisis?' asked Alix.

'Your father's life was one long crisis,' said Carrie. 'And we were well rid of him.'

Alix undid her hair so that it fell in front of her face. 'Are you sure?' she asked.

'What?'

'Are you sure we were well rid of him?'

'I don't want to talk about it,' said Carrie firmly. 'It's in the past.'

She never wanted to talk about it. The day he'd left, Carrie had bundled all the things he'd left behind into a bag, driven straightaway to the dump at Dunsink and thrown them in.

John had rung the house one day to ask when he could pick up his stuff and Carrie had laughed wildly and told him anytime but he'd have to be quick before it all rotted away completely. Wyn had told the story to Alix one night when Carrie had gone out and left them with a baby-sitter who spent the entire time reading a romantic novel and wiping tears from her eyes.

'So what are you going to do about Paul?' asked Carrie.

'I don't know.'

'Do *you* want to marry and have children?'

Alix bit her lip.

'Just because it didn't work for me doesn't mean it won't work for you.' Carrie said the words she'd said to her daughters a thousand times before. Wyn had believed them so much that she'd married at twenty-one.

'I'm meeting Paul next week,' she told Carrie. 'We'll have a chat then. I'll let you know.'

'Why don't you come into the salon beforehand?' suggested Carrie. 'I'll do you up, make you look so wonderful he won't know what hit him.'

Alix laughed. 'He'd get a fright if I suddenly turned up

113

in full metal jacket make-up. Thanks, Carrie, but I don't think so.'

'Come in anyway,' said her mother. 'I'll give you a massage. Then, no matter what happens, you'll be ready for it.'

'Maybe,' said Alix.

'Absolutely,' said Carrie.

'Thanks for calling.'

'Look after yourself.'

Alix replaced the receiver and finished her beer.

Chapter 10

A lix peered at the laptop on the desk in front of her and wondered if she needed glasses. She needed to make the print on her slides much, much bigger. But that meant cutting down on the information on each one.

She sighed and rubbed the bridge of her nose. She'd been working on the presentation for Anatronics all afternoon and she was tired. She looked through her glass window at the dealing room. Dave and Jenny were both reading the newspapers. Gavin was on the phone.

He worked hard, she thought ruefully. He was keen and he was arrogant but he worked harder than the other two put together. Dave was quick-witted and good at analysing trends. Jenny was methodical and got on well with the customers. But Gavin was all of those things as well as possessing a drive that neither Jenny nor Dave seemed to have. Alix knew that it wouldn't be long before Gavin would be looking for a promotion. Or another job.

She bit the tip of her finger. This was the first time she'd ever felt threatened by anyone in the dealing room. This was the first time she'd ever balked at giving someone extra responsibility because she knew that they wanted it. If she gave Gavin too much opportunity he could simply walk all over her. And she'd worked too hard to let someone walk all over her.

He was gesticulating as he spoke, obviously making the case for whatever trade he was trying to get the customer to do. His face was intense as he concentrated on the prices on the screen in front of him.

Of course he could always fly too high, Alix mused, as she watched him nod vigorously and begin tapping details of a trade on the keyboard. He could take one risk too many and end up out on his ear. She'd seen it happen before. It had almost happened to her.

She shuddered as she remembered. She'd been working in London at the time, dealing Kiwi, which was slang for New Zealand dollars. She'd been building a long position in them, confident that the New Zealand dollar was going to appreciate in value. She was almost at the limit of the amount she was allowed to hold when Rik Johnson, the financial controller of a beef processing plant, had called her saying that he needed to buy a million US dollars and sell Kiwis. The trade would push her over her limit but she knew that she could sell Rik's Kiwis easily enough and return to her correct position.

She bought the Kiwis, and almost straightaway the US dollar had roared upwards because a headline appeared on her Reuters screen saying that the US had fired a missile at Iraq. People were buying US dollars and selling other currencies because they always did whenever there was the faintest threat of military action. The value of the Kiwi had plummeted as the dollar soared.

Even remembering it now made Alix feel sick. She'd known that she should just cut the position and at least get back inside her limits but she couldn't believe that the US had really fired a missile at Iraq. She sat there for a minute as the profit and loss spreadsheet in front of her assimilated the new exchange rates. The numbers all turned red. What had been a small profit was turning into a significant loss before her very eyes.

And then, just as she was about to call another trader and cut the position, a US official's denial of the alleged missile-firing flashed across the screen. As quickly as it had gone up, the dollar came down again. The numbers in front of Alix had turned from red to black. Not only that, but the dollar fell lower than it had been before the news story broke. She cut the position straightaway.

Afterwards, Logan McDonald, the chief dealer, had called her into his office and asked her why she'd gone over her limit. She'd explained but he was furious.

'Those limits are for our protection. You can't just choose to break them whenever you like. You know the rules. I can fire you for this, Alix.'

She'd stared at him. 'But I made money for us.'

'That makes no difference. You broke the rules.'

She couldn't believe it. 'Are you going to fire me?'

He'd gazed at her for a moment, then shrugged. 'Not this time. Maybe you've learned something. But if you break a limit again, Alix, you're out.'

She hadn't broken a limit again, even though there were times when she wanted to. Whenever she felt really strongly about anything she talked to Logan about increasing the limit. Sometimes he did, sometimes he didn't. But she'd played by the rules every time.

She walked out into the dealing room.

'How are things going?' she asked.

'Not bad,' said Dave. 'Couple of late trades, nothing too exciting.'

'And you, Gavin?'

He looked up at her in surprise. 'What about me?'

'What was the last trade you did?'

Suddenly, he looked very uncomfortable. 'Me?'

'Yes, you.'

'Small foreign exchange,' he said. 'Nothing much.'

'Tell me about it.'

'We bought some dollars. We were a little bit short anyway. It was only a hundred thousand.'

She nodded. 'Who was the client?'

'Anatronics,' said Gavin.

She regarded him thoughtfully. 'Did they ask for me?'

Gavin looked even more uncomfortable. 'Yes,' he admitted eventually. 'But I said that you were busy. You did say that you didn't want to be disturbed and I thought that, for a hundred thousand dollars, you probably didn't.'

'You made a decision,' said Alix. 'It was entirely up to you.' She smiled at him and walked back into her office.

'Shit,' said Gavin as she closed the door behind her.

'I told you you should have called her,' said Jenny. 'She wants that account.'

'Well, let her fight for it,' said Gavin defiantly.

'Who d'you think would win?' Dave asked Jenny lazily. 'Our lovely leader or the young Turk?'

'Fuck off, Bryant,' said Gavin.

'Evens?' suggested Jenny.

Dave raised his eyebrows. 'You're that negative on our boss?'

Jenny flushed.

118

'I won't deal,' said Dave. 'I might be tempted to swing things one way or the other if I did.'

'Dave.' Alix opened the door. 'Can you find the report on the Far East that Guy sent over last week? I want to rob some info out of it.'

'Certainly,' said Dave. He grinned wickedly at Jenny and at Gavin. 'I always follow orders.'

∾

Alix took the laptop home and practised her presentation in front of the bedroom mirror. She never used notes when she spoke and she hated it when other people did. She liked to give the impression that she was simply talking to the people in the room, with each topic flowing easily from the one before. The slides helped to keep her focused and the graphs helped to keep her audience focused too.

She ran through the presentation three times. When Paul had lived with her, she'd always do the last practice run in front of him. He understood enough about finance to ask occasional questions and he would tell her whether or not the whole thing was boring. But she didn't need him to listen to the presentation. It would simply have been nice to have had his encouragement.

She picked out her purple suit before she went to bed. She knew that the purple was striking and that people remembered it. The skirt was calf-length and narrow and the jacket fitted to her waist. The suit made her look tall and commanding and gave her confidence.

∾

119

The meeting with Anatronics was at eleven o'clock. The markets weren't busy, and by the time she was leaving, Dave was already reading the sports supplements while Jenny was leafing through the *Guardian*. Gavin was doing a technical analysis study on the future direction of the South African rand.

'I'll be back by lunchtime, Dave,' she told him as she slung the laptop over her shoulder. 'This shouldn't take too long.'

'See you later,' said Dave. 'Have fun.'

She made a face at him then turned to Gavin. 'By the way, have you any particular recommendations for their yen cash flow?'

Gavin looked up from the graph. 'Not really.'

'Why? I thought you wanted this account.'

He glared at her. 'I want what's best for the company.'

'Oh, I see.' She beamed at him. 'That's great news, Gavin. I'm so pleased to hear it.'

Alix opened the sunroof of the BMW as she turned onto the M50. It had been cloudy until now but suddenly the sun had come out and she was hot. Alix looked enviously at the planes parked around the airport terminal buildings as she drove by and wished that she was heading off herself. A holiday would be nice, she thought, as she pressed harder on the accelerator. A relaxing, sun-soaked holiday where she could read a good beach book and forget about Paul and Gavin, Carrie and Wyn.

Anatronics shared a modern building in an industrial estate just off the motorway – a couple of miles past the toll plaza, Matt Connery had told her, the second exit and then to the left.

She could see the building, as he'd described it, from the motorway. She indicated and took the exit, then slowed down to find the entrance to the industrial estate.

This was one of the things she really liked about going to meet clients. When she was in the bank, using the telephone and the Reuters screens to trade, the reality of what she was doing always seemed remote. But when she went to see a client, when she walked around their offices or their factories, it all became more real to her and she knew that finance wasn't just about shifting money all around the world. She could help these companies be more profitable. If her advice was right, both the company and the bank would benefit.

She pulled into a space marked 'Visitors' and pushed open the glass door of the building. She gave her name to the receptionist and sat down on one of the steel and canvas chairs. She picked up the *Irish Times* business supplement and began to read it.

The jobs pages were crammed with advertisements. 'Head of Treasury for World Name in Banking,' she read. She wondered who that could be. The ad had been placed by a leading recruitment company.

'Surely you're not thinking of moving?' Matt Connery had appeared behind her and she jumped. She'd been half watching the lifts opposite, expecting to see him arrive from there.

'I just like to keep aware of what's going on.' She smiled at him and folded the newspaper. 'I'm already the head of treasury for a world name in banking.'

He laughed. 'We're in the boardroom. It's on the second floor.'

She picked up the laptop and her briefcase and followed him across the small reception area.

'We're hoping to move from here in a few months,' said Matt as he pressed the button in the lift. 'We're sharing this building with three other companies and it's getting rather crowded.'

'Is that because you're expanding or because the others are?' asked Alix.

'Both.' He gestured to her to step out of the lift before him. 'We've taken on some more people but so has everyone else here. It's good news for industry generally, though.'

'Absolutely.' Alix followed him into a room dominated by a large chrome and glass table. There was a projection screen at one end.

'Is this all you need?' asked Matt.

'It's fine.' She nodded.

'Let me round up the posse and we can get underway.'

She stood in the boardroom and stared out of the window. She could see the motorway where cars, lorries and freight containers whizzed past. It was busy, she thought. The economy was still strong.

She attached a lead to the projector, switched on the computer and called up the presentation. She experienced the usual frisson of fear that somehow it wouldn't work, that the disk had been corrupted and that she'd look like a complete fool. But Power-Point whirred into action and the Europa Bank logo appeared on the screen.

Her heart was beating faster now. It always did just before she made a presentation. She could never decide whether she was nervous or excited. She wiped the palms of her hands against her skirt.

'Alix, this is Michael Hollis, our managing director.' Matt re-entered the room followed by four other men. 'And this is Josh Redmond, another director. We also have Peter Carmody and Declan Barr with us today.'

'Gentlemen.' Alix shook hands with them in turn. 'Thank you so much for coming along.'

'Thank you,' said Michael Hollis, 'for taking the time to come across the city to see us.'

'No trouble,' she said. 'My pleasure.'

She cleared her throat and looked at the men sitting round the table. She wanted to make them all believe in her and her ability to deliver. The fact that they'd done a few small deals with her was incidental. There was a lot more business that Anatronics would be in a position to do and she wanted to make sure that Europa Bank got all of it.

Matt Connery smiled encouragingly at her. He imagined that she must be nervous. It couldn't be easy, he thought, for such a beautiful girl to walk into a room of five men and start talking about forwards and options, caps and collars. He'd heard most of this from her already, from the time he'd called in to see her in Europa Bank. He smiled a little at the memory of her sitting on the steps to the bank, puffing away at her (last) cigarette. She'd been embarrassed, he knew. As though she'd been caught out doing something she shouldn't. That had made her seem more vulnerable and she'd compensated, he thought, by being incredibly businesslike in the meeting with him.

There was no doubt that she knew her stuff. Michael Hollis had just interrupted her and asked her to explain the pricing of an option. And she hadn't faltered for a moment, she broke it down into steps so simple that a school child could have understood.

Matt was fascinated by her. She looked absolutely wonderful in the purple suit with the unbusiness-length skirt and the tight jacket which was cut a tiny bit lower than he would have expected. Her green eyes glittered as she spoke and the sun caught the auburn tones in her hair.

Was she always this cool? he wondered. Was she the sort of

girl who put her career before everything or was she, secretly, a homebird who only wanted to meet the right man before she settled down into a life of suburban bliss?

He couldn't see her settling down into a life of suburban bliss somehow. But he really wanted to know what she was like outside of working hours.

He remembered her on the night of the Europa Bank reception. Still cool, still professional, even when he'd wandered up to the dealing room and found her sitting there in the dark.

There had to be more to her than he was seeing now, he thought. Then he remembered her words when he asked her what she did in her spare time. 'I go to the gym and I shoot.' She looked like a woman who went to the gym. She looked toned and healthy although Matt thought that there were dark smudges under her eyes. But that could always be make-up, he told himself. You never know with women and make-up. He wondered what she was like when she was shooting. Did she wear camouflage gear and paint on her cheekbones? Did she stand up in front of the target or shoot lying down?

He shifted in his seat. It wasn't a good idea to think of her lying down.

'Any further questions?' Alix looked around at them. 'Matt?'

He dragged his mind back to the meeting. 'I don't think so.'

'Michael? Josh?'

'Tell us about the people in your team,' said Josh. 'I know you're the person in charge, but what about the people who work for you? How good are they?'

'Excellent,' said Alix briskly. 'Dave Bryant, who's the senior dealer, has nearly ten years' experience in the markets. He worked in London and Frankfurt before coming back to

Dublin. Jenny Smith has been with the bank for seven years. She's hugely experienced in all types of corporate business. Gavin Donnelly was with Hypo Bank before he came to us.'

'That's the guy I've been speaking with,' said Matt. 'I thought he was the senior dealer.'

Alix regarded him calmly. 'Gavin is a very experienced member of the team.'

Michael Hollis stood up. 'Thanks again, Alix. We'll look over the stuff you've left with us and decide what to do about forward cover in both the Far East and the States. But we're really happy with what you've done for us so far.'

'Great.' She unplugged the laptop. 'Anytime you have any questions, give me a call.'

They shook her hand and filed out of the room until only Matt Connery remained.

'You were good,' he said.

'It's my job.' She zipped up the holder for the laptop.

'You get so passionate about it.'

'Not passionate,' she said. 'It makes sense for companies to manage risk. That's all I do. Talk to you about managing risk.'

'What sort of risks do you take yourself?' he asked.

'Me? Personally?' She raised her eyebrows. 'I'm not a risk-taker. I take risk for the bank, of course, but that's entirely different.'

'What about the shooting?' asked Matt.

'The shooting?' She grinned at him. 'Very, very risk-free. There's a range officer to make sure no one walks out onto the firing range by mistake. I have a special sling to protect my arm. And I always wear my earplugs.' She picked up her bags.

'Would you like to go to lunch?' asked Matt.

She looked at her watch. It was a quarter past twelve. 'I told them I'd be back by lunchtime,' she said.

'Surely this very experienced team can manage without you?' Matt's blue eyes twinkled at her.

'Touché.'

'So you'll lunch with me?'

'I'm hungry,' she confessed. 'Talking always makes me hungry.'

She rang the office before she left. The markets were still quiet. Both Dave and Gavin were out and Jenny was looking after things.

'But I might as well be out too,' she told Alix. 'It's boring.'

'Not to worry. If it's still like this when I get back you can head home.'

'Great, Alix, thanks.'

'I won't be too late,' said Alix. 'I think we're only going to the pub for lunch. There isn't much else around here.'

She followed Matt's black Audi to the Spawell leisure complex which offered food and drink as well as a par-three golf course, go-karting, tennis and snooker.

'Gosh,' said Alix. 'Everything for the busy executive.' She looked out to the driving range where all the booths were occupied despite it being a Friday.

'It's always busy,' said Matt. 'What would you like to eat?'

'Soup and a sandwich is fine,' Alix replied. 'I'm hungry, but I couldn't eat much more.' She sat down at a table near the window.

'Are you sure that's all you want?' Matt looked at her doubtfully.

Alix nodded. 'Truly. I don't eat a lot during the day.'

'OK.' He ordered the same for both of them and sat down beside her.

She caught the faint smell of Polo aftershave. She had bought Paul some Polo aftershave once. She suddenly missed him with an intensity that hurt.

'Alix? Are you all right?' Matt looked at her anxiously.

'Of course,' she said. 'Why?'

'You looked – strange.'

'I'm fine,' she said dismissively. 'Do you come here often?'

'Pardon?'

'For lunch, I mean.' She looked around the crowded bar area. 'Is this a local for you?'

'Sometimes,' he replied. 'We're not exactly in the same class as the financial services sector when it comes to flashy restaurants.'

'I try not to spend too much time in flashy restaurants,' she told him. 'Not good for the waistline.'

'You seem to have a pretty good waistline from where I'm sitting,' he said. 'All that time in the gym, I suppose.'

'You remember a lot about me,' said Alix. 'The gym, the shooting. You don't need to know all that.'

'I like knowing the people I deal with,' said Matt. 'I like the relationship to be more personal.'

She looked at him thoughtfully. 'What do you mean by personal?'

'Not personal,' he said hastily. 'Friendly. I mean friendly.'

'That's OK,' she said. 'I want to make sure we have everything straight. I don't do personal with my clients.'

'Who do you do personal with?' Matt could have kicked himself. The question had formed in his head and spilled out before he had a chance to stop it.

'I don't think that should matter to you.'

'I know,' he said. 'I'm sorry.'

A barman arrived with their food. Alix sprinkled salt onto her soup.

'It's bad for you,' said Matt. 'Too much salt.'

She put down her spoon. 'If we gave up everything that's bad for us we'd never do anything. I like salt.'

'What else do you like?'

'You really do want to know personal things, don't you?'

Matt shook his head. 'Sorry, forget it. You rang the office, didn't you? What's going on in the markets?'

Alix felt more comfortable now that they'd switched back to business talk. 'It's quiet,' she told him. 'Although the European Central Bank will be releasing their monetary policy statement next week. Should have a bit of action then.' She outlined her view on the European Central Bank's monetary policy.

Matt Connery listened to her but the words went over his head. He was too busy wondering what Alix Callaghan would be like in bed.

⌒

She got back to the office at three o'clock. Neither Gavin nor Dave were back from lunch. Jenny was playing Solitaire on the computer.

'How did the presentation go?' asked Jenny.

'Pretty good.' Alix sat down in her chair and put her feet up on the desk. 'They didn't ask anything I couldn't answer and they liked some of the hedging ideas.'

'Where did you go for lunch?'

'The Spawell. A soup and sandwich with Matt Connery.'

'Is he the tall, blond guy that was at the reception?'

Alix nodded.

'No wonder you don't want Gavin to have the account.' Jenny grinned wickedly at her. 'Why should you give up a hunk of muscle like that!'

'What?'

'Alix! He's absolutely gorgeous. Don't tell me you hadn't actually noticed!'

Alix frowned. 'Of course I noticed he's good-looking, Jen. I'm not blind. But he's not my type.'

'He's probably married,' said Jenny gloomily. 'The gorgeous ones always are.'

'He might be.' Alix shrugged. 'I didn't ask.'

'Was he wearing a wedding ring?'

She shrugged again. 'Don't think so.'

'Oh, Alix, you're absolutely hopeless. If you're going to be like that you might as well just marry Paul and have done with it!'

Marry Paul. If he'd asked her to marry him instead of bleating on about settling down and having babies, what would she have said? Alix sighed. She would have said yes, because she always imagined she would marry him some-day. And she would have expected life to go on exactly as before.

'Alix? You OK?'

'Yes, absolutely.'

'Is everything all right between you and Paul?' asked Jenny. 'I thought that maybe—'

She broke off as Dave walked into the dealing room carrying a new golf club. 'Dennis gave it to me to try out,' he said. 'Looks good, doesn't it?'

'Great,' said Alix, relieved that she didn't have to talk to Jenny about Paul. She wouldn't have been able to lie to Jenny about him. She'd almost told her anyway. 'Who's Gavin lunching with?' she asked.

'Dunno.' Dave took a couple of practice swings with the club and almost put it through one of the screens. 'Oops, sorry, Alix.'

'Dave, how much have you had to drink?'

'Not much,' he assured her. 'We shared a bottle or two of Faustino and had a couple of beers.'

Alix sighed. 'Why don't you head off, Dave? It's quiet here anyway and there's no point in you hanging around.'

'They're still in the pub,' he told her. 'I was going to stay but I thought I'd better come back.'

'Decent of you,' she said. 'But feel free.'

'In that case, I'll see you on Monday.' He left the room whistling cheerfully.

'You might as well go yourself, Jenny,' said Alix. 'There's nothing happening.'

'OK, if you're sure.'

Alix nodded. 'Go ahead.'

She liked being in the room on her own. She liked knowing that information from all over the world was being concentrated on the screens in front of her.

She couldn't imagine giving it all up and having babies. Despite her grey hair and her biological clock. But she couldn't imagine doing both either. She didn't really believe it was possible to have it all. A lot of the time, she thought, it was difficult enough to have the part of it she had.

It was nearly half past four when Gavin returned. He looked surprised to see her there.

'I thought you'd stay out to lunch,' he said. His words were slurred.

'Just as well I didn't,' she said, 'since you decided to.'

'If I'd been you I would have stayed,' he told her. 'I would have stayed and I would have made sure that the Anatronics guy only ever wanted to talk to me.'

'I know,' said Alix.

Gavin blinked at her. 'How do you know?'

'I've seen people like you before,' she said. 'I know how you work.'

'Roy Dunphy offered me a job,' said Gavin. 'Corporate trader in Banco Andalucia.'

'And are you going to take it?' asked Alix.

Gavin shrugged.

'After all, there aren't so many corporate trader jobs these days. Since the euro, half of us have been wiped out. We're having to concentrate more and more on other options.'

'I might take it,' said Gavin. 'Or I might wait for your job.'

'It'll be a long wait,' said Alix. 'And you still have to think about Jenny and Dave.'

'Write off Jenny for a start,' said Gavin. 'She doesn't really care. And Dave wants to get out of trading.'

'Does he?' Alix kept her voice calm but she was surprised. She thought that Dave liked what he was doing.

'Ultimately,' said Gavin. 'He wants to be head of compliance.'

'Poacher turned gamekeeper.' Alix smiled.

'But I'm good,' Gavin told her. 'I'm the best dealer here.'

'Do you think so?'

'Yes,' said Gavin. 'I know I am.' He swayed a little on his feet.

'Why don't you go home,' said Alix. 'Or go back to the Harbourmaster – I think that's where Dave is. You and he can keep hatching your great career development plans. And when you've sobered up a bit, you can remember this conversation and feel embarrassed.'

'You could never embarrass me.' He stared her straight in the eye. 'Never.'

'We'll see,' said Alix.

꙳

She went to the gym after work and pumped iron until she was lathered in sweat. Then she went home, watched *Die Hard with a Vengeance* on TV and went to bed.

Chapter 11

Someone was chasing her. The road was long and straight and there was nowhere to hide. She could hear the sound of her attacker gaining on her and she tried for one last, desperate surge. But her legs were tired and someone seemed to have wrapped them up in heavy sacking because it was getting more and more difficult to move. And her pursuer was closing in now, she could hear the sound of his breathing over the bell ringing—

It was the phone. Alix emerged, tousle-headed, from the duvet which had wrapped itself around her as she slept. She was trembling with tension from the dream, from the fear of being caught.

'Hello.' Her voice shook.

'Alix? Are you OK?'

'Of course I am, Carrie.' She sat up in bed. The summer sun streamed through a chink in the curtains. 'I was asleep.'

'For heaven's sake!' Carrie sounded disgusted. 'It's ten o'clock on a glorious Saturday morning. What are you doing in bed?'

'Do you really want to know?' asked Alix.

'Oh! Alix! Don't tell me that you've actually—'

Alix laughed. 'I was having a nightmare, to tell you the truth. I'm kind of glad you called.'

'What sort of nightmare?'

'The chasing one,' said Alix.

Carrie murmured some words of sympathy. Alix had always had the chasing nightmare, even as a little girl. Carrie remembered her daughter coming into her bed, shaking with fright, terrified to go back to her own room and the shadowy someone who was running after her.

'It's OK,' said Alix impatiently. 'I'm fine now.'

'Well, get your ass out of bed and get in to the salon,' ordered Carrie. 'I have a cancellation for a twelve o'clock aromatherapy massage and it'll do you the world of good.'

'I don't need a massage,' said Alix. 'I need to do some shopping.'

'You've plenty of time for shopping,' said Carrie. 'Come on in. My God, loads of other women would kill for a free massage.'

'I'll pay you,' said Alix automatically.

'Not this time,' said Carrie. 'I want to give it to you. Cheer you up a bit.'

'I don't need cheering up,' Alix told her. 'I'm great. Honestly.'

'Everyone needs cheering up,' said Carrie. 'Twelve o'clock, Alix. See you then.'

Alix sighed as she got out of bed. She knew her mother was trying to be kind and supportive and she truly appreciated it. But she wasn't sure that she was ready for Carrie's questions yet or for her undoubted sympathy. She still hadn't got over the feeling of wanting to cry whenever she thought of Paul, even though she knew that she was being ridiculous.

She had a quick shower and pulled on a T-shirt and jeans. She'd been telling Carrie the truth when she said she needed to go shopping – there was virtually no food left in the apartment. She'd eaten the half-dozen Marks and Spencer dinners over the past couple of weeks – at least, she'd heated them up then discovered that she wasn't really hungry. There was no powder for the dishwasher (or maybe it was the washing machine), she needed toothpaste and dental floss, and, above all, she needed more beer and more wine.

Paul had always done the shopping. Paul was an efficient shopper who knew the prices of things and who always made sure that they didn't run out of any essentials. Even beer and wine.

Alix hated supermarkets. She felt ridiculous pushing a trolley around when she was only shopping for one, but those wire baskets weighed a ton when you put washing powder in them. She wished she'd checked whether it was dishwasher or washing-machine stuff that she needed. Not knowing meant that she had to buy both.

'Are you a club card holder?' asked the girl at the checkout.

Alix looked at her in bewilderment. 'Club card?'

'Do you have an in-store card?' the girl asked patiently.

'I don't think so,' said Alix. She shook her head. 'No, I don't.'

'Would you like to apply?'

Alix knew that there was a queue of impatient people behind her.

'Next time,' she said hastily. 'When I've more time.'

She paid for the purchases and carried them to the car. Were they club card holders? she wondered. Paul had never mentioned it to her. Not that it made any difference, she told herself. But it would have been nice to know.

She parked her car in Drury Street car park and made her way to Carrie's salon. She was dreading meeting her mother. She was afraid that she'd cry and, after the awful day when John Callaghan had walked out, she'd never cried in front of her mother again. Carrie had wanted them to be strong. Alix had wanted to be strong for her mother. She didn't want Carrie worrying about her, thinking that she couldn't cope. Besides, Carrie didn't cry. Carrie hadn't sat around and wondered what she should do with her life. Carrie had got on with things, worked at her business, earned success.

But it would be nice, Alix thought wistfully as she pushed open the door of Destressed, to have the kind of mother you didn't mind seeing you cry.

'Alix! You look . . .' Carrie Callaghan regarded her daughter thoughtfully, 'not as bad as I expected.'

'Well, thanks.' Alix gave her mother a peck on the cheek. 'You look wonderful, as always.'

'Thank you.' Carrie glanced at her reflection in the wall mirror. 'I do my best to advertise my work.'

She was a good advertisement. At fifty-five she was an elegant woman, fine-boned, with ash-blonde hair and eyes which were the same intriguing shade as her daughter's. Carrie's white shirt and navy trousers emphasised the trim body of a woman who looked after herself.

'Hi, Alix!' Samantha Sullivan, Carrie's twentysomething assistant, opened the door of one of the treatment rooms and glanced over the reception area. 'Having the works, are you?'

'Just a massage,' replied Alix.

'Nice,' Samantha smiled. 'Carrie, I forgot to mention that

Mrs Burton will be in at three for her facial. She changed it this morning and I knew you wouldn't mind.'

'Of course not,' said Carrie. Bernadette Burton was the wife of a senior government minister but, as Carrie said to Alix while she lay on the massage table, she was as nice as anything and wouldn't change an appointment without good reason.

'So is there anything I should know about government policy?' asked Alix.

'Nothing I could tell you,' said Carrie primly. She poured some oil onto Alix's back and began to knead her muscles. 'Good God, Alix, you're even more tense than usual!'

'Yeah, yeah.' Alix heard this every time her mother gave her a massage.

'I mean it,' said Carrie. 'Your shoulders are completely knotted. This business about Paul must be getting to you.'

'It's because I was busy yesterday.' Alix shifted a little to make herself more comfortable. 'I had a presentation to do and it took up a lot of time. The others left the office early and there was a settlements problem with some Greek drachma.'

'So that's why you're tense and that's why you had the chasing dream? A piddling little presentation and something wrong with Greek drachma?'

Alix sighed. 'It wasn't a piddling little presentation, it was a very important account. And three billion drachma had been paid into the wrong bank. Could have been very costly.'

'So the Paul thing isn't upsetting you at all?' Carrie's tone was neutral.

'Of course it's a bit upsetting,' Alix mumbled. 'Naturally it's making me a little tense.'

'Tell me about it.'

'I've told you already.'

'Not about the French woman, you haven't.'

I will *kill* Wyn, thought Alix viciously. I will tear her limb from limb. 'Honestly, Carrie,' she said mildly, 'haven't you and Wyn anything better to do than talk about me?'

'I told you before, we worry about you.'

'Worry about me!' Alix snorted. 'What's there to worry about? I have a good job, a nice apartment and a decent car. There's no need to worry about me. Ouch!'

Carrie prodded her daughter just below her shoulder blade. 'Very tense,' she said. 'Very, very tense.'

'You're making me tense,' said Alix. 'Look, I know you and Wyn love your gossipy evenings and telephone conversations and everything but there's nothing wrong with me and it's up to me to decide what I want to do about Paul.'

'Are you sure that it's not up to Paul to decide what he wants to do about you? Or his French girl?'

'Will you *stop* talking about this French woman,' snapped Alix.

'But she must be part of the equation.'

'She was a catalyst,' said Alix. 'Paul admitted that. But he hasn't run off with her or anything. She isn't even in the country.'

'Is he?'

'Yes,' said Alix shortly. 'He is.'

She hoped he was. She hoped he was at home tapping away on a keyboard, writing something against a deadline. She didn't like to think that he might be in Paris with Sabine. He couldn't be in Paris with Sabine. He didn't have time. He was working too hard – too busy to meet her earlier in the week.

'Tell me about her anyway,' Carrie said.

'Her name is Sabine,' Alix sighed. 'She's a designer. He met her in Paris.'

'And?'

'What?'

'What did they do in Paris?'

'For heaven's sake, Carrie!' Alix tried to turn over but her mother's hands on her shoulders prevented her. 'I don't bloody know.'

'You should,' said Carrie. She tipped some oil onto Alix's thighs and began to massage them.

'Maybe I don't want to know,' Alix admitted.

'It's hard for a man living with a successful woman,' said Carrie. 'And when he gets to Paul's age and starts thinking about a family, maybe it gets harder.'

'He could have talked to me about it.' Alix buried her head in the towel at the top of the table. 'We could have worked it out.'

'And now?'

Alix was silent for a moment. 'If I decide he's worth it, then I'll get him back,' she said.

'You're done,' said Carrie. 'Lie there for a couple of minutes and relax.'

She walked out of the room and Alix closed her eyes. She hated to think about Carrie and Wyn talking about her. She hated the fact that she was the object of their concern. Of their sympathy. She didn't want to be the object of anyone's sympathy. She was OK. She could cope.

The piped music was restful. She stopped raging at her mother and her sister and let Dvorak's New World Symphony soothe her.

'What are you doing for the rest of the day?'

Alix jumped, she hadn't heard Carrie open the door. 'I'm going to dinner with Terry and Wyn tonight,' she said. 'Where I will tell my bloody sister to stop gossiping with my bloody mother about me.'

'I told you, we weren't gossiping.' Carrie stood beside her daughter. 'Going anywhere nice?'

'I don't know,' said Alix. 'They want me to make up the numbers. Some business thing of Terry's.'

'Let me give you a facial,' suggested Carrie. 'You might as well look good anyhow.'

Alix screwed up her face. 'You mean I don't?'

'Let's just say that every little helps.'

Alix enjoyed facials. She decided to let her mother have her way.

❧

It was still warm by the time Alix was dressing for dinner. She chose a long, floaty dress in burnt sienna by Ghost, which emphasised her willowy frame and made her look both serene and elegant. She wore the gold earrings and gold necklace that Paul had bought her the previous Christmas. She'd intended to wear the emerald jewellery that she'd bought herself but had suddenly wanted something that Paul had given her. She sprayed herself with Dune which was her favourite evening perfume.

She wondered about tonight's dinner party. Wyn enjoyed entertaining and would happily cater for dozens of people, given the opportunity. Paul had never really liked going to Wyn's parties, although he always seemed to enjoy himself once he was there. At least, thought Alix as the taxi she'd ordered turned into Wyn's driveway, I won't have to worry if he's having a good time.

Nobody else had arrived. The only other car in the drive was Terry's.

'Hi, Alix! You look lovely!' Wyn smiled at her as she held open the front door.

'Hi, Wyn.' Alix kissed her on the cheek. 'So do you.' Wyn was wearing a pastel-pink linen dress and looked cool and refreshed in the warmth of the evening. 'Am I the first?'

'You're the only,' Wyn told her. 'We're not eating here tonight.'

'We're not?'

Wyn shook her head. 'Terry's booked Roly's.'

'Oh.' Alix was surprised. She rarely went out to dinner with her sister and her husband.

'We felt it would be best,' said Wyn. 'Otherwise Cathal might feel overwhelmed.'

'Overwhelmed?' Alix looked at her sister suspiciously. 'Who is this Cathal person? And who else is coming along?'

Wyn was saved from answering by Nessa and Aoife hurling themselves out of the kitchen and along the hallway to wrap their arms round Alix.

'Yes, yes, of course I brought you something,' she said in response to their eager questions. 'Don't I always?' She handed them each some sweets. 'Only for heaven's sake don't eat them all in one go. You know your mother doesn't approve.'

'Oh, she doesn't mind really,' said Nessa calmly. 'She never lets us eat sweets normally, that's why we like it when you come, Alix.'

'It's so nice to be wanted.' Alix grimaced.

'Terry! Are you ready yet? Alix is here!' Wyn shouted up the stairs to her husband.

'Of course I am,' he answered as he came downstairs. 'No need to yell, Wyn.'

'I thought you were beautifying yourself.' She smiled at him and kissed him on the lips.

'OK,' said Terry. 'Are we ready?'

'Sure.' Wyn opened the living-room door. 'Girls, see you later. Behave yourselves and do what Miranda tells you. Miranda,' she looked at the baby-sitter, 'get them to bed by ten.'

'OK, Mrs Mitchell.' Miranda looked up from the book she was reading.

'See you.' Wyn blew a kiss at her daughters. 'Be good.'

Alix followed her sister and brother-in-law outside. Terry unlocked his Audi and held the door open for Alix.

'Tell me about tonight,' said Alix as Terry started the car. 'Why are we going to a restaurant? Who else is going to be here? What does this Cathal bloke do?'

She saw Wyn and Terry exchange a quick glance.

'Wyn!' She leaned forward. 'What is tonight all about?'

'It's not about anything,' said Wyn. 'It's just dinner, that's all.'

'But who else is going to be here?' asked Alix urgently. 'Who—'

'The four of us,' said Terry. 'You and Cathal. Wyn and myself.'

'Is this some sort of set-up?' demanded Alix. 'You've never had a dinner party for one person before. What exactly is all this about?'

'Cathal Moran is a really nice bloke who works in our finance department,' said Terry quickly. 'You'll like him, Alix. You'll have a lot in common with him.'

'Will I?'

'Absolutely,' said Wyn. 'Truly, Alix, he's really sweet. And he's just come back from two years in Brussels. He doesn't know anyone.'

'Wyn.' Alix's voice was dangerously low. 'Is this some kind of blind date?'

'I wouldn't put it like that,' said Wyn. ·

'How exactly would you put it?'

'It's just a dinner engagement.'

'Is this a business dinner or a social dinner?' asked Alix.

'A bit of both.'

'I don't believe it.' Alix flopped back into the seat. 'I don't believe you two! You're setting me up with some bloke I've never met before. What on earth has got into you?'

'Oh, come on, Alix.' Wyn turned to look at her. 'I told you, Cathal's a decent guy. He's lonely. We thought it would be nice if—'

'Well, you bloody thought wrong!' said Alix angrily. 'I'm not going to dinner with someone I haven't met before and I'm not taking part in some ridiculous dating game you've set up.'

'Alix, be reasonable,' said Terry. 'It is partly business. Cathal is an up-and-coming member of the company. I want to take him under my wing a bit.'

'Terry, I don't want to get involved with up-and-coming people,' said Alix. 'I know enough of them already.'

'Oh, be a sport, Alix. Besides, you might like him.'

Alix gritted her teeth. 'I don't want to like him.'

'That's being silly,' said Wyn. 'You're cutting off your nose to spite your face.'

I wish I'd cut off yours, thought Alix, seething with rage, then you wouldn't keep sticking it in my business.

She was still angry as she followed Terry and Wyn up the stairs into the restaurant. Normally she liked the buzz of conversation, the chink of glasses, the clatter of crockery. But all she wanted to do now was to go home. She hated being manipulated like this.

Cathal Moran was already at the table. He stood up as they arrived and Alix guessed he was around six feet tall. He had sandy hair, grey eyes and a light tan that covered a cheerful, freckled face.

'Hope we didn't keep you waiting,' said Terry.

'Not at all.' Cathal smiled at them. 'Nice to see you again, Wyn. And this must be Alix.' He held out his hand to her.

Alix grasped it firmly and shook it. 'Hi.'

'I've heard so much about you,' said Cathal.

'I've heard so little about you,' said Alix wryly as she sat down.

'What do you want to know?'

'I haven't decided yet.' Alix took a menu from the waiter and opened it.

'Anyone like a drink?' Terry asked.

'Gin and tonic,' said Alix.

'Same for me,' Cathal nodded.

'Martini,' said Wyn.

'And I'll have a gin and tonic too,' Terry told the waiter.

The four of them studied their menus in silence. Alix peeped over the top of hers and quickly looked away when she realised that Cathal was observing her. I'll kill them, she thought again. They'll wish they'd never been born! What on earth was Wyn thinking about, agreeing to this charade?

144

She kept her menu open until well after the others had closed theirs.

'How were the markets this week?' asked Cathal when she finally put the menu down on the table.

'Quiet,' said Alix.

'Are the Brits going to cut interest rates?' he asked.

Alix shrugged. 'Hard to say.'

'Is it likely? Do you think they should?'

'Since none of the economists agree, it probably doesn't matter an awful lot what I think.' God, she thought, you sound so petulant. It's not his fault he's been dragged out here too. 'But yes,' she added, 'I think they should.'

'So is it as exciting working in a dealing room as everyone says?' asked Cathal. 'I remember when I was in college, so many of the guys wanted to give financial services a go.'

'It's a job,' replied Alix. 'I enjoy it.'

'But what about the male-dominated part of it?' Cathal asked. 'Don't you find it difficult giving orders to a load of men?'

'No.'

Wyn stifled a giggle and Cathal sighed. 'That's me put in my place.'

Alix shrugged. 'I'm sorry, but people ask me that all the time. It doesn't make any difference to me whether I work with men or women. Men are more confrontational, certainly. Women try to be more helpful. But at the end of the day you either make money or you don't and it doesn't matter whether you're a man or a woman then.'

'I worked for a woman once.' Cathal buttered a slice of tomato bread. 'She was pretty good. But she gave it up to have babies.'

Alix tensed. She didn't want to get into this particular debate.

'But Terry tells me that you've no interest in children.'

She flicked an angry glance at her brother-in-law who was unconcernedly looking around the restaurant.

'Alix is very good with children,' said Wyn. 'She treats my two daughters like they were her own.'

No, I don't, thought Alix. If they were my kids I wouldn't bring them Bertie Bassett sweets every time I came home. I wouldn't play hospitals with them and let them inject me with the meat baster!

'I like children,' said Cathal. 'Although I'm certainly not in a rush to settle down and have any!' He beamed at Alix who smiled weakly in return.

The waiter came with their drinks and took their dinner order. Alix gulped some gin and tonic.

'Have you ever made a whole heap of money?' asked Cathal. 'Or – worse still, I suppose – lost it?'

'I've done both at various points,' replied Alix. 'And making it is certainly better fun.'

'You make a lot of money, don't you?' said Wyn.

'For me or for the bank?' Alix asked.

'For the bank, of course.'

'I suppose I do.'

'And what do you do for recreation?' asked Cathal. 'I knew a dealer in Brussels who was into hang-gliding. He'd jump off the edges of cliffs on his hang-glider! Had dreadful trouble with his life assurance.'

Alix smiled slightly. 'I don't do anything half as hazardous.'

'What about the shooting?' asked Terry.

'That's not dangerous,' Alix laughed. 'Unless you're a piece of paper!'

'Remember when you took up judo?' Wyn made a face at

Alix. 'And you did some throw and dislocated your shoulder? Poor Carrie nearly had a fit.'

'That was years ago,' Alix reminded her. 'And someone threw me. I just didn't land properly.'

Cathal smiled and leaned back in his chair. 'At least it means that you can look after yourself, Alix,' he said. 'And whoever you go out with too. No worrying about muggers at any rate.'

'I guess not,' she said as the waiter put her roulade of crab in front of her. 'I guess not.'

He wasn't bad, she admitted to herself as she touched up her make-up in the ladies'. He kept quizzing her about her life but she couldn't blame him if he was a direct sort of guy. And, during the meal, he'd lightened up a bit, related some stories about his work in the European Commission in Brussels. But she didn't find him remotely attractive. They'd both reached for the salt at the same time and his hand had brushed against hers and she felt absolutely nothing. He'd smiled at her then, a kind of complicit smile, but it had left her cold.

She wished Terry and Wyn hadn't set this whole evening up. It wasn't fair on her and it certainly wasn't fair on Cathal who seemed to have been living the life of a monk in Brussels, if his stories were to be believed. No time for anything but work. No wonder he was pleased to be home.

She ran her fingers through her hair and leaned towards the mirror. The roots were beginning to show a little grey again. She bit her lip. She wondered what Cathal thought about grey-haired women.

He lived in Ranelagh and offered to share a taxi home with her.

'Good idea,' said Wyn.

'I was going to walk,' said Alix. 'It's not far. And it takes Cathal out of his way.'

'Not really,' he said. 'But if you want to walk, I'll join you as far as your apartment. Make sure you get home safely.'

Alix groaned to herself. She'd realised, almost as soon as the words were out, that she'd made a mistake to talk about walking. 'Don't feel as though you have to,' she told him. 'I walk quite fast. As exercise.'

'I could do with some exercise myself after that meal.' Cathal patted his stomach. 'Terry, it was great. Thanks very much.'

'No problem,' said Terry as he signed the Amex slip. 'We like to make sure everyone feels welcome in the firm.'

'I feel very welcome now,' said Cathal. 'Wyn, thanks for giving up your Saturday night.'

'Cathal, it's not like my Saturdays are a riot of entertainment.' She grinned at him. 'It's dreadful to need an excuse for my husband to take me out.'

It was warm outside. The gentle breeze drifted along the road and rustled through the trees of Herbert Park. Alix pushed a strand of hair out of her eyes.

'We'll be off then,' she said. 'I'll give you a call, Wyn.'

'Yes, do.' Her sister kissed her. 'Safe home.'

'It's OK, Wyn, she has me to look after her,' Cathal said. 'And she *is* a judo expert, isn't she?' He grinned at them. 'See you Monday, Terry.'

'See you, Cathal.' Terry and Wyn walked hand in hand to their parked car.

Alix wished she had pockets so that she could shove her own hands into them.

'I like your brother-in-law,' said Cathal as they began to walk. 'He's friendly. So's your sister.'

'Yes.'

'I thought you would be more outgoing,' he said candidly. 'I always thought that dealers were the in-your-face sort.'

'And is that the sort you prefer?' asked Alix.

'Not at all.' Cathal took her arm. 'I like you, Alix.'

She felt herself flinch. 'I like you too,' she said. 'But I've got to be honest with you, Cathal, I'm not looking to go out with anyone right now.'

'Why not?'

'I'm really still in a relationship.'

'Not according to Terry,' said Cathal calmly. 'According to Terry you've split up with your boyfriend.'

'Have you been talking to him about me?' she demanded.

'Only chatting.' Cathal steered her across the road. 'So don't get uptight about it, for heaven's sake!'

'Look.' Alix stopped walking and turned to him. 'I don't know exactly what Terry's agenda is, or yours, or Wyn's. But the truth of the matter is that I haven't yet split with the man I've known for the past three years. And even if I had I'm not ready to go out with someone new yet. And even if I was, I don't know if that person would be you.'

Cathal raised his eyebrows. 'Don't tell me I fall down on all your requirements?'

She smiled at him. 'Of course not. But I'm not ready to jump into the whole going-out thing again. Honestly, I'm not.'

'Hey, I'm not ready for any great commitment either,' said Cathal easily. 'Let's wait and see, OK?'

'OK,' she said.

They walked in silence back to her apartment. She didn't ask him in for coffee and he didn't try to kiss her goodnight.

She was still going to kill Wyn. And Terry. And anybody else who tried to mess with her life.

Chapter 12

Alix unlocked the apartment door, went straight into the kitchen and rummaged in the bottom drawer of the fitted unit to find her emergency packet of cigarettes. Despite the fact that she'd left all the windows open, the apartment was like an oven. She opened the patio door and stepped out onto the balcony. The air was milky-warm on her bare arms.

Alix lit a cigarette and breathed in the smoke. Part of her was disappointed in herself for lighting it in the first place. Another part of her was grateful for its soothing properties. She inhaled again and the tip of the cigarette glowed in the darkness.

She thought about Cathal Moran as she leaned on the balcony rail and stared into the inky blackness of the canal. He definitely wasn't her type. She wasn't exactly sure what her type of man really was, since all of her boyfriends had been very different. But she knew, somehow, that it wasn't Cathal.

There'd been quite a few boyfriends when she was still at school, but none of them had lasted very long. It wasn't that she'd had any problem grappling with them in the laneway beside her home, or that she'd been shy about trying alcohol or cigarettes or doing any of the things that Carrie hoped she wouldn't do, it was just that she grew bored with them very quickly. What was the point, she'd once asked Wyn, in wasting time with blokes that just weren't interesting? Practice, Wyn had told her, but Alix had shrugged and said she didn't need any.

Sophia Redmond, who'd been her best friend at college and who had worked with Morgan Stanley in New York for a couple of years before being headhunted back to London, had once told her that she never let men get close enough.

Alix had retorted that she'd let far too many of them get close. But she knew that Sophia wasn't entirely wrong. There was always a point in her relationships when she panicked, when someone wanted more commitment than she was prepared to give. And that was the point at which she would call it a day. She had always been the one to call it a day.

'You definitely have a problem,' Sophia told her the day after she had split up with yet another boyfriend, a solicitor named Christopher Symmons. 'You just can't hack togetherness.'

'Not at all,' she'd replied briskly. 'I just haven't met my type yet.'

And now, standing alone on the balcony of the apartment which she'd bought herself five years earlier, she wondered if she ever would.

She thought it had been different with Paul. She hadn't expected to fall for a journalist who thought her job was a heap of rubbish even though the subsequent article made her sound like a cross between Margaret Thatcher, Kate Moss and Ulrika Jonsson. *'Callaghan needs very little sleep. She hits the hay around midnight and is up before six most mornings. But you wouldn't know it to look at her. She is tall and slender with an arresting face and eyes that glitter like a pair of emeralds. But it's not all work for Callaghan. Friday nights see her drinking pints with the lads and she never once during this interview complained about sexism in the workplace.'*

She'd had to endure a lot of stick from her colleagues in the bank after that had appeared. But she hadn't cared. For the first time in her life she liked someone ringing her in the office, or waiting for her in reception or cooking her dinner at night. Paul had seen her as someone to take care of and she'd enjoyed the way he looked after her. She'd *allowed* him to look after her. She'd let him get close and she'd opened up to him and now it looked as if that had been a terrible mistake.

So now she was supposed to start all over again. Meet new men. Find out about their likes and dislikes. Learn what made them tick. She shuddered. She wasn't ready for all that. She didn't want to do it all over again. She'd been right never to get involved before. And she wasn't going to become some manic thirtysomething looking for a man, any man.

Was this how people saw her now? A solitary, ageing female for whom they would have to trawl their lists of acquaintances to find a remotely suitable man? Instead of Alix Callaghan, have-it-all, successful, envied financial dealer who lived with an attractive, articulate man, she would now be Alix Callaghan, single, depending on her job for fulfilment but never quite finding it. She was an Alix Callaghan that deserved sympathy because she was thirty-two and had wasted three years of her life on a bloke who was quite prepared to run off with the first available blonde that came into his life. Alix Callaghan, the odd number at dinner parties. Alix Callaghan who'd probably end up looking through the lonely hearts columns of newspapers and afraid to ring up any of them in case they were sickos.

She finished her cigarette and flicked it over the balcony and into the canal. She was ashamed of herself for doing that because she was firmly anti-pollution as far as the canal was concerned, but she'd felt like doing something bad. She recognised the feeling from her childhood, when she'd deliberately drop a plate when drying the dishes or splash a tidal wave of water over the side of the bath when she was getting in. Carrie would look at her impatiently and ask her if she was born clumsy and Alix would stick out her jaw and say, yes, she was.

She could see Carrie now, in her imagination, standing in the living room looking out at her and asking if she just wanted to stay alone forever. Because, she could almost hear Carrie say, you'll have to make an effort, Alix. Most of the good ones have been snapped up by now.

The phone rang and startled her. She went back inside and picked up the receiver.

'Hello?'

'Hi, Alix.'

'Who's that?'

'How quickly they forget!' The man's voice was amused. 'It's me. Cathal.'

'Cathal! How did you get my number?'

'I got Wyn to write it on the back of the business card you gave me,' he told her. 'I really didn't want to call you at work.'

God, thought Alix, Wyn was really pushing it. She was going to have a real heart-to-heart with Wyn. Tell her that she, Alix, was perfectly capable of looking after her own love life, thank you very much. And stop bloody interfering.

'I rang to say that I enjoyed tonight,' said Cathal.

'Did you?'

'Oh, absolutely. I like Terry and I like Wyn. But, obviously, it was you I liked the most.'

Alix made a face at the phone. This was the corniest line she'd ever heard. She said nothing.

'So I was wondering if you'd like to get together again sometime?'

She sighed. 'I thought I told you—'

'You said you weren't ready for commitment. I understand. Neither am I. But there's nothing wrong with us being friends.'

'I'm not a great believer in the theory that men and women can be good friends,' said Alix wryly. 'Sex usually complicates matters sooner or later.'

'Hey, it was you that brought up sex, not me. Just remember that in the future, will you?' Cathal sounded amused, and despite herself, Alix smiled.

'Thanks for ringing,' she said. 'But I've got to go, Cathal. I'm very tired.'

'So what about another night?'

'Maybe,' she compromised. 'I'm honestly not sure.'

'How about I call you next week?' suggested Cathal. 'Give you a bit of time to think about it.'

'Yes, fine.' Suddenly Alix wanted the conversation to be over. 'I've got to go, Cathal. 'Bye!'

'Goodbye,' he said, but he was already talking to a dialling tone.

She poured herself a gin and tonic and went back outside.

∽

Cathal stood on the pavement opposite her apartment and wished that he could see the balconies on the other side of the block. He was sure she'd be sitting on the balcony. He'd hoped she'd ask him up. The fact that she hadn't made him feel very uncomfortable. He was beginning to lose his touch.

He sighed and put his mobile phone back in the pocket of his jacket. Then he flagged down a taxi to take him home.

❧

Alix couldn't sleep. She turned over in the double bed and pushed the light summer duvet away from her. She'd never been so warm in her life, not even on the holiday in Greece when there'd been a heat wave that had sent everyone, tourists and natives, scurrying for cover.

She wondered what Paul was doing now. It was difficult to imagine that, at the exact same moment, he was living his life, not even thinking about her, not caring about her. When she tried to picture him, the images of Sabine cluttered her memories so that she couldn't separate the pictures of Paul from the visions of his latest love.

He doesn't love Sabine, she told herself fiercely. And he isn't going to move in with her and have babies. It's a revolting concept. If he wants babies, he can have them with me.

But she found that concept even more revolting.

❧

She started to sneeze at three o'clock. She sat up in the bed and reached for a tissue. Her eyes hurt and her head throbbed. Though it was still warm in the room, she shivered. Bloody hell, she thought, don't tell me I'm coming down with a cold. We've had the hottest summer in living memory and I might have a cold. Bloody wonderful!

She pulled on a T-shirt and went into the kitchen. Her throat was hurting now and every bone in her body ached. She poured herself some orange juice. She peered blearily at the carton as she closed it again. Best before 15 July. Out of date. If the cold didn't kill her, the orange juice probably would.

She got back into bed and pulled the duvet around her. She was shivering now, really cold. She wished that she had someone – anyone – to cuddle her. Selfish bitch, she told herself, wrapping herself even more tightly in the duvet. Whoever it was wouldn't thank you for giving them the flu.

She tossed and turned, alternately cold and hot, before falling into a fitful sleep around six o'clock. She opened her eyes again at seven, wished that she had her gun handy so that she could shoot the magpie that was screeching outside her window, and then suddenly fell into a deep and dreamless sleep.

The phone woke her. She was tired of the phone waking her, she thought, as she reached for the receiver.

'Hello?'

'God, Alix, you sound rotten.'

'Thanks, Wyn.'

'What on earth did you and Cathal get up to last night?' Her sister chuckled. 'It wasn't that late when we left you.'

'It wasn't late when he left me either. Hold on a second, will you?' Alix dropped the receiver on the bed and reached for another tissue. Her nose was sore. She bet it was red.

'You OK?' asked Wyn.

'More or less,' replied Alix. 'I've got a cold.'

'Poor thing.' Wyn didn't sound in the slightest bit sympathetic. 'Do you need anything? Will you be OK?'

'I need peace and quiet,' said Alix. 'And I'll be fine.'

'I just called to see how you and Cathal got on,' said Wyn. 'But I'll phone back if you like.'

'No need.' Alix lay down, holding a tissue to her nose

and the phone to her ear. 'There was no getting on, as you put it.'

'Alix, he's a perfectly nice guy. What's wrong with him?'

'Nothing,' Alix told her. 'Absolutely nothing.'

'Didn't you have a decent conversation as you walked home? Did you ask him in for coffee?'

'Really, Wyn, don't be ridiculous. Of course I didn't ask him in for coffee. What d'you take me for? If I'd asked him in for coffee we would have ended up in bed and I didn't want to go to bed with him.'

'You don't have to go to bed with everyone you invite into the apartment for coffee,' said Wyn waspishly.

'Well, Cathal Moran would have expected it,' said Alix.

'Not necessarily.'

'Yes necessarily.'

'But—'

'Look, Wyn, he's a perfectly decent bloke and all that but there's really no need for you to try and fix me up with someone. I'm capable of looking after myself.'

'We weren't trying to fix you up.' Wyn sounded hurt. 'Terry had asked Cathal about dinner ages ago. We would have invited you and Paul if you'd been able to hang on to him.'

'What do you mean, "hang on to him"?' demanded Alix.

'Oh, come on,' said Wyn. 'You've got to face facts. He's dumped you for some French crumpet and he's not coming back. All this shit about space and everything is just a sop to his conscience.'

'Actually,' said Alix as she burrowed even deeper beneath the duvet, 'Paul and I are meeting for a drink on Wednesday. So you can just forget about your stupid matchmaking plans with Cathal. Thanks all the same!'

'A drink? You and Paul?'

'I told you but you didn't believe me.' Alix blew her nose. 'It *is* all about space and time and working things out.'

'He'll probably just tell you it's all over,' said Wyn.

'Gee, thanks for your support!'

'These on-again-off-again things seldom work out,' Wyn told her. 'And I'm not trying to be mean to you, Alix. All I'm saying is that you can't hang about any more. You've wasted your three best years with Paul. You need to get out there and find someone else before it's too late.'

'For Christ's sake!' Alix was so annoyed that she sat up, even though it made her head ache. 'You're talking as though I was on my last legs, Wyn. I'm thirty-two years old, not a candidate for the Sunnyside Home for Retired Gentlewomen. I have a great life as it is. I don't need someone in it. I might choose to have someone in it, but that's entirely different.'

'You're nearly thirty-three,' Wyn told her. 'Terry and I didn't manage to have kids straightaway. It might be the same for you. Next thing you know you're in your late thirties, childless and struggling to conceive. And don't tell me that's rubbish because it isn't. It's exactly what'll happen. You just don't hear your bloody clock ticking because you're obsessed with that stupid job!'

'I don't need to hear any clock ticking,' said Alix furiously. 'And who says I want any kids anyway? And even if I did, it's up to me to decide when to have them.'

'No, it's not,' said Wyn. 'You might decide when you'd like to have them and your body might disagree. You've got to face facts, Alix. You can't control everything.'

'I don't need to control everything.'

'Of course you do,' said Wyn. 'You plan, you manipulate,

you do exactly what you want when you want. You control, Alix. But you can't control your biological clock. It's doing its own thing and it isn't waiting for you.'

'You can be a real bitch sometimes.' Alix blew her nose again.

'I'm just telling you stuff you don't want to hear,' said Wyn.

'Well, thanks for waking me up and reminding me that I'm an ageing single woman with nothing to look forward to.'

'You can look forward to another date with Cathal.'

'No, I can't.'

'Why not?'

'Because he's not my type.'

'Oh, for crying out loud!' Wyn's tone was sheer exasperation. 'Of course he's your type. Corporate. Businesslike. Works out in the gym. Exactly like you, Alix. Exactly.'

'Then maybe that's why he isn't my type,' said Alix triumphantly.

'Alix,' said Wyn gently, 'believe me. One day you'll wake up and there won't be any of your type left.'

'Goodbye, Wyn,' said Alix.

'I'm only trying to—'

'I'm going back to sleep,' said Alix. 'I want to get rid of this cold by tomorrow. I have a busy day at the office ahead of me.'

But her cold got worse, not better. By four o'clock in the afternoon she'd gone through an entire box of Kleenex for Men and her nose was like a red beacon. Her throat was sore and her eyes continually watered.

She sat, shivering, on the sofa and watched black-and-white movies on TV while trying to read the business section of the *Sunday Times*. The last time she'd had a cold like this, Paul had brought her hot toddies and made her stay in bed. But she didn't like staying in the double bed on her own. She wished he was here now, to rub her aching shoulders and tell her that she'd be better before she was twice married. Huh, she thought miserably, how right he was.

She found a bottle of Night Nurse in the bathroom cabinet and took a dose at seven o'clock. Then she went back to bed and fell asleep.

✑

For the third day in a row, the phone woke her. She picked up the receiver and tried to say hello, but a strangled croak was all that came out of her mouth.

'Alix, is that you?'

'Yes,' she rasped.

'It's me, Jenny. When you weren't in by eight I thought I should ring. You know you have a meeting with Des and the finance guy from Sorrento Products at ten, don't you?'

Alix glanced at the alarm clock. She'd forgotten to set it the previous night. But she never slept as long as this. Thirteen hours! It must have been the Night Nurse.

'I've got a slight cold,' she said.

'What?'

'A cold,' said Alix.

'You sound terrible,' said Jenny. 'Do you want me to cancel the meeting? Or let Dave go instead?'

'No,' Alix croaked. 'I'll be in. I have a lot of stuff for that meeting.'

'Are you sure?' asked Jenny doubtfully. 'It sounds like more than a cold to me, Alix.'

'I'll be there,' said Alix painfully. 'Don't worry.'

She hauled herself out of bed and into the shower. The hot water helped but she still felt rotten. She stood in the bathroom, wrapped in a blue-and-white striped towel, and wished, for the first time ever, that she didn't have to go in to the office.

She dried her hair and pulled it back and secured it with a tortoiseshell clip. Her face was blotchy, as though she'd spent the night crying. Her skin was sensitive and stung when she applied some foundation.

But the make-up made her look less haggard. She sprayed herself liberally with Issey Miyake perfume. She hoped she hadn't been too heavy-handed. Her nose was so blocked that she couldn't smell a thing.

∽

There was an air of quiet efficiency about the dealing room. Jenny was on the phone to a dealer in London, Dave was chatting to one of their customers and Gavin was plotting a moving average graph of sterling two-year bond prices.

Alix went into her small office and logged on to her computer. She opened the file with the material for this morning's meeting. The light of the screen made her eyes water. She took out her compact and checked her nose. Despite the foundation, it was still red.

'Line two, Alix,' said Jenny over the intercom. 'Charlie Mulholland for you.'

'Can you take it?' Alix whispered. 'I'm trying to save my voice.'

'Sure.'

Alix took an Extra-Strong Fisherman's Friend lozenge from the box she kept in her drawer. The menthol taste nearly blew her head off but didn't unblock her nose.

She printed some graphs for the meeting and went through the notes she'd made the previous week. She knew what she needed to talk about.

Then she sat back in her chair and read the *Irish Times*. She didn't have the energy to care about anything else.

Eileen Walsh, Des's secretary, called Alix to tell her that Brian Nicholls of Sorrento Products had arrived and the meeting was in the boardroom.

'I'll be right there,' said Alix.

'Are you OK?' asked Eileen. 'You sound awful, Alix.'

'Just got a sore throat,' Alix told her. 'I'll be fine.'

She gathered up her notes. As she stood up, the room seemed to spin round her and she had to grab the edge of her desk to steady herself. Her heart was pounding. She flashed an anxious look through the glass wall at the other dealers but they hadn't noticed anything. Alix blew on her palms which were beginning to perspire. She still felt dizzy and light-headed as she walked into the dealing room.

'I'll be in the boardroom,' she told Dave. 'Give me a shout if anything dramatic happens.'

'Nothing dramatic will happen,' said Dave confidently. 'Martin Dardis is thinking about taking a five-year swap – that'll suit our position if he deals. But it's the only imminent interest we have at the moment.'

'OK,' said Alix. 'I'll leave things in your capable hands.'

'You should be at home,' said Jenny. 'You look terrible, Alix. Have you got a temperature?'

Alix shrugged. 'I feel a bit odd,' she admitted. 'But I'll be OK.'

She left them and walked downstairs to the boardroom. She knew that she should have stayed at home. If this had happened a couple of weeks ago, Paul would have made her stay at home. He'd have brought her honey and lemon and medicinal alcohol and told her to stay in bed.

But she couldn't have stayed in bed today. It was vital that she didn't miss any meetings with clients, especially any that involved the managing director of the bank too. She wasn't going to give Dave Bryant or Gavin Donnelly or even Jenny Smith the slightest opportunity to show how brilliant they were. She was the head of treasury. She was the one in command. And she was going to make sure it stayed that way.

'Hello, Alix.' Brian Nicholls got up when she walked into the room. 'It's nice to see you again.'

'And you,' she said as firmly as she could.

'Are you all right?' he asked.

'Touch of a sore throat,' Alix replied. 'So don't expect me to do too much talking!'

'That'll be a change,' said Des Coyle. 'Usually we can hardly shut you up.'

'How unfair.' She smiled at him.

'OK,' said Des. 'Let's go through the proposal with you, Brian. I think you'll find we've covered all your concerns.'

Alix listened while Des outlined the scheme whereby Brian's company borrowed cheaply in the US market and then swapped the proceeds back into euros. Every so often Des asked her a question and she supplied the right answer. But it seemed to her as though he was talking to her from a huge distance and his words were fuzzy and indistinct.

She yawned.

'Tired?' asked Des tersely.

'Of course not,' she answered quickly. 'My sinuses are blocked. I'm just trying to unblock them.'

'I've got a great spray at home,' said Brian. 'You should try it. I can't remember the name – my wife buys it for me. I'll check it out, though. Let you know.'

'Thanks, Brian.' She smiled at him.

'Now,' Des brought the meeting back to business, 'about the three-year borrowings . . .'

Alix could hardly keep her eyes open. It wasn't that she was tired, she simply wasn't able to concentrate. Des's words became more and more indistinct.

Her eyelids were like lead. They were closing and there was nothing she could do about it. Her whole body was relaxing. The boardroom seemed to recede into the distance.

She tried to keep conscious but it was slipping away from her. She slid, slowly and inexorably, from the chair and onto the boardroom floor.

Chapter 13

When she came to, the first person she saw was Eileen Walsh who was kneeling beside her, holding a glass of water.

'Oh, Alix!' she cried. 'Are you OK?'

'Of course.' Alix tried to sit up. 'I don't know what came over me. I'm perfectly all right.'

'You're certainly not perfectly all right,' said Eileen sharply. 'You gave everyone a terrible fright.'

'I just fainted,' protested Alix. 'It's not such a big thing.'

'Would you like to sit with your head between your knees?' asked Des. 'That's what you're supposed to do.'

'No, honestly.' Alix was burning with embarrassment. 'It's just this cold. My head was so blocked up that I got dizzy. That's all.'

'You're dreadfully pale,' said Brian Nicholls.

Oh God, thought Alix. He's still here. I collapsed in front of a client. Des will never forgive me. 'I guess I'm not as well as I thought.' Alix tried grinning at him but it took a lot of effort.

'You shouldn't have come in if you felt like this,' said Des.

'I didn't want to miss seeing Brian,' said Alix.

'That's very flattering.' Brian smiled at her. 'But Des is right. You should be at home in bed, Alix.'

'You're right,' she agreed. 'As soon as we're finished here, I'll go home.'

'You'll go home right away,' said Des. 'You're not fit to be here.'

'Honestly, Des—'

'Alix,' he said firmly. 'We can finish this meeting without you. We've already covered the foreign exchange swap anyway. There isn't anything else major, and if we need something, we can give Dave a call.' He turned to Eileen who was still holding the glass of water. 'Phone for a taxi, will you? Tell them to be here as soon as possible.'

'Des, I—'

'No arguing, Alix.'

She managed to get up from the floor and sit on a chair.

'Des is right,' said Brian. 'You should put your head between your knees.'

'I'll just sit here quietly,' said Alix. 'I'm much better now.'

The three of them sat in silence. Alix wished she could think of something bright and witty to say so that she could distract them from the fact that she'd keeled over in front of them. Fainting in front of the managing director and an important customer was awful. How could she appear efficient and commanding when Brian Nicholls had seen her spread out on the floor? It was hardly the image of an executive woman in control of her life. She was prepared to bet that Brian had never before been at a meeting where one of the participants had fainted. He might well, she supposed, have been at drinking sessions where a business colleague had collapsed, but that was an entirely different situation. She sighed. This was a catastrophe. It just underlined how absolutely crap the last few weeks had been.

'Taxi's here!' Eileen poked her head round the door and smiled brightly at Alix.

'Take your time,' warned Brian. 'Don't rush things.'

'I'm much better now, Brian,' said Alix, although the floor felt unsteady beneath her. 'I probably just need a few more hours in bed.'

'Don't come in tomorrow,' said Des. 'In fact, you might be better off staying out all week.'

'Absolutely not,' said Alix. 'I'll be right as rain tomorrow.' She followed Eileen out of the room and to the taxi.

'Are you sure you're OK?' asked Eileen. 'You really are as white as a ghost.'

'I'm OK,' said Alix. 'Thanks, Eileen. I'm sure I gave them a bit of a shock.'

Eileen laughed. 'Poor Des nearly collapsed himself! He came running out of the boardroom and I thought someone had died.'

'He hasn't quite got rid of me yet.' Alix smiled feebly. 'Apologise to him for me, will you?'

'Why should you apologise?' Eileen stared at her. 'You're sick, Alix. You should be at home in bed. You shouldn't have come into the office in the first place.'

Alix nodded.

'Why on earth did you?' asked Eileen. 'Any of the others could have stood in for you. Des would have understood. And I'm sure Dave wouldn't have minded meeting Brian.'

I'll bet he wouldn't, thought Alix miserably. Dave would have sat there and talked about golf and rugby and they would have had a very convivial meeting, everything would have been sorted out and it wouldn't have ended with Dave conking out on the boardroom floor.

She got into the taxi and closed her eyes. She could just imagine Des and Brian back in the office, talking about her. Thinking that she wasn't up to the job. Des would be wondering if it was all getting too much for her. She rubbed her eyes and put her hand to her forehead. It was burning hot. She'd better get the taxi to drop her at the doctor's. She hated going to Dr O'Neill but if she'd picked up some sort of bug then she'd better just get some antibiotics to shift it.

She leaned towards the driver. 'Can you drop me on Baggot Street, please. Near the bridge.'

'Sure.' The driver glanced in his mirror. The woman looked haggard, he thought. Her face was white and her hair, damp and escaping from the clip that held it back, snaked across her face. He hoped to God that she wasn't going to pass out in his taxi.

❱

Des asked Eileen to bring coffee for himself and Brian.

'She didn't look very well,' said Brian. 'I thought as much even when she came into the room.'

'She hasn't been one hundred per cent for the last few weeks,' said Des. 'I was chatting to Dave – you know Dave, don't you, the senior dealer? He said she'd had to go home early a couple of times.'

'She's not pregnant, is she?' asked Brian. 'You know the way they get when they're pregnant. Theresa kept falling asleep when she was having James. Couldn't take her anywhere without her eyes closing.'

'I don't think Alix fell asleep,' Des said dryly. 'It was more dramatic than just falling asleep!'

'She could be pregnant all the same,' Brian laughed. 'Either that or she's got a new bloke and she's spending so much time in the sack that she's not getting any sleep. He might have her completely worn out.'

Des laughed. 'She's been living with the same guy for a few years. Maybe he's been taking Viagra.'

'Or maybe she has!' Brian laughed too. 'Actually, she's not at all bad looking, is she?'

'She's a bit of all right,' nodded Des.

'Have you— ?'

Des shook his head. 'I wouldn't dare. To be honest, I thought she was one of those chic lesbian types at first. Didn't seem to even notice men and *so* cool. But I was wrong about that.'

'Could be a ruse,' said Brian. 'Maybe her bloke's gay. Maybe it's all a cover! And the strain of this double life caused her to collapse.'

Des chuckled. 'You've been watching too many TV soaps. Anyway, she'd better not keel over again. I'm running a bloody bank, not a hospital.'

'Well, since you're running a bank you'd better give me those facility documents to sign. Might as well get the formalities over and done with.'

'Great,' said Des. He passed over a sheaf of paper. 'Always nice to do business with you, Brian.'

'And you, Des,' said Brian as he signed on the dotted line.

∽

Alix sat in Dr O'Neill's waiting room. She'd thought that it would be a quick visit to the doctor – nip in, collect a prescription, and nip out again. She hadn't counted on the number of people who were there ahead of her. She'd been waiting nearly an hour already and she was beginning to feel as though she would collapse again. She flicked through the year-old copy of *Cosmo* but, much as she wanted to, she couldn't concentrate on the article about 'Getting a Man and Keeping Him'.

'Alix Callaghan?' The receptionist was bright and cheerful and ushered Alix into the doctor's surgery.

'Hello, Alix.' Geraldine O'Neill smiled at her. 'Haven't seen you for a while. How are you keeping?'

'Not very well, obviously.' Alix's throat was absolutely killing her now and talking was even more painful than it had been earlier.

'My goodness!' Geraldine raised an eyebrow. 'How sore is that?'

'Very.'

'OK,' said Geraldine briskly. 'Let's have a look at you.'

Alix let the doctor listen to her chest and look at her throat and take her blood pressure. It was nice to have someone worrying about her and someone else in charge.

'Have you felt sick at all?' asked Geraldine as she took Alix's temperature.

Alix shook her head and immediately felt dizzy again.

'It's a virus,' said Geraldine. 'I know that isn't awfully helpful, Alix. But there is a bug going around. I'm surprised you haven't been sick, most people tend to throw up as well as everything else.'

'Charming,' murmured Alix.

'I'll prescribe something for you. But you really need to rest. Take a couple of days off and stay in bed.'

'I can't do that,' said Alix. 'We're busy in the office now and I—'

171

'Don't be ridiculous,' Geraldine told her. 'You're not indispensable. What do they do when you're on holiday?'

'That's different,' protested Alix feebly. 'We have time to organise and plan things then.'

'Well, you can organise and plan three days at home. Minimum,' said Geraldine firmly. 'What's your diet been like lately? Leaving aside the bug, you look rundown, Alix.'

'There's nothing wrong with my diet.'

'Plenty of fresh fruit and vegetables?'

Alix thought of the straw basket on the kitchen counter where a couple of dusty apples (bought by Paul) lay uneaten.

'Yes,' she replied.

'It doesn't look like it to me,' said Geraldine. 'Do you cook a meal in the evening?'

'I eat out at lunchtime quite a lot,' said Alix.

'And what do you eat when you're not lunching?'

Alix shrugged. 'It depends.'

'Eat properly,' said Geraldine. 'Especially now. Come back to me in a few days. You should be feeling a lot better by then, but I want to have a look at you again.'

'You don't think there's anything seriously wrong with me?' Alix was suddenly alarmed by the look of concern on the doctor's face.

'Of course not,' said Geraldine. 'I just want to give you another check, that's all.'

'OK.' Alix opened the door.

'Look after yourself,' said Geraldine.

'I will.'

Alix walked slowly to the chemist and handed in her prescription. She felt utterly exhausted now, hardly able to stand up. The walk back to the apartment was even worse. But when she got inside she immediately phoned the dealing room.

'Yo, dealers.'

Alix grimaced. 'Hello, Gavin.'

'Alix? Is that you?'

'Yes,' she said. 'And if I ever hear you answer the phone like that again—'

'Sorry,' said Gavin, though he didn't sound very sorry. 'We're having a good day, Alix. Although you're not, I hear. Are you OK?'

'I'm fine,' she said. 'Put Dave on, will you?'

'Hi, Alix.' Dave sounded very cheerful. 'What's all this I hear about you throwing yourself at Brian Nicholls?'

Alix smiled faintly. 'It wasn't deliberate, I assure you. Is everything OK there?'

'Great,' said Dave. 'We did the swap trade with Martin Dardis. Markets are trading in tight enough ranges but we've executed a few client orders and everything is under control.'

'Good,' said Alix. 'I was supposed to meet Steve Pearson for lunch. Will you call and cancel for me?'

'Sure,' said Dave. 'I guess you'll be out for the rest of the week.'

'Depends on how I feel,' Alix said. 'I've got some anti-bs from the doc. If I'm OK tomorrow I'll be in.'

'Don't rush,' Dave told her. 'Everything's fine here. Take your time.'

'I will,' she said and hung up.

Take your time, she thought as she crawled into bed. They'd want her to take her time, of course they would. Dave – despite Gavin's protestations to the contrary – would be only too pleased to have an opportunity to prove himself. Gavin would be delighted to have her unexpectedly out of the picture for a couple of days. And Jenny . . . Alix sighed. She thought she could count on Jenny but she couldn't be certain. Jenny never said anything about wanting to have more responsibility or moving on within the dealing room. But if the opportunity was there, Alix was sure that the younger girl would take it. Hell, she'd take any opportunities she could if she was Jenny. But she doubted, somehow, that Jenny wanted to be the one in charge. At the same time, the girl was good at aligning herself with people of influence. She was very friendly with all of the other managers and Des Coyle liked her a lot.

Alix rolled over in the bed. Bloody body, she thought angrily. Letting me down at a time like this.

◠

She woke up later that afternoon. Her throat still hurt but she didn't feel quite as light-headed as earlier in the day. She had a raging thirst, though, and it was still an effort to get up and go into the kitchen for a drink. There was only the out-of-date orange juice in the fridge. She drank it anyway. It couldn't make her feel any worse.

The sheet on the bed was damp with sweat. She wished she had the energy to change it but she just moved to the other side of the bed.

She lay on her side and thought of Paul. She wished he was here now to look after her. She didn't want to be in the apartment all by herself when she felt so miserable. She couldn't remember when she'd last felt like this. A tear slid down her cheek and plopped onto the pillow.

Damp sheet and damp pillow, she said to herself. Not a good idea. I'll probably catch pneumonia.

The next time she woke up it was dark. She had to blink a couple of times before she could focus on the digital clock. Four a.m. People died at 4 a.m., she reminded herself. Your body is at its lowest ebb then. She reached for the clock to check that she'd set the alarm. Despite what everyone said, she didn't want to stay out of work for another day. She didn't want to leave Dave and Gavin and Jenny to plot against her. And she didn't want to spend a whole day on her own in the apartment, feeling miserable.

But when the radio clicked on at six o'clock, Alix couldn't drag herself out of bed. She'd go in for the afternoon, she told herself as she hit the off button. She needed to sleep.

∽

Gavin answered the phone. He almost said 'Yo, dealers' but at the last minute realised that it could be Alix and instead gave the preferred 'Europa Bank, dealers' greeting.

'Hi, can I speak to Alix Callaghan?'

'Who's calling?' asked Gavin, although he recognised the voice.

'This is Matt Connery, Anatronics.'

'Hi, Matt. It's Gavin Donnelly here.' Gavin hit a couple of keys on his computer terminal and a graph of the dollar/yen exchange rate for the past two days appeared. 'Alix is out of the office today. Can I help?'

'Is she ever in the office?' Matt sounded aggrieved.

'She's a very busy person,' said Gavin. 'She tends to be out a lot. Although this time, I'm afraid, it's just a common or garden cold that's laid her out.'

175

'She's off sick?'

'Probably just as well she didn't come in,' said Gavin. 'Even if you don't feel that bad in yourself, you hate to infect other people in the room.'

'I need to sell some yen buy dollars,' said Matt. 'It's not huge, forty million yen.' Forty million yen was less than three hundred thousand dollars. Small money in foreign exchange terms.

'One fifteen forty-five,' he said.

Matt hesitated. 'Actually, I—'

'I can do forty-four and a half,' said Gavin swiftly. He'd pitched the price a little on the expensive side. He wanted to see how in touch Matt Connery was with the current exchange rate. The difference was less than a thousand dollars, but it was the principle that mattered.

'OK,' said Matt. 'Can you pay the dollars to our account at Chase. The yen will be coming from Bank of Tokyo.'

'That's fine,' said Gavin. 'Thanks for the trade, Matt.' He paused for a moment. 'We should get together for a bite to eat sometime.'

'Perhaps,' said Matt.

Gavin called up his Microsoft Outlook calendar. 'I'm free on Thursday. Would that suit you?'

'I can't meet you this week,' said Matt. 'I'm busy every day.'

'Tell you what,' Gavin said, 'I've got some tickets to the pro-am golf tournament in Portmarnock on Friday next week. I'm taking a few clients. Why don't you come along to that? It should be a good day.'

'I'd like to,' Matt told him. 'But I'm not sure about my schedule. Let me get back to you.'

'Fine,' said Gavin. 'I'll keep a place for you anyway. You can let me know next week.'

'OK,' said Matt. 'When do you expect Alix back into the office?'

Gavin gritted his teeth. 'Not certain,' he said lightly. 'To be fair to her, she doesn't usually stay out for very long if she's ill. But that's not always a good idea. You know yourself, you think you're fine and the next thing you've relapsed and you're out for another few days.'

'Does she get sick that often?' asked Matt. 'I didn't get the impression she was a sick kind of person.'

'Oh, you know women!' Gavin laughed. 'There's always something.'

'If she rings in, tell her I'd like a chat,' said Matt.

'Sure,' replied Gavin. 'And in the meantime I'll book up this trade. If there's anything else you want, don't hesitate to call. And let me know about Portmarnock.'

'Of course,' said Matt.

Gavin disconnected the call and looked at Dave and Jenny who were staring at him.

'What?' he demanded.

'That was really mean,' said Jenny. 'You've made Alix sound like some hypochondriac.'

'It's not my fault she flaked out.' Gavin was inputting the dollar/yen trade.

'It's more than just a cold,' objected Jenny. 'And she hasn't been out sick in years. Listening to you, anyone would think she's out every couple of weeks!'

'Hey, it's business, that's all.' Gavin looked at her impatiently. 'She'd do exactly the same thing.'

'I don't think she would,' said Dave. 'But who cares. Anyway, it was a good idea to offer him the Portmarnock tickets.'

Gavin grinned. 'I know. I'll have to bump someone off the trip if he accepts, though. Right now, I don't have any spare.'

'I can get you one if you're stuck,' said Dave. 'But you'll owe me.'

'Great, thanks.'

'Alix will be pissed off at you,' Jenny told him.

'Oh, come on, Jen! He's turning into a good customer. Looks like we're getting his trades exclusively. She'd want me to look after him.' Gavin pressed the 'enter' button on the keyboard to commit the trade to the system. 'And that's all I'm doing.'

'I know,' said Jenny. 'And looking after yourself too.'

Gavin shrugged. 'We all have to look after ourselves. It's the business, after all.'

⁓

Alix still felt as though she was detached from reality but she thought her temperature had come down and she didn't feel as shaky as she had earlier. She'd spent the entire day in bed, drifting in and out of sleep, and she had to admit that it had been the best thing for her. It was now half three and she leaned across to pick up the phone.

'Europa Bank, dealers.'

'Hi, Jenny.' Alix was pleased to find that her throat wasn't quite as sore either. 'How are things?'

'Alix! You feeling any better?'

'Improving, thanks,' replied Alix. 'I thought about coming in this morning, but I couldn't stand up.'

'You poor thing.' Jenny was sympathetic. 'It's one thing to

feel like that after a night on the beer, it's quite another when you're actually sick!'

'My doctor told me that there's a bug going round,' said Alix. 'So you'd better take care. She's been advising me to overdose on fruit and vegetables.'

'I'll keep it in mind.' Jenny laughed.

'Anything happening?' asked Alix. 'Is it busy?'

Jenny glanced at Dave and Gavin who were watching her intently. 'Busy enough,' she said. 'The dollar is trading in a very narrow range but the bond has been doing well and we picked up some five-year treasuries which are in profit.'

'Great,' said Alix. 'Any decent client trades?'

'No,' answered Jenny. 'All less than half a bar.' Less than half a million was considered small by the dealers, though some of their clients thought even fifty thousand was a huge sum.

'Nothing I should know about?' asked Alix.

'Not a thing,' said Jenny uncomfortably. 'We're all slaving away for the good of the bank.'

'That's what I like to hear,' said Alix. 'How's Gavin?'

'Gavin?' Jenny looked at him and he made a face at her. 'He's fine. Do you want to talk to him?'

'No,' said Alix. 'I'm sick. I don't want to jeopardise my recovery.'

Jenny laughed. 'I'll tell him you were asking for him. Will you be in tomorrow?'

'Absolutely,' said Alix. 'There's a management meeting at lunchtime. I really need to be there for that.'

'Don't push yourself,' cautioned Jenny. 'If you're still feeling shaky you should stay out. Dave can go to the management meeting.'

'I'm sure he can,' said Alix dryly. 'But I'd like to be there myself.'

'It's up to you,' said Jenny. 'We might see you in the morning.'

'You will.'

'Take care, Alix.'

'You too.'

Alix hung up and lay back on the pillows. The simple conversation had exhausted her. And she felt sure that Jenny was being reticent about something. She hoped she'd feel better tomorrow. There wasn't a chance in hell that she was going to let Dave go to the management meeting.

In the dealing room, Dave looked at Jenny. 'Well?' he asked.

'She might be in tomorrow,' said Jenny.

'What did she say?' Gavin's tone was truculent.

'Just asked what was going on. You heard the conversation.'

'You didn't say anything about Matt Connery.'

'Why should I?' asked Jenny. 'It was a small trade, Gavin. It doesn't matter in the great scheme of things.'

Gavin grinned at her. 'You're not bad,' he said. 'For a woman.'

Jenny threw a bottle of Tipp-Ex at him but he ducked just in time and it hit Mike Keogh, one of the settlements people, as he opened the dealing-room door.

❧

At four o'clock, all of the TV stations were showing variations on cookery programmes. Alix sat in front of the screen, the duvet wrapped round her, while she watched someone concoct a cordon bleu meal out of a couple of squashed tomatoes and some herbs. Paul could do that, she thought. Paul could rummage around in the fridge and come up with the ingredients for something wonderful. Although even Paul would be hard pressed to find anything worth eating in the fridge right now. Despite her shopping expedition, the contents of Alix's fridge were still sparse. The freezer was packed to capacity with meals for one, but the fridge only contained the remains of the out-of-date orange juice, an almost out-of-date jar of mayonnaise, half a carton of milk and a packet of Easi-Singles cheese. There was some beer and some wine, of course, but beer and wine weren't exactly what she needed right now.

The intercom buzzed and Alix jumped in surprise. Who was looking for her? The thought that Paul might have rung the office and discovered she was ill flitted through her mind. And when he discovered that she was sick, he'd rushed to be with her! She tried not to think like that but she couldn't help it. It almost made her feel better.

'Who is it?' she asked.

'Delivery for Callaghan, Apartment 2A.'

'Come on up.' She pressed the door release, and while the delivery man was coming up the stairs, pulled on a pair of jeans. She'd only been wearing a T-shirt beneath the warmth of the duvet. She pulled a brush through her hair.

She looked through the security window of the door. The delivery man was holding a bouquet of flowers.

'Sign here,' he said when she'd opened the door.

'Thank you.'

She took the flowers into the apartment and ripped open the envelope on the card that accompanied them.

'Sorry you're ill,' said the message. 'Get well soon.' It was signed Matt Connery, Anatronics Industries.

181

Chapter 14

The next morning Alix woke at her usual time of six o'clock. She shook her head experimentally to see if she still had a headache, but it seemed OK. She swung her legs over the side of the bed and stood up. A little shaky, she thought, but at least she didn't feel as though she was going to fall over.

She got ready for work slowly, not wanting to provoke any sudden feelings of dizziness. By the time she'd dressed in the checked Chanel suit that she'd bought in Paris the previous year, she felt more like her old self. She wore more make-up than usual to hide the pallor of her cheeks. She looked at herself in the mirror and was pleased with the reflection. Not perfect, she thought, but at least she'd lost the haggard look.

She picked up her car keys and closed the bedroom door behind her. There was no way she would be able to walk to the office today and anyway, for the first time in weeks, it looked as though it might rain.

The living room was full of the scent of Matt Connery's flowers. Even though her sinuses weren't completely clear, she could still smell the combination of carnations and tiger lilies. She looked at them in the porcelain vase, hurriedly shoved in so that the beautiful arrangement of the florist had been ruined. She'd rearrange them when she got home.

What had the man been thinking of? she wondered. Why on earth would he send her flowers? She knew that he was attracted to her – God, she told herself, at thirty-two (nearly thirty-three, as Wyn had reminded her) she could tell when a man was attracted to her. But sending flowers! Completely over the top. Besides, he was a client. And she knew nothing about him. He could be married, for all she knew. Probably was. At her age, the pool of unmarried, available, heterosexual men diminished substantially.

Flowers! It was such an old-fashioned thing to do. And sweet, but she had never been turned on by sweetness. She liked her men with a touch of iron. She wondered who had given Matt her home address. Not the bank – it was strictly against their policy to give out telephone numbers, let alone addresses. Perhaps he'd looked her up in the phone book. She wondered if he'd sent flowers to the other A. Callaghans too. It seemed an awful lot of effort. He must be married, she decided. Unmarried blokes wouldn't bother. 'Anyway,' she said out loud, 'I am not ready to start all this new relationship stuff. If that's what I wanted, there's always Cathal Moran.'

Traffic was light at that hour of the morning. She turned into the car park under the Europa Bank building. Because she often walked to work, she'd told people in the bank that they could use her space if it wasn't occupied by eight thirty. She was surprised to see it already occupied by a five-year-old green Mazda coupé. She glanced at her watch. Twenty-five to eight. But maybe nobody had expected her in today – the story of her collapse at the meeting had probably gone through the bank like a dose of salts. All the same, it was infuriating. There was a very limited number of spaces and she didn't want to rob someone else's. She drove back out of the complex and parked on a double yellow line outside the building, her hazard lights flashing. She ran up the steps and told the security guard at reception to keep an eye on the car. 'I'll be back to move it in a couple of minutes,' she promised. 'I know it's early and there shouldn't be any of those clamping maniacs around, but please watch out for me.'

'Sure,' he said. 'But I won't be able to stop them, you know.'

Dave and Gavin were already in the dealing room.

'Do you know who owns the Mazda in my space?' asked Alix as she walked in. 'I know everyone has assumed I'm at death's door, but robbing my space is a bit much to take.'

'Actually, it's mine.' Gavin shrugged. 'Sorry, Alix, I didn't think you'd be in today. I knew you wouldn't mind.'

'I mind the fact that you decided I wouldn't be in,' she said waspishly. 'Now you're just going to have to move it.'

'Give me five minutes,' said Gavin. 'I'm waiting on a call from Hans Mueller in Frankfurt. He was checking some data for me. He said he'd call back before eight.'

'I'm sitting on a double yellow outside,' said Alix. 'I don't want to be clamped.'

'You won't,' said Gavin.

'Forget it,' said Alix. 'I'll take it round to the public car park.'

'I'll pay for your day's parking,' said Gavin without looking up from his computer.

'It's OK,' said Alix. 'It doesn't matter.'

She hurried down the steps of the building. As she reached her car, she saw a van marked 'Ace Security Services' approaching. The bloody clampers, she thought, and rammed the BMW into first. If she'd been clamped then she'd certainly have made Gavin pay.

She would have to do something about Gavin. He was becoming more and more arrogant. She should really do something about Dave and Jenny too. Both of them were senior to Gavin but neither of them seemed prepared to show any authority over him. Jenny didn't have the killer instinct that would drive her to the top, but she couldn't understand why Dave allowed his subordinate so much leeway. Maybe Gavin had been right when he'd told her that Dave didn't want her job. Maybe Dave didn't care any more. But she did! And she would have to confront Gavin sooner rather than later.

She was about to leave the car park when the threatened rain began to fall. Not a soft, drizzling rain as she had expected, but a torrential downpour. Fat raindrops bounced off the pavement and rivulets of water ran along the gutters. She groaned. She didn't have an umbrella in the car. She looked up at the sky. It didn't look as if it was going to stop and it was only a five-minute walk back to the office. But she'd be soaked in five minutes.

She stood, undecided, for another couple of seconds before she decided to make a run for it. By the time she reached the bank she was drenched and the Chanel suit was clinging to her.

She went into the ladies' and tried to dry her soaking hair under the hot air dryer. Although she kept a second suit in the office, she didn't want to walk into the room looking like a wet rag. Her efforts with the dryer had a limited effect but she was marginally more comfortable when she walked into the dealing room.

By then, Jenny had arrived and the three dealers were chatting about the day ahead.

'The futures position is at our target level,' Dave was saying as she pushed open the door. 'But I think we can run it a little more.'

'No technical resistance,' said Gavin. 'Should be good for another ten ticks anyway.'

'What futures position?' asked Alix.

'Hi, Alix!' Jenny beamed at her. 'Good to have you back. How are you feeling?'

'Great,' she said. 'Especially after walking back from the car park in a bloody monsoon.' At least Gavin looked a little guilty, she thought. Though not half guilty enough.

'I'm sorry,' he said as he looked at her wet clothes. 'I really didn't think you'd be here today. And I would have moved my car.'

'It's OK,' she said. 'I can change into my other suit. But first of all, what futures position?'

'We're long some gilt futures,' said Dave. 'The gilt crapped out yesterday afternoon and we thought it was time to buy. It picked up in late trading and we ran with it. We're up twenty-five grand at the moment.'

'Excellent,' said Alix. 'What else did we do?'

'Not a lot, to be honest,' said Dave. 'A few client trades. We put a couple of swap prices into the market but no one dealt. Fairly routine stuff.'

'Leave the report on my desk, will you?' she said. 'In the meantime I'll change my clothes.'

Her emergency suit was a black Donna Karan that she'd bought in New York but which she hadn't liked when she got it home. It was good as a standby and had been called into use a couple of times, notably the day Dave had accidentally dumped a full cup of coffee into her lap five minutes before she'd had a meeting with Guy Decourcelle and the rest of the Paris management team who'd flown to Dublin on one of their infrequent but nerve-wracking fact-finding missions. She kept a pair of black shoes in her office too. The day the French managers had come over, she'd been wearing her favourite office colour of chocolate brown. Unfortunately she'd also been wearing brown shoes which had clashed horribly with the black Donna Karan. She'd noticed Guy looking at her shoes and imagined him thinking that no French girl would dream of wearing a black suit and brown shoes. Even if they'd cost her a fortune in Milan.

She felt better once she was wearing dry clothes, although her teeth had chattered alarmingly while she was peeling off the damp Chanel. But now, dry and with her make-up retouched, she felt able to face the day.

They were on the phones again when she returned. She smiled briefly at them and walked into her glass-panelled office. They were still running Dave's futures position, she noted. Very profitable. She picked up the list of yesterday's trades and looked through it.

Dave had been right, most of them were small client trades. The biggest had been Martin Dardis's swap, but none of the foreign exchange deals had exceeded half a million. She turned over the page and saw the name Anatronics at the top. She couldn't believe it. Matt Connery had dealt again. And she'd been out again. She looked at the figures. Not a big trade. They wouldn't have made much on it.

'Gavin!' she called, and he indicated that he was still on a phone call. 'When you're finished,' she mouthed.

It was nearly five minutes before he came into her office. 'Yes?'

Alix ignored the aggression in Gavin's voice. 'I see our good friend Matt Connery dealt yesterday.'

'It was another small deal,' said Gavin.

'That's fine.' Alix smiled at him. 'He didn't ask you anything about swaps, did he?'

'No,' replied Gavin. He looked at her anxiously. 'Should he have?'

She shrugged. 'Not necessarily. I just wondered. Did we make much out of the deal?'

'Not a lot,' admitted Gavin. 'It's too small.'

'If only these bloody clients knew how little we make out of them,' said Alix. 'That's OK, Gavin. Thanks.'

He turned to walk away but she stopped him. 'Did Connery ask for me?'

'I told him you were sick,' said Gavin. 'It was true.'

'I know,' she said. 'That's fine.'

He turned again and she stopped him for a second time. 'He didn't ask you for my address by any chance?'

'Your address?' Gavin swivelled around. 'Your home address?'

'Yes.'

'No,' he said. 'Why should he?'

'Don't mind me,' she said. 'It's nothing.'

'He didn't ask for anything.' Gavin regained his composure. 'But I've asked him to the pro-am in Portmarnock. I'm sure he'd enjoy it.'

'I thought you'd used up all your invitations,' said Alix.

'Dave had one spare.' Gavin grinned. 'I owe him but it's worth it to get Connery for a day out and check out exactly what sort of business he has to do.'

'Great idea,' said Alix.

'It's my account,' Gavin said abruptly. 'I've done all the work and all the small, shitty deals. When the big one comes, it's my account.'

'Let's wait for the big one, shall we?' said Alix. She was getting tired of being nice to Gavin.

'When it comes, I'll be ready,' he told her.

'Fine,' she said.

⤚

She was finding it hard to concentrate. Her head was buzzing and her eyes were tired. The computer screens made them water and she constantly had to wipe them with a tissue. Jenny giggled and told her that she looked as though she was going to burst into tears at any minute. Alix muttered that you never knew, she just might.

At twelve o'clock, Eileen Walsh called to say that the management meeting had been cancelled. Des was stuck in another meeting, she told Alix, and he wouldn't be back in time.

Alix gritted her teeth. She could have stayed at home after all and done some more recuperating. She'd really only come in because of the management meeting.

The rain had stopped and the sun was beating down again so she decided to stroll downtown and buy herself something new to wear for her drink with Paul. She wanted him to know that she'd had time to go shopping and look after herself and that she hadn't gone into some kind of decline.

She spent significantly more than she meant to on a canary-yellow dress in Debenhams. As she brought it (and the earrings, silver chain and bright red Lancôme nail varnish which she'd also bought) back to the office she thought, ruefully, that Paul wouldn't even notice that it was new. Paul never noticed what she wore, unless it was a particularly short skirt.

She phoned RTÉ when she got back. 'Paul Hunter, please.'

'Paul's desk.' The girl who answered sounded young and busy.

'Is Paul there?'

'No, he's out for the day.'

'When will he be back?'

'Not until tomorrow,' said the girl. 'Can I take a message?'

'No,' said Alix slowly. 'It's OK.'

'Sure?'

'Yes. Thanks.'

Shit, she thought. Where was he? Had he forgotten about their drink? Or was she supposed to meet him in Kiely's like the last time? Her head was beginning to ache. She rubbed her temples. As she glanced downwards, she saw the trading report with the Anatronics deal listed on it. She should phone Matt Connery and thank him for the flowers. But really, she thought angrily, he'd put her in a dreadful position. It was far too personal a thing to have done. Maybe she should stop thinking of the account as one she wanted to handle and just tamely hand it over to Gavin. But she couldn't do that. Not now. Not when the account had become something of a battle zone for them.

She smiled as she thought of Gavin's expression if she rang Matt now and started thanking him profusely for his thoughtfulness. Poor Gavin would have a coronary. It'd almost be worth it just to watch him.

But she didn't want to phone Matt Connery. She didn't want

to have to thank him for doing something she hadn't needed or wanted him to do in the first place.

She was uncomfortable with the idea of a man sending her flowers. Paul had never done anything like that. Paul wasn't into romance very much and that was one of the things that Alix liked about him because she wasn't into romance either. They'd never bought each other Valentine cards, or had candlelight dinners or walked hand in hand along the beach. Theirs had been a practical relationship with lots of very exciting sex thrown in. But just because they didn't waste time on heart-shaped boxes of chocolates, it didn't mean that they didn't love each other.

Or maybe it did. Alix picked up a pencil and snapped it in half. Maybe Paul had only pretended not to be interested in flowers and champagne and jewellery and silly cards. Maybe he'd already sent Sabine hundreds of exorbitantly priced stupid gifts. Like furry teddy bears with 'I love you' stamped across their stomach. Alix had told him that if he ever sent her a furry teddy bear with something ridiculous stamped on its stomach she'd leave him.

She pushed Paul to the back of her mind while she decided what to do about Matt bloody Connery and his bloody bouquet of flowers.

Eventually she went into her office and dialled the Anatronics number.

'Matt Connery,' she said when the phone was answered.

'I'm sorry,' said the receptionist, 'Matt is out of the office today. I don't expect him back until Friday.'

'Right!' Alix exclaimed.

'Pardon?'

'I'm sorry. I – can I just leave a message for him?'

'Certainly.'

'Could you say that Alix Callaghan called to say thank you?'

'Of course. Does he have your number?'

'It's Europa Bank,' said Alix. 'He has the number.'

'Fine, Alix. I'll pass on the message.'

'Thank you.'

'No problem.'

Great, thought Alix as she hung up. Now he knows I got the flowers and called him. So I've gained kudos for ringing, without having to talk to him. An outcome which she decided was very satisfactory.

❧

She left the office at half four. By that time her eyes were smarting and she was feeling light-headed again. She wanted to go home and sleep before meeting Paul. Or before he called. Or before she decided that she had to call him. I won't, she told herself. I won't call. I'm not going to demean myself by running after him.

'If Paul phones, will you tell him I've gone home?' she asked Jenny as she picked up her shopping.

'Of course,' said Jenny. 'Are you sure you were right to come in today, Alix? You look awfully pale.'

'I'm just tired,' Alix told her. 'I'll be OK.'

'See you tomorrow,' said Jenny.

'Yeah, Alix. See you tomorrow. Look after yourself.' Dave's voice was sincere and, unaccountably, Alix felt tears prick at her eyes.

'Thanks.'

'If you're sick again, don't come in tomorrow,' said Gavin. 'I really don't want to catch whatever it is you're harbouring.'

If I cry, thought Alix looking at him, it'll be tears of rage before I tear you limb from limb!

Des Coyle rang the dealing room fifteen minutes after Alix had left.

'She's gone home, Des,' said Dave. 'She was feeling tired.'

'If she wasn't better she shouldn't have come in at all,' said Des. 'Are you busy, Dave? I need to talk to someone about Polish zloty.'

'What I know about Polish zloty could be handwritten on a microchip,' said Dave. 'But I'll give you the benefit of my expertise. Do you want me to drop down to your office?'

'Yes, good idea,' said Des.

Dave left the dealing room and strolled down to the managing director's office. In Europa Bank, the dealing room was on the third floor. Somewhat unusually, Des Coyle had his office on the floor below but it was a significantly bigger office than he otherwise would have had. It was L-shaped and had a view across the Liffey as well as down towards the port. Unlike the dealing room where everything was utilitarian, Des's office had a thick-pile blue carpet, blue-grey wallpaper and modern pine furniture. He also had some original paintings by a local artist (who the bank's design consultant said would one day be very famous) hanging on the wall.

'Hi, Des.' Dave strode across the office and sat in the grey leather chair in front of the desk. 'How's it going?'

'Jim Rothwell has asked me about this zloty thing.' Des pushed a piece of paper in front of Dave. 'What d'you think?'

Dave skimmed through the paper. 'Looks OK to me,' he said. 'Who are you getting to do the swap?'

'Don't know,' said Des. 'Who do you advise?'

'Don't you want Guy Decourcelle's mob to do it?'

'Do you trust them not to go after the client? Try to nab the whole deal for themselves?'

Dave made a face. 'I'm not sure. It's possible but I don't think they'd deliberately shaft us. Let me talk to Guy.'

'OK,' said Des. 'Tonight?'

'Not a chance,' Dave laughed. 'They're an hour ahead of us, you know. Guy is doubtless sitting in a brasserie with some French tart as we speak. He's certainly not in the office.'

'And tell me,' Des leaned back in his chair, leather, like his visitor's chair, but with a higher back and much more padding, 'what's the story with Alix?'

'Alix?' said Dave carefully. 'What kind of story do you want, Des?'

'This bloody so-called cold. Keeling over in the boardroom. Going home early. What's behind it?'

'I don't know.' Dave stretched his hands over his head. 'Maybe it is just a virus. But, I have to be honest with you, Des, we were wondering if there was something wrong with her before this. Remember I mentioned it to you? She left the office early a couple of times. She's forgotten one or two meetings. And she's giving poor old Gavin a terrible time.'

'What d'you mean?'

'Nothing he does is right,' said Dave. 'He's made some pretty decent calls, following some tips he's got from guys he knows in the States. She wouldn't let us position ourselves on the back of some of them, and we would have made money. She doesn't like him very much and it's clouding her judgement.'

'Is she broody?' asked Des. 'God knows, she's in her thirties.

Even the most career-minded of them get broody in their thirties.'

'She hasn't said anything,' Dave replied. 'But she could be. Des, you know how it is with women. They think they want it all – the career, the promotions, the management positions. But do they really understand what it's about? Let's face it, if she is getting broody she'll drop this job like a hot potato.'

'Do you like her?' asked Des.

Dave considered the question. 'I respect her,' he said eventually. 'But people have to earn respect and they can lose it just as quickly.'

'Is she coming in for the rest of the week?'

'It doesn't much matter about tomorrow. But she has to be in on Friday because Gavin is taking some clients to the pro-am and I have a meeting with Arnie Daly in the afternoon. So there won't be enough cover if she doesn't come in.'

'I'll be at the pro-am myself,' said Des. 'Who's Gavin taking?'

'About half a dozen people,' Dave said. 'Including that new guy, Connery, from Anatronics. Gavin's doing really well with that account.'

'Great,' said Des. 'Tell him to keep up the good work. He's not a bad golfer himself, is he?'

'Plays off twelve,' said Dave, 'but he could be better. If he spent more time on the course he'd get down to single figures.'

'Encourage him to take guys out for golf,' said Des. 'It always pays off.'

'Sure.' Dave smiled. 'Anything else?'

'No,' replied Des. 'That'll do for now. Let me know what you think about Decourcelle and the zlotys.'

'Will do,' said Dave. 'I'll give you a call tomorrow.'

'Great. Doing anything interesting this evening?'

Dave shook his head. 'I'm working on some technical analysis charts. Good time to get them done, when the markets are closed.'

'It's all nonsense to me,' said Des cheerfully, 'but if we make money out of it, I don't care whether or not you read tea leaves.'

'Sometimes I think they'd tell us just as much,' joked Dave as he got up from the chair. 'Talk to you tomorrow.'

'Sure thing,' said Des and returned to the folder in front of him.

Dave whistled lightly as he ran up the stairs. A good evening's work, all told, he thought. He looked at his watch. He'd hang around for another twenty minutes in case Des called again. Then he'd go home. He hated technical analysis and Gavin had done the charts hours ago anyway.

Chapter 15

The phone was ringing as Alix opened the door to the apartment. Paul! she thought in relief as she dropped her shopping on the floor and rushed to pick up the receiver before the answering machine clicked in.

'Hi, Alix! It's me. What on earth are you doing home at this hour?'

Alix's heart sank as she recognised Sophia's voice. 'Hi, Soph,' she said, trying to sound enthusiastic. 'I left the office early.'

'You guys sure have it easy in Dublin,' joked Sophia. 'It's a nightmare over here. I'm up to my tits in work and London is like an oven.'

'Poor thing.' Alix smiled despite herself. 'Plenty of securitisation going on then?'

Sophia also worked in financial services. Her job was to repackage a range of small, individual loans into one big loan, turn it into a single bond and sell it to institutional investors. The concept of securitisation had first emerged in the States where nobody was sure how successful it would be. But securitisations had been very successful and, because many financial institutions had hedged their bets and shunted women into their securitisation departments, it was one area in financial services where women could do sensationally well. Sophia was

197

one of those women. She earned almost three times as much as Alix, and if you took her bonuses into account, almost three times that again. She lived in a small but perfectly located townhouse in Chelsea, took three holidays a year, and loved her work.

'We put together a very exciting ship leasing package,' Sophia told Alix. 'Excellent yield, AAA rating, was a blow-out. Everyone wanted a piece.'

'Good for you,' said Alix.

'So – why are you at home?' asked Sophia again. 'I rang your office and some very rude bloke told me you'd skived off early!'

'Probably Gavin,' said Alix. 'If that's all he said, I'm lucky. Gavin and I aren't exactly seeing eye to eye at the moment.'

'Oh, dear.'

'I'll tell you about it sometime,' said Alix. 'But not today. It wouldn't do my blood pressure any good.' She flopped into the armchair. 'I'm home because I caught some kind of bug over the weekend and I've been off work for a couple of days. We were supposed to have a management meeting today so I went in. But I was wrecked by four, that's why I came home.'

'Poor you,' commiserated Sophia.

'Why are you calling?' asked Alix. 'Any news?'

'Well . . .' Sophia paused teasingly. 'A bit.'

'Come on, Soph, tell me.'

'It's so funny really.'

'What is?'

'Richard and me. We're getting married!'

'Sophia!' Alix nearly dropped the phone. Her friend had been seeing Richard Comiskey since the beginning of the year. Alix knew that Richard and Sophia were practically living together but she'd never thought about them actually getting married. 'Congratulations,' she added.

'That's not all.' Sophia giggled.

'What?' asked Alix, although she felt a tremor of suspicion already.

'We're going to have a baby!'

Alix said nothing.

'Alix? Are you still there?'

'Of course I am,' she replied. 'It's just – I'm shocked. I mean, is congratulations the right word? Did you want the baby?'

'If you'd asked me this last year, I would have said no. But, oh Alix, yes – I'm thrilled.'

'Then I guess it's congratulations again.'

'I know it sounds really hormonal and stupid and everything. But I haven't felt so wonderful in ages.'

'That's great,' said Alix.

'I know I'm supposed to be feeling tired,' Sophia went on, 'but I don't. I feel terrific.'

'That's great,' said Alix again. 'I'm really pleased for you.' To her, the words sounded incredibly banal.

'Thanks.' Sophia giggled. 'I know I'll probably hate it when I swell up and can't see my toes, but right now all the good things have happened – like my hair shines and my skin is ultra-clear!'

'So what you're saying is that I should cancel my membership to the gym and get pregnant instead?'

'Somehow I can't imagine you pregnant, Alix,' said Sophia. 'But I couldn't imagine me pregnant either, so I guess if you and Paul want to go ahead . . .'

'I doubt it,' said Alix dryly.

'Is everything OK?' Sophia caught the tension in her friend's voice. 'You and Paul are all right, aren't you?'

Alix sighed. She didn't like keeping things from Sophia. Theirs was the kind of friendship where they didn't speak to each other for ages but when they did, it seemed like the time between calls had never existed.

'We're struggling,' she said finally.

'Oh, Alix!' Sophia was full of sympathy. 'What's the matter?'

'Paul's going through a phase,' said Alix. 'He's changed jobs – full time in RTÉ now – and he's talking about settling down and starting a family ourselves.'

'But isn't that what you want?' asked Sophia. 'I know you love your job, Alix, but I thought that maybe by now you'd feel as though you can let go a little.'

'Having babies doesn't mean I have to give up work,' Alix said sharply. 'Are you going to?'

'I'm not sure,' said Sophia honestly. 'Sometimes I think it would be so wonderful, not having to buy the kind of clothes I hate wearing just because I'm supposed to look businesslike, not having to get up at five thirty in the morning, not having to argue all the time with the sharks on the twenty-second floor – oh, yes, sometimes it sounds great.'

'But . . .'

'It's been my life,' said Sophia simply. 'It defines who I am. Since I left college, Alix, I've been like you, living for my work. And now I don't know if I want to do that any more.'

'I still do,' said Alix. 'But I don't know if I could do it and have kids. And I know Paul wouldn't want it. It'd mean such a change in our lives . . .' She faltered as she realised that she'd been speaking as though she still lived with Paul. As though he hadn't walked out on her. She wanted to tell Sophia the truth. But she couldn't. Besides, she reasoned, Paul might come back. What was the point in telling her if Paul came back in the end?

'I know exactly how you feel,' said Sophia. 'And financially the whole thing is a non-starter. But sometimes you need to look beyond the money, don't you? You need a jolt to make you decide. Mind you, this isn't a jolt I'd recommend for everyone!'

Alix laughed. 'So what are you going to do? Give up? Get a nanny? Make Richard give up?'

'I haven't decided yet,' Sophia answered. 'But I feel as though my life has moved on to a whole new level. The things that mattered to me before don't matter as much. I can't explain it, Alix.'

'When are you due?'

'End of January,' said Sophia. 'Poor little mite will demand to go back in because it'll be so cold.'

'Are you going to have it there or come home?'

'Oh, here,' said Sophia. 'We're getting married here too.'

'When *are* you getting married?' The news about the baby had pushed Sophia's wedding plans out of Alix's mind.

'As soon as we can. Probably next month.' Sophia laughed. 'I know it's terribly sudden and I thought about coming home for it, but we've decided to just get it done here then come home and celebrate. Mum and Dad are coming over but we're keeping it a small event, Alix. I'm not really into all this wedding schmaltz.'

'I'm in shock,' Alix told her. 'This morning you were my only other unmarried, living-with-someone, childless friend. Now you're defecting!'

'I feel terribly grown-up,' said Sophia. 'I know it's weird, Alix, but suddenly I remember all the mad things I've done and they seem so trivial and silly.'

'Remember the night of Cliona O'Brien's party?'

'Don't remind me,' said Sophia. 'Do you know, I never even spoke to that bloke afterwards? I could have got pregnant then, Alix – I was so bloody careless!'

'I guess God was looking out for you.'

'So was my mother,' Sophia said. 'And she gave me a right earful. And what about that rave we went to with Josie and Tara? Remember, in Southampton?'

'I will never forget it,' said Alix. 'And every time I see anything about Ecstasy on TV, I wonder if I did myself irreparable damage.'

'I think if anything was going to happen to you, it would have happened by now.' Sophia sighed 'It was eight years ago.'

'I've never taken anything since,' said Alix. 'Part of it was great, but it wasn't me, somehow.'

'That's because you lost all your inhibitions and just had a good time,' said Sophia. 'I haven't seen that happen before or since.'

'I have good times,' said Alix. 'I go to the pub. I drink. Sometimes I smoke – though I'm trying not to. I might have inhibitions but I'm not repressed, you know.'

'I know, I know.' Sophia was surprised at the vehemence in Alix's voice. 'Listen, I'd better go. I'm supposed to be at a marketing meeting in fifteen minutes and I need to run through some details with the troops first. But I wondered if you'd like to come over, Alix. I'd love to see you.' She laughed. 'Before I get married!'

'I'd love to come over,' said Alix, although it was the last thing in the world that she wanted to do. 'Maybe next week, Sophia. I've been putting off a few London meetings for a while. I could set them up and then meet you.'

'Perfect,' Sophia told her. 'Give me a call when you get things sorted.'

'OK,' said Alix. 'I'm glad you rang. And I'm really glad about you and Richard. And the baby.'

'Thanks,' said Sophia. 'Take care of yourself, Alix. Get rid of the cold! And give my love to Paul.'

'Yes, sure,' said Alix. 'I will.'

She replaced the receiver and stared into space. Sophia! The one person she always felt she understood. The one person who definitely understood her. Sophia had now joined the ranks of the disposable nappy and breast-is-best brigade. Sophia was already thinking in terms of her future life outside financial services. Why, thought Alix, why do we have to make a bloody choice?

She glanced at her watch. It was after five o'clock. She wondered what she should do about Paul. She really didn't want to ring him at RTÉ again. And she certainly didn't want to phone him at his mother's home. Besides, if she called him, he'd know that it mattered to her. She didn't want him to know how much it mattered. So she'd wait for him to phone. If he did.

I don't believe it, she said to herself as she curled up in the chair. I'm sitting beside the phone like some lovesick adolescent. I never did this when I was sixteen.

She sat beside the phone for almost an hour but it didn't ring. She was annoyed with herself for caring so much, and furious with Paul for not calling. Maybe she should ring after all, she thought. She was a mature adult, for heaven's sake. There was no need to sit around and wait. If she knew whether or not she was meeting him, then she could plan what she wanted to do for the rest of the evening. Go to the gym, perhaps. Or the shooting club.

She couldn't go to the gym, of course. She was far too exhausted to lift weights or pound the treadmill. And she wasn't feeling strong enough to go to the shooting club either. She'd never be able to support the weight of the gun.

She decided to take a shower. One of the rules of waiting for the phone to ring was to be doing something else. Preferably something that made it difficult to answer straightaway. The shower would be perfect for that.

But in case he called, she switched on the answering machine.

Actually, she thought as she shampooed her hair, it would be good if he rang while she was in the shower. Getting the machine would teach him that she didn't need to hang around and wait for him. Not that he probably cared either way. She stood under the jet of water. Her emotions were all over the place. She didn't know what she wanted him to feel. She didn't even know how she felt.

She was wrapping a towel round her when the phone rang. She stubbed her toe on the bathroom door as she hurried into the living room.

'Hi, I'm sorry we can't take your call but don't hang up. Leave your name. Leave a number. We'll get back to you.'

'Hi, Alix, it's me. Have you got someone else living with you? Who's the "we" on the machine? I just—'

'Paul! I'm here!' she interrupted him. 'Sorry, I was busy, that's why the machine was on.'

'Always busy,' he joked.

'You know how it is,' she said noncommittally.

'Are we still meeting tonight?' he asked.

'Whatever suits.'

'I'm in Dundalk at the moment,' he told her. 'Had to interview someone up here so I'm on the way back right now.

I can meet you if you want, but I've got to see someone else at around half nine.'

'You sound busier than me.'

He laughed. 'It's been all go since I took this job.'

'Why don't we meet for a quick drink,' she said. 'After all, it wasn't ever going to be anything else, was it? What about seven thirty in the Beggar's Bush? It's convenient for me, and for you if you're coming over the toll bridge.'

'That sounds OK,' said Paul. 'I'll see you then.'

'OK,' said Alix. 'Looking forward to it.' It was amazing, she thought, how she was talking to him as though he was a client all of a sudden. Looking forward to it! She'd never talked to Paul like that before.

She went back into the bathroom and rubbed down with the towel before hanging it neatly on the towel rail.

Once she'd dried her hair, she did her nails with her new Lancôme varnish. Alix rarely wore varnish because her nails weren't really long enough. She used the computer terminal so much that it was impossible to have long nails, and whenever she was particularly tense, she bit the nail of her little finger so that it was usually shorter than all the rest. But right now, they were almost uniform in length, the little fingernail a couple of millimetres shorter but not so much that Paul would notice.

∽

She arrived at the pub early. It was only a five-minute stroll from her apartment, but she couldn't sit around any longer. The rain that had persisted on and off for most of the day had stopped and the clouds were beginning to break up. Quite suddenly, it was warm and humid.

There were a few people sitting outside the pub when she arrived. She looked inside for Paul without any real hope of seeing him, and when he wasn't there, she ordered a bottle of Miller and took it outside. She knew that she wasn't supposed to drink with the antibiotics, but she was only going to have the beer. She couldn't sit on her own in a pub and drink mineral water.

It was nearly fifteen minutes later before a blue Rover drew up at the pavement and Paul got out. Alix felt her heart miss a beat as she saw him. He looked even more handsome than before – his hair was shorter, he was wearing a pair of stonewashed Levi's which she hadn't bought him and didn't recognise, and a blue Nike top. Paul had always hated branded clothes.

She was glad that she'd decided against wearing the yellow dress she'd bought at lunchtime after all. She hadn't wanted to look dressed-up for Paul and that was exactly how the yellow dress had looked. So she'd chosen a black Kookai top and her black tight-fit denims which she normally had to squeeze into but which, following her loss of appetite over the past few weeks, were now easier to wear. They made her look thin, she knew, and much younger. She'd pulled her hair back into a loose ponytail, unlike the more severe look she used for work, and she was wearing the new silver earrings and chain.

'Hello!' She waved at Paul and he walked over to her and kissed her on the cheek.

'Hi,' he said. 'Can I get you a drink?'

'Let me get you one,' said Alix.

He shook his head. 'What do you want?'

'A bottle of Miller, please.'

'OK.' He smiled at her and his eyes turned vivid blue. 'Back in a jiffy.'

She sat back in her seat, aware of the relief she felt that he'd shown up. She'd had a horrible feeling he might phone and say that he was sorry, he'd been delayed, he couldn't make it. She took her mobile phone out of her bag and switched it off.

'Here you are.' Paul put the drink in front of her. 'God, it's hot again, isn't it?'

She nodded. 'I got caught in the rain earlier. It's hard to believe it's so nice now.'

'Hottest summer since I can remember.'

'Makes it very hard to work,' said Alix. 'You see the blue skies outside and it seems such a shame to be cooped up indoors.'

'Not something that ever worried you before,' said Paul casually.

'It hasn't been this hot before.' Alix was determined not to argue with him. She'd planned her strategy in the time since he phoned. She was going to be relaxed and composed. She wouldn't let him ruffle her and she wouldn't try to score points off him. Serenity would be her watchword.

'So how is the new job?' she asked.

'It's great,' replied Paul. 'I wish I'd taken the plunge before now, Alix. I really do. I know people knock RTÉ and say that national radio and TV is bland and boring – and maybe sometimes it is – but we're working on some really interesting stories and there's so much more in terms of resources! I'm doing stuff I would have liked to do before but didn't have the backup myself. Best thing I ever did. Honestly.'

'That's great,' she said.

He told her about the interview in Dundalk and how he'd had to work to get the confidence of the interviewee and how, eventually, he'd got the story he wanted to get.

'Sounds like you're really enjoying things,' said Alix.

'I am.'

'New car?' She nodded at the Rover.

'Yes.' He looked a little guilty. 'I know I've been anti-car in the past, but I need it now.'

'You never minded borrowing the BMW,' she reminded him.

'But I felt bad about it,' he said.

She laughed. 'Not so's I noticed.'

They were silent for a moment.

'So how have you been?' asked Paul. 'How are things in the big bad world of capital markets?'

'It's been busy,' she answered. 'I'm still having arguments with Gavin Donnelly. Little shit is getting cockier by the day. We've had a few really good days but a few truly horrible ones as well. I'm a little behind budget for the year, but I guess I'll be able to make it back.'

'I admire you,' he said.

'Pardon?'

'I admire you. I always have. You're so – so much in control of yourself. Of your life. Of the people around you.'

She stared at him. 'No, I'm not.'

'You are, Alix. Of course you are.'

'Wyn says that too.'

'There. You see. We can't both be wrong.'

'Of course you can. I'm not in control of anything.'

'You know exactly what you want from life and you've got it,' said Paul. 'If that's not control, I don't know what is.'

'How do you know I've got exactly what I want from life?'

'Because you light up every time you talk about work.

You should see yourself – animated, knowledgeable. I envy you.'

You're just saying that, she thought. You're saying it so that I can't burst into tears and beg you to come back.

'I've been sick,' she said.

'You don't look it,' he told her. 'You look wonderful.'

She was glad he'd said that. It had taken Rimmel concealer, Clarins fake tan and Dior face bronzer to look healthy. She'd sat in front of the mirror and thought that she looked like shit earlier.

He grinned suddenly. 'But you must have been ill. You're wearing your crotch-cutting jeans and you haven't squirmed in your seat once yet.'

She blushed. Paul had always called them crotch-cutters but she hadn't expected him to notice that she was wearing them. 'How come you spotted I was wearing them without the giveaway wriggling?'

'I'm clued in to fashion at the moment,' he explained. 'Doing a piece on double-dealing in the rag trade.'

'Does that explain the Nike top and Levi jeans?' she asked.

'No.' He looked abashed. 'I just thought I should treat myself.'

'Do you miss me?' The question was out before she had a chance to stop it and she was furious with herself. She hadn't meant to ask.

He looked uncomfortable. 'I hate living with my mother. Maybe you were right about her, Alix. She's dreadfully over-bearing. And she asks me when I'm going to be home!'

Be serene, she told herself as he avoided the question. Don't push it.

'I miss you,' she told him. 'Are we in the Superclub?'

209

'What?' He looked at her in amazement.

'Superclub. Or whatever it's called. Club card. In the super-market. They asked me when I went shopping and I didn't know.'

He roared with laughter and people at the next table turned to look at them. 'Only you could ask a question like that, Alix.'

'I just wanted to know.'

'Yes,' he said. 'We – or at least I – have a club card. It's in my name but it's the apartment's address. Do you want it?'

'No,' she said in annoyance. 'I just wanted to know if it was something you'd joined.'

'Take the card.' He took his wallet from the pocket of his jeans. 'I don't need it. Mum is doing the shopping. I'm just giving her a fortune in cash.'

'No,' she said. 'You'll need it when you move to Malahide.'

'It's probably a different supermarket out there.' He grinned at her. 'You might as well have this.'

She shook her head. 'I hate that bloody supermarket. I think I'll just buy things as I need them.'

'That's hopelessly uneconomic,' said Paul.

'I don't care.' She was trying very hard not to sound petulant but she knew she did.

Paul drained his glass.

'Do you want another?' she asked.

He hesitated.

'I do,' she said. 'You've plenty of time.' She got up and walked inside. She shivered. Her eyes were beginning to water again. Maybe she shouldn't have drunk two bottles of beer.

She carried his pint and her mineral water outside.

'Water?' He looked at her drink in surprise.

'I shouldn't be drinking any alcohol,' she explained. 'I'm on antibiotics.'

'What exactly is wrong with you?' he asked.

'Don't know,' she said laconically. 'It's not too bad. Wasn't good the first day but I feel OK now.'

'Are you really sick?' he asked. 'Have you been throwing up?'

'No,' she answered. 'But I've had headaches, scratchy throat, that sort of stuff. I'm much better.'

'Have you been off work?'

She nodded. 'Couple of days.'

'You must have been really bad,' he said. 'I don't remember you ever staying off ill.'

She grinned at him. 'What about the night we went to Drogheda?'

'Close,' he said. 'But it doesn't quite cut it.'

It had been when they'd first started living together. Paul had taken her to the Boyne Valley Hotel for dinner and then shocked her by saying that he'd booked a room for the night.

'You can't do that,' she'd told him. 'I've got to go to work in the morning.'

'So what?' he'd said. 'Take a day off.'

'I can't just take a day off.'

'Why not?'

'I just can't!'

But when the phone had rung at half five the following morning, she'd replaced the receiver and snuggled up to him. They'd only been asleep for three hours. After dinner, they'd gone to the room and made love. Just as she'd been falling asleep, Paul had rung room service and ordered a bottle of champagne. He'd insisted on making love while drinking

211

champagne. It hadn't been a very successful exercise in terms of champagne consumption, but it had been hugely erotic. And then they'd taken a bath together because both of them were covered in champagne and that had led to another bout of lovemaking. Alix had told him that she'd never believed a bloke could do it three times in one night. Paul had told her that he hadn't expected to!

So she'd been in no mood to get out of bed at the crack of dawn the next morning and drive to work. She'd tried to drift back to sleep again but she couldn't. So she'd slid out of bed.

'Where are you going?' Paul had woken up just as she was slipping into her shoes.

'Work.'

'Alix! Forget about work! Come back to bed.'

'I can't,' she'd told him. 'I have to go in. I'll be late as it is.'

'Phone in sick,' he'd mumbled. 'God knows, after all the wine and champagne you should feel a little under the weather.'

'I feel great.' She'd kissed him on the forehead and gone to work, even though it had been impossible to concentrate on anything all day.

'Why don't you take some time off?' Paul broke in on her thoughts.

'Too busy,' she said.

'Always too busy.'

She could hear the coolness in his voice. She said nothing and the silence between them became awkward. Paul looked at his watch.

'Before you go,' Alix put her hand on his arm, 'I need to know. Have you been talking to Sabine?'

'Of course,' he said simply.

'What – what is your relationship with her?' Alix hated herself for asking.

'I told you before. And it hasn't changed.'

'When are you moving out to Malahide?' She changed the subject.

'Ten days,' he said thankfully. 'Weekend after next.'

'It'll seem strange, I guess.'

'Not as strange as living with my mother.'

'I suppose not.'

'Alix.'

'Yes?'

'I don't know about Sabine. I truly don't. But I know that I want something different from a relationship than what we had.'

'You liked what we had in the Boyne Valley.'

'I know,' he said. 'And I never stopped enjoying that part of our lives. It's just that there's more to it than making love.'

'I know,' she said.

'I care about you a lot.'

'Do you?'

'Of course I do. Alix, there's so much about you that I love. It's just that I think your priorities are different to mine.'

'What makes you so sure?'

He shrugged.

'You don't really know me at all,' she said. 'You only think you do.'

'I'm pretty certain I do,' he told her. 'Look, I'd better go, Alix. I have to drop home before I go out again.'

'OK.'

He stood up but she stayed where she was.

'It was nice meeting you but I don't think we should see each other for a while,' he said.

'Sure.'

'Do you want a lift back to your apartment?'

'No,' said Alix. 'I'll sit here for a little longer.'

'Are you certain?'

'Yes.'

'OK.' He kissed her on the cheek again. 'Take care of yourself.'

'And you.'

She watched him as he walked to the car and unlocked the door.

If he waves before he gets in, she said to herself, he still fancies me.

She held her breath as he opened the door. He looked back at her, waved, and got in.

She waited until he'd driven away before lighting a cigarette.

Chapter 16

Alix didn't know whether it was the result of the drinks or the cigarette or whether it was simply meeting Paul again, but she felt wretched by the time she got back to the apartment. Her head was pounding, her palms were sweating and every so often she shivered violently.

She sat in her favourite armchair and turned on the TV. Why was the scheduling so bad during the summer? she wondered. Why did producers assume that anyone actually watching TV at nine thirty in the evening was either mentally subnormal or had the memory of a goldfish? The episode of *Friends* they were showing was one that she'd seen at least three times already on this station.

It would be nice though, she thought tiredly, as she watched Jennifer Aniston serve cups of coffee, to have a job where you didn't have to think. And people who cared about you no matter what. She couldn't see Jennifer's character having to worry about junior members of the café plotting to take over her best clients. And if Jennifer was feeling sick with some ridiculous virus she'd happily stay at home while her charming and reliable friends called around to make her cups of coffee and hand out slices of comfort cake.

The thought of coffee and cake made Alix feel ill. She jumped out of her chair, sprinted to the bathroom and was sick in the shower tray.

Oh, God, she groaned as another wave of nausea hit her. Please don't let me puke again. Please.

Better out than in. She clutched at the shower door and tried to tell herself that she was better off for having dumped her granary roll and two bottles of Miller. Dr O'Neill had been surprised that she hadn't thrown up already. At least she was now conforming to the symptoms of the bug. Geraldine O'Neill had also told her to take a minimum of three days off work.

Alix ran her fingers through her damp hair and leaned against the relative coolness of the tiled wall. She should have done what the doctor ordered and she shouldn't have had anything to drink. Haven't you got any bloody sense? she asked herself as she rinsed out the shower.

She dragged herself back to the armchair. Her head, which had felt as though it was going to explode while she was actually being sick, wasn't pounding quite so much now. But she still felt horribly shaky and was shivering violently.

'This is what it would be like if you were pregnant,' she said out loud. Running to the bathroom and puking your guts up every morning. That's what it's like and you'd absolutely hate it. This is what's going to happen to Sophia and she'll regret every minute of it. So, Alix, you've no regrets. You're better off. You'd be hopeless, useless, absolutely dreadful at being pregnant.

But – if it meant having Paul back in her life? Would it be worth it then?

She turned off the TV. She could hardly focus on the screen. She'd be better off in bed. Besides, a decent night's sleep would make all the difference.

It didn't. She tossed and turned all night. At three o'clock she was sick again.

~

She phoned Wyn at seven the next morning.

'I'm really sorry,' she said. 'But I feel terrible. I got up to go to work but I couldn't even stand up without wanting to be sick. I think I should go to the doctor again, but I'm afraid I wouldn't make it to her surgery without passing out.'

'For goodness' sake, Alix!' Wyn was alarmed by the desperate tone in her sister's voice. 'Why didn't you ring me last night? I would have come straight over.'

'I thought I'd be better by now,' said Alix. 'I thought I'd be OK once I got to sleep.'

'I never heard anything so ridiculous in all my life,' said Wyn sternly. 'Why don't you ring the doctor, get her to make a house call? I'll be over as soon as I get the girls to school.'

'Will she do house calls?' Alix was rarely ill – the last visit she'd made to the doctor was for her regular smear test.

'Of course she'll do a house call,' said Wyn impatiently. 'She probably has set times for them.'

'I thought you had to go to doctors,' Alix muttered. 'I didn't think they'd come to you any more.'

Dr O'Neill began her surgery at eight. Alix phoned at a quarter to, and was astonished when the receptionist said that Dr O'Neill did house calls from ten-thirty to twelve. But it would be nearer twelve when she got to see Alix. She had a number of other calls first.

My God, Alix thought as she hung up. Half of the country is obviously down with this bug.

She lay on her back and closed her eyes. She didn't want to feel like this. She wanted to be better. She wanted to be back at work. She wanted to see Gavin Donnelly licking her boots. She smiled weakly at the thought of Gavin licking her boots and then reached out for the receiver to phone the bank.

'Not again, Alix!'

Dave's tone made her flush. She didn't like the implication that she was making it up. 'I was throwing up all night,' she said. 'I feel awful. The doctor is calling around twelve. I'll give you a shout afterwards.'

'It doesn't much matter today,' said Dave. 'There's no news out and no one has meetings. But you know that Gavin is going to the pro-am tomorrow and I have a meeting at half two. That'll leave Jenny on her own.'

'I'm perfectly well aware of the situation tomorrow, Dave,' she said with an authority she didn't feel. 'And I'll be in the office in time to cover for you, so don't worry about it.'

'It's not me that's worrying,' said Dave. 'If you're not here, you're not here. But you know Des. He'll burst a gasket if he finds out that you're out again.'

'Dave, the last time I was out sick you didn't even work for the bloody bank,' she snapped. 'So just don't give me all that shit. I've said I'll be in and I will.'

'OK, OK. Keep your knickers on,' said Dave. 'Although I suppose it should be keep your pyjama bottoms on, shouldn't it?'

She smiled weakly. 'If I wore pyjamas.'

He laughed. 'See, you're getting better already.'

She'd only just hung up from her conversation with Dave

when the buzzer to the apartment sounded. She walked unsteadily to the monitor and peered at it.

'If you gave me a bloody key I wouldn't have to get you out of bed,' said Wyn. 'Hurry up and let me in.'

Alix released the entrance door and waited for her sister to reach the apartment.

'Hi,' she said as she opened the door. 'Come in.'

'Jesus, Alix. You look like shit.'

'Thanks.'

'I mean it.' Wyn's eyes were troubled. 'What's supposed to be the matter with you? I thought you just had a cold.'

'According to the doctor it's some sort of bug. I went on Monday because I felt bad at work. It's doing the rounds apparently. So I suppose I'm giving it to you by making you fuss over me. I'm sorry.'

'There's no need to be sorry,' said Wyn. 'I'm your big sister. I'm supposed to fuss over you.'

'Like you did when I had chickenpox?'

'Most kids would have been happy that their sister loved them enough to try and pick off their spots,' said Wyn. 'Now get into bed! Did you phone the doctor?'

'She'll be here around twelve.'

'Fine,' said Wyn. 'I'll stay with you until then.'

'You don't have to.' Alix was already feeling better now that there was someone with her. 'I think I'm over the worst.'

'Get into bed,' said Wyn again. 'And try to get some sleep. I'll make myself coffee.'

Alix made a face. 'I don't think I have any milk,' she said. 'I came home in a bit of a hurry last night and I forgot to call into the shop.'

'How could you forget milk?' Wyn stared at her. 'Why don't

219

you stock up when you go to the supermarket? It lasts long enough.'

'Wyn, don't panic about milk. Maybe there's some there.' Alix crawled beneath the duvet and pulled it round her.

'I won't panic,' said Wyn dryly. 'Now, go to sleep.'

Alix closed her eyes and listened to the sound of her sister pottering around in the kitchen. It was nice to have someone here to look after her. To worry about things. She definitely didn't feel as ill now that Wyn was here.

Wyn filled the kettle and plugged it in. She looked around the tiny galley kitchen and sighed. Alix didn't seem to use the kitchen for cooking. A week's supply of newspapers (including four Sunday papers all with a range of supplements) were stacked up on the counter. A bundle of Bloomberg financial magazines were piled onto the cooker. A sheaf of bills was in imminent danger of floating down from the top of the microwave.

The kettle boiled. Wyn opened a cupboard door and took out the silver tea caddy that she'd given Alix as a present when she had moved into the apartment. It contained one crumpled tea bag. Wyn sighed and opened the fridge. There was just enough milk for one cup of tea.

After she'd drunk the tea, and when she'd looked into the bedroom to find Alix sleeping soundly, Wyn emptied the remainder of the best before 15 July orange juice down the sink and dumped the carton in the refuse sack, as well as the Easi-Singles (which were also past their best before date) and the half-empty jar of mayonnaise.

The only other items in the fridge were two cans of Miller and a bottle of Chardonnay.

Had Alix any food in the house at all? Wyn asked herself.

Whenever she'd visited in the past, there'd seemed to be plenty of fresh fruit, edible cheese and enough milk for as much tea and coffee as you could drink.

She opened the door of the freezer and leaped out of the way as two frozen Beef Byrianis fell out and almost hit her on the head. She picked the packets off the floor and squashed them back into the freezer alongside four Thai green curries for one and a spinach lasagne.

Honestly, Alix, she thought crossly. You should be eating better than this. It's no wonder you've caught a bug.

She took an envelope from the pile on the fridge and wrote 'Gone to shops – won't be long' on it. She propped it on the bedside locker where her sister would be sure to see it, took the keys from the worktop and let herself out of the apartment.

She'd been gone about fifteen minutes when Alix woke up. She blinked a couple of times and rolled over very slowly. It took her a few minutes to focus on Wyn's note.

Shit, she thought. Wyn would no doubt have done a complete snoop around the kitchen, found it to be completely devoid of food and was now marching through the supermarket looking for fresh produce to counteract the scurvy which Wyn was no doubt assuming she had contracted. She'd meant to do a proper bout of shopping this weekend. She'd even written some things down on a list. But now Wyn would think that she'd gone to pieces completely and she'd start lecturing her on not letting herself go simply because she'd been dumped by her boyfriend. Wyn was a great lecturer about how to get over being dumped by your boyfriend – probably because she had so much practice at it when we were younger, thought Alix viciously, as she thumped her pillow.

She lay on her back and stared at the ceiling. It was nice to have mean thoughts about Wyn who was so irritating when she got into her elder sister mode. Meddling elder sister mode, thought Alix as she recalled last Saturday's blind date with Cathal Moran, organised by her brother-in-law and aided and abetted by his wife.

Wyn was so happy in her marriage and so happy with her kids that it sometimes drove Alix to distraction. She seemed to have found exactly the right person in Terry. How had they known? wondered Alix. How had Wyn been so sure that it was right to marry Terry when she was only twenty-one? And when it was right to start a family? Was everything always bloody perfect for her? Wyn never stopped telling her that it was all very well being a modern career woman but that sooner or later she would want to settle down. Her sister had made such an easy transition from potential high-flier to wife and mother, thought Alix. But she knew she couldn't be like that herself. Yet people seemed to expect it. If you didn't want a horde of screaming children, there was something wrong with you. Even Sophia had sold out. Alix groaned.

The apartment door clicked open.

'Are you OK?' Wyn pushed open the bedroom door.

'I'm fine,' said Alix.

'I thought I heard you moan.'

'You did.' Alix smiled faintly at her. 'But not because I felt bad. Just because I'm stuck here and haven't the bloody energy to get up.'

'You can stay there until the doctor comes,' said Wyn. 'I'm going to fill your fridge. Honestly, Alix. Miller and Chardonnay!'

'Life's little essentials,' said Alix.

'Well, I've bought you milk and eggs and cheese and fruit. I got you some bread and sliced ham. And some tomatoes. And tea bags.'

'Thanks,' said Alix. 'There's some money on the worktop.'

'It wasn't expensive,' Wyn told her sternly. 'It's a lot cheaper to buy decent fresh produce than half a dozen Marks and Spencer's Thai curries.'

'Are there really half a dozen there?' asked Alix. 'I didn't see any before I went shopping.'

'Don't be facetious.'

'Don't be disapproving then.'

'Ungrateful wretch.' But Wyn smiled at her before she went back to the kitchen.

❧

Geraldine O'Neill arrived at half past eleven.

'I didn't think you were that bad, Alix,' she said as she sat on the bed beside her.

'I wasn't,' said Alix. 'I felt miles better yesterday. Then it suddenly came over me again and I was sick.'

'Thought you should have been sick.' Geraldine shoved a thermometer under Alix's tongue. 'Any aches and pains? Neck? Joints?'

Alix shook her head. 'Not specifically,' she mumbled.

'Shivering and sweating?'

Alix nodded.

'Feeling light-headed again?'

Alix nodded.

'Did you stay in bed like I told you?'

Alix shrugged.

Geraldine took the thermometer out of her mouth and looked at it. 'Don't tell me you went to work.'

'I came home early,' said Alix defensively.

'And then you went to bed?'

'I had to meet someone.' She felt herself blush. Wyn, who'd been sitting in the chair by the window, gazed at her sister speculatively.

'Did you have anything to drink?'

'Like?'

'Like alcohol,' said Geraldine.

'Just a bottle of beer.'

'For goodness' sake!' Geraldine looked at her angrily. 'You had to be carted from your office to my surgery. I tell you that you have a particularly nasty bug and to stay in bed for three days. You proceed to go back to work and meet friends in the pub. Honestly, Alix. Are you actually surprised you've had a relapse? Not that you were ever really better in the first place.'

Alix looked at her sheepishly. 'Sorry.'

'So you should be.' Geraldine strapped a blood-pressure pad round Alix's arm. 'When I say stay out of work I mean stay out of work. What is it with people that they feel this need to rush back to the office? You work in a bank, don't you? Surely there's plenty of people who can cover for you.'

'I'm a dealer,' said Alix. 'I'm in charge of the dealing room, Geraldine. I had to go in yesterday. It was important.'

'Don't be stupid,' said Geraldine. 'Your health is far more important than jumping up and down and shouting buy and sell and whatever other rubbish it is that you do.'

'It's not rubbish,' said Alix. 'It's—'

'Relax, relax. You'll burst the monitor.' Geraldine grinned at her and Alix made a face. 'OK,' said Geraldine finally. 'You *are* taking the tablets I prescribed already?'

'Yes,' said Alix.

'I want you to take these as well.' She scribbled another prescription and handed it to Alix. 'Start today. Finish the course. Also, stay in bed today and tomorrow.'

'But I can't stay in bed tomorrow,' protested Alix. 'Honestly I can't.'

'Of course you can.' Wyn got up from the chair and walked over to the bed. 'You're staying there and you're not getting up. I'll make sure of that.'

'You don't understand.' Alix wished she could get through to them. 'I can't just stay out. I'm needed.'

'No you're not,' said Geraldine brutally. 'If you were run over by a bus they'd have to get on without you. And that's exactly what they'll do tomorrow.'

Alix bit her lip. She had no doubt that they could get on without her, but she didn't want Dave Bryant telling Des that she had let them down. She felt herself grow even hotter at the thought.

'Come to the surgery on Monday evening,' said Geraldine as she repacked her bag. 'Five thirty until seven.'

'OK,' said Alix.

'And do what I said. Your immune system is weakened. I don't want you to pick up anything else.'

'What exactly is the matter with me anyway?' asked Alix.

'Viral infection,' said Geraldine. 'Covers a multitude, I know. But that's what it is. You'll be fine in a few days but you really must stay in bed and rest. I mean it, Alix. Even Saturday and Sunday you should take it easy.'

'I always take it easy at the weekends,' said Alix.

Wyn showed Geraldine out then came and sat on the edge of Alix's bed. 'What did she mean, carted to her surgery?' she asked.

Alix made a face. 'I was ill at work. They sent me home.'

'How ill?'

'I felt bad,' said Alix. 'I fainted.'

'Alix!'

'Lots of people faint,' said Alix. 'It wasn't a big deal.'

'You're not pregnant or anything, are you?' asked Wyn suddenly.

'Don't be absolutely ridiculous,' retorted Alix. 'How the hell could I be? Paul doesn't live here any more.'

'I thought, perhaps, that before he left—'

'Give me some credit,' said Alix. 'When I told him I didn't want kids, I meant it.'

'Did you meet Paul last night?' asked Wyn.

'Of course. I told you I was going to meet him.'

'But you were ill.'

'So what?'

'It was bloody stupid to meet him if you weren't feeling well!'

'Don't be ridiculous,' said Alix. 'You sound like the sort of mother Carrie isn't.'

'She'd want to know if you were being stupid.'

'Oh, give me a break,' Alix snapped.

'It's your business, I suppose,' said Wyn. 'But why don't you make a clean break of it? What's the point in clinging to him? You're not the clinging type, Alix.'

'I think he's making a mistake, that's all.'

'Do you love him?' asked Wyn.

'Of course I do.'

226

'Are you sure?'

'Don't give me that shit.' Alix closed her eyes. 'I can do without the lectures, thanks.'

'No one ever broke it off with you before, did they?' continued Wyn. 'You were always the one.'

Alix shrugged.

'I just wonder if you're trying to hang on to him simply because you can't believe that anyone would want to leave you,' said Wyn.

'Wonder all you like,' said Alix. 'I'm sick, I don't want to talk about it.'

'I'm sorry,' said Wyn. 'Honestly I am.'

Alix opened an eye.

'I'm so used to seeing you up and about and in control of things that I can't imagine you don't feel well enough to argue with me.'

Alix smiled weakly. 'I enjoy arguing with you. Usually.'

'Oh, Alix. I just want you to be happy,' said Wyn. 'Really I do. But it seems to me that Paul has a point. After a certain age people's priorities change. They did with me.'

'Come on, Wyn. You always wanted a husband and kids.'

'Yes, but not straightaway. It was just that when I met Terry—'

'Love's young dream.' Alix yawned.

'A career isn't everything,' Wyn continued. 'And everyone says that yours is a young person's game. And you're not as young as you were, Alix.'

'Thirty-two is hardly old, Wyn.'

'But it's different to when you're twenty-two.'

Alix sighed. 'I really don't want to talk about this any more. I'm tired.'

'I'll let you get some sleep,' said Wyn. 'I want to wash out your fridge anyway.'

Alix closed her eyes. Arguing with Wyn had exhausted her. She tried to think about Paul and babies, but she was asleep within five minutes.

⌒

When Wyn had finished cleaning Alix's kitchen she tiptoed into the bedroom, took the prescription and went to the chemist to get it filled. Although she was sorry that Alix was ill, she couldn't help enjoying her role in looking after her. Alix was so damned independent, she thought as she crossed Haddington Road. She hated the idea of not being able to do everything for herself. Wyn remembered her when they were children, pulling her tricycle up the hill at the back of their house, determinedly trying to keep up with her elder sister and her friends. Alix's four-year-old legs struggled to keep up, but when Wyn (in a sudden fit of sibling duty) turned round to help her, Alix struggled away from her. 'I can do it myself!' she'd cried, tugging at the handlebars of the bike and pushing Wyn out of the way. And she had.

But Wyn couldn't understand why Alix always seemed to want to test herself. The high-pressure job in a male-dominated industry. Taking part in shooting competitions at the shooting club. Pushing herself to the limits in the gym. Alix had once invited Wyn along to the gym with her. Wyn had agreed, looking forward to a gentle jog on the treadmill and a leisurely swim afterwards. She'd been astounded to see her sister push herself through what seemed to Wyn, at least, a punishing regime of bike, treadmill, rowing machine and weights.

'You're not training for the bloody Olympics,' Wyn commented sourly as she watched Alix use the shoulder press.

'I like it,' her sister said. 'It makes me feel good.'

But there had to be something wrong with someone who felt that they needed to push themselves all the time, thought Wyn. There wasn't any need for Alix to do everything she did.

The chemist was busy and Wyn had to wait for Alix's prescription. She'd lecture Alix about taking the tablets, she said to herself. She knew that her sister would be just as likely to forget about them once she felt the slightest bit better.

And she'd better make sure that Alix didn't even consider going in to work in the morning. Perhaps she should call round, just to be certain.

'I said I wouldn't go in and I won't,' Alix said when she woke up two hours later. 'Though I do feel a lot better now.'

'Maybe you do, but you won't if you go to work tomorrow.'

'I told you, I'll stay home.'

'Fine,' said Wyn. 'The doctor said that you should stay in bed. I'll call round at nine, see how you're doing.'

'There really isn't any need,' Alix protested.

'I'd like to,' said Wyn. 'If you give me a spare set of keys you won't even have to get up.'

'Really, Wyn—'

'It's no trouble at all.' Wyn smiled sweetly at her. 'I wouldn't be much of a sister if I left you to suffer all on your own, would I?'

❧

Alix waited until after three to phone Dave.

'I'm sorry,' she said. 'I'm not going to be able to make it in tomorrow.'

'Fuck it, Alix!' Dave sounded annoyed as she knew he would. 'You know I'll be out in the afternoon. And you know Gavin's taking people to Portmarnock! We need you here.'

'It seems that my bed needs me more,' said Alix dryly. 'I'm sorry. I feel a lot better but my doctor – and my sister – have both absolutely forbidden me to get up. So you'll have to manage without me. Is there any chance you can reschedule your meeting?'

'Are you crazy?' asked Dave. 'You know what it's like trying to get to see Arnie. He's put me off twice already.'

'I'm really sorry, Dave. But Jenny can cope and you could ask Mike Keogh to help with the phone lines. It probably won't be that busy anyway. There aren't any economic releases due and it'll probably be one of those quiet Fridays where everyone goes home early.'

'You know that's rubbish,' said Dave gloomily. 'You know how it's always when you're short of people that something really major breaks and it's a complete nightmare.'

'I'll phone in the morning,' said Alix. 'See how things are.'

'Things are fine, to be honest,' said Dave. 'It's not that we can't manage, Alix. It'd just be nice to have the bodies around.'

'It's great to feel wanted,' she muttered. 'Look, if there's a problem, just call me. The phone is right beside me.'

'Sure,' said Dave. 'We'll see you on Monday.'

'Absolutely,' said Alix. 'Monday.'

She lay back and closed her eyes again. She wondered which was worse for her health, work when she was ill or to be away from the office when she just knew that those bastards were waiting for an opportunity to shaft her.

〜

It was Carrie, not Wyn, who called round the following morning. Alix was in the kitchen inspecting the new contents of her fridge when her mother rang the bell.

'Where's Wyn?' asked Alix as Carrie walked into the apartment.

'I told her I'd call to see you this morning. She rang me last night.' Carrie picked up the kettle and began to fill it. 'You should be in bed.'

'I'm much better,' said Alix. 'And there wasn't any need for Wyn to ring you.'

'You're my daughter,' said Carrie. 'I need to know these things. And Wyn was right to tell me.'

Alix sighed. She supposed that Wyn had enjoyed ringing Carrie and telling her that she was sick and alone. They probably had a nice girly discussion about poor, solitary, deserted Alix who was doomed to a life of single womanhood.

'Go back to bed,' said Carrie. 'I'll bring you in a cup of tea.'

'Coffee,' Alix told her. 'I was going to make coffee.'

'Tea is better for you.'

Alix gritted her teeth and went back to bed. There wasn't any point in arguing.

She was watching CNN on the portable TV when Carrie brought a mug of tea and a slice of toast in to her.

'Thanks.' Alix took the tray from her.

Carrie picked up the remote control and turned off the TV.

'Oh, switch it back on!' Alix cried. 'I was watching a piece about the Tokyo markets.'

'Nothing you can do about the Tokyo markets from your

231

bed,' said Carrie briskly. 'So there's no need for you to be watching it.'

Alix said nothing.

'So.' Carrie sat on the edge of the bed. 'What the hell is all this about?'

'All what?' asked Alix defensively.

'Collapsing at work! Too ill to get to the doctor's surgery.' Carrie's eyes were full of concern. 'Alix, I'm worried about you.'

'I have a bug,' said Alix. 'According to the doc, lots of people have it. It's no big deal. I know I was very sick, but you know me, Carrie, I always had a flair for the dramatic when it came to illness. Remember all my stomach upsets as a kid? Puking everywhere and right as rain next day. There's no need to fuss. It's the same now.'

Carrie looked at her daughter thoughtfully.

'But I was worried yesterday,' Alix conceded. 'I knew I was pretty shaky and I thought I should go back to the doctor. So I did what you have to admit was the most sensible thing I could have done and asked Wyn to come over.'

'How come you were so susceptible to this bug?' asked Carrie.

'Who knows?' Alix shrugged.

'I'll tell you,' said her mother. 'You were as tight as a drum when you called into the salon. You looked tired and unwell. And it's all because of this thing with Paul.'

'Oh, Carrie, for God's sake! It's nothing to do with Paul.'

'You miss him, don't you?'

'Well, of course I miss him,' snapped Alix. 'It's only been a few weeks.'

'But according to Wyn you're convinced he'll come back.'

'He might.'

'What makes you say that?'

'I just know.'

'And if he does, what then?'

'What do you mean?'

'Are you going to change for him?'

'Change?'

'Alix. Cop on. Paul wants to settle down and have a family. A reasonable enough desire at his age. And at yours. So it seems to me that the only way you're going to get back together is to settle down and have a family.'

Alix put her half-empty mug on her bedside locker. 'Maybe. Maybe not.'

'Alix, when you want to have children it's a really strong desire. If Paul feels like this now, there's nothing you can do to change him.'

'I never said anything about changing him.'

'I can see it in your eyes,' said Carrie. 'You're thinking that somehow you can get him back and make him forget this children nonsense. Maybe promise to do something about it next year.'

Alix squirmed uncomfortably in the bed.

'It's not like that,' Carrie continued. 'You can't just put him off. If you truly don't want kids, then you should forget about Paul.'

'Thanks for your support,' said Alix tartly.

'I'm only trying to help,' said Carrie. 'Make you see how things are.'

'And if I give in to Paul and have a kid before I'm ready, then everything will be OK.' Alix laughed shortly. 'It sure worked for you, didn't it?'

'Alix!' Carrie went white. 'You don't know anything about that. Anything at all!'

'Oh, come on,' said Alix. 'You're a businesswoman, Carrie. You settled down and had kids. And he still walked out on you. Lot of good that did you.'

'First of all,' said Carrie, keeping her voice as steady as she could, 'both of us wanted children. I wasn't a businesswoman. I worked in a beauty salon. I had to change when he walked out on us. That was nothing to do with you or Wyn. It was about him and me.'

'And who wanted children in the first place?' asked Alix. 'Him or you?'

'We both did,' answered Carrie.

'But, like most men, he couldn't take it once we were born.'

'Alix, you weren't the reason he left.'

'We weren't enough reason for him to stay,' she said.

Carrie rubbed her temples. 'It was nothing to do with you,' she said again. 'Or Wyn.'

'But the point is,' said Alix, 'men are not necessarily the best people to decide that they want kids. I've heard them in the office, you know. Blokes who talk about the wife and kids as though they were talking about some encumbrance. Having to go home is a duty to them half the time. And any time there's a crisis, it's the wife who has to run around picking up the pieces. She's the one who takes time off if one of the children gets sick. She's the one who has to make sure they've got the right stuff for school. She's the one who remembers birthdays and is rushed to a frazzle at Christmas. Meanwhile blokes stay late at the office and go for pints after work and look at Christmas as one long party season! And as soon as their wives get pregnant they're ogling every girl in the office.'

'It's not like that,' said Carrie.

'Yes it bloody is,' snapped Alix. 'If you're a working mother you're guilty for working and guilty if you give it up. Nobody looks at you in the same light any more. Actually, even if you're not pregnant, once you get married they're waiting for the announcement almost straightaway. I've worked really hard, Carrie. Really, really hard. I've had to do all they do and more. I'm not ready to give it up to have kids.'

'So you're not ready to spend the rest of your life with Paul.'

'He's started a new job,' said Alix. 'He's really happy there. I bet he's not quite so eager to start a family too.'

'I wouldn't bet on it,' said Carrie.

'You hardly know him,' Alix told her.

'I know people,' said Carrie. 'Most men like to have a wife and family. You might not think that, but they do.'

'They like to have a wife and family so that they have something to moan about in the office,' said Alix.

'Why are you so bloody cynical?' demanded Carrie.

'I'm not. I'm just practical.'

Her mother sighed. 'Don't you ever want to have kids?'

'Maybe,' said Alix. 'But I'm still young.'

'Not getting any younger.'

'Oh, don't you start! Listening to Wyn you'd swear I was ready for HRT.'

'You get more pleasure out of your children than anything else,' said Carrie softly. 'More than work, more than anything.'

'I'll take your word for it.' Alix leaned back against the pillow.

'It's true,' said Carrie.

Alix closed her eyes.

Carrie watched her for a moment, then took the tray back into the kitchen.

Chapter 17

When Alix woke up again it was midday and she felt a hundred times better. She slid out of bed and wrapped her towelling robe round her.

Carrie was sitting in the living room watching Jerry Springer on TV.

'How on earth can you look at that rubbish?' asked Alix.

'It makes me laugh.' Carrie turned to look at her. 'How are you feeling?'

'Much better,' replied Alix. 'I've stopped shivering and my head doesn't hurt any more.'

'Good.' Her mother smiled. 'But you should still stay in bed, Alix. There's no point in rushing things.'

'I feel fine,' Alix protested.

'You probably felt fine the other day,' said Carrie. 'Please, Alix. Just for once do what someone else tells you.'

Alix sighed. 'OK. But I need to ring the office and check how things are going.' She ran her fingers through her hair and wrinkled her nose. 'And I want to take a shower. I feel so grubby.'

'Go ahead,' said Carrie. 'It's a good idea. You'll feel better.' She reached for her red and white striped canvas bag. 'Here. Use this. Aromatherapy shower soap. It'll relax you.'

'Thanks.' Alix took the sample bottle her mother gave her. 'You don't need to stay with me. I know Friday is a busy day for you.'

'I told Samantha that I'd be in around three,' said Carrie. 'I'll make you some lunch and then I'll go.'

Alix sat down on the sofa beside her mother and hugged her. Carrie looked at her in astonishment.

'We don't hug very often,' said Alix. 'And I do love you, you know.'

'Don't be an idiot,' said Carrie, but she hugged Alix back.

Before she showered, Alix logged on to her computer to check on markets. It looked as if it was a quiet day, the graphs were all within very narrow ranges. She picked up the phone and dialled the office.

Jenny answered.

'How are things, Jenny?' asked Alix.

'Great,' said Jenny. 'Actually, you've picked a reasonable enough day to be out. Forex markets are quiet and there isn't too much going on in fixed income. The Footsie's up ten, so nothing much there either.'

'What have you done for cover this afternoon?'

'Mike will sit in for the afternoon,' said Jenny, 'though, to be honest, he probably won't have anything to do. The phones haven't been ringing much this morning.'

'Good,' said Alix. 'Can you put me on to Dave for a second?'

'Sure,' said Jenny. 'He's just finishing up a call. How are you feeling, Alix?'

'Much better,' she replied, 'but the doctor was adamant that I shouldn't come in. So I thought I'd better listen to her for once.'

'You were right,' said Jenny. 'Hang on, I'll pass you on to Dave now.'

'Hi, Alix. How are things?' asked Dave.

'Not bad. Listen, Dave, did you send the table of historical rates to Gary Hafford? I left it on my desk and I completely forgot about it.'

'He rang yesterday,' said Dave. 'I didn't know it was on your desk so I re-ran it and sent it by e-mail.'

'Thanks,' said Alix. 'Anything I need to know about?'

'Nope,' said Dave dismissively. 'It's been pretty quiet so you don't have to worry too much. Did a nice five-year swap with Charlie Mulholland yesterday. We were going to run it because the market was moving slightly in our favour and I liked the position. Then we were asked for a price in the interbank market and dealt. So we picked up ten basis points on five million.'

'That's great,' said Alix.

'Gavin did a trade with Christie Reardon and we made another four grand on that. So, even though it's been quiet, it's been profitable.'

'Excellent,' said Alix. 'I presume he's got everything organised for the pro-am this afternoon.'

'Yes. He's sent them the tickets and they're meeting in the clubhouse for a pint and sandwiches first. I told Gavin to order toasted bacon, egg and sausage. Portmarnock is famous for it.'

'Ugh,' said Alix. 'I was feeling OK until you said that.'

'Will you be back on Monday?' asked Dave.

'Absolutely,' said Alix. 'I'm much better.'

'See you then,' said Dave.

'Right,' Alix said. 'Tell Gavin to have a good time. And you have a good meeting with Arnie.'

'Sure.' Dave clicked out of the line.

Gavin looked up from his monitor. 'So, how is she?'

'Sounds OK,' said Dave. 'Hard to tell. She said that you're to have a good time today.'

'Huh,' said Gavin, 'bet she hopes it's a disaster.'

'She's not like you.' Jenny stretched her arms over her head. 'She probably *does* hope it goes well.'

'It will,' said Gavin. 'It will.'

❧

He'd been afraid that some people wouldn't show up, but by half past one they had all arrived. Even Matt Connery, whom Gavin had been the most doubtful about.

'Hi, Matt,' he said as the taller man was shown over to their table. 'Nice to meet you. Gavin Donnelly.' He extended his hand.

'Hi, Gavin. Nice day for it.' The sun was shining from a clear blue sky and the breeze was from the south-west.

'Sure beats the hell out of sitting in the office,' said Gavin.

'Wouldn't mind being on the course myself.' Matt sat down beside him. 'Though they'd have me arrested for wanton destruction. I like watching golf, but I'm not a great player.'

'Member anywhere?' asked Gavin.

'We've got corporate membership in the K Club,' said Matt. 'But I don't usually use it. Too embarrassed.'

'Can I get you a drink?' asked Gavin. 'And a sandwich? We're on toasted bacon, egg and sausage.'

'Sounds good to me.' Matt grinned. 'And a pint of Carlsberg, please.'

'Coming up.' Gavin was pleased at how the day was going

so far. Some of the clients knew each other already, but those that didn't were getting along well and Matt Connery looked pleased to be there. Gavin knew that the right sort of corporate entertaining was worth its weight in gold. Some clients liked gold-card-style entertaining – brash and obviously expensive. Others preferred events like today's, a relaxed day out in an informal atmosphere. And as long as they didn't have to put their hands in their pockets they were happy. Everyone enjoyed being entertained.

'Feel free to follow whoever you like,' said Gavin, after they'd finished the sandwiches. 'I thought what we could do is to meet up in the tent for a beer around four, four thirty, and then we could head back to Gibney's in Malahide for a few more. For those of you who drove here, if you want to leave your cars in Malahide later, I've organised drivers to drive you and your cars home.'

'Sounds good,' said James Morrissey, one of Gavin's best clients. James was twenty-four and worked in an insurance company. He got on well with Gavin and both of them often went on drinking binges together.

'Excellent.' Niall Baldwin added his approval.

'Great,' said Gavin. 'Let's go.'

They split up as they walked towards the course, James and Niall electing to follow Darren Clarke and his partner, a minor television celebrity. Joe Fitzgerald, Martin Dawson and Eddie Byrne wanted to camp at the ninth. 'I come to grief here every time,' said Martin. 'I want to see how the celebs get on.'

'Any preference?' Gavin asked Matt Connery and Dermot Doyle. He would have liked to go with James and Niall but today was work and both Matt and Dermot were his newest accounts.

'Think I'll just watch a few of them teeing off,' said Matt.

'Good idea,' said Gavin.

'I'll join you shortly,' Dermot told them. 'I see someone I know over there – won't be long.'

Gavin and Matt strolled to the first tee where Padraig Harrington was chatting to his caddy.

'Do you play much?' asked Matt.

Gavin shrugged. 'Not as much as I'd like, to be honest. I used to play every day but I don't get the time these days.'

'Busy at work?'

'Yes,' said Gavin. 'We're doing really well right now. Got a lot of new clients, fresh interests.'

'What's Europa Bank like as a place to work?' Matt applauded a long, straight drive from Harrington.

'It's good,' said Gavin. 'Lots of freedom, flexibility. If you think something is worthwhile you're encouraged to go for it. Most of the time.'

'And Alix Callaghan? It must be unusual to work for a woman in the dealing area.'

'Oh, Alix is a legend,' said Gavin easily. 'She's very committed to the job. At least, she used to be.'

'Used to be?'

'I suppose people's attitudes change as they get older,' Gavin mused. 'I don't think she has as much time for it as she used to have. But maybe I'm wrong.'

'What makes you say that?'

'Hard to define,' said Gavin. 'Just an impression I got. Between ourselves,' he leaned towards Matt, 'I think there's a bit of boyfriend trouble. And you know how the girls get when things aren't going smoothly in that department.'

'What sort of boyfriend trouble?'

'I don't know.' Gavin laughed. 'We were putting bets on her getting either pregnant or married in the next few months. But Jenny – she's our other female dealer – Jenny thinks that Alix's current relationship might be going through a rough patch.'

'Why is that?'

'Womanly intuition, I suppose – oh, great shot!' Gavin applauded the club pro's drive.

'She did a great presentation for us,' said Matt.

'What?'

'Alix. She did a great presentation to the board.'

'She's good at that,' Gavin conceded.

'Why didn't she come out today?' asked Matt.

'She's not really into golf,' said Gavin, 'which is a huge disadvantage in this business. Also, she has a feminist thing about Portmarnock's non-lady membership. It's stupid, really. Half the major deals get done on the golf course. Anyway, she's still out sick.'

'She's been out all week,' said Matt.

Gavin shrugged again. 'That's what I mean about not being as interested.'

'What is she interested in?' asked Matt.

'Do you know, I haven't a clue,' said Gavin. 'She goes shooting, that's all I know. Hi, Dermot. Did you see that drive? Brilliant, wasn't it!'

'Wish I could do that,' said Dermot Doyle glumly. 'I always hook mine. Always.'

～

Alix was glad that Carrie had left. She was pleased to be on her own again, feeling reasonably OK and checking the computer every so often to see how the markets were doing. She felt incredibly guilty to be out of the office when she was feeling so much better. It wouldn't have done her any harm to sit at the desk simply to answer phones as necessary. But Jenny was right. The markets were quiet and it probably was a good day to be out.

She turned on the TV. Another one of those cookery programmes! Why did they go to all that bother with garnishes and colours and making everything look so attractive when it all tasted pretty much the same in the end? Alix thought about the business lunches and dinners she attended where the waiters brought the food to the table with such a flourish and hovered around anxiously checking whether or not everything was OK when nobody really cared what it tasted like. All they wanted to do was to talk about the bigger, better and more important deals that they'd done. Sometimes the stories they told were even true!

Food was for refuelling, Alix thought, as she watched the chef slice vegetables at an incredible speed. She was a burgers and chips person really, not a timbale of crab with cherry tomatoes and fresh basil.

The phone rang and she jumped.

'Hello,' she said.

'Alix. How are things?'

'Who's that?' she asked.

'Oh, come on! Don't tell me you've forgotten already!'

'Cathal?' she guessed.

'Exactly. I said I'd call this week and I left it until the very end of the week so that you wouldn't think I was pressuring you. I gave your office a buzz but they said that you were out today. Doing anything nice?'

'Actually I've been out sick,' said Alix. 'I caught some kind of bug at the weekend and it pretty much flattened me all week.'

'Hope it wasn't anything you ate in Roly's!' Cathal laughed.

'No, more of a flu thing,' said Alix.

'Are you feeling better now?'

'Much,' said Alix.

'I was wondering if you'd like to go to dinner tonight?'

'Oh, Cathal, that's nice of you. But the doctor said I was to stay in bed for the next couple of days.'

'That doesn't sound too good,' said Cathal. 'Are you sure you're OK?'

'I'm fine,' said Alix impatiently. 'But I went back to work when I shouldn't have and I relapsed. So I'm following her instructions to the letter this time.'

'Maybe I could drop round for a while,' suggested Cathal. 'I could bring some pizza or Chinese or Indian food, if you like?'

'That's really good of you, but I'm not hungry,' said Alix. She laughed. 'One good thing about being ill. You lose weight without having to try.'

'You don't need to lose weight,' said Cathal. 'You're perfect the way you are.'

'Thanks,' said Alix. 'But even so, Cathal, I'd prefer to be on my own right now.'

'Are you certain?'

'Yes,' she said. 'Besides, I might still be infectious. Wouldn't like to be the cause of you catching anything.'

'It'd almost be worth it,' said Cathal.

'I've got to go,' Alix told him. 'It's time for my tablets.'

'OK,' said Cathal. 'I'll give you a call next week, see how you are. Monday, maybe.'

'I – oh, OK.'

'Take care, Alix.'

'Sure.'

Shit, she thought, as she stared unseeingly at the TV. Cathal Moran was a nice guy but definitely not for her. Wyn, of course, didn't see that. Carrie wouldn't see that either. Alix sighed. She didn't want a new relationship. New relationships were far too much trouble. Finding out about someone. Discovering their likes and dislikes. Having to endure an evening of country music or heavy metal simply because some bloke thought it would be fun! Then having to decide whether or not to go to bed with them afterwards.

No, she decided. Far too much trouble.

~

Gavin had managed to stick with Matt Connery for most of the afternoon. He'd discovered that Anatronics was thinking about taking over another animation company and that, if so, they'd be looking for new financing facilities. They might borrow on the US private placement market, Matt told them. They hadn't decided yet.

Gavin had asked about their future foreign exchange and interest rate business. Matt said that they were happy with their current arrangements – foreign exchange was shared between Europa and another bank, with Europa getting the lion's share. Borrowings were mainly with an American bank at the moment. Deposits were shared.

'Are you happy with what we're doing for you?' asked Gavin.

'Sure,' Matt replied. 'Otherwise I wouldn't call.'

'What about other business?' Gavin asked him. 'Options, perhaps?'

'Haven't decided which route we're going down,' said Matt. 'Alix left some pretty good information packs with us after her presentation. We're still thinking about it.'

'She goes into everything pretty thoroughly,' said Gavin.

'I liked her.' Matt grinned at him. 'Nothing fazed her. Our MD asked some ridiculous question about pricing something and her answer was so clear and precise that even he understood it. And all without blinking an eye!'

'Sounds like she really impressed you.' Gavin knew that he was gritting his teeth.

'I like women with brains,' said Matt.

'She's only part of the Europa Bank team,' said Gavin as lightly as he could.

'Oh, I know,' said Matt. 'And don't worry, Gavin. I appreciate all you've done for us.'

'Great,' said Gavin. 'Thanks. Can I get you another drink?'

Des Coyle, the managing director of the bank, was at the bar.

'Hi, Gavin,' he said. 'Having a good day?'

'Yes.' Gavin beamed at him. 'They're all enjoying it. Weather's been great, everything's working well.'

'Who's that guy I saw you with?'

Gavin glanced back towards Matt who was chatting to James Morrissey. 'Matt Connery, Anatronics. We've been doing some small forex trades for them. A little bit of deposit business too. But they'll be much bigger, Des. And I'm working hard to make sure that when they deal in size, we'll be ready.'

'Excellent,' said Des. 'In the meantime, fill 'em with food and drink and keep 'em entertained.'

'Exactly.' Gavin smiled.

'I believe you're a bit of a demon on the golf course yourself.' Des took a sip from his beer.

'Oh, could be better,' said Gavin.

'Dave told me you play off twelve.'

'As I said, could be better.' Gavin laughed.

'Where are you a member?'

'Here, actually,' said Gavin. 'My father's a member too.'

'I'm in Woodbrook,' said Des. 'We must have a round together sometime.'

'That would be great.' Gavin nodded at him.

'I'll look at my diary on Monday. Let you know.'

'Thanks, Des.' Gavin gathered up the drinks he'd ordered.

'Have fun,' said Des.

'Absolutely.'

Yes, thought Gavin as he walked back towards the group of clients, yes, yes, yes!

Chapter 18

Alix felt nervous as she took the lift to the third floor on Monday morning. She couldn't understand why she should feel this way, she'd never felt anxious on her return from her fortnight's holiday which she took every May, or her week's skiing at the end of January. Those times she bounded enthusiastically back into the office, eager to know how things had gone in her absence. Now she was nervous.

She was in before anyone else. She sat at the dealing desk and called up the deals for the previous week. It had been busy enough, she thought ruefully, and a lot of trades had been done for her own clients. Charlie Mulholland had dealt. So had Christie Reardon. So had a number of her smaller accounts. And so had Matt Connery. Another foreign exchange deal, less than half a million dollars again, executed by Gavin Donnelly.

She should let him have the account. It didn't matter in the scheme of things. She was still the head of treasury. She was the one who called the shots. She was in control. So why was it, she thought, biting her lip, that she felt as though she was the one who was being outmanoeuvred at every turn?

'Good morning, Alix. Are you better?' Jenny smiled at her as she walked into the room.

'Completely,' Alix assured her. She watched in surprise as

Jenny came round to sit at the desk beside her. 'What are you doing?'

'Dave thought it would be a good idea if we switched,' explained Jenny. 'He's going to sit beside Gavin. He said that he'd be able to keep an eye on him that way.'

'Did he?' Alix tapped her pen on the edge of the desk. 'And Gavin said?'

'Gavin was delighted. Oh, Alix, you know he and I don't get along that well. To be honest with you, I wanted to move.'

'And nobody thought of waiting until I was back to ask me?'

'We didn't think you'd mind,' said Jenny. She looked quizzically at Alix. 'Do you? We could always switch back, I suppose.'

Do I mind? Alix asked herself. Or am I being paranoid? Are those bastards really out to get me?

'No, I don't mind,' she lied. 'How was business in my absence?'

'Oh, fine,' said Jenny. 'No traumas. Dave is working on some Polish zloty deal with Guy Decourcelle at the moment. It looks like it's actually going to work! The bank gets fees and the dealing room ends up with cheap six-month dollars.'

'Really.'

'Yes. Dave wasn't too sure about the mechanics of it but he had a long conversation with Guy who pretty much set him straight and the whole thing will be closed this week or next, we hope.' Jenny beamed at her.

Now I'm praying that the zloty deal will go wrong, Alix realised. I'm hoping that the whole thing will blow up in their fucking scheming faces and that we lose a fortune! This is not me, she tried to tell herself. I believe that when one of us makes money, we all make money. Don't I?

'Good morning!' The door banged open and Dave walked in. 'How's the patient?'

'Better, thanks,' said Alix.

'Good. Not infectious any more?'

'Hopefully not.'

'We had a good week while you were out.' Dave took off his jacket and hung it over the back of his chair. 'Did you see the profit and loss?'

'Yes.'

'Pleased?'

'Of course.'

'You don't sound very pleased,' said Dave peevishly. 'If I'd been out and the room had ended up making the guts of a hundred grand on the week, I'd be pretty pleased.'

'Would you?' asked Alix. She looked up and caught Dave's eye. They stared at each other for a couple of seconds before he looked away.

'Profit is profit,' he said abruptly.

'And I see you've done a bit of moving around the place too,' said Alix.

'It was a good idea,' said Dave. 'I thought it would be helpful if I sat next to Gavin for a while. Keep an eye on him, that sort of thing. He's awfully bright, Alix, but inclined to lose it a bit sometimes.'

'So I noticed. We'll see how it works out. Anything on the agenda for today?'

'Morning all!' Gavin walked in carrying a bag of doughnuts. 'Anyone want breakfast?'

'Jesus, Gavin, doughnuts?' Jenny wrinkled her nose. 'At this hour?'

'Why not?' he asked. 'Very nutritious they are too. I think. Alix, would you like one?'

'Thank you.' She took one covered in pink icing and sugar strands. 'How did it go for you on Friday?'

'Absolutely fucking brilliant.' Gavin grinned broadly at her. 'Great day, Alix. Super weather, course was playing great, everyone had a good time.'

'And they all showed up?'

'Oh, yes. We walked around for a while, followed a few of the matches. Then we had a couple of beers. A couple of them left after that but Niall, James and Matt came back to Gibney's where we had a few more.'

'And what time did you finish up?' asked Alix.

'Around eleven.' Gavin smirked. 'I tell you, those blokes will be eating out of the palm of my hand. I was so good to them. They won't dream of dealing anywhere else.'

'I don't want to disillusion you, but most of us feel like that after corporate outings,' said Alix dryly. 'And the gratitude lasts only as long as it takes to get a competing quote that's better than the one you gave them.'

'She's right,' said Dave. 'But I must say, I thought Matt Connery enjoyed himself.'

'How do you know?' asked Alix.

'Because I called out to Gibney's myself,' said Dave. 'But of course Paul wouldn't have told you.'

She stared at him, aghast. 'Paul?'

'He was there,' said Dave. 'We were both talking to him. Gavin and me. He was telling us about his new job in RTÉ.'

Alix felt her throat constrict. 'He's mad about the job.'

'Bloody hell, yes. So I said that you must hardly see him at all these days and he said not bloody likely since he was moving out to Malahide. He'd been doing some DIY around the house. You didn't tell us anything about that, Alix. That he'd given you the boot.'

Alix stared wordlessly at Dave.

'Still, he's not with some other woman,' Dave assured her. 'At least he wasn't on Friday night. He was with a gang of very arty types!'

'What's the story, Alix?' Jenny looked at her wide-eyed.

'There isn't a story,' said Alix briskly.

'But why have you and Paul split up? Is that what was wrong with you? You were upset about it and didn't want to come in?'

'Don't be absolutely ridiculous,' snapped Alix. 'I certainly wasn't upset about Paul. I had the flu.'

'Psychosomatic,' said Gavin.

'I was at the doctor,' said Alix. 'I had to take antibiotics.' God, she thought, why am I even telling him this?

'Probably brought on by stress, though,' said Jenny. 'After all—'

'Jenny, forget it,' said Alix. 'It doesn't matter.' She punched a few letters on her keyboard. 'We've work to do. Dave, you'd better give us a rundown on last week. And don't leave anything out.'

The three dealers exchanged knowing glances while Alix stared unseeingly at the screen in front of her. She felt humiliated. She should have told them before now so that they would have found out on her terms. By keeping it quiet, by pretending it hadn't happened, she'd made herself look a complete fool. She scrolled through the computer worksheet, ignoring Jenny's sympathetic glances.

'The main thing for this week is the zloty transaction.' Dave didn't look directly at Alix. 'I'm going to Paris tomorrow morning to tie up some details with Guy.'

'Tomorrow?' Alix glanced up at him.

'Flight out tomorrow morning,' he told her. 'We're meeting in Europa Bank at two.' He grinned. 'I'm looking forward to that – I haven't been in the new dealing room yet and you said that it was fabulous, Alix.'

'Yes,' she said. 'It is.' *De l'audace, encore de l'audace, et toujours de l'audace!* she thought wryly.

'Anyway, I'll be back Wednesday and I have a meeting with Des and Jim Rothwell at lunchtime to go through the whole thing.'

'How about me?' Alix looked at him. 'Am I involved in this meeting?'

'If you like,' said Dave. 'It's up to you.'

'We'll see,' she said.

'Apart from the zloty . . .'

But Alix didn't hear the rest. She was thinking about Dave and Guy in Paris working out the deal, dividing up the profit, being pleased at how things were panning out. She could see Dave chatting expansively to Guy and maybe going to some club with him later that night – something that she couldn't (and wouldn't) have done. And she could almost hear them swap stories about her. Guy would probably tell Dave that she must be frigid because he, Guy, had offered her a good time and she'd refused. And Dave would tell him that Paul had dumped her and that she'd been off work for a week with an imaginary illness. She felt herself grow hot and cold at the thought.

'Are you all right?' Jenny looked at her anxiously. 'You're

very flushed, Alix. Are you sure you should be back in the office?'

'I'm fine,' she snapped. 'Come on, let's get to it.'

At eleven o'clock, when the markets were quiet, she called down to Des Coyle's office.

'Alix!' He stood up as she entered the room. 'How are you feeling?'

'Much better, thanks, Des.'

'What was wrong with you?'

She shrugged. 'Some kind of viral infection, according to my doctor. I thought I'd shaken it off but she was right. I needed to stay in bed for a few days.'

'Everything went OK in your absence,' Des assured her. 'You've built up a strong team, Alix.'

'Yes,' she said, 'I have.'

'You know Dave is involved in the zloty transaction?'

'Sounds like a good deal,' said Alix. 'We'll end up with cheap dollars and Jim ends up with cheap funding. Good for both of us.'

'Dave worked hard on it.'

'He tells me he's going to Paris tomorrow.'

'Yes. He needs to go through the final details with Guy and he thought it would be better if they could sit down and look through the papers together.'

'I agree,' said Alix.

'Anything else on the cards for this week?' asked Des.

'Not yet,' she said. 'I have to reschedule a few meetings, that sort of thing.'

'Don't push yourself too hard,' said Des. 'These viruses are hard to shake off. You might think you're OK and the next thing you know you've relapsed. Take it easy.'

'Sure,' she said.

Not a chance, she thought, as she walked back upstairs. She was going to work even harder. The current trauma in her life was caused by her work. If it was causing her pain personally, she was damn sure she was going to make it pay dividends professionally. She certainly wasn't going to let anyone in the dealing room push her out of her job.

The others were all on the phone when she walked back into the room. Another line rang and she picked it up.

'Europa Bank, dealers. Alix Callaghan,' she said.

'Hello, Alix. Feeling better?'

'Matt?' she said cautiously. Because so much of her work was done on the phone she was adept at recognising voices. But it seemed like ages since she'd last spoken to him.

'Yes,' he said. 'How are you?'

'A lot better,' she said. 'I believe you had a good time on Friday with Gavin.'

He laughed. 'It was fun.'

'I rang,' she said uneasily. 'To thank you.'

'For what?'

'The flowers.' Her voice had dropped to almost a whisper. The others were too busy to listen to her anyway.

'Oh, you're welcome. Gavin told me you were sick and I just thought – it was probably very silly of me.'

'No,' she said. 'It was nice.'

'Nice,' echoed Matt. 'That sounds – boring.'

Alix laughed. 'Sorry.'

'And are you feeling better?'

'I'm fine,' she said.

'Good.'

There was a moment's silence.

256

'What can I do for you?' asked Alix.

'Actually, I didn't ring to trade,' said Matt. 'I rang to invite you to lunch.'

'Lunch?' said Alix.

'Yes.'

'I have to tell you I'm not a great lunch person,' she said. 'I get a bit edgy. Want to get back to work, you know.'

'It's not any old lunch,' Matt assured her. 'We're having a preview screening of a new animated movie we've been working on. A few of our other business partners will be there. I thought you might like to come along.'

'Oh.' Alix smiled. 'That sounds interesting.'

'It'll be fun,' said Matt. 'Next week. I'll send you a formal invitation but I thought you'd probably forget about it if we just did that. So I wanted to ask you personally.'

'I wouldn't have forgotten,' she protested. 'Not if you sent a formal invitation! What d'you take me for? But I'm glad to come.'

'Good,' said Matt. 'You should get the invitation by tomorrow. I'll look forward to seeing you.'

'In the meantime, is there anything we can do for you?' Alix laughed. 'Spot, forward, interest rates?'

'No,' he chuckled. 'I think I did the month's dealing while you were out. Sorry about that.'

'No problem,' she said. 'I'm sure Gavin looked after you very well.'

'He did.'

'Well, thanks for the call,' said Alix.

'See you next week,' said Matt.

She disconnected the line. Gavin was looking at her suspiciously.

'Who was that?' he asked.

'Matt Connery.' She smiled at him.

'What did he want?'

'To ask me to lunch,' said Alix.

Gavin stared at her.

'But he did mention that he'd had a great time on Friday,' she told him. 'It sounded like he really enjoyed it.'

'Good,' said Gavin shortly and Alix suddenly felt a lot better.

~

'Would you like to go for a sandwich?' Jenny asked Alix at twelve thirty. 'I'm starving.'

'Depends on what the guys want to do.' Alix looked across the desk at Gavin and Dave. 'Anything planned?'

Dave shook his head. 'I want to do some work on the zloty transaction for tomorrow,' he said. 'I'm going to order a roll or something. I can stay here.'

'And you, Gavin?'

'I'll stay here too,' he said.

'OK.' Alix smiled at Jenny. 'A sandwich it is.' The smile didn't reach her eyes. She still felt under pressure. Dave was going to Paris instead of her; Gavin was undoubtedly raging that Matt Connery had asked her to lunch and was probably plotting his revenge; and Jenny was going to pump her for information about her break-up with Paul.

'My treat,' said Jenny as they sat at one of O'Reilly's outside tables.

'If you like,' said Alix.

'So, how are you feeling?' asked Jenny.

Alix sighed. 'If anyone else asks me how I'm feeling I'll scream. You've asked me already. I'm better.'

'I didn't mean about being sick,' said Jenny. 'I meant about Paul.'

'I'm fine about Paul,' said Alix.

'What happened?' asked Jenny. 'If you don't want to talk about it, that's fine, but I thought you and Paul were for life, Alix. You always seemed so close. If I had to make a price on anyone splitting up, it wouldn't have been the two of you.'

'How sweet,' murmured Alix.

'So what went wrong?'

'First of all,' Alix unfolded her paper napkin, 'nothing went wrong, as you put it. Paul and I are going through a difficult patch. We both want different things from the relationship. We decided it would be a good idea to live apart for a while.'

'So he hasn't dumped you?' asked Jenny.

'When you get to my age you'll discover that relationships are more complicated than dumping or being dumped,' said Alix.

'Says who?' Jenny cut her roll in half.

'Says someone who knows,' said Alix.

'But don't you think it would be better to work things out together?' asked Jenny. 'I mean, it seems to me that being apart is a backwards step.'

Alix regarded her thoughtfully. 'Maybe it is. But we took it anyway. And I think it's a good idea. Besides, it's not as though we're not speaking or anything like that. I met him on Wednesday.'

'Maybe that's why you were sick on Thursday!' Jenny giggled. 'Couldn't stand the sight of him.'

'It wasn't like that.' Alix smiled.

'But you have to admit that it's odd that you got sick after he – after you decided to live apart.'

'Not at all,' said Alix.

'But you're never ill,' protested Jenny. 'I don't remember the last time you were out of the office.'

'I do.' But it had been a long time ago. 'Anyway, Jenny, it doesn't matter, it's a personal thing and nothing to do with work.'

'I wasn't even suggesting it had anything to do with work.' Jenny looked surprised. 'I just thought you might like to chat about it, that's all.'

'Thanks, but I'm fine,' said Alix.

'Just because you're my boss doesn't mean I don't care if you're upset,' said Jenny.

'I'm fine,' repeated Alix firmly. 'What I'd really like to know is how the blokes reacted to my being out for another couple of days.'

'I thought they'd argue more,' said Jenny, 'but actually they worked quite well together. I suppose because Dave was doing the zloty thing and Gavin was all fired up about his golf outing.'

'Which went well,' said Alix.

'I guess so.' Jenny emptied a sachet of sugar into her coffee. 'He was pretty happy about it this morning, wasn't he?'

Alix nodded.

'You're still the head of treasury,' said Jenny. 'Nobody is as good as you.'

'Thanks for the vote of confidence.'

'Dave isn't as assured. Gavin is too reckless.' Jenny took a sip of coffee. 'You're still better than both of them.'

'And if I wasn't, would you tell me?'

Jenny made a face. 'I don't know,' she answered honestly. 'I suppose I would.'

'If you think I'm losing it, I want you to tell me,' said Alix. 'It's important to me, Jenny.'

'OK.' Jenny nodded. 'I'll tell you.'

~

'She's pissed off at you.' Gavin propped his feet up on the desk and looked at Dave.

'Maybe.'

'She wants to go to Paris.'

'Tough,' said Dave.

'We've rattled her.'

Dave grinned. 'I know.'

'What do you want?' asked Gavin. 'You said you didn't want her job, but you do, don't you?'

'It'd be good on my CV,' said Dave. 'I don't necessarily want it forever, but head of treasury sounds a damn sight better than senior dealer.'

'And senior dealer sounds better than dealer,' commented Gavin.

'We haven't got rid of her yet,' said Dave.

'But if she leaves?'

'Actually,' Dave clasped his hands behind his head, 'this Paul thing makes it a bit less likely, don't you think? After all, we were assuming that she was getting broody and thinking of settling down, which might have made her chuck it in. If she's finished with Paul it seems to me a lot less likely.'

'Bugger!' Gavin took his feet off the desk. 'I never thought of that!'

'Of course, she might be so distraught that she'll blow it anyway,' mused Dave.

'Perhaps she'll want to move abroad,' suggested Gavin. 'She might ask for a transfer to Paris.'

Dave looked at his colleague thoughtfully. 'That's an idea. Maybe I should suggest it to Guy. Ask him if he thinks Alix would work well there.'

Gavin's eyes brightened. 'Brilliant idea.'

'That's me.' Dave grinned at him. 'Planning ahead.'

∽

Alix sat on the balcony and sipped a glass of water. She was still on a no alcohol regime. She'd called into Geraldine O'Neill's surgery on the way home and the doctor had told her that she was much better but that she should still take it easy. Geraldine had suggested that Alix take a week off. Alix had laughed and told her that she'd just had a week off.

'Somewhere hot and sunny,' Geraldine advised. 'Relax, Alix. You're awfully tense.'

Alix was fed up with people telling her she was tense. Anyone would be tense if they had to go into Europa Bank every day and face the concerted effort that was Gavin and Dave. It was funny, she mused, how she now thought of them as Gavin and Dave not Dave and Gavin. All of the pressure was coming from the younger man. Until Gavin had arrived, Dave had been happy to work with her and for her.

She flushed as she remembered their comments about Paul. They must be thrilled to think that he'd dumped her. To them it was a sign of strength. Poor, feeble Alix, distraught at her lover's departure, gets sick. Poor, feeble Alix spends the best part of a week at home sobbing her eyes out. She gritted her teeth. They could think what they liked. She knew the truth. She knew that she could get Paul back. If she went about it the right way.

If she knew what the right way was.

Chapter 19

Alix had learned the art of travelling light years earlier. For her trip to London she packed a pair of black trousers, a silk blouse and a white shirt – a combination which covered either a dressed-up night out or a sloppy night out. She also packed a very fine cashmere top just in case. Including her toilet bag, underwear and a pair of very light black leather Italian shoes she'd bought in Florence, everything fitted into a small overnight bag which she could carry onto the plane. Alix hated having to wait for luggage after a flight. Given that a part of her day was taken up with work, she wore a simple Principles suit which made her look efficient and businesslike. Alix quite happily mixed designer labels and multiple-store clothes. If they looked good she didn't care where her clothes came from.

Alix knew that she should feel guilty about using a trip to London to see her friend, but she didn't care. At least, not much. She could justify the journey, though, because she had two meetings lined up before she was due to meet Sophia and she knew that she could make it worthwhile.

She took a cab from City Airport to Chase Bank's wonderful building at London Wall, where she had a very agreeable meeting with Colin Harper, a dealer she'd known for years.

Then she strolled back to Bishopsgate for her second meeting, this time in NatWest.

Russell Cobham, the specialist US company where Sophia worked, also had a building in Bishopsgate, so after another successful meeting, Alix walked up the street to meet Sophia.

'You can go up.' The security guard handed Alix an ID badge. 'The fourteenth floor.'

Alix waited for the lift while she fiddled with the tag. It always irritated her that so many of these security badges were designed to clip onto the top pocket of a suit. Very few women's suits had top pockets. As usual, Alix ended up clipping the badge to the waistband of her skirt where, she thought, it looked absolutely ridiculous.

Russell Cobham had redecorated the offices since Alix had last visited Sophia a year earlier. Gone were the ultramodern clear plastic seats, chrome uplights and glass tables that had been in the reception area before. They'd been replaced with maroon leather seats, green shaded lamps and heavy mahogany tables. In a period of recent market volatility, Russell Cobham were clearly trying to look serious and long-term. She sat in one of the leather seats and waited for Sophia.

'Alix! How are you?' Sophia beamed at her. 'How was your day? You look fantastic!'

'Thanks.' Alix kissed her friend on the cheek. 'My day was fine. And you, Soph, you look absolutely wonderful.'

Sophia Redmond was almost as tall as Alix, with honey-coloured hair coiled into a loose knot on the back of her head, and hazel eyes.

'I feel wonderful.' Sophia's eyes sparkled. 'Well, I do now. This hasn't been an exactly great week for me. I've got the most wretched heartburn and I haven't slept a wink.'

'You'd never guess.'

'I fake it,' said Sophia solemnly. 'That Christian Dior face stuff you gave me last Christmas is a godsend!'

Alix laughed. 'Glad you found a use for it.' She stepped back and looked at her friend. 'Sophia, are you sure you're pregnant? Only you don't seem to have put on an ounce of weight.'

Sophia turned a circle so that Alix could look at her. 'It's all in the cut,' she said. 'The jacket hides the bump so well. It's vital, you know, not to look as though you're going to pop at any minute. It scares them if they think you might go into labour during office hours!'

'Well, you don't. You look as efficient as ever.'

'Thanks,' said Sophia. 'Do you want to come into my office? I just need to finish something on the computer and then I can leave.'

'OK. If you don't mind having someone hanging around while you work.'

'It's nothing much,' said Sophia. 'But I want to get it finished. You know how it is.'

Alix nodded and followed her along the corridor. To her right was a huge dealing room where men, mainly dressed in jeans and casual shirts, were shouting prices at each other. Occasionally, someone in a suit joined the fray. There were no women.

'We decided on a dress-down policy for Fridays,' said Sophia as they walked past the room and into an adjoining office. 'But I couldn't be bothered to get casual maternity outfits for the office. It was bad enough having to buy the more formal stuff. And my leggings are too scruffy. Anyway, sit down anywhere. I'll only be a couple of minutes.'

Alix sat in one of the visitor's chairs and picked up the *Wall*

Street Journal. One of the things about working in financial markets was that she always wanted to read everything she possibly could about what was going on in the world. However, she rarely had the time to read anything. Her news was gleaned from the TV and the radio and the constant headlines that scrolled up on the Reuters and Bloomberg screens in her office. It was nice to simply sit back and read newsprint for a change.

Sophia's phone rang and she swore softly. 'No, Ramon,' she said. 'I can't come to a meeting at six . . . yes, I know it's vitally important but only to you . . . of course we'll still be able to do it on Monday . . . if anything goes horribly wrong you can e-mail me at home . . . yes, I believe you can handle it yourself . . . I wouldn't have suggested it otherwise . . . OK, Ramon . . . have a good weekend.'

Sophia was warm but efficient, thought Alix. She wondered if she was warm enough herself. Sophia had been sympathetic and friendly with Ramon. It was a long time since Alix felt she'd been sympathetic and friendly with anyone in Europa Bank.

Her friend sounded so much more at ease than she did.

'Finished,' said Sophia with satisfaction a couple of minutes later. 'I think that package will be pretty impressive for my presentation next week.' She logged off her computer and rubbed her eyes. 'I wish they'd invent a screen that didn't tire you out.'

'Are you supposed to sit in front of that all day?' asked Alix. 'In your condition, I mean?'

Sophia grinned. 'I don't sit in front of it all day. I used to. But actually, I spend more of my time at meetings than anything else these days.'

'And do you prefer that?' asked Alix.

'Sometimes,' Sophia admitted. 'But I like doing the research. More fundamental.' She smiled at Alix. 'Ready to go?'

Alix nodded.

'Do you want to go straight back to the house?' asked Sophia. 'Get rid of the travel stuff, freshen up?'

'Yes, please,' said Alix.

'And after that, do you want to eat posh or homely?'

Alix laughed. 'Oh, homely, I think. I'm not really a posh person, Soph. You know that.'

'Come on, then.' Sophia smiled. 'Let's grab a cab and book something homely.'

'Richard won't be home for ages,' said Sophia as she unlocked the door of the house. 'He never gets in before seven and he plays indoor soccer on Friday nights with a gang from work.' She rubbed the base of her spine. 'Just thinking about indoor soccer makes my back ache. Do you want to bring your stuff upstairs? The usual room, Alix.'

'Thanks.' Alix carried her bag up the stairs to the pretty blue and white painted bedroom while Sophia went into the living room and poured herself a Malvern water. She really wanted a gin and tonic but she was trying very hard to be a good mother to her unborn child.

'Drink?' she asked as Alix walked into the room. 'I'm on water myself but there's loads in the cupboard. Although there are plenty of things Richard will share with me, abstinence isn't one of them.'

'I see his point of view.' Alix poured herself that gin and tonic that Sophia would have liked. 'Cheers.'

'Cheers.' Sophia raised the glass of water. The two friends smiled at each other.

'So.' Sophia placed her glass on the coffee table. 'Do you want to have a shower and all that sort of thing and hit the restaurant early? Or do you want to fall into intimate gossip straightaway and send out for food when you're too drunk to walk?'

'I haven't been too drunk to walk in a long time,' said Alix. 'And I'd really love to have a shower.' Now that she was here, face to face with her friend, she found that she wasn't ready to spill her guts about Paul. Not yet.

'Fine,' said Sophia calmly. 'I'm glad you said that because I'm going to wallow in the bath for twenty minutes. It's soothing. I'll give the restaurant a call and book us in for seven. It's only a five-minute walk.'

'Sounds good to me,' said Alix.

She sipped her drink while Sophia made the reservation. It was good to be somewhere different, she thought. Good to be away from Dublin, even for a couple of days. She suddenly realised how sick she was of being alone in the apartment every night and how poor her social life had been in the last few weeks. Except on the occasions she'd met Paul, she hadn't been to a pub or to the cinema since he had left. The only other events she'd been to were the bank's tenth anniversary night and the blind date that Terry and Wyn had so ridiculously organised for her. She gritted her teeth as she remembered it. Other than that, she'd been to the shooting club once and the gym once. And that was all. The rest of the time she'd sat around and wondered when Paul was coming back. Of course, she had been sick. She had to allow herself a whole week of being unable to go anywhere. She drained her glass and stood up.

'See you here in about half an hour?'

Sophia nodded. 'Take your time, Alix. We're not in a rush.'

Alix laughed. 'You used to be a very rushed kind of person as far as I remember, Sophia Redmond.'

'I still am.' Sophia grimaced. 'But I'm trying to chill out a bit more. For the sake of junior. My gynaecologist tells me to be calm. And you know how it is, Alix. Women are always supposed to do what their gynae tells them.'

'I don't know how it is exactly,' Alix grinned, 'but I'm pretty sure that your gynaecologist is terrified of you.'

'I wish.' Sophia finished her water. 'I was hoping for a sympathetic woman. I got a man who is wonderfully reassuring but talks to me as though I have a mental age of about ten.'

'Never mind,' said Alix. 'I'll ask you lots of hard questions later. Get your intellectual level back to its peak again.'

⌒

They strolled down the road to the Italian restaurant, enjoying the warmth of the evening sun on their backs.

'Wonderful Indian summer,' remarked Sophia.

'Fabulous,' agreed Alix. 'Remember last year? Rain and hurricanes and all sorts.'

'You went to Mexico, didn't you?'

Alix smiled wistfully. 'Cancun and Playa del Carmen. It was wonderful.'

'Where did you go this year?'

'Majorca. Pollensa. We had a good time.' She flicked an imaginary strand of hair out of her eyes. 'We always had a good time on holidays.'

Sophia was silent.

'And all the time I didn't know that he was yearning for a suburban house, a dog, a cat and two point four children.'

'Cross over here,' said Sophia. 'That's the restaurant.' She pointed at a green and white striped awning over a huge picture window.

'Looks good,' said Alix.

'But homely.' Sophia grinned at her as they walked inside.

Although it was early, the restaurant was almost full. Alix and Sophia sat at a table near the window and looked at the menus.

'I get ravenously hungry,' remarked Sophia. 'But as soon as I start to eat I feel full. I'll just have a pizza.'

'Same for me.' Alix closed the menu.

'Wine?' asked Sophia.

'Only if you're having a glass.'

Sophia shook her head. 'As an incubator I'm not supposed to drink. And although I had a few glasses before I realised that Sophia junior was on the way, I've decided I'd better do things properly.'

'Fine by me,' said Alix. 'We'll just have Pellegrino.'

Sophia gave the order to the waiter who returned a moment later with the mineral water.

'Cheers.' Sophia raised her glass.

'Cheers.'

'So, Alix.' Sophia looked thoughtfully at her friend. 'Do you want to tell me what the story is with Paul?'

Alix exhaled slowly. 'I – suppose so.'

'It's really upset you, hasn't it?'

'More than I thought,' admitted Alix.

'Why?'

'I don't know.' Alix ran her finger round the rim of her glass.

'We don't have to talk about it now,' said Sophia. 'We don't have to talk about it at all if you don't want to. We're supposed to be having fun!'

'I think that was part of the problem,' said Alix wryly. 'Paul thought I was having too much fun.'

'Too much fun?' echoed Sophia.

'He complained that I was still living my life as though I was twentysomething when, in fact, I should be settling down and thinking of starting a family.'

'And you don't want to?'

'Settle down and start a family?' Alix smiled at Sophia. 'It's a bit callous of me to say no when that's exactly what you're doing.'

'Starting a family yes, settling down no!' Sophia laughed. 'Do I look settled down to you?'

'You looked very efficient in the office,' said Alix. 'And you look almost normal now.'

Sophia was wearing a loose denim shirt over a pair of jeans. 'Maternity jeans,' she hissed earlier when Alix had expressed surprise that her friend could fit into jeans. 'They have an elasticated waist.'

'Anyway it's not how you look, it's how you feel,' Sophia said. 'I didn't think that I'd ever feel maternal, Alix, but I have to confess that I do now.'

'You see,' Alix sighed. 'That's what everyone says. That if you get pregnant you suddenly change. But Soph, I'm not ready to change yet. And I didn't think Paul was either.'

'But he has changed,' said Sophia. 'So what are you going to do about it?'

'It's what he's done about it,' Alix told her. 'He's moved back into his house in Malahide and he's got some French bird who's going to move in with him.'

'Alix!' Sophia stared at her. 'You didn't tell me all this before!'

Alix didn't reply as the waiter arrived and placed their Quattro Staggione pizzas in front of them.

Sophia made no attempt to pick up her knife and fork, but continued to stare at Alix.

'Don't look at me like that,' said Alix uncomfortably.

'Alix, you've split up with your boyfriend of three years and you've waited until now to tell me? When did this happen?'

'About a month ago,' said Alix.

'Had he moved out when I phoned?'

Alix nodded.

'And you didn't say anything?'

Alix squirmed in her seat. 'I wasn't sure about it. Whether or not he'd come back. I . . .' She didn't finish the sentence and looked miserably at her plate.

'You'd better tell me the whole lot now,' said Sophia. 'And don't leave anything out.'

So Alix told her. Her voice wavered when she said that Paul and Sabine had met at a Europa Bank bash in Paris. 'If I hadn't brought him along he'd never have met her,' she finished bitterly. 'And everything would still be OK.'

'Well, maybe not.' Sophia finally ate a piece of pizza. 'I mean, he can't have suddenly decided he wanted to rush off and start procreating.'

'I suppose not,' said Alix tiredly. 'But I didn't know he was thinking like that. And Soph, she doesn't even look like the sort of woman who wants to jump into the whole family scene. I only vaguely remember her, but in the photo – admittedly not a very clear photo – she looks about seventeen and she has that blonde spiky look that school kids have. Part of me thinks the baby thing is just an excuse. But he didn't need that sort of excuse.'

'This Sabine is a designer?'

'That's what Paul told me. But afterwards I remembered meeting the designer. I'd say she's more of a decorator or painter or something.'

'Arty,' said Sophia.

Alix nodded.

'Maybe not very businesslike.'

'Possibly not.'

'And therefore not as threatening as you.'

'Oh, for heaven's sake, Sophia! I'm not threatening.' Alix placed her knife and fork firmly on her plate.

'In the business sense,' said Sophia. 'In the money stakes, Alix.'

Alix shook her head. 'I can't believe it's all about money.'

'But Paul said so,' Sophia told her. 'You said that he threw it in your face that you earn more than he does. He obviously resents that.'

'But it's so silly,' objected Alix. 'It was never an issue before.'

'So maybe it's an issue now because he's older and you're still doing better than him.'

'I don't see why,' said Alix mutinously. 'I loved him, Sophia. I thought he loved me. If there was a problem, why couldn't he talk about it?'

'I don't know,' answered Sophia. 'But talking isn't exactly what most men are good at.'

Alix smiled faintly. 'I suppose you're right.'

'So what are you going to do now?' asked Sophia. 'Now that you're single all over again?'

Alix pushed her half-eaten pizza away. 'I don't feel single all over again,' she said. 'In fact, I don't want to be single all over again. I want to work it out with Paul.'

'But, Alix, what can you work out? Unless you've decided that you want your career to take a back seat to your relationship?'

'Have *you*?' asked Alix fiercely. 'Is that what you're planning, Sophia? To give up the struggle at Russell Cobham and stay at home with the baby?'

Sophia took a sip of Pellegrino. 'No,' she said honestly. 'But that's not an issue between Richard and me. And maybe I'll feel differently about it when the baby is born. Maybe there are other things besides boardroom battles and avoiding getting stabbed in the back.'

'Not for me,' said Alix.

'Why?'

She stared at Sophia. 'Because that's the way it is. I like my job. I want to keep doing what I'm doing. Maybe in five years or ten years or something I'll change.'

'Maybe in five years or ten years it'll be too late,' said Sophia.

'Oh, don't you start!' Alix banged her fist on the table. 'Wyn's already had a go at me about my bloody biological clock! I expected something different from you.'

'I can't tell you anything different,' said Sophia reasonably. 'And I'm only stating a fact, Alix. In ten years you'll be in your forties. It's not exactly easy to start conceiving in your forties.'

'Why is it so hard to have what you want?' asked Alix.

Sophia shrugged. 'I don't know.'

'But you have what you want.'

'I didn't know I wanted it until I had it,' said Sophia gently. 'And I still don't know if I can have it all.'

Alix rubbed her eyes. 'I don't want it all,' she said miserably. 'I just want it to be the way it was before. I was happy, Sophia. I truly was. Paul and me – we just seemed to work, you know? And Europa Bank was such a good place for me too.'

'Was?'

Alix sighed. 'They're having a go at me in the dealing room,' she said. 'I haven't been on top form lately, Soph. Obviously. And they scent blood. Dave Bryant – remember him? You met him last year – Dave is supposed to have said he doesn't want my job, but I know he does. And he's aided and abetted by Gavin Donnelly. We hired him last summer. He's a good trader, or at least he will be, but he's so ambitious! He brokes clients into deals that they probably shouldn't do and it's made us lots of money but one day it'll all go wrong. And I'll be caught in the crossfire.'

'Don't be silly,' said Sophia.

'And there's an account that we're fighting over,' said Alix. 'I mean, it's crazy, Soph, it's only a small account. It has the potential to be big, but it's peanuts at the moment. But it's become a kind of symbol of the clash between us. Gavin keeps booking trades with them and I'm keeping tabs on him and I won't allocate him the account even though I probably should. It's so stupid. And I can't help myself!'

Sophia looked at her sympathetically. 'But that's business, Alix. It happens all the time.'

'I know,' said Alix. 'But I could cope with it when Paul was around. I just can't seem to cope now.' To her surprise and horror she started to cry. She rubbed at her eyes with her napkin.

'Are you all right?' asked Sophia.

She wanted to say yes, she was, but the tears were flowing freely now and she couldn't speak. Sophia watched her in silence. She had never seen Alix like this before. In all the time that she'd known her, Alix Callaghan had been the most self-contained person she'd ever met. Even on the occasions when she'd got blazingly drunk, Alix had never truly lost control of herself. When, for the one and only time, they'd taken drugs and Alix *had* let herself go, she'd been embarrassed afterwards and refused to take anything ever again.

'You just want to draw experiences in,' Sophia said to her the next day. 'And you don't let anything out.'

Alix had laughed and told her friend not to be so stupid. But Sophia was right. She didn't let herself go. Yet now she was sitting in a restaurant, a public place, and crying as though she was never going to stop.

'Here.' Sophia pushed a clean tissue at her.

Alix took it wordlessly.

'What's upsetting you more?' asked Sophia. 'The situation with Paul or the situation at work?'

Alix scrubbed at her eyes. 'I don't know,' she muttered. 'They're entwined, Sophia. Don't you see?'

'Maybe.'

'As long as I was with Paul everything was OK. Since he moved out, my life has been a disaster. Work is a shambles, my social life has fallen apart. I've had the flu – and you know me, Soph, I'm never ill. I can't seem to control anything any more.'

'And controlling things is important?'

'Don't try to psychoanalyse me,' said Alix sharply. 'It's not all about control. It's about your life moving the way you expected.'

'So what do you want to do?' asked Sophia.

'I wish I knew.' Alix smoothed her hair. 'I have no idea what I want to do.'

'Do you love Paul?'

'Of course I bloody love him,' she said. 'Christ, Sophia, what do you think this is all about? I'm a basket case because I hate him?'

'I'm only trying to help,' said Sophia.

'I know. I'm sorry.'

'So you love Paul and you want him back. But to get him back you have to oust Sabine. And you have to want children. And give up your job.' She looked at Alix. 'Is that it?'

Alix sighed. 'Probably.'

'Are you ready to do all that?'

'Why does it have to be one thing or the other?' she asked. 'Why can't I have Paul, keep my job and think about babies?'

'Did he ever talk about it before?' asked Sophia. 'Was this a complete bolt from the blue?'

Alix considered the question. 'We talked about it,' she admitted. 'I told him that I wasn't ready.'

'When?'

'Last January.'

'So you had some idea.'

'I didn't think he was serious.' She began to cry again. 'I'm a fucking idiot, Sophia. He was trying to tell me stuff and I wouldn't listen. He's right. I *am* selfish. I *am* self-centred. I *don't* care enough about other people. As long as I'm happy I don't think about anyone else's happiness.'

'That's not true,' said Sophia.

'It is.' She buried her face in her hands while Sophia gazed at her in disbelief.

'Stop crying, Alix,' said Sophia.

'I can't.' The tears were streaming down her face and she was shocked by them. She was crying in a crowded London restaurant where people could look at her and point their fingers at her and wonder what on earth was wrong with the girl in the white shirt. This wasn't her. It wasn't.

'Alix,' said Sophia gently. 'Please stop crying.' She reached out and took her friend's hands from her face.

'I want to, but I can't.' Alix gulped.

'It's probably really good for you but you'll make yourself sick.'

'I hate my life,' she blurted. 'I've got it all wrong, Sophia. I was so fucking smug about my job and my boyfriend and my lifestyle. And now it looks as though I've lost them all.'

'Don't be utterly ridiculous,' said Sophia sternly. 'You may have lost Paul but you haven't lost your job. And what's a lifestyle except something in the Sunday supplements?'

Alix smiled through her tears. 'You're right, I suppose.'

'Come on.' Sophia let go of her hands. 'Let's settle the bill and go back to the house.'

'OK,' said Alix.

Sophia gestured to the waiter who brought the bill.

'Let me.' Alix handed her credit card to the waiter. 'Cheap counselling,' she said to Sophia. 'I'd have to pay a lot more to a professional.'

'We have until Sunday to sort out your life,' said Sophia. 'Don't worry, it'll cost you a fortune.'

Chapter 20

Alix had regained her composure by the time they got back to the house. Which was just as well, because Richard had returned from his indoor soccer match and was watching TV, his feet propped on the coffee table in front of him.

Alix smiled at him, told Sophia that she was tired and wanted to go to bed, and disappeared upstairs before either of them could object.

'What's wrong with her?' Richard asked in surprise.

'Man trouble.' Sophia sat down beside him. 'Oh, Richard, I'm so glad I found you!'

'Me too,' he said. He pulled her closer to him. 'I love you, Sophia.'

'I love you.' She snuggled into the crook of his arm.

He kissed her gently on the eyes. 'I love every single bit of you.'

'Even the new, fatter bits?' she asked.

'Especially the new, fatter bits.'

She sighed with pleasure as he opened the button of her jeans. 'She's broken up with Paul.'

'Oh?' Richard didn't care about Alix.

'And she doesn't know what she wants any more.'

'I know exactly what I want,' said Richard. 'And it's right here beside me.'

❦

Alix could hear them. She tried not to listen but she couldn't help it. She hid her head under her pillow and thought about the dollar/yen rate and how the dollar had strengthened again following its weakness after the rate cut and concentrated fiercely on American economic policy for the months ahead.

❦

Her eyes were puffy the next morning, the lids still red.

'You look like you have hayfever,' said Sophia. 'Wear your sunglasses, nobody will notice.'

Richard had gone out for the day.

'I feel like I'm driving him out of your home,' said Alix. 'I didn't mean to come over here and just dump everything on you, Soph.'

'You didn't,' said her friend. 'He's gone to a cricket match, and let me tell you, he's delighted not to be dragged around Mothercare or its equivalent this morning!'

'All the same—'

'All the same nothing,' said Sophia. 'I thought you might like to go shopping. A little bit of retail therapy never did anyone any harm. And we didn't get to Harvey Nics last time you were here.'

Alix smiled at her. 'No, we didn't.'

'So what are we waiting for?'

❦

It was certainly true that buying things helped. When they returned to Sophia's house later that day, Alix had inflicted serious damage to her credit card and was surrounded by a mound of shopping.

'I'll never fit all that into my bag,' she told Sophia. 'I think I lost my reason this afternoon.'

'You lost your misery anyway.' Sophia was glad to see that Alix no longer looked pale and drawn. 'Who cares, Alix. It was fun.'

They had fun that evening, too, when Richard insisted on taking them to dinner and booked a table in Orrery, Terence Conran's fashionable restaurant which, Alix remarked, was falling over itself with modern chic.

'Thanks for everything,' she told Sophia the next day as she got into a cab to go to City Airport. 'I had a good time and I feel miles better.'

'Anytime you feel you're on the verge of a breakdown, just let me know.' Sophia grinned at her.

'All I need now is to figure out what I want to do with my life,' said Alix. 'Shouldn't be too difficult, should it?'

Sophia shook her head. 'The day any of us knows what we want to do with our lives will be the day! I wanted fame and fortune as a prominent female investment banker. What am I going to get? Nappies and regurgitated milk, that's what.'

'But you're happy with it,' said Alix. 'Which is what matters.'

'You'll be happy once you've sorted yourself out,' Sophia told her. 'Just get out there again. Be single! Have fun.'

'Sure.' Alix smiled at her. 'That's exactly what I'll do. And I'll think of you when I'm having it!'

'I rather hope you'll think of more exciting things.' Sophia's eyes were full of amusement.

'Goodbye, Soph. I'll give you a call next week.'

'Take care, Alix.' She waved at the cab until it had turned the corner and was out of sight.

⌒

It was bedlam at Dublin Airport. A dozen flights seemed to have arrived all at the same time and the arrivals area was a seething mass of irritated and tired travellers. Alix was glad that she'd managed to squeeze so many of her new purchases into her bag and had managed to get away with carrying a couple of Harvey Nichols bags onto the plane too. At least she was able to avoid the hysteria that was the baggage hall and walk straight out into the terminal building.

It was equally crowded. A young girl with an enormous rucksack banged into her and Alix turned round in annoyance. The girl smiled and shrugged apologetically. 'I'm sorry,' she said in heavily accented English.

Alix bit back the angry words that she'd been about to snap. Be cool, she told herself. Peaceful. Relaxed. Don't drive the tourists away. Sophia had told her that she was too tense. Carrie was forever telling her that she was too tense. Perhaps, only perhaps, they were both right.

The backpacker walked towards the exit and Alix stared in front of her. Because only a few yards away was Paul, scanning the new arrivals for someone. He looked great, she thought, dressed in jeans and sweatshirt but looking fashionable rather than scruffy. She almost went over to him but some instinct stopped her. She stood, indecisively, clutching her bags.

'Sabine!' She didn't hear him but she could see the name on his lips. And then a blonde girl pushed her way through the throng and almost threw herself into his arms.

Alix thought she was going to be sick. She stood, rooted to the spot, while Paul kissed Sabine on both cheeks and then, more passionately, on the lips. She felt uncomfortable as she watched them. Sabine was holding Paul's head, pushing her fingers through his hair, pulling him closer to her. Alix could almost feel the heat of Paul's fingers through her own clothes, could almost taste him on her own lips.

The pair finally parted. Alix moved out of sight, blending in with a group of holidaymakers who had just returned from Spain. But, she thought, even if she'd been standing right beside him, Paul wouldn't have noticed her. His eyes had been only for Sabine. His embrace had been only for Sabine.

Had he ever looked at her like that? As lovingly, as intimately as that? She wasn't sure. She swallowed and felt sick again.

They were walking out of the building now. Alix followed at a distance and watched while Paul paid for his parking ticket. She moved towards the machine as soon as they had left. She wondered where he had parked, whether she would see them leave.

She paid for her own ticket and walked to her car in a daze. Her hands were shaking as she unlocked it and threw her bag and her shopping inside. The retail therapy had worn off already. She felt as awful as she had the night Paul had told her that it was over between them.

She started the engine and drove slowly out of the car park. It was ridiculous to think that she would see them leave and there was no reason to. She knew where they were going.

Back to Paul's house in Malahide. Where they would make love. Passionately, as she and Paul had once done.

Alix's grip tightened on the steering wheel. She couldn't get the image of them out of her mind. Paul tracing his fingers from Sabine's throat to the blonde hair between her legs. Perhaps she wasn't a real blonde, thought Alix suddenly. Maybe Paul would discover that the collar and cuffs didn't match – something that, if it was there to be discovered, he'd probably discovered already. He'd implied that he hadn't been to bed with Sabine in Paris, but how did she know that for sure? Perhaps he'd been sampling Sabine's delights even while she lay sleeping in the comfort of her room in the Georges V.

The car behind her blasted her with the horn as she veered out of her lane. She corrected instantly, her heart pounding.

At the roundabout leading onto the motorway, Alix saw the blue Rover. She knew that it was Paul's car. She recognised the registration instantly. Paul used to tease her about her ability to remember a car's reg even if she'd only seen it once before and they would laugh at the fact that she found it so much easier to remember numbers than names. She'd seen the registration of the Rover when he'd waved goodbye to her outside the Beggar's Bush.

Without knowing why, she turned left at the roundabout and, at a careful distance, followed the Rover.

Although Paul's address was in Malahide, his house was in a development that stretched between the pretty harbour town and the inland town of Swords. When they'd first met, he'd wanted her to move into the house with him. But it was two miles away from the train station and the faster, electric trains didn't run as far as Malahide which meant that she would have had to get a lumbering diesel train to the office. Since the town had grown so rapidly over the past few years the traffic into the city was dreadful. That was why she had persuaded Paul that it was a much more practical proposition to rent out his house in Malahide and move into the apartment with her.

But Paul had loved living in Malahide. Alix had teased him, told him that he was, after all, living in a suburban semi not a bijou cottage beside the sea. And he'd laughed, said she was right and agreed to rent out the house.

The Rover indicated left and turned into the estate. Alix, a good distance behind, indicated too. She wasn't too worried about Paul noticing the BMW. He never recognised cars, never mind their registration numbers.

She turned right, then left and slowed down to a crawl as she saw Paul and Sabine get out of the Rover. Paul lifted Sabine's case out of the car and carried it up the path. As Alix drove slowly by, he opened the door and the two of them disappeared inside the house.

Alix was horrified to find that she was crying again. This is ridiculous, she told herself as she wiped the tears from her eyes. I worked all of this out. I'm a single girl with nothing to worry about. So what if he wants to live with somebody else? Why should I care?

But I want him back, she moaned out loud. I don't want him to be living with her. I don't want him doing the things to her that he used to do to me. I don't want him to forget about me. I want him back!

～

'How was the trip?' asked Jenny as Alix walked into the office the next morning.

'Good,' she said briefly.

'Any news from our pals in London?'

'Like what?' asked Alix.

Jenny shrugged. 'I don't know.'

'Then don't ask stupid questions.'

Dave and Jenny exchanged glances.

'Get out of the wrong side of bed this morning?' asked Dave cheerfully.

'Oh, shut up, Bryant,' snapped Alix. 'I'm not in the mood for your brand of humour this morning.'

'You're never in the mood for anything these days,' said Dave. 'Is it because of Paul?'

Alix glared at him. 'It's absolutely nothing to do with my personal life whatsoever, Dave. And I resent the implication that I can't cope with something as trivial as a bloke moving out of my apartment.'

'Keep your knickers on, Alix.' Dave stared at her in amazement. 'I was only trying—'

'Yes, well, don't try,' she said. 'If you want to do something useful you could go to the forex meeting for me this morning. I'm sure their particular brand of humour and innuendo will suit you.'

'Alix, fuck off,' said Dave.

'Don't talk to me like that,' she said furiously.

'Alix, fuck off,' said Dave again.

'Alix,' said Jenny gently. 'Lighten up, can't you?'

Alix exhaled slowly. She knew that she was being ridiculous but she couldn't help it. She felt as though she was a pot about to boil over. She clenched her fists and bit her lip.

'I'm sorry, Dave,' she said. 'I'm a bit preoccupied today. I didn't mean to snap at you.'

'That's OK,' said Dave guardedly.

Alix pulled her hair back from her face and refastened her tortoiseshell clip. 'Where's Gavin this morning?' she asked, trying to keep her tone friendly.

'He had a dentist's appointment,' said Jenny.

'Oh, yes.' Alix nodded. 'I remember.'

She took a copy of the *Financial Times* from the bundle of newspapers on the desk and opened it. Her hands were still shaking. They hadn't stopped shaking since she'd seen Paul and Sabine at the airport. She'd lain awake for most of the night thinking about them and, when she'd finally fallen asleep, it was to dream about them. She felt utterly exhausted.

~

'Europa Bank, dealers.'

'Hi, Alix.'

'Cathal?'

'Yes. I left a message on your machine. Didn't you get it?'

'I'm sorry, Cathal,' said Alix. 'I was away for the weekend and I didn't get back until late last night.'

'I said you could ring anytime until midnight.'

'I know. But I was really tired.'

'How about tonight?' asked Cathal. 'I wondered if you'd like to go for a drink.'

'It's good of you, Cathal, but—'

'Listen, Alix, I understand you don't want some long-term thing. That's fine by me. But, come on, you've got to live a little.'

'I know,' she said.

'Quick drink,' urged Cathal. 'You choose the venue.'

She didn't want to go for a drink with Cathal. 'Smyth's,' she said, naming the pub that was practically next door to her apartment.

'Great,' said Cathal. 'See you there, half eight?'

'Half eight,' she agreed tiredly.

Jenny grinned at her. 'Got a date, Alix?'

'Oh, nothing special,' said Alix.

'You're a fast worker,' said Jenny. 'Paul just out the door and you've got someone else already. Alix, you're incredible.'

'I haven't got someone else.' Alix couldn't help smiling a little.

'Sounds to me like you have. How do you do it?' Jenny looked at her ruefully. 'When I split up with Ruairi I didn't go out with anyone for months. Not that I didn't try!'

'How did you try?' asked Alix.

'Clubs, pubs, dinner parties – I did the lot.' Jenny laughed. 'I even went to evening classes because I thought there might be a few eligible men there.'

'What sort of evening classes?' asked Alix.

'Computer studies,' said Jenny.

'But you know everything there is to know about computers,' said Alix.

Jenny made a face. 'I know. I thought I could impress them with my knowledge. But they were all teenage wimps.'

Alix chuckled. 'Too young for you?'

'Too young, too boring.'

'And now?' asked Alix.

'I've had a couple of dates but there's nobody special,' said Jenny. 'You know that.'

'What are you doing about it?'

'Nothing,' said Jenny. 'I'm kind of enjoying things the way they are.'

❦

Alix examined her hair for grey as she stood in front of the bathroom mirror. A few strands, nothing too serious, although she was due to visit Tina again soon. She gathered her hair and pulled it back into a knot.

Alix the confident, she thought, as she looked at her reflection. Alix the poised. Alix the control freak. She let her hair go and it swung in front of her face. She'd wear it loose tonight even though it irritated her like that. She pulled on a pair of grey trousers and a black T-shirt. She looked dull. But that was the way it was going to be.

Cathal was already in the pub when she arrived, a pint of lager in front of him. Alix smiled at him and he stood up and kissed her on the cheek.

'What can I get you?' he asked.

'White wine, please.'

He went up to the bar and got her a drink. 'So,' he said as he sat down again. 'Where were you for the weekend?'

'London,' said Alix. 'Business mainly.'

'You look tired,' said Cathal.

'Thanks,' she said.

'I'm sorry.' He looked at her in contrition. 'I didn't mean—'

'It's OK.'

They sat in silence for a moment.

'Would you mind if I smoked?' asked Alix.

'Well, sure, no problem.' Cathal looked at her in surprise. 'I didn't think you smoked.'

'Only sometimes,' she said as she took the packet of cigarettes out of her bag and lit one. 'Do you?'

He shook his head. 'How are you feeling after your bug?' he asked.

'Oh, much better,' she told him. 'It was pretty awful at the time but I seem to have shaken it now.'

'Lots of people seem to have had it,' he said awkwardly.

'I guess.' Alix inhaled deeply. 'Though no one else in the office managed to catch it from me.'

Cathal drained his glass. 'I'm going to get another. Would you like one?'

Alix looked at him in surprise. 'I've hardly started this.'

'I'll get you another anyway,' said Cathal and went to the bar.

⌒

It wasn't a good evening. Alix didn't feel like talking and Cathal was finding it heavy going. Every so often he'd light upon a topic that she was interested in and he thought that he'd finally managed to reach her, but she'd close up again and sit silently, waiting for him to think of another conversational gambit. She is very attractive, he thought as he watched her, but attraction can only do so much. She doesn't seem to have any life in her at all.

This was a mistake, thought Alix. It wasn't fair on Cathal and it wasn't fair on her. She wasn't ready for an evening in the pub with a bloke she hardly knew.

'Would you like one for the road?' asked Cathal.

She shook her head. 'I truly am tired,' she told him. 'I think I should get to bed.'

'OK.' He sounded relieved and that amused her. 'I'll walk you home.'

'Not that it's much of a walk,' she observed as she slipped on her jacket.

He laughed. 'Do you like living here?'

'Oh, yes,' she told him. 'I can walk to almost anywhere – although I have to confess that I usually drive. I'm not really the most environmentally friendly of people. I just throw glass jars into the rubbish which I guess is probably high up on the list of environmental crimes.'

'I'll have to report you to the green police,' Cathal warned her as he took her by the arm. She almost pulled away from him but she didn't.

'Here we are,' she said apologetically. 'Thanks for the drink.'

'Anytime,' said Cathal.

She looked at him and said uncomfortably, 'Would you like to come in for a coffee?'

He smiled at her. 'I don't think so, do you?'

'No.' The relief in her voice was clear.

'I'm sorry I wasn't the man you were looking for,' said Cathal.

'I'm sorry,' said Alix. 'I was a horrible person to take out tonight. I should have said no from the start.'

'Oh, I probably wouldn't have listened,' said Cathal. 'I needed tonight to get you out of my system.'

'And I'm out now?' She smiled faintly at him.

'I think so.' Cathal grinned at her.

'That's something,' she said.

'Goodnight, Alix.' He kissed her lightly on the cheek.
'Goodnight, Cathal.'

She watched him for a moment as he turned and walked towards Baggot Street. Then she took her keys from her bag and let herself into her empty apartment.

Chapter 21

'So the complete upgrade will cost us around twenty-five thousand.' Mike Wallis, Europa Bank's chief accountant, looked around the boardroom table. 'But I think it's worth it. It'll increase our processing speed enormously.'

'What do you think, Alix?' asked Des. 'You've been using that system for the past six months.'

Alix continued to stare out of the window at the mountains in the distance.

'Alix,' repeated Des. 'What do you think?'

'Oh, sorry.' She blinked and looked at the five men present. 'I didn't realise you were talking to me.'

'Alix, you've been out of it for nearly the entire meeting,' said Des. 'What on earth is wrong with you?'

She couldn't tell him that she was thinking about Paul and Sabine. She couldn't say that she hadn't been able to get them out of her mind for the past two days, ever since she'd seen them together. When she was least expecting it, when she felt sure that she was engrossed in whatever she was doing, she would suddenly imagine them together and she wouldn't be able to stop thinking about them. She'd been picturing Sabine telling Paul that she was pregnant and Paul's ecstatic response. Him telling her that it was the best moment of his life. That he loved her more than anything. And then she'd imagined another scenario, one in which Paul suddenly realised that the whole baby thing had been the most awful mistake and he cursed himself for ever leaving her in the first place.

She dragged her mind back to the conversation the management group had been having about computer upgrades.

'Twenty-five thousand sounds fine,' she said, glad that she could absorb a conversation while thinking about something else.

'You haven't had any problems?' asked Mike.

She shook her head. 'No. We had a few crashes at the start but that was due to the defaults on the software package we were using. When we changed some of the settings, everything was OK.'

'Right.' Des closed the folder. 'That's the lot. I'm stopping at the Galloping Green for a pint on my way home. Anyone heading in that direction is free to join me.'

The rest of the group stood up. 'I will,' said John Collins, the credit manager, as he looked at his watch and saw that it was nearly seven. 'I'm gasping for a drink.'

'Me too.' Kieran Dougherty slipped his jacket on.

'I can't,' said Alix. 'I promised the others I'd meet them in O'Reilly's. We're celebrating the closing of the zloty deal at last.'

'What was the problem?' asked Des. 'I was getting worried.'

'Nothing serious,' Alix told him. 'It was a settlement thing, nothing intrinsically wrong with the deal.'

'It was a great deal,' said John. 'And the client is delighted.'

'The best sort of deal is one where we're all happy.' Des patted John on the shoulders. 'And you did well to come up with the client, John.'

'I think Dave deserves some of the credit,' said Alix. 'After all, he did all the hard work.' What am I saying? she asked herself. Why am I praising him? Would he give me the credit for it if our roles were reversed?

'I've spoken to Dave already,' said Des.

'Oh.' Alix wondered what the managing director had told her senior dealer. That one day he would have her job? That they'd move her somewhere else? Transfer her to London? Or Paris? Don't be paranoid, she told herself. You don't have to imagine conspiracies in everything.

'By the way,' said Des to the room at large, 'don't forget about the Institute dinner next month. It's in the Shelbourne. Black tie. Boring, I know, but it has to be done.'

'Hilary will kill me,' said Mike Wallis. 'I seem to be out at something every night.'

'She won't kill you this time,' said Des. 'This is the one where you get to bring your wife.'

'I don't *have* to bring her, do I?' Mike looked horrified.

'Actually, yes,' said Des. 'We're trying to make things a little less stuffy. We thought that spouses would be a good idea.'

'It's a dreadful idea,' said John.

'Tough,' said Des firmly. 'The decision was taken at the spring general meeting. There are two dinners a year. One will be without partners, the other with.'

'We can come on our own if we want, though, can't we?' asked Alix.

'Oh, I'm sure Paul will have a good time,' Des told her. 'He can write about us if he wants.'

Alix had assumed that Des would know. She was certain Dave would have told him. In a man-to-man-type conversation, Dave could have said that the reason she was behaving like a basket case was that Paul had walked out on her. And that she was in denial about the whole thing.

I *am* in denial, she told herself as she walked across the Matt Talbot Bridge. I don't want to believe he's with Sabine. I don't want to accept that it could possibly be over between us.

The pub was heaving with people. They'd spilled outside the building onto the tiny patio in front and onto the pavement outside. You'd swear they were serving free beer, thought Alix as she pushed her way inside. And it was only Wednesday.

'Alix! Over here!' Gavin waved at her.

'Why is it so crowded?' she gasped. 'I thought we'd be able to have a quiet kind of celebration but this is bedlam.'

'There's a twenty-first party going on,' Gavin told her. 'A gorgeous bit of stuff, Alix. Legs up to her armpits. Look at her, over there.'

'I'm sure she hasn't noticed you,' Alix said as she turned to look at the object of his admiration. The girl was striking, with jet black hair that hung to her tiny waist, piercing blue eyes and legs which, as Gavin had said, were long and shapely and shown to best advantage in the short skirt she was wearing.

'I'm pretty certain she has.' Gavin winked at her.

'What would you like to drink?' she asked.

'Heineken,' said Gavin.

'And you?' She turned to Dave and Jenny.

'Same,' said Dave.

'Miller,' said Jenny.

Alix ordered the drinks. 'It's warm enough outside,' she said. 'Do you guys want to stay in here or go out?'

'Oh, stay here,' said Gavin. 'We've got a much better view of the action here.'

Jenny made a face. 'You're so bloody childish, Donnelly.'

'She wants me,' he told her. 'I can see it when she looks at me.'

'Are you out of your mind?' asked Alix. 'She's probably seen you flashing your gold card around or something and thinks that you have money. Little does she know!'

'After this year's review, I'll have a lot more.' Gavin looked at Alix, the challenge in his eyes. 'I deserve it.'

'You deserve something, all right,' said Alix.

'Money talks,' said Gavin. 'I work hard, I'm entitled to the reward.'

'We're here to celebrate Dave's deal tonight,' Alix said firmly. 'Not talk about future bonuses.' She raised her glass at Dave. 'Well done, Mr Bryant.'

'Thanks,' said Dave.

'I never asked what you thought about the Europa building in Paris?'

'Fantastic,' said Dave. 'It's exactly the sort of place that makes you feel the money flowing.'

'I know what you mean. What did you think of the dealing room?'

'Pretty neat,' he said. 'I liked the way the desks are grouped. And so far it hasn't got the complete bombshell look of most dealing rooms. But give it time.'

'What about the quotations?' asked Alix.

'Bloody silly.' Dave made a face. 'I wouldn't want to be sitting with a losing trade looking at some tripe spouted by Napoleon Bonaparte.'

Alix grinned. 'My sentiments exactly.'

She felt almost normal again. The tension between herself and her colleagues seemed to have disappeared. She told a joke and even Gavin laughed. They weren't so bad, she thought, it was just that she was so sensitive right now. But she'd get over it. She had to face the fact that Paul was out of her life forever. She could do that. But she wasn't going to let anyone else in.

'Alix?' Jenny's eyes were glazed.

'Yes?'

'What happened?'

'What do you mean, what happened?'

'Between you and Paul.'

'It's really none of your business, Jenny.'

'I know,' said Jenny. 'But I wanted to ask anyway.'

'We were getting on each other's nerves,' said Alix. 'We decided to live apart for a while.'

'So it's not a permanent split?'

Of course it was a permanent split. She'd seen him walk up the pathway to his house carrying Sabine Brassaert's suitcase. How much more permanent could it be?

She shrugged. 'Who knows?'

'Will you bring him to the Christmas party this year?' asked Jenny.

'I might.'

'I like him,' Jenny told her. 'He's a decent kind of bloke.'

Oh really, thought Alix. Decent enough to be tearing the clothes off that French bitch while I was asleep in my hotel bedroom. *Our* hotel bedroom. That was pretty decent, all right.

'He's not the worst,' she said.

'Anyway, I hope you two get back together,' Jenny sighed.

'Thanks,' said Alix dryly. 'And what about you?'

'I'm working on it.' Jenny made a face. 'I have a date for tomorrow night.'

'Really?'

Jenny nodded. 'I met him at Anna's wedding. He was a friend of the groom. I wasn't expecting to meet anyone there, so maybe it's a good sign.'

'Maybe it is,' said Alix. 'Love is funny like that. When you're looking for someone he never comes along.'

'I think that's a watched pot you're thinking of.' Jenny grinned at her.

'Whatever,' said Alix. 'I'll await your detailed report with interest.'

Gavin and Dave had joined in the twenty-first birthday celebrations. Gavin had his arm round the exotic-looking birthday girl, while Dave was chatting to someone else in the group.

'How do they do it?' asked Jenny.

'I don't know.' Alix smiled at her. 'You're surprised because you know them. You can't understand why anyone would be bothered with them. But girls that have never met them before probably think they're attractive and rich.'

'Gavin certainly gives that impression.' Jenny watched him as he bought a bottle of champagne.

'He's young,' said Alix.

'You're very understanding all of a sudden.'

'Maybe I'm mellowing in my old age.' She grinned at Jenny.

'You? Mellow?' Jenny laughed. 'That'll be the day, Alix. That will definitely be the day.'

～

She'd only had three bottles of beer because she'd driven in to work. The security guard at reception smiled at her as she walked into the building. 'Can't stay away?'

'I love it so much,' said Alix. 'I'll be in the dealing room for about ten minutes and then I'll leave.'

'Fine,' said the security guard.

She went upstairs and let herself into the room. She switched on the screens. The Nikkei – the index of the Japanese stock exchange – was higher. The yen was stronger. That was OK, they were running a small position in yen and an upward move suited them. She sat at her desk and watched the numbers change in front of her – red if the price was lower than the previous price, blue if it was higher. The market would end a lot higher, she thought as she watched the blue numbers outweigh the reds.

She closed her eyes. It was comfortable here. She felt contented. She liked the rise and fall of the numbers on the screen, the muted bleep every time an important news item was announced, the feeling that she was connected to the entire world. It was better than being in the pub. Better than being at the gym. Better than being at the shooting club. And much, much better than being at home on her own.

~

She kicked off her shoes, flopped on the sofa and flicked the remote control. She pressed the buttons in quick succession but there was absolutely nothing worth watching on TV. Even the news was boring – Sky was running a piece about a dog who'd walked over a hundred miles to get home when his family had accidentally left him behind at the seaside. How could you accidentally leave a spaniel behind? she wondered.

Didn't anyone miss him drooling all over the back of the car? She switched off the TV and opened the balcony doors.

It was cool tonight. Until now the summer had been hot and stifling. For the first time in weeks the breeze that blew across the balcony had the chill of autumn in it. Alix shivered and rubbed her arms.

She walked back into the living room and closed the door behind her. She picked up her jacket and slipped on her shoes again. She had to go out.

She pretended to herself that she didn't know where she was going, but of course she did. She didn't bother with the toll bridge but drove through the city centre and Fairview and turned left for Malahide. It was about eight miles to Malahide from Fairview. She passed through a variety of suburban developments before emerging onto the narrower, more countrified part of the road at Kinsealy where the enormous detached houses reminded her that a number of seriously wealthy people lived around here. She drove by the estate of the ex-Taoiseach, the disgraced Charlie Haughey, and wondered if all the wealth he had accumulated over the years compensated for ending up in court. Money isn't everything, she muttered as she overtook a bright orange Nissan Micra.

If she'd had less money maybe Paul would have cared about her more. She shook her head. It wasn't as though she was loaded, for God's sake! She was well-off, but that was a completely different thing. She couldn't afford to chuck in her job and become one of those half-envied, half-despised people, the ladies who lunch. She smiled to herself. If she gave up work she wouldn't get out of bed early enough to lunch!

The traffic lights were red at the junction to Paul's house. She glanced at herself in the rear-view mirror as she waited for them to change. She looked OK. A bit tired, maybe, but OK.

The lights turned green.

The house was in darkness. Alix hadn't expected it to be dark. She glanced at the clock on the dashboard. Nearly half eleven. Maybe they'd gone to bed. She grimaced. Paul had never been keen on going to bed early. That had been one of the things they argued about, her complaining that she had to be up early and needed to be asleep before midnight, Paul telling her to go ahead, he'd join her later. But if she went to bed before him, she'd invariably wake up when he slipped under the duvet beside her and slid his hand between the warmth of her thighs. She'd wake up and she'd say 'not now' but he'd know that it didn't take much to make her change her mind and she'd already be moving her body closer to him, warm with desire herself.

He made her feel that way. He was the only man who ever had.

And now he was doing it with Sabine. She couldn't let it go on like this. He needed to be told that it was a mistake. Shown that it was a mistake.

She got out of the car and slammed the door. Her footsteps echoed loudly on the pathway. She stood in the pool of light cast by the lamp in the porch. He should have turned off the porch light before going to bed, she thought. He was careful with money, he wouldn't want to waste electricity like this.

She took a deep breath and pressed the doorbell. Her mouth was dry but her palms were sweating.

She could picture them, stopping in the very act of making love, faces shocked, wondering who could be calling to the

303

house this late at night. And worried, because people only called late at night if there was something wrong.

She waited for the lights to come on but nothing happened. Perhaps they were hoping that the caller would go away. Perhaps they'd been asleep and were only now waking.

She pressed the buzzer again, holding it down for longer this time.

Nothing stirred.

They must be out. She clenched her fists in annoyance. She was ready to confront them and they weren't there to be confronted! Where were they? Had Paul taken Sabine away for a few days? A kind of honeymoon in Ireland? A few nights at a luxury hotel in the country where they'd be waited on hand and foot?

She banged on the door in her frustration and the house alarm went off.

Shit, she thought, as her heart thudded in her chest. She ran down the pavement and jumped into the car, praying that nobody had seen her, that the residents of Marina Cove didn't have a neighbourhood watch scheme. If she started the car now perhaps some interfering old biddy with nothing better to do, who was already looking out of the window, might take down the registration. And then the police would call to her apartment. Her imagination ran riot as she thought of the police coming round and warning her for – what? Breaking and entering? Well, hardly. Causing a disturbance? Possibly. Being a total fucking idiot? Definitely, if that was at all possible.

She crouched down in the driving seat and hoped that no one had seen her.

Of all the bloody stupid things you've ever done, this has to rate as the most stupid, she muttered as she banged her head on the steering column.

Now that she was bent down like this, she wondered when she could get up. She couldn't see anything. Maybe there were people already peering into the car to find out who the potential burglar was. She groaned.

It seemed like at least half an hour, but was in fact only ten minutes later, when the alarm stopped. She sat up cautiously and peeped out of the window.

The front door was open. Paul and Sabine had obviously arrived home from an evening out.

'I can't see anything.' Paul's voice carried across the road.

'Are you sure?' It was the first time she'd heard Sabine speak. The French accent was unmistakable.

'It was probably the cat from next door,' Paul told her. 'Sometimes he manages to set it off.'

'You don't think there is a need to worry?'

'Of course not, *ma chérie*,' he said.

Ma chérie. Alix nearly threw up.

'OK, then. You are coming inside?'

'Yes. In a moment.'

Alix ducked down again as Paul walked to the side of the road. She held her breath but there was no furious rapping on the window of the car. He didn't wrench the door open and haul her outside. She was right about his inability to recognise cars.

Alix heard the front door close and she sat up again. The light was on in the front bedroom, the blue curtains drawn. She saw Paul's silhouette as he walked across the room, then the main light was turned off and the fainter glow of a bedside lamp was all that was left.

You're such a bloody, bloody fool, she told herself as she started the car. They'd be right to lock you up and throw away the key. You shouldn't be let out on your own. You crazy, stupid cow.

Chapter 22

When she finally got to sleep that night Alix had the chasing dream again. She was grateful when the radio alarm clicked into life the next morning even though she was still exhausted. The dream always made her feel tired the next day, as though the chase had been for real, as though she'd run throughout the night.

She pushed back the duvet and then she remembered Paul. Surely she hadn't driven out to Malahide for some ill-defined showdown. Surely she hadn't set off the alarm on his house by banging on the door. And surely she hadn't been hiding in her car while he checked for nonexistent burglars.

She felt a wave of guilt and embarrassment wash over her. I'm acting like some neurotic teenager, she thought. If any of them in work ever got to hear about last night – she shuddered at the idea.

I will put it out of my mind, she told herself firmly. It was mad, impetuous and incredibly silly but no harm has been done. Forget about it, that's the best thing.

∽

'Alix, it's your sister on line two,' Jenny called.

'Thanks.' Alix picked up the phone. 'Wyn, how's it going?'

'All right,' said Wyn. 'And you?'

'I'm fine.'

'Good.'

Alix waited for Wyn to say something else.

'Wyn? Are you still there?'

'Yes,' said Wyn.

'Is something wrong?'

'Not exactly wrong,' said Wyn.

'What then?' Alix was impatient. It had been a busy day, she had lots of paperwork to do and she didn't have time to waste in roundabout conversations with Wyn. That was the worst thing about her sister, she could never get to the point quickly.

'I had a phone call from Carrie,' said Wyn hesitantly. 'At lunchtime.'

'And?' Alix glanced at her watch. It was almost five o'clock.

'Dad's back.'

The numbers on the screen in front of Alix blurred.

'What did you say?'

'I said that Dad's back.'

'Back where?'

'Back here, of course. Don't be so bloody silly.'

'I'm sorry.' Alix cleared her throat. 'I didn't mean – I just said the first thing that came into my head.'

'It's OK,' said Wyn. 'I was a bit dazed myself.'

'What does he want?' asked Alix. 'And how's Carrie?'

'I don't know. I wanted to call over but she said no. She phoned from the house. He was there.'

'In the house? She let him into the house?'

'Apparently so,' said Wyn.

'Is she mad?'

'I suppose she thought it'd be OK. Alix, do you realise that they're still married?'

'I know they're still married,' snapped Alix. 'Of course they're still married. Didn't I have a row with her last year about getting a divorce?'

'Yes. I remember.'

'So because she's still married to him she feels that she can let him into our house.'

'Her house,' said Wyn.

'We both lived there too,' said Alix. 'It's our house. It's not *his* house!'

'Calm down, Alix,' said Wyn.

'I am calm. I just don't want him barging in on our lives and upsetting Carrie all over again. Why is he back? What does he want?'

'I don't know,' said Wyn. 'Carrie wants us to call over to her tonight.'

'And will he be there?'

'No,' Wyn answered. 'I asked that. He's staying in a guest house. He won't be anywhere nearby.'

'OK,' said Alix. 'Just so long as she doesn't think that there's going to be a great family reunion or anything.'

'I hardly think so,' said Wyn. 'I don't think she wants him back in her life either. Alix, it was nearly thirty years ago. Everything is completely different now.'

'I know.' Alix sighed. 'It's a shock, Wyn.'

'Yes,' said her sister.

'What do you think? How do you feel?'

'To be honest?'

'Yes, to be honest.'

'I don't know how I feel.' Wyn sounded bewildered. 'I

don't know why he's back. What he wants. I don't know
how I should feel.'

'What time?' asked Alix.

'Sorry?'

'What time does she want us to come over?'

'I don't know. Some time after tea, I suppose. I didn't ask.'

'That's not like you.' Alix laughed shortly.

'No. I know. Alix, do you want to come here first?'

'Yes,' said Alix. 'I'll go home and change and then come
over.'

'OK.' Wyn sounded relieved.

'See you then,' said Alix.

'See you,' said Wyn.

Alix stared at the screens in front of her. The numbers and
the graphs were just meaningless whirls. A news headline,
giving details of the Federal Reserve's latest monetary policy comments, scrolled past her without registering in her
consciousness.

Her father was back. Dad. She hadn't thought of him as
Dad for a long time, hadn't thought of him at all. She didn't
want to think about him. She bit her lip.

'Are you OK, Alix?' Jenny looked at her in concern.

'What?'

'Are you OK?'

'Yes, fine, Jenny. I'm sorry. Just a domestic problem.
Nothing serious.'

'Sure?'

'Of course.' Alix smiled at her. 'I was miles away there for
a moment.'

'I know,' said Jenny. 'Alix, is it all right if I head home
now?'

'Sure,' said Alix. 'Everything has gone through to settlements?'

Jenny nodded.

'You seem very cheerful.' Alix suddenly registered Jenny's eagerness to be off. 'Anything special planned for tonight?'

'Yes.'

'Oh?'

'I'm going out,' said Jenny.

'Anywhere nice?'

Jenny shrugged. 'I don't know. I'm meeting Mike.'

'The guy you went out with last night? You're seeing him again?'

'Yes.' Jenny looked defiant.

'Go for it,' Alix told her. 'Have a good time. Obviously you like him.'

'We got on,' said Jenny simply.

'What does he do?'

'He's an electrician. He has his own company.'

'That'll be useful when the fuses blow,' Alix grinned.

'Well, hopefully we'll generate enough electricity of our own.'

'Jenny Smith!' But Alix was laughing. 'Enjoy yourself tonight.'

'Thanks.' Jenny picked up her bag.

Alix finished the report she'd been writing then stood up. 'I'm off myself, Dave. See you tomorrow.'

'Fine,' said Dave. 'I'll be heading home shortly.'

She glanced at Gavin's empty seat. 'I thought he was coming back this afternoon.'

'The client's offices were in Stepaside,' said Dave. 'I guess he thought it was too much hassle to come back.'

'He should have phoned,' said Alix. 'I couldn't care less

311

whether he was here or not, Dave, but he should have phoned.'

'Normally he would.'

'Perhaps.' Alix stretched her arms over her head. She didn't know why she was bothering about Gavin. She didn't know why she'd had a conversation with Jenny about her new boyfriend. She didn't know how she could be thinking about anything else other than the fact that her father was back. And she didn't want him in her life.

❧

Wyn opened the door before Alix had time to ring the bell.

'Terry's taken the kids over to his mother's,' she said as Alix walked into the living room. 'I told him to bring them home in about an hour. I didn't want anyone here, Alix.'

'That's OK.'

'D'you want tea?'

Alix shook her head.

'Coffee?'

'Wyn, this isn't a social get-together,' she said. 'I don't want anything to eat or drink. I couldn't drink anything anyway.'

'I know.' Wyn pulled at the bottom of the sweatshirt she was wearing. 'I can't help myself. It makes things more normal.'

Alix sat on the sofa and motioned her sister to sit beside her. 'Everything is normal,' she said. 'There's nothing for us to get frazzled about. The man is in Ireland after spending most of his life in the States. As far away from us as he could possibly be.' She looked at Wyn. 'There's no need for us to get upset about it. He means nothing to us. He wasn't there when we were kids and now we don't need him. If Carrie wants us to meet him we can say no. We're not under any obligation to him.'

'I remember it,' said Wyn blankly. 'The day he left. I remember Carrie screaming and crying and throwing his things into bags. I remember she wouldn't take a tissue from me. I remember her tearing a photograph of him in half.'

Alix reached out for her hand. 'It was a long time ago.'

'What do you remember?' asked Wyn.

She hadn't wanted him to leave. She'd known there was something dreadfully wrong. She'd seen Carrie crying and she'd started to cry too. And she'd held on to him. And Carrie. And she hadn't wanted him to leave.

'Being afraid,' said Alix slowly. 'Knowing that there was something awful happening. Knowing I couldn't do anything about it.'

Wyn squeezed her hand. 'Carrie called him an uncaring bastard,' she said. 'That's what I recall the most. "Get out, you uncaring, selfish bastard," she said.'

'It doesn't matter why he left,' said Alix. 'The point is that he did.'

'But why wouldn't Carrie ever talk about it?' asked Wyn. 'I questioned her over and over and she just wouldn't say anything. And then, I suppose, I got tired asking.'

'Anyway, you could never be sure she'd tell us the truth,' said Alix.

'Is there something wrong with us that we didn't ask?' wondered her sister. 'That we never tried to find out?'

'Carrie didn't want us to find out,' said Alix. 'And I didn't want to hurt her by delving into the past.'

'But he's our father,' Wyn said. 'We should want to know about him.'

'Why?' asked Alix fiercely. 'What did he ever do for us?'

Wyn drove them to Carrie's house, one of a small red-bricked terrace in Ranelagh. They'd lived in Clontarf when John had been around and for a few years afterwards until Carrie, who needed the money for the salon she'd decided to open, sold the rambling old seafront house and brought them across the city to Ranelagh. Alix liked Ranelagh but she always remembered the sound of the sea in Clontarf.

❧

Carrie saw the car pull up outside the house. She took a couple of deep breaths and closed her eyes. She waited until the doorbell rang before going to open the door.

'Hi, Carrie.' Alix dropped a kiss on her mother's cheek and walked past her into the front room.

'Hi, Carrie.' Wyn did the same.

'I'm glad you came over.' Carrie sat down on one of the newly re-covered armchairs. She smoothed her already smooth hair and looked from one to the other of her daughters who sat side by side on the sofa.

They were angry, she could see. And confused. Alix stared back at her, eyes like emeralds. Wyn's gaze was more troubled, less aggressive.

'Your father was here today.' Carrie's voice wavered a little and, for a moment, she was afraid she was going to cry. She took another deep breath and exhaled slowly. The two girls watched her carefully. 'He wanted to know how you were.'

'Huh,' snorted Alix. 'First time in his life he cared.'

'Alix.' Wyn placed a warning hand on her sister's arm.

'No,' said Carrie. 'Alix is right.' She sighed. 'Almost right.'

She smoothed her hair again. She wasn't good at this. She'd never been good at talking to them. Not about serious things anyway. Especially with Alix. At least with Wyn she could have easy, gossipy conversations about the salon and about her clients. And sometimes about Alix. But they never talked about each other.

Carrie had never felt like a real mother to her girls. She'd encouraged them to call her by her Christian name and to think of themselves as partners in her life. And so they talked to her as an equal, but they never came to her with their troubles. And she never shared hers with them. It had seemed right until today. But now she wasn't certain.

'I was very angry when your dad left,' she said. 'Really angry.'

'I remember,' said Wyn.

'I thought he'd betrayed us.'

'Why?' asked Alix.

'Leaving us was a betrayal,' said Carrie cautiously, 'of everything I thought we were.'

'What did you think we were?' asked Wyn.

'Happy,' said Carrie simply. 'I was happy. I had the two of you, I had your father. I worked a couple of days a week in Sheri's salon. I was happy about things.'

Alix gripped the edge of the sofa.

'I didn't know that John wasn't happy.' Carrie looked carefully at both of them. 'Truly I didn't. I knew that there were *times* when he wasn't happy but that's not the same. I thought it was because of work – you know how it is with work, sometimes you hate it, sometimes you love it.' This was hard, she thought. She'd practised this talk for hours but it was still hard when the two of them were sitting in front of her, staring at her. 'So I didn't know that he was really unhappy.'

'Why was he really unhappy?' asked Wyn.

'Because he'd met someone else.'

They sat in silence.

'Who?' asked Alix eventually.

'John worked for IBM,' said Carrie. 'At that time, of course, it was business machines not computers. He sold accounting machines, ones that posted items to ledgers. He was good at it. He was good at the mechanical end and he was good at the numbers end.' She smiled faintly. 'He was better at the numbers than the machines. He could total a column of figures almost just by looking at them.'

'Like you, Alix,' said Wyn.

Alix said nothing.

'He sold them to a company called Addtrex. I've no idea what they did. But there was a girl in the ledgers department called Imogen Hogan. He started going out with her.'

'Going out with her!' spluttered Wyn. 'He was married to you! What was he playing at?'

'Imogen Hogan was beautiful,' said Carrie. 'Really beautiful. I saw her photograph. She had dark hair and huge eyes and I could see why he'd fall for her.'

'But he shouldn't have fallen for her,' said Alix. 'What about us?'

'Don't be naïve,' Carrie snapped at her. 'How many of your married friends are completely faithful to their husbands?'

'I don't have that many married friends.' Alix thought about Guy Decourcelle who'd offered dinner and maybe more in Paris. And of Des Coyle who, though in his view very happily married, had conducted an affair with one of the temps in the accounts department for six months until she left Europa Bank.

'How did you find out about her?' asked Wyn.

'The photograph,' replied Carrie. 'Stupid sod had left it in his shirt pocket. I knew straightaway even though he tried to deny it at first. But he admitted it eventually.'

'So you threw him out,' said Alix.

'I think these things can be worked out,' said Carrie. 'I told him that. I said he could stop seeing her and we'd forget about it.'

'That was decent of you,' said Wyn.

'It was probably very stupid,' said Carrie. 'But, you know, it's really easy for people to tell you what to do in those circumstances. To say that you should throw him out and never see him again. To say that you shouldn't trust him any more. I was married with two small children. I didn't want to throw him out.'

'So why did you?' Alix closed her eyes and remembered it more vividly than ever before. She was sitting at the dining-room table, doing a jigsaw of a cow. She could see it clearly, big wooden pieces coloured black and white. And blue pieces for the sky. She'd put a piece of sky in place when she heard her mother begin to cry. She'd sat, frozen, on the chair. Wyn had been sitting on the floor, playing with a set of Dinky cars. She jumped up and hurt her foot when she stepped on one of the cars. They'd run into the hallway together and John had been standing there with a suitcase in his hand.

'Where are you going?' Alix had asked. 'Where?'

And then the shouting and screaming had started and Carrie was crying and Wyn had shoved tissues at her but Carrie hadn't even noticed.

'She was pregnant,' said Carrie.

Alix and Wyn stared at their mother.

'What?' whispered Wyn.

Carrie was silent for a moment. She'd practised this bit too but it was hard to stay calm. It was history now, she reminded herself, and she could cope with it. It didn't have the power to hurt her as it had before.

'She was pregnant,' repeated Carrie. 'And he wanted to be with her.'

'And us?' asked Alix. 'Didn't he want to be with us?'

Carrie got up from the armchair and walked to the window. 'Of course,' she said. 'He offered to take you with him. So that you could be a family together.' She stared out at the quiet cul-de-sac.

Alix and Wyn exchanged glances.

'I'm glad you didn't give us away,' said Wyn shakily.

'I thought about it.' Carrie continued to look out of the window. 'Because I thought that maybe it would be better. I was trying to be rational about it, but how can you be? And I said to myself, come on, Carrie, think about what's best for the children.'

'And you told him to sod off,' said Alix.

Carrie smiled. 'Actually, yes, I did.' She turned to face them again. 'I told him that he was a bastard to even suggest it and that if he thought he was getting his mitts on my beautiful children he could think again.' She sighed. 'I don't want to be truly horrible but I think he was relieved in the end.'

'So he left,' said Wyn.

'Yes,' Carrie sighed. 'He left and he went to work for IBM in the States and Imogen went with him.'

'And the baby?' asked Alix. 'Our father's daughter?'

'Yes,' said Carrie. 'She looks just like her mother.'

'You've seen her?'

'Only a photograph,' said Carrie. 'She's very pretty.'

'What's her name?' asked Wyn.

'Kate.'

I have another sister, thought Alix in wonderment. A half-sister, but still someone connected to me. By blood. It felt strange.

'So why is he here?' asked Wyn. 'Is there some drama with Imogen and Kate? Has one of them got a terminal disease or something? That's usually the way with the long-lost mother or father or son or daughter, isn't it?'

Carrie smiled faintly. 'Only in the movies, dear. Both Imogen and Kate are in perfect health.'

'So what does he want?'

'A divorce, for starters,' said Carrie. 'They didn't bother about getting married before but they want to now. Because Kate was married last year and she's having a baby. And they want to be legitimate grandparents.'

Alix laughed. 'You're not serious?'

'Oh, I am,' said Carrie. 'You know, when he left to be with Imogen, it was all very romantic as far as he was concerned. She was so lovely and fragile and waif-like he couldn't help himself. That's what he told me, anyway. And they thought it was even more romantic to live together and not get married because it meant that they were together for love and not for the piece of paper.'

'Oh, for heaven's sake!' exclaimed Wyn. 'That's so bloody old-fashioned.'

Carrie smiled. 'That's John.'

'But why did he insist on leaving us for her?' asked Alix. 'It might be romantic to have an affair, but afterwards?'

'He said that he cared about me a lot and he loved both of you immensely,' said Carrie. 'But he said he couldn't live without Imogen.'

'What shit.' Alix grunted.

'Her parents didn't talk to her for months,' said Carrie. 'Actually, I felt sorry for her. He took the job in the States and dragged her with him. She didn't have a job and she was quite sick with the baby. I guess it wasn't so romantic then.'

'Have they been back here before?' asked Wyn. 'In Ireland?'

'A few times, apparently,' said Carrie. 'To see her family.'

'And he wasn't in touch?'

'He phoned,' said Carrie. 'But I didn't want to see him.'

'Did he want to see us?' asked Alix.

Carrie sighed. 'Of course he did. But he didn't come back for five years. So he wasn't exactly pining, was he? And I thought it would be too upsetting for both of you. The next time he came was when Alix was in hospital with appendicitis. I didn't think it would do you any good, Alix, to see him appear in the ward carrying a bunch of grapes.'

'I'd have thrown them at him.'

'You were only thirteen, Alix,' said Wyn.

'That wouldn't have stopped me.'

'Anyway,' said Carrie, 'he stopped asking after that.'

'But he never sent cards or anything,' said Wyn. 'Never.'

'He did the first year,' said Carrie. 'And after that, no, he didn't.'

'And now he wants to see us?' asked Alix.

'If you like,' Carrie said.

'I hate him,' said Alix. 'I've always hated him.'

'You don't know him,' Carrie told her. 'You hate what you think he is.'

'How do you feel?' asked Wyn suddenly. 'You met him here. In this house.'

'I didn't mind,' said Carrie. 'It's my house. I was OK.'

'Does it upset you?' asked Alix.

Carrie bit her lip. 'I'd be wrong if I said it didn't. But you don't feel it so much after time. And I've been happy since.'

'But you haven't had anyone else,' said Alix.

'Biblically, you mean?' Carrie smiled at her daughter.

Alix blinked. 'Oh!'

'To love,' said Wyn hastily. 'A partner.'

'I've been happy,' said Carrie. 'Honestly I have. I have both of you and a business that's very successful. I don't need a partner.'

'All the same.' Wyn shrugged expressively.

'I know you've been very lucky with Terry,' said Carrie. 'And I think it must be the most wonderful thing in the world to have a happy-ever-after kind of marriage. But it's worked out for me. I like the way my life is.'

'I don't want to see him,' said Alix.

'Don't rush into it,' Carrie said. 'Think about it.'

'I do,' said Wyn. 'I need to see him.'

'You should think about it too,' said Carrie. 'We can set it up in a couple of days.'

'OK,' said Wyn.

Carrie heaved a sigh of relief. 'Does anyone want a drink? I'm gasping for some vodka.'

'Great,' said Alix.

'Yes,' said Wyn.

'Right,' said Carrie.

Chapter 23

They left Carrie's house at nine o'clock. Because she was driving, Wyn had drunk only one glass of vodka. Carrie had had quite a few and Wyn thought that Alix had too.

The sisters were silent as Wyn drove down the narrow road where Carrie lived to join the steady stream of traffic in Ranelagh village.

'Are you all right?' asked Wyn as they waited for the lights to go green.

'Fine,' said Alix.

'What do you think?' asked Wyn.

'Of what?'

'Oh, for God's sake, Alix! Of everything.' The lights changed and Wyn crunched the gears.

'Take it easy,' said Alix. 'You'll destroy the car.'

'I know what I'm doing.' Wyn gritted her teeth and shoved the gearstick into first.

'She seemed OK,' said Alix.

'Carrie?'

'Wyn, there wasn't anyone else there.'

'I know, I know.' Wyn thudded the car into third gear. 'I'm sorry. I'm kind of distracted.'

'Are *you* all right?' asked Alix.

Wyn glanced in her rear-view mirror, indicated and pulled the car in to the side of the road. 'I don't know.' She bit her lip.

'Do you want me to drive?' asked Alix.

'Are you out of your mind?' Wyn said. 'You and Carrie were knocking back vodkas. We'd be stopped for sure.'

'I wasn't,' said Alix. 'I had one but I kept topping it up with lemonade. Carrie didn't notice.'

'Neither did I,' said Wyn.

'If you want, I'll drive,' Alix said. 'Honestly, Wyn, I'm fine.'

'It's OK,' said her sister. 'I can do it. It's just – oh, Alix, I don't know! How could she not have told us! He left her because of a woman he'd got pregnant. And he preferred her to us. And that other baby to us.' Wyn's face was contorted with pain. 'Why?'

'I don't know,' said Alix gently. 'I don't know.'

'I loved him,' said Wyn. 'He used to bring things home for me. He called me his princess.' She laughed shortly. 'I suppose all fathers call their daughters princesses. But I thought he meant it. I though I was special. *We* were special.'

'Yeah, well, we weren't,' said Alix.

'I know.' Wyn turned to look at her. 'You probably don't even remember him very well.'

'Well enough,' said Alix. 'Well enough to have wanted him to stay.'

'I could understand it if she was young and beautiful and not pregnant,' said Wyn. 'I could understand that! At least he'd be running away for something more glamorous than Carrie and Wyn and Alix. But he was just exchanging us, Alix. Exchanging us for someone else with a kid.'

'Stop,' said Alix. 'I don't want to talk about it any more.'

'But we have to talk about it.' Wyn wiped her eyes. 'We have to figure it out.'

'I don't want to figure that bastard out!' Alix clenched her fists. 'I don't give a shit about him. No more than he does about you or me. I'm not going to meet him and I couldn't care less about his wife or his daughter or his bloody granddaughter either.'

'Oh, God,' said Wyn. 'I'd forgotten about the grand-daughter. We're related to that child. I've never been an aunt before.'

'It's great.' Alix smiled wryly at her. 'You get to be real nice to them and then leave them if it becomes too hectic. Anyway, Wyn, you're only some kind of step-relation to the kid and you're never likely to see her anyway so I don't know what you're worrying about.'

'But the other one. Kate. She's our half-sister, Alix.'

'I don't care what she is,' said Alix. 'She means nothing to me. I didn't know about her before and I don't know about her now. Come on, Wyn. Either drive or let me drive. I don't want to sit here all night.'

'OK, OK,' said Wyn. She put the car into gear and moved off. 'Aren't you curious, though?' She shot a glance at Alix. 'Don't you want to know what she looks like?'

'No,' said Alix.

'Or what *he* looks like now?'

'Definitely not,' said Alix.

'Maybe he's sorry,' said Wyn. 'Maybe he regrets it.'

'Like shit he regrets it,' snorted Alix. 'He's back to sort out his affairs. Get a divorce from Carrie. Marry the lovely, fragile, has-to-be-looked after Imogen. Play happy fucking families with his granddaughter! You think he cares about us? Think again, Wyn.'

'But you can't just blot people out of your mind,' said Wyn. 'I mean, Alix, he must have thought of us sometimes. Carrie said he wanted to see us.'

'After five years! He obviously wasn't all that gutted, was he?'

'How do you know? Maybe he was.'

'Wyn, you live in a fantasy world, didn't anyone ever tell you? Where fathers love their children and mothers love their husbands and everything is happy ever after.'

'Don't be stupid.' Wyn rubbed her eyes and slowed to let a car out in front of her.

'You've been lucky,' said Alix. 'You married Terry and you had the kids and everything has worked out for you. So you think that everyone should be like you.'

'No, I don't,' said Wyn. 'And I resent the implication that I'm so one-dimensional that I can't see outside my own family. I'm not stupid, Alix.'

'No, you're not.' Alix smoothed back her hair in a gesture that was a carbon copy of Carrie's. 'I'm sorry, Wyn. I'm pretty thoughtless sometimes.'

'I love Terry,' said Wyn. 'He's been good for me, Alix. And I love my kids more than anything else in the world. I don't know how anyone could ever leave their children, I really don't. And I can't see how you could ever stop thinking about them if you did. But I know that some people can. And maybe, for whatever reason, it's easier for men to leave them. I just wish it hadn't been our father that had done it.'

'We're better off without him,' said Alix.

They drove the rest of the way in silence. Alix leaned back

in the seat and closed her eyes. She had a thumping headache. She was glad that Wyn was doing the driving.

She remembered him coming into the bedroom one night. Walking lightly because he thought they were asleep. She should have been asleep but something had woken her. Alix hadn't been the sort of child to cry when she woke up. Usually she just lay in her bed and looked around her, not afraid of the dark.

He leaned over the bed and saw that her eyes were open.

'Why aren't you asleep?' he whispered.

'I am,' she said.

'With your eyes open?'

'They're nearly closed.'

He smiled and kissed her on the cheek. He pulled the sheet up to her neck. 'Sleep well,' he whispered.

'I love you,' she said.

She didn't want to remember things like that. They weren't real. She'd probably dreamed it anyway.

❧

Terry was in the living room. He looked up when they walked in.

'How was it?' he asked.

'OK,' said Wyn uncertainly. Then she began to cry.

He jumped up from the sofa and put his arms round her. Gathered her close to him and stroked her hair. 'It's all right,' he murmured. 'It's OK.' He looked at Alix who was standing at the door watching them. 'What happened?' he mouthed silently.

She shrugged.

Terry kept his arms round Wyn who leaned against him. Alix sat on the sofa and said nothing as he held her tightly and comforted her.

I want someone like that, she thought. The pain of wanting seared through her. I want someone to care about me the way Terry cares about Wyn. I want someone who'll comfort me when I feel bad, who'll be there when I need him the most. She shivered.

Terry led Wyn to the sofa. She sat down beside Alix, her face tear-stained.

'Do you want to tell me about it?' asked Terry.

'The news from the front is that good old Daddy, who abandoned us and Carrie, left us for another woman who was pregnant with his child,' said Alix lightly. 'He's returned to the old sod because he wants a divorce from Carrie – not that she has much say in it anyway, I suppose. The reason for this sudden desire to disentangle himself from her is because he wants to marry his girlfriend. Her name's Imogen. The daughter, their daughter, is pregnant and they want to be legitimate grandparents.' She laughed shortly. 'He also claims to want to see us. But I guess that's just to make things sound good.'

'Your father has another child?' Terry stared at her in amazement.

'Hardly a child at this point,' said Alix. 'She must be at least twenty-nine.'

Terry held Wyn's hand. 'I'm not surprised you're upset,' he said. 'You're probably in shock.'

'It's only hitting me now.' Wyn's voice was shaky. 'I just can't believe it. I thought that he'd left because of work. Because he thought it was so important. That's what Carrie used to say when we were small. That he'd left us for work. She wouldn't ever say anything else. Eventually we stopped asking. But even when I didn't believe that any more I still never thought he'd left us because of another child.'

'If it was another woman I could understand,' said Terry. 'But a woman and a kid.'

'His kid,' said Alix.

'How do you feel about it?' Terry asked her.

She shrugged. 'What's there to feel? The man obviously didn't give a shit about us. Why should I get upset about things now? He only wants to see us as some kind of sop to his conscience, I guess. He never really cared about us.'

'Perhaps he did,' said Terry.

'Oh, don't you start!' Alix looked at him in disgust. 'Carrie, despite refusing to talk about him when we were kids, was trying to make excuses earlier. He's a shit, he always was a shit and he always will be a shit. And I'm not going to waste any emotions feeling sorry for him or wondering about him or even remembering any of it.'

'He's your father,' said Terry gently.

'A biological accident,' Alix told him. 'Who cares who our father is? The facts of the matter are that Carrie brought us up and Carrie did everything for us and she made us stand on our own two feet and accept nothing from anyone and she was right. So I won't get mushy and sentimental over someone who had no more than a bit part in my existence.'

Terry was silent. Wyn blew her nose.

'You're so strong, Alix,' said Wyn. 'I'm your older sister. I should be the strong one. But it's you. You could always stand up for yourself.'

'No one else will do it for you,' said Alix harshly. Then she smiled. 'Well, for you, Wyn, I suppose Terry will.'

Terry patted Wyn on the hand and got up. 'I'll put the kettle on,' he said. 'I think you could both do with some tea.'

'Thanks,' said Wyn. She leaned back in the seat. 'I feel exhausted.'

'Me too,' said Alix.

'Do you think he ever thought about us?' asked Wyn.

'I couldn't care less,' said Alix.

'But what if he regretted it?' Wyn looked anxiously at her. 'What if he used to sit at home and think about us and wish he hadn't left Carrie.'

'His loss,' Alix said shortly.

Terry brought tea and biscuits in to them. They sipped the hot drinks, cupping their hands round the bright red mugs. He switched on the TV but it was only for background noise. None of them watched it.

Alix closed her eyes. She wished that John hadn't come back to Ireland. She wished Carrie had never told her about Imogen and Kate. Despite not wanting to think about them, she couldn't help imagining what they were like. The fragile Imogen and her equally fragile daughter. So unlike herself and Wyn, both of whom were tall and strong and healthy-looking. Unlike Carrie who, in many ways, looked fragile too. Alix gritted her teeth. Did they get their sturdy bodies and dark hair from John? She remembered him, of course, but only as the sort of memory that floats into your head when you're not trying to find it. Whenever she really tried to think about him, she couldn't visualise him at all. But he was dark, she remembered that much. And Carrie was fair. At least, Alix conceded, she was fair now. Perhaps she hadn't been quite so blonde when she was younger.

Thinking of Carrie's hair colour made her think of her own grey strands. Visible signs of being older. Wiser. But she didn't feel either of those things. She felt exactly the same as she'd always done. She yawned.

'Tired?' asked Terry.

She shook her head. 'Not really. I suppose it's been a long day.'

'You should go to bed early. Get some sleep,' he told her.

'I should do that every night.' She smiled faintly at him. 'Never quite manage it, unfortunately.' She stood up. 'You're right, though. I'll head off. Leave you two in peace.'

'You don't have to rush away,' protested Wyn. 'Stay the night if you like.'

'Don't be daft,' said Alix. 'I haven't even got a change of things with me. I'm fine, Wyn. Besides, I have a busy day at work tomorrow.'

'You sure?'

She nodded. 'Absolutely.'

Wyn stood up and kissed her on the cheek. 'We'll always have each other,' she said.

'Don't be so dramatic,' Alix grinned. 'What you mean is we're stuck with each other.'

Wyn made a face. 'Sure. That's exactly what I mean. But I love you, Alix.'

'And I you.' Alix gave Wyn a hug. 'Take care.'

'Safe home,' said Wyn. 'Sleep well.'

Terry and Wyn stood at the door and waited until Alix had turned out of the driveway before they went back inside.

'Was it really difficult?' asked Terry.

'It's just that your life isn't what you thought it was,' said Wyn falteringly. 'I always thought there was just Alix and me. And Carrie. As far as I was concerned, John existed, and I suppose I assumed that he'd have another relationship, but I never, ever thought of children. How naïve could I be?' She looked at him in puzzlement. 'I mean, it was odds on that he'd have another family. But it just never occurred to me.'

'It's not something I'd think about either,' said Terry. 'How do you think Alix is taking it? She seems pretty OK.'

Wyn shrugged. 'You know Alix. Shocked at first and then she kind of made a joke of it. Dismissive. Light-hearted. Said it didn't matter.'

'And is that what she really thinks?'

'I wish I knew.' Wyn leaned her head against her husband's shoulder. 'I really wish I knew.'

⁓

Alix turned the key and walked into her empty apartment. She went over to the computer and checked the level of the dollar. Slightly stronger. She wrinkled her nose. She didn't want it to be slightly stronger. But then, nothing was as she wanted it these days. So it wasn't entirely surprising that the dollar wasn't doing her any favours either.

She pushed open the bathroom door and peered at her face in the huge mirror over the sink. She could see Carrie in it. In the shape of her eyes. In the lift of her mouth. In her cheekbones. All of that was Carrie. But her thick dark eyebrow, weren't like Carrie's. Carrie's were finely arched and their shape had as much to do with nature as with their owner's skill with tweezers. The green and grey colours of

331

her eyes weren't Carrie's either. Carrie had blue eyes. Like Wyn.

He was a shit, she told her reflection. A complete and utter shit who walked out on us and who wouldn't stay. Even though Carrie begged him. He didn't love us then and he doesn't love us now.

She switched off the bathroom light and went to bed.

～

It was five o'clock when she woke up, heart thumping. She hadn't had the chasing dream. She didn't know why she was suddenly sitting upright in the bed, trembling with fear. She listened for the sound of someone in the apartment but everything was quiet.

She slid out of the bed and pulled her dressing gown round her. She peeped out of the window but there was nothing to be seen. She tiptoed out into the living room and checked the patio doors but everything was closed. Then she head a muffled thud and a stifled laugh from the apartment next door.

Three girls shared the apartment next door and it looked as if at least one of them was having a very late night. She sighed. Lucky Fiona or Meredith or Yvonne.

She looked at her watch. She was wide awake now and she knew that she would never get back to sleep. She might as well get dressed. She could go into the office early. Get a few things done.

But an hour later she didn't feel like going into the office. It seemed a suddenly pointless exercise to sit in the dealing room for an hour and a half ahead of everyone else. She could do some early trades, perhaps, but she didn't feel in the right frame of mind for trading.

What does Kate do? she wondered. Besides being married and being pregnant. What is her career? And is she going to give it up now because of her child? John's grandchild.

Why had he walked out? How could he walk out?

Alix picked up the keys to her car and let herself out of the apartment. The sky was lighter as she slid behind the wheel and turned the key. She drove down Haddington Road and towards the toll bridge. Then she took the coast road northwards, round the estuary, until she was in Malahide village.

This is crazy, she told herself. You're being stupid.

She drove through the village and turned towards Paul's estate. You are not to drive past his house, she told herself. He could be up. He could see you. Although Paul was never out of bed before eight. But Sabine might be. Doing whatever arty thing it was that she did. She might like to paint in the early morning.

Alix slowed down as she drove past his house. It was silent, curtains closed, a pint of milk on the doorstep.

A pint of milk. It looked so bloody domesticated.

The tears stung her eyes as she accelerated past the house and back to the main road.

Chapter 24

In the end, Alix was late getting into the office. She hurried up the stairs, too impatient to wait for the lift. The others had started the morning meeting without her.

'Sorry,' she said as she slipped into her seat. 'Traffic.'

'We were just talking about the UK unemployment data,' Dave told her. 'Lots of talk that they'll be worse than expected. The gilt market looks like it'll open lower.'

'Fewer people out of work and it's bad for the market,' sighed Alix. 'I can never quite get my head around that.'

Jenny smiled. 'You're not meant to get involved in the moral dilemma.'

'I don't,' said Alix. 'But I think it's crazy that we say that the numbers will be "worse". They're not worse for the people who've got a job for the first time.'

Dave and Gavin exchanged glances.

'I didn't realise you were a bleeding heart,' said Gavin.

'Now you know,' Alix said. 'So if you ever lose your job, Gavin, you'll take comfort from the fact that I'm feeling very sorry for you.'

'Thanks. But I won't lose my job,' he told her. 'I'll only ever move onwards and upwards.'

She laughed suddenly. 'I believe you, Gavin. I truly do.'

An hour later she opened her diary and sighed. Meetings, meetings and – she'd almost forgotten – her lunch date with Matt Connery. Not a lunch date, she told herself, a viewing of their computer-animated movie. It would be interesting, she thought, if it wasn't for the fact that the idea of being around Connery was an uncomfortable one. She wished he hadn't sent her those damned flowers. How could she sit near a man who'd sent her a magnificent bouquet of carnations and tiger lilies and not feel uncomfortable? It messed up the whole basis of a business relationship to have one party sending the other flowers.

At least Paul had known better.

She flushed as she thought about having driven out to Malahide this morning. Of all the stupid things she'd done, that was the most stupid. Well, no, it wasn't, she reminded herself. Her previous trip to Malahide when she'd set off the house alarm had been even more stupid. In fact, she thought, her behaviour over the past few weeks had been littered with stupidity.

Her first meeting of the morning was with Des Coyle. She walked into his office and sat down in the visitor's chair, stretching her long legs out in front of her.

'You look a lot better,' Des told her. 'You've got some colour in your cheeks again.'

'Thanks,' she said, although she was acutely aware that the colour in her cheeks was more to do with the embarrassment she still felt about her early-morning activities than anything else.

'Completely recovered?' he asked.

'Of course,' she replied. 'It wasn't all that bad, Des. I should have taken the time off earlier, that's all.'

Des leaned back in his seat. 'You work hard,' he said.

'You pay me to work hard,' said Alix. 'And I try to do my best.'

'I'm sure you do.'

She was suddenly aware of an edge in his voice. 'Is everything all right?' she asked.

'Why wouldn't it be?'

'Because I know you,' she told him. 'And it sounds to me like you have something to say to me and you're not quite sure how to say it.'

Des sat up straight. 'Why don't you beat about the bush?' he complained. 'Why do you always have to come to the point so quickly?'

'Beating about the bush just wastes time,' said Alix. 'What's the matter?' She kept her eyes focused on his face, something she knew made him feel awkward.

'I was chatting to Dave while you were out,' said Des cautiously. 'He tells me that there have been some problems in the dealing room lately.'

'Problems?' Alix stared at him. 'What sort of problems?'

Des shrugged. 'Between you and young Gavin Donnelly.'

'Oh, for heaven's sake!' Alix looked at him in disgust. 'Gavin Donnelly is an ambitious young bloke who wants to barge his way to the top. Fine, I can understand his point of view. But it's my job to run the dealing room in the best and most profitable way possible. And letting Gavin do exactly what he wants all the time doesn't achieve that objective.'

'Dave says that you won't listen to Gavin.'

'Rubbish,' Alix snorted.

'He says that you resent him.'

'Give me a break!' Alix sighed. 'I don't resent him, Des. I just want to keep him under control, that's all.'

'What about the Anatronics account?' asked Des. 'What's the problem there?'

'There's no problem,' said Alix. 'It's an account that I put a lot of work into but Gavin did the first trade. And he wants to keep looking after it. I just haven't allocated it to him, that's all.'

'Why?'

'Do you know, Des, I'm not certain,' answered Alix slowly. 'Maybe it's because I'm not sure he'll deal with it in the best possible way.'

'But he gets on well with the finance guy – what's his name?'

'Matt Connery,' said Alix.

'Exactly. Connery. He invited Connery to the pro-am in Portmarnock and they had a great time.'

'I'm glad,' said Alix.

'So if he's prepared to put the time in entertaining this guy, why shouldn't he get any of the rewards?'

'I never said he wouldn't get any rewards,' said Alix. 'I just said I haven't allocated him the account yet. I might. I might not.'

'It's not like you to be undecided,' said Des.

'I'm not undecided,' said Alix. 'Anyway, I'm meeting Mr Connery for lunch today. He's invited me to a showing of their latest movie.'

'Oh.' Des looked slightly abashed.

'So, don't worry, Des. We have the account well covered and it shouldn't matter to you whether Gavin or I talk to Matt

Connery because either of us is perfectly capable of dealing with the business.'

'Sure,' said Des hastily. 'I just wanted to make certain that everything was OK, that's all.'

'Anything else bothering you?' asked Alix.

Des sighed. He'd wanted to bring up the subject of a possible transfer to Paris for Alix but he didn't feel that this was the most appropriate time. He'd given Guy Decourcelle a call while Alix was out sick and Guy had been quite positive about the idea. 'We can use a girl like Alix,' he'd said enthusiastically. 'There are plenty of areas where her experience would be a tremendous asset.'

Des had told Guy that he'd have a chat with Alix, see how she felt about the whole idea. He couldn't imagine she'd feel anything but elated at the idea of working in Paris. Particularly since she'd been dumped by her boyfriend.

Dave Bryant had told him about that the previous evening when they'd bumped into each other in the car park. As far as Des was concerned, Paul's departure explained a lot. It explained Alix collapsing at the meeting with Brian Nicholls. It explained her absences from work. It explained the slightly distracted air that she'd had at the last few meetings. Des knew that women fell to pieces whenever their relationships broke up. It was the way they were. And Alix, despite her efficiency and her desire to be the best dealer in the world, was still a woman who'd been dumped by her boyfriend. She'd be better off working somewhere else for a while. But he wasn't going to suggest it today. He had a feeling that she might hit him if he did.

Alix knew that there was still something bothering Des. She could see it in his eyes and in the false cheerfulness that he showed throughout the rest of the meeting. She knew that it was something to do with the dealing room. She just didn't know what. What she did know was that she was going to kill Dave Bryant. Going behind her back to Des like that! Just as she'd anticipated he might. They were so bloody predictable, she thought angrily, and so bloody male!

✎

Her next meeting was with Linda, one of the bank's accountants. They went thought the profit numbers for the first half of the year and Alix's estimates for the second half.

'I hear you were sick,' said Linda when they'd finally finished going through the accounts. 'Keeled over in the boardroom.'

'I'm never going to live that down,' sighed Alix. 'No matter what I do in the bank now, the defining moment of my career will be collapsing in front of Des.'

'Eileen tells me that he was white as a sheet when he came rushing out of the room looking for her.' Linda chuckled. 'I bet he hadn't a clue what to do.'

'It was more embarrassing than anything else,' said Alix. 'He was embarrassed, I was embarrassed and I'm sure Brian Nicholls will never deal with us again!'

'He signed the facility letter,' said Linda practically.

'That's true.' Alix smiled then yawned.

'How's Paul?' asked Linda idly as she closed the folders on her desk.

Alix glanced at her. Linda wasn't even looking at her, had asked the question casually, with no ulterior motive.

'We're not together right now,' said Alix.

'Oh?' Linda looked up from the folders. 'I'm sorry, Alix. I didn't realise.'

Alix shrugged. 'It doesn't matter.'

'But you were living with him for ages, weren't you?'

'Three years,' said Alix.

Linda smiled sympathetically. 'Plenty more fish in the sea.'

'Right,' said Alix.

'No point in settling down with one person too soon,' said Linda brightly.

'Absolutely,' said Alix. 'How about you and Michael Devlin?'

'Still together,' Linda told her. 'Just about.'

'Really? Or are you saying that to make me feel better?'

Linda laughed. 'No. We fight like cats and dogs. But I like it really.'

'And you've no plans to settle down and have kids?'

'Not yet,' said Linda blithely, 'but I'm only twenty-five, Alix. I've buckets of time.'

Alix returned to her office and stared at the Reuters screen. She'd be thirty-three in less than three weeks. Turning thirty hadn't bothered her. Why did she now feel older when she'd always thought of herself as young?

～

The reception area of Anatronics Industries was crowded with people. A woman wearing a badge with her name, Maria, welcomed Alix and handed her a glass of champagne.

'I wasn't expecting to see quite so many people,' said Alix.

'It's a big event for us,' said Maria. 'This is the first piece we've done in Ireland. We're very happy about it.'

'Great,' said Alix. She looked around. 'Is Matt Connery here?'

'He's about somewhere,' Maria told her. 'But I haven't seen him in a while. He's probably with the banking blokes – they were chatting about money earlier.'

Alix smiled. 'I'm sure I'll find him.'

She wandered through the crush of people, sipping her champagne appreciatively. Alix liked champagne. Especially Moet. She stood beside one of the large windows and gazed at the cars and trucks whizzing along the motorway. It would be interesting to work in a manufacturing company, she thought. It must be very satisfying to develop a product, produce it, sell it and make a profit. Sometimes financial services seemed very mundane in comparison.

'Alix Callaghan! How are you?' She turned to see Thomas Hewitt, who'd once worked for Europa Bank but had left to join one of their competitors the previous year.

'Thomas. Nice to see you.' She smiled at him.

'I didn't expect to see you here,' said Thomas. 'I thought John Collins might be, since we did a joint facility for Anatronics.'

'Maybe he is.' Alix glanced around. 'Although he didn't mention it to me.'

'Much nicer to see you,' said Thomas. 'Are you keeping well?'

'Yes, thanks,' she said. 'And you? How are Evelyn and the kids?'

'Oh fine,' Thomas told her. 'Actually, Alix, we're expecting number three any day now.'

'You're not!' She looked at him in surprise. 'I thought Evelyn said that she wasn't going to have any more.'

'You know women.' He sighed. 'As soon as Greta started in

341

Montessori, Evelyn came over all broody again.' He laughed. 'I didn't mind, actually. I love the kids.'

'Give her my regards,' said Alix.

'Of course,' Thomas said. 'What about you, Alix. Any news?'

'What sort of news?'

'You know. Wedding bells, that kind of thing.'

'Not at all,' she said firmly. 'I'm not that kind of girl.'

'Not what kind of girl?' Matt Connery appeared at Thomas's shoulder and looked from Alix to Thomas. 'Welcome, by the way,' he said. 'Sorry I didn't get to you earlier but more people came than we thought.'

'Good turn-out,' said Thomas.

'Yes.' Matt looked pleased. 'Do you two know each other? I thought rival bankers would spit at each other or something.'

Alix smiled. 'You have the completely wrong impression of financial people,' she told him. 'And Thomas and I are old friends.'

'Ah,' said Matt. 'So what kind of girl are you, Alix?'

'Pardon?'

'As I arrived you were saying you weren't that kind of girl. What kind of girl are you?'

'A very ordinary kind,' she said, 'who has to go to the ladies' room and freshen up.' She handed her empty champagne glass to a waiter who was hovering nearby. 'If you'll excuse me, gentlemen.' She strode across the room, leaving Matt and Thomas together.

'I like her,' said Thomas. 'I used to work in Europa. Lots of the dealers had no real time for what went on in credit, but Alix was always interested. She was one of the most helpful people I knew.'

'I like her too,' said Matt, 'although I don't seem to be able to have a conversation with her for more than ten seconds at a time.'

Thomas looked at him speculatively. 'And what conversation would you like to have?' he asked.

Matt grinned. 'Keep your filthy thoughts to yourself, Hewitt. My motives are entirely pure.'

'Oh really?' Thomas raised an eyebrow. 'I'm not sure how successful you'll be if you're interested in her. She's been living with some bloke for a few years.'

'So I believe,' said Matt. 'Still, you never know.'

'He's a journalist,' Thomas told him. 'A bit pretentious, like most of them. He wrote some awful guff about Alix in one of the business magazines. She really struggled with her credibility for months afterwards. Everyone in the bank gave her such a hard time.'

'Why?' asked Matt.

'Oh, it was all about how good-looking she was and how wonderful and how talented.' Thomas laughed. 'And, of course, by the time it was published they were actually living together. So they gave her an even worse time. Didn't bother her, though. She toughed it out.'

'She's tough all right,' said Matt.

'Heart of gold, though,' Thomas told him. 'And, according to her boyfriend, she's a wow between the sheets.'

❧

Alix undid her hair and brushed it. She peered at it in the mirror. Definitely more grey again. It seemed to reappear with indecent haste. She'd colour it later in the week with the colour she'd bought while in the chemist to pick up vitamins. She was trying to take Geraldine O'Neill's advice and look after herself more but she kept forgetting to take the vitamins. She repinned her hair at the back of her head. They grey wasn't really noticeable. Then she did her lipstick and sprayed herself with Tommy Girl. Though I should probably be wearing a more mature perfume, she told herself. As befits my elderly creaking body. She fastened up the jacket of her maroon silk suit and walked back into the room.

Michael Hollis, the director who'd been at the presentation she'd done for Anatronics, was giving a speech. Alix listened idly as she leaned against the wall. She glanced at her watch. She was feeling tired and very slightly light-headed from the champagne. She hoped that Michael wouldn't talk for too long.

Fortunately he didn't. He invited them in to see the movie, which lasted half an hour. Alix thought it was very clever and she could see how it would achieve Michael's objective of being both educational and entertaining for its target six- to eight-year-old audience.

When the movie was finished, they were ushered into another room where a buffet lunch was being served. Alix was starving. She hadn't eaten since lunchtime the previous day. She hadn't felt like eating last night and of course she'd skipped breakfast in her ridiculous flight across the city to Malahide this morning.

What was going through your head? she asked herself as she queued up for some chicken fricassee. Did you actually want to see Paul? Or Sabine? And do you want to see Dad? The thought came into her head before she could stop it. She tried to push it away but she couldn't. Right now she could remember him again. More clearly than ever before. Images hurtled into her head. Of him picking her up after she'd fallen from the swing in the back garden. Dusting the dirt from her knee and kissing her on the forehead. 'You're OK, my little angel,' he said. 'Daddy loves you.'

She closed her eyes. It was too real. Too close.

'Alix?'

She opened her eyes again. Matt Connery stood beside her, a look of concern on his face.

'Are you all right?' he asked.

'Yes,' she said hurriedly. 'I'm fine.'

'You looked as though something had upset you,' said Matt.

'Not at all,' she told him.

'I thought perhaps you were feeling unwell again.'

'Everyone keeps going on and on about my so-called illness,' she said impatiently. 'I had a bug, that's all.' She handed her plate to the chef who piled it with rice and chicken.

'But you've regained your appetite.' Matt grinned as he looked at her plate. She laughed and he was pleased to see that it was a genuine laugh.

'You've probably told them to feed everyone up so they'll go away thinking nothing but nice thoughts about the company.'

'Maybe,' said Matt. 'I can't take the credit or otherwise. The organisation was nothing to do with me.' He led her to one of the small tables.

'The organisation was excellent.' She sat down. 'And so was the movie.'

He nodded. 'The guys here know what they're doing. All I have to do is to make sure that we keep the financing on an even keel and don't do anything stupid.'

'I won't let you do anything stupid,' said Alix.

'Thank you.' He smiled at her and held her gaze until she suddenly busied herself with her food.

'I should thank you again myself,' she said without looking up.

'Oh?'

'For the flowers. You really shouldn't have done that, you know.'

'I know.'

She glanced up at him.

'It was crass of me really. I don't know why I did it. It must have been embarrassing for you.'

'Embarrassing?'

'I know that you live with someone. I didn't think of that possibility. I'm sorry.'

'It's OK,' she said. She smiled faintly at him. 'Actually, I thought you were married.'

'Married!' He looked at her in astonishment. 'Why on earth would you think that?'

'It was such a – a – gesture,' she said. 'It's the kind of thing a guy who's trying to seduce a woman does.'

'Well, yes, maybe,' admitted Matt. 'But it doesn't mean he has to be married.'

'It's like you've done it before,' she said.

'Bloody hell.' He put down his fork. 'You really see the worst in me, don't you?'

'Not at all,' she said cheerfully. 'I'm just covering all the angles.'

'And have you been living with this guy for long?' Matt picked up his fork again.

'Why?'

'Curiosity,' he said.

'None of your business,' she responded.

'I guess not.'

'Absolutely not.'

'I like you,' he said and smiled at her.

Their eyes met and Alix was the first to look away.

She liked him too. Sitting at the table chatting to him she realised that he was an interesting person to talk to. He'd only been with Anatronics a few months. Before that he'd worked in the States and in Malaysia.

'I was lucky,' he told her. 'When the Asian economy went down the toilet I thought I might have to take any job that came along. But then our parent company in the US offered me something in California and off I went.'

'Must be nice to have worked in a number of different places,' she said.

'Yes. Good experience. But eventually you want to come home.'

'Why?' she asked.

'I don't know.' He considered the question. 'Roots maybe? I've no idea. But I was delighted to have the chance to get home.'

'And you don't miss California or Malaysia?'

He shook his head. 'Not in the slightest.'

Her mobile rang and she jumped. Matt turned away while she took the call.

'You asked me to call if you weren't back by half three,' said Jenny. 'It's half three now. Are you having a good time?'

'It's fine,' said Alix.

'Are you coming back?'

'I have to,' Alix told her. 'I'm supposed to meet that guy from Dresdner Bank at half four.'

'What guy from Dresdner Bank?' asked Jenny. 'You haven't got an appointment in your diary. Oh!' she said. 'There's someone with you.'

'Got it in one, Ms Smith,' said Alix. 'I'll be back shortly.' She ended the call and put the phone back in her bag. 'I've got to go,' she told Matt.

'That's a pity,' he said. 'I was enjoying our conversation.'

'So was I,' said Alix. She stood up. 'But I really must be off.'

'Let me see you to the lift,' said Matt.

'It was a very enjoyable lunch,' she said as the lift doors opened. 'And anything we can do to help, just let us know.'

'Sure.'

The doors began to close and Matt suddenly pressed the button again. Alix looked at him in surprise as he got into the lift beside her.

'I could do with some fresh air,' he said. 'I'll see you to your car. You're OK to drive, aren't you? Or would you prefer me to order you a cab?'

Alix shook her head. 'I had a glass of champagne when I arrived, that's all.' She yawned and put her hand over her mouth. 'Oh, I'm sorry.'

'Late night last night?' asked Matt.

'Late enough.'

You'll always be my best little girl. Her father had held her over his head. Why could she suddenly remember all this stuff when she'd never been able to remember it before? And she'd only been three years old. It wasn't as though people remembered much of their life at the age of three.

The lift stopped at the ground floor and Matt followed her out.

'Goodbye, Matt.' She held out her hand.

'Goodbye.' His handshake was firm and confident.

'Don't forget to call us with your next trade,' she said.

'I won't. But will I be dealing with you or with Gavin?'

'Does it matter?' she asked.

'I suppose not,' said Matt. 'He's efficient. And I enjoyed myself out in Portmarnock.'

Alix nodded. 'I believe it was a good day.'

'Yes, it was,' said Matt.

'I'm glad you enjoyed it.' She unlocked the car.

'Drive carefully,' said Matt.

'I will.' She got into the car and drove swiftly away.

Matt watched as she indicated and moved onto the main road. He rubbed his chin thoughtfully. What was it about the girl that attracted him so much? Her looks? Her brains? The fact that she was living with someone else?

Forget about her, he told himself. It's not worth the grief.

Attractive and uncomplicated, thought Alix. But I'm not interested.

Chapter 25

For the first time in weeks, Alix didn't feel tired when she woke up the following morning. She got out of bed as soon as she awoke and pulled open the bedroom curtains. The sky was clear blue and cloudless, marred only by the long white streak from a plane thirty thousand feet higher. She stood at the window and wondered where the passengers in the plane were going. Somewhere nice, she hoped. Not somewhere boring and businesslike. Somewhere people could have fun.

She needed to have fun again. She'd go to the shooting club which was always fun. When Paul had lived with her she used to go most Saturday mornings. She missed the discipline. And she felt, very strongly, that she needed some discipline in her life right now.

She dressed in a pair of loose cotton trousers and pulled on her long-sleeved T-shirt followed by a sweatshirt. Even on the warmest days it could be cold at the shooting club, located on the north-facing side of the mountains. She pulled her hair back from her face and into a tight plait so that she wouldn't be distracted by stray wisps floating into her line of vision. Right, she thought, ready for the fray.

There were a lot of cars already at the shooting club grounds. A surprising number, thought Alix as she locked the BMW and walked towards the clubhouse. There must be a competition on. Shit, she thought. If there was a competition she might not get the opportunity to shoot. And now that she was here, she desperately wanted to shoot.

'Hi, Niall,' she said as she walked into the small room that was the clubhouse. 'How are things?'

'Alix!' He smiled at her. 'I thought you'd given up.'

'I've been busy.'

'You said that the last time you were here. You mentioned trips to Paris and London and other exotic destinations.'

'London, exotic?' She raised an eyebrow.

'Maybe not exotic,' he conceded. 'But different.'

'You're right, though,' she said. 'I've been away quite a bit and there's been lots of things going on. So I haven't had the time to be here. Sorry.'

'I don't mind,' said Niall. 'But you'll be a bit rusty for this morning.'

'I didn't realise there was a competition today,' she said.

'But you'll enter for it?'

'Is there space for me to enter?'

'Of course. But I'd better warn you that Darren Sherlock is shooting so you'll have stiff competition.'

She shrugged. 'It's not the winning, it's the taking part.'

'Oh, Alix!' Niall laughed. 'You know quite well that as far as you're concerned, it's always been the winning!'

He was right, of course. Alix collected her ammunition and walked outside. Winning was important. What was the point of competing if you didn't think you had a chance?

'Hi, Alix.' Darren stood beside her. 'Haven't seen you in a while.'

'Been busy,' she said laconically. 'I believe you're tipped to win today.'

He laughed. 'They always tip me to win. That's just to put the pressure on.'

'You won't be getting much pressure from me,' she told him.

'You should practise more,' said Darren.

She shook her head. 'I enjoy it and I want to win. But I can't afford the time.'

'Pity,' he said. 'You could be really good.'

'Bet you say that to all the girls,' she teased and Darren blushed.

Alix smiled as she watched him walk back to the clubhouse. She liked Darren; he was only nineteen but he was a skilled shooter. He wanted to compete in the Olympics one day.

She was one of the first to shoot. She pushed her earplugs into her ears, took up her prone position and sighted the paper target. She allowed her breathing to become slower and settle into a steady rhythm. Her mind was clear of everything except the target. The faces that had haunted her dreams over the past few weeks disappeared. There was nothing but herself and her rifle and the target.

Her first shot was high and to the left. She was surprised. She adjusted her sight. The first five shots didn't count as part of the competition. After that, she had five shots at each of four targets. The maximum score was 200. Her best ever was 196. She knew that there was no hope of beating Darren Sherlock today but she wanted to give him a run for his money. She kept her breathing slow and steady as she aimed at her first target.

She was shooting well, despite her lack of practice. When

she'd completed all four targets she estimated her score to be around 190. There were a couple of shots she wasn't sure about.

'How did you do?' asked Darren as she walked back to the clubhouse, removing the single point sling she used to help steady her aim.

'Your title is safe,' she told him. 'Unless you were out on the town last night.'

'I wish,' he said.

'How's Angela?'

Darren made a face. 'I haven't seen her in a few weeks. We've decided to cool it a bit, Alix.'

'Oh. I'm sorry to hear that.'

'No need.' He beamed at her. 'It was getting too involved, to be honest with you. She wanted to know where I was every minute of the day. It's kinda nice to be cut loose again.'

'I suppose it is,' said Alix.

She walked to the observation point to watch the other shooters. Why couldn't she think of how nice it was to be cut loose again? Why was it that the thought of Paul still had the power to hurt her so much? Why couldn't she just bloody well get over him?

'Dad!' She heard Darren call to his father who was also a member of the club.

'Hi, Darren. Have you shot yet?'

She looked round at them. Father and son stood beside each other, discussing the event, completely at ease in each other's company. Darren was laughing at something his father had said and the older man clapped his son on the back. Alix gritted her teeth. Fathers were a sensitive subject with her. She wasn't going to think about hers. She'd successfully kept him out of her mind all day. She wasn't going to allow him to invade her thoughts now.

Darren won the competition with a score of 198. Tony Leehy was second with 193. And Alix was third with 191.

'Are you coming for a drink?' asked Niall. 'We're going down the road for one.'

She shook her head. 'I don't think so. I've things to do.'

'Are you sure you're OK, Alix?' he asked. 'You've seemed – oh, I don't know, unlike yourself all day.'

'What am I supposed to be like?' she asked lightly.

'I don't know,' admitted Niall.

'Your imagination is getting the better of you,' she said. 'I'm fine. I just don't have time to go for a drink, that's all.'

'No problem,' said Niall easily. 'Hope you'll start dropping by more often again.'

'I will,' said Alix. 'I had a good time today.'

⁓

After the noise at the shooting club, her apartment seemed unnaturally quiet. I should have gone for a drink with them, thought Alix, as she leafed through the *Irish Times*. I'm becoming completely anti-social.

The phone rang and she jumped.

'Hello,' she said.

'Hi, Alix. How are you?'

'I'm fine, Wyn.' Alix put the paper to one side. 'And you?'

'I'm OK. I rang earlier but you didn't answer.'

'Sorry,' said Alix. 'I forgot to switch the machine on.'

'I was worried about you.'

'Worried?'

'On your own. I thought maybe – well, I don't know what I thought really.'

'Oh, Wyn, don't be such an idiot,' said Alix crisply. 'What on earth did you think I was doing?'

'I just thought you might be upset.'

'Well, I'm not,' said Alix. 'Are you?'

'Of course I am,' said Wyn. 'I don't understand you, Alix. You seem to shrug off life's great events as though they mean absolutely nothing.'

'What the hell are you talking about?' demanded Alix.

'Things like Dad. Things like Paul. Nothing seems to bother you.'

Alix almost laughed out loud. Just as well my darling sister didn't see me running down Paul's driveway and diving into my car after banging on his door and setting off his alarm, she thought. 'Of course things bother me,' she told Wyn. 'I just get over them quicker.' She felt as though she should cross her fingers at the lie.

'I don't know how you can sweep Dad out of your life so easily,' said Wyn.

'As easily as he did it to us,' Alix told her. 'Nothing to do with him is ever going to bother me.'

'But what about Imogen and Kate?'

'What about them?' asked Alix. 'They won't interfere with me and I won't interfere with them. Simple.'

Wyn sighed. 'I can't just put it to the back of my mind, Alix.'

'Don't,' said Alix. 'Just don't complain because I can.'

'We're different, I suppose.'

'Yes,' said Alix. 'And it's a good thing.'

355

'There was something else I wanted to ask you,' said Wyn.

Alix grimaced. She wasn't comfortable with this conversation. 'What?' she asked.

'Any chance you could drop over tonight and baby-sit?'

'Sneakily done, Wyn Mitchell,' Alix laughed. 'You ring up and pretend to be all concern for me when in reality you only want to know if I'll be fit enough to look after your kids!'

'It's not like that,' protested Wyn.

'Oh, isn't it?' Alix chuckled. 'But, yes, I'll come over. Seven o'clock be OK?'

'Perfect,' said Wyn with relief.

'See you then.' Alix replaced the receiver and picked up the paper again.

When she'd finished both the Simplex and Crosaire crosswords she went into the bathroom to investigate the hair colour she'd bought. It was an auburn shade, close enough to her own. She opened the box and read the instructions. Alix had always liked messing with paints when she was a child. She put colouring her hair into the same category – plenty of messing around with tubes and bottles. She hoped that they were telling the truth when they said that the eventual colour of her hair was nothing like the purple mess on top of her head now. She looked at her watch and timed twenty minutes.

The phone rang with a minute to go.

'Bugger,' she said out loud as she wiped some colour off her ear and picked up the receiver. 'Hello.'

'Hi, Alix.'

She felt herself freeze on the spot. She said nothing.

'Alix? Are you there?'

'Yes, yes. I'm here. How are you, Paul?'

'Great,' he said cheerfully. 'And you?'

'I'm great too.'

'Good to hear,' he said.

She waited for him. She wanted to talk, to gabble at him, to find out why he'd called. But she waited.

'You're probably wondering why I phoned,' said Paul.

'Yes,' she said.

'I hope you don't mind.'

'Why should I mind?'

'It's just that I was wondering if you'd do me a favour.'

'A favour?' she repeated.

'I'd really appreciate it,' he said. 'And it's not as though you haven't done it before?'

'Done what?' she asked suspiciously.

'Been on TV.'

'On TV? You want me to go on TV?'

'It's a programme about women who've made it,' said Paul. 'It's right up your street, Alix, and you know you're good at interviews.'

'Women who've made what?' she asked acidly.

'You see, that's exactly the kind of thing they're looking for,' said Paul. 'Wit, sarcasm, a bit of a putdown with a sense of warmth.'

'A sense of warmth!'

'Oh, be a sport, Alix. Say you'll do it.'

'What sort of format is it?' she asked. 'What do they want to talk about?'

'Business,' explained Paul. 'The series is about women in business, or any successful women. The idea is to try to go for women who aren't in traditional roles but who are successful in more male-dominated areas. Like finance. Or engineering.

357

We've nabbed a wonderful engineer named Anastasia Moran. Does anything sound less like an engineer to you than someone called Anastasia? And we've got a woman who runs a trucking company and used to drive articulated lorries, plus a woman who's a flying instructor. So it's not boring old suits, Alix, these are good women.'

'In fact, I'm the boring suit,' she said.

'Well, yes, I suppose so.'

'Thank you for those words of comfort.'

'So what do you think? Will you do it?'

'What show?' she asked.

'New show. Twenty-minute interviews. Different one each time,' he said. 'Not me this time, unfortunately. Haven't quite managed to get myself in front of the camera yet.'

'If that's what you want, I'm sure you will,' said Alix dryly.

'Maybe,' said Paul. 'To tell you the truth, I'm not sure what I want.'

Was he happy? she wanted to ask him. He sounded happy about work. But he was asking for a favour from her when she was sure he'd rather not. Was he happy at home? Or had his dreams of domestic bliss begun to evaporate? Did he suddenly realise that work could be even more fulfilling?

'When?' she asked.

'Fairly soon,' he said. 'We'll broadcast before the end of the year.'

'And the questions are all about work?'

'About what it's like,' Paul told her. 'You know, dealing with macho blokes all the time. Putting up with the harassment.'

'I've never been harassed,' she told him. 'Unless it was by you, looking for something to eat.'

He laughed. 'People would be afraid to harass you,' he said. 'I never did, Alix. I was far too scared.'

'I don't believe that for a moment,' she said. 'OK, I'll do your interview thing. Where do they want to do it?'

'I'm not sure,' said Paul. 'I'll get back to you on that.'

'OK.'

'Alix – thank you.'

'Anytime,' she said.

She was glad he'd asked her. He could have suggested Sabine as a successful arty, interior design sort of type, but obviously she wasn't successful enough. So it was all very well for her to wander around the house in Malahide looking blonde and babyish and pretty but that wasn't much good to Paul when he was putting together a successful women show. He'd come to her. He'd come back to her. She smiled and leaned back in the chair. Then she remembered the hair colour. She leaped out and scrubbed at the upholstery with a tissue. It was an interesting shade of purple and orange.

'Shit!' She ran into the bathroom. Talking to Paul, thinking about him afterwards had knocked her schedule out of the window. Her hair would be some ridiculous shade by the time she'd rinsed off the colour and dried it.

But it was OK. A little more purple than she'd expected, perhaps, but all of the grey was successfully covered which was the main thing. And it was gleaming under the high-intensity bathroom light. She looked good, she thought. Good and healthy and OK with her life. Maybe things were finally getting better again.

❧

Wyn opened the door before Alix rang the bell. She looked tired, thought Alix, even though she was dressed up and wearing more make-up than usual.

'Saw the car pull up,' explained Wyn.

'Are you going anywhere nice?' Alix hung her linen jacket on the coat stand.

'Terry is taking me to dinner,' said Wyn as she led Alix into the kitchen. 'I think he feels it would be good for me to get out.' She laughed shortly. 'As though I'm going to stay indoors and never move again.'

'He probably thinks that if you're out and about you won't be brooding on the John and Carrie situation,' said Alix.

'Probably.' Wyn sat on a stool at the breakfast bar. 'But I honestly don't feel like it, Alix. He doesn't have to drag me out like this. I know he's probably worried because I was so upset – and I'm still upset – but he's carrying it a bit far.'

'He worries about you.' Alix sat beside her. 'And I think it's nice that he does.'

'Have you spoken to Carrie?'

Alix shook her head. 'I thought about ringing but I wasn't sure what to say. I don't want to meet him and I couldn't think of anything else to talk to her about. Have you?'

'Of course,' said Wyn. 'But I call her a lot more than you anyway, Alix. She's fine.'

'I assumed she *was* fine,' said Alix. 'After all, she's known everything all along. It's only you and me who've been taken for idiots.'

'I said that to her.' Wyn sighed. 'I got quite ratty with her. Said that she should have told us everything before now. That it was unfair to keep it from us.'

'And she said?'

360

'That she was trying to protect us.'

'What utter bullshit.' Alix slapped her hand on the counter. 'Protect us from what?'

'Feeling hurt, I suppose.'

'And she thinks this way is better? Give me a break.' Alix looked disgusted.

'It wasn't her fault,' said Wyn forcefully.

'I know. I know. And I'm not blaming her or anything like that. But I'm not going to fall in with her wish that we can all bury the hatchet.'

'Do you think that's what she wants?'

'I haven't a clue,' said Alix. 'But I think she feels bad about not telling us everything before now. So she wants us to do something she'll feel better about.'

'But I can't see her feeling better about us meeting Dad.'

Alix shrugged. 'You know her better than I do, Wyn. You've always been closer to her. You figure it out.'

Wyn said nothing.

'Do you still want to meet him?' asked Alix eventually.

'I think we have to,' said Wyn. 'I think we owe it to ourselves.'

'Go ahead,' Alix said. 'I don't mind whether you see him or not. But I won't. And that's final.'

'Why?'

'I just won't,' said Alix obstinately. 'I've no interest in seeing him either to please Carrie or to please you.'

'I think you're making a mistake,' said Wyn.

'I don't,' Alix said.

⌣

Terry brought Wyn to Jacob's Ladder for dinner. They sat near the window and watched the crowds of people bustle through the city streets.

'She won't meet him,' said Wyn suddenly.

Terry replaced his glass of Beaune on the table. 'Why?'

'She says she's not interested in meeting him.'

'In that case there's nothing you can do about it, Wyn.'

'But she's his daughter. He's our father! Surely that means something.'

'Doesn't have to,' said Terry.

'It does to me.' Wyn's eyes were bright.

'You can't make her meet him,' Terry told her. 'And you shouldn't try.'

'I know.' Wyn sighed. 'I just think it would be the right thing to do.'

'Maybe. Maybe not.' Terry reached over and took her hand. 'People have to make up their own minds, Wyn. And what's right for you might not be right for your sister.'

'I worry about her,' said Wyn.

'For heaven's sake! What do you need to worry about Alix for?'

'Because she's on her own. Because she's lonely. Because she has a tough job and sometimes I think she takes on too much.'

'What about Paul?'

Wyn shook her head. 'I can't see anything coming of that. He's living with the French tart now.'

'Wyn!'

'Come on,' said Wyn angrily, 'they got together on a business trip to Paris. That French girl probably threw herself at him.'

362

'That's a bit judgemental, don't you think?'

Wyn shook her head. 'The French think differently about things.'

'Really and truly, Wyn, you're getting very insular. That's completely untrue. This French girl was no more likely to throw herself at him than any Irish girl. Or American. Or English. It's more likely that, bored out of his mind listening to Alix gibber on about swaps and options, he threw himself at the French girl. What's her name?'

'Sabine,' Wyn snorted.

'If the relationship was OK it wouldn't matter how many Sabines were in the room,' said Terry. 'A whole army of them could walk in here right now and I wouldn't take my eyes off you.'

'Oh, Terry.' Wyn smiled at him.

'Don't worry about everything so much,' he said. 'You decide what you want to do about meeting your Dad. Let Carrie solve Carrie's problems. Let Alix make her own decisions. Don't take it all on yourself.'

'You're right.' Wyn began to butter her bread roll. 'I can't help it sometimes.'

'You know, you and Alix are really very alike,' said Terry thoughtfully. 'Both of you have very set ideas about what you want from life. And both of you want things to go as you plan them.'

'I'm not as bad as Alix!' Wyn looked at her husband in horror and he laughed.

'No.' He leaned across and kissed her on the forehead. 'You're unique, Wyn. And I love you.'

⌢

Alix sat in the children's bedroom and read Enid Blyton to Aoife and Nessa. She wished the two girls would go asleep. But they'd been full of energy, running around the house, playing hide and seek and fighting with each other over the slightest thing. And when she'd finally got them to bed they insisted on a story. And another. And another. Now, finally, Nessa's eyes were closed although Aoife was struggling to stay awake.

Were we like that? wondered Alix. Did we scream and fight and give Carrie all sorts of grief? She couldn't remember. She remembered Carrie shouting at her occasionally. She remembered giving Wyn a black eye (justified at the time because Wyn had robbed her Fuzzy Felt game). But she didn't remember running out of the house when bedtime came around, or hiding behind the sofa and refusing to come out or clutching a chair and forcing her mother to prise her fingers loose one by one.

But, she thought, as Aoife finally closed her eyes, they probably had done all those things. Time just changed your perspective on them.

Chapter 26

There was something comforting about the fact that it was a busy day in the dealing room and that she was about to have a row with Gavin Donnelly. The last few days had been far too full of emotional stuff for Alix's liking. Every time she tried to push the situation about her father to the back of her mind, Wyn would phone begging her to meet him. And when she wasn't wrestling with that particular dilemma, she kept musing about Paul and the TV interview.

She couldn't help hoping that he'd asked her to do it so that he could get closer to her again. She tried to tell herself that she was mistaken, but she didn't think so. His tone had been so different when he talked to her, friendly and caring rather than simply polite. She felt certain that she could get him back if she really wanted to. She just needed the right set of circumstances.

But neither John nor Paul was her foremost thought right now. She had to deal with the fact that Gavin had gone to lunch with Niall Matthews without booking a trade. And that he hadn't arrived back until three o'clock. And that nobody had known about the trade until he returned in high good humour – having consumed a bottle of Cabernet Sauvignon. And, worst of all, that because Gavin hadn't booked the trade nobody knew that they were long dollars and Jenny had bought more.

Very unusually, this hadn't cost them any money. Normally if a trade was booked incorrectly or somehow overlooked, they always lost money on the position. But foreign exchange markets had been quiet and the dollar stable, so it hadn't mattered.

That, as Alix said sharply to Gavin, was hardly the point.

'I've said I'm sorry,' said Gavin stubbornly. 'And I am. But anyone could have made that mistake.'

'No they couldn't,' retorted Alix. 'You're the only one who's bloody careless about inputting your deals. When was the last time anyone just "forgot" to put one in?'

Gavin sighed. 'Cut me a bit of slack here, Alix. I work hard. I contribute. No need to treat me like a child.'

'I'm not treating you like a child,' she said. 'I'm merely pointing out that if everyone walked off without checking what they'd done we'd lose a fortune.'

'But, hey, we didn't lose anything, did we?' He beamed at her. 'So we got away with it. Lucky, I know, but better to be born lucky than smart, don't you think?'

She gritted her teeth. 'Gavin, I have to tell you that your attitude is getting right up my nose. And not only that, it's bloody unprofessional. Now, I'm telling you that I want you to shape up, take more care, cut back on the boozy lunches and the afternoon golf outings and get your act together.'

'Des told me to take clients golfing,' said Gavin truculently.

'Perhaps he did,' said Alix. 'And I'm telling you to cut back.'

'How do you think he'll feel about that?' asked Gavin.

'Gavin, I don't give a fuck how he feels,' said Alix. 'I'm your boss and I'm telling you what I want. OK?'

He shrugged. 'Suit yourself.'

'I will,' she said. She got up and walked to the door. 'I'll be in the accounts department if you're looking for me.'

She walked out of the dealing room and exhaled slowly as she closed the door behind her. She was shaking. That little shit, she thought. 'Des told me to take clients golfing.' I'll kill him. I'll kill him and I'll kill Des and I'll fucking kill Dave Bryant too who's probably laughing his head off right now.

She walked down the corridor and into the ladies'. She needed to cool down for a minute. She hated having to reprimand anyone. She did it when she had to, but it left her feeling drained afterwards. Maybe, she thought, this is why men are supposed to be better at the cut and thrust of office politics. They don't mind yelling at each other.

When she'd calmed down she went to see Linda Crossan. The accountant was looking through a bundle of reports when Alix walked into her office.

'Hi.' Linda pushed the papers to one side. 'What can I do for you?'

'Nothing,' said Alix. 'I just came for a spot of refuge.'

'Refuge?'

Alix sighed. 'I needed some peace and quiet. I've had to yell at Gavin Donnelly for not inputting a trade and I couldn't stay there.'

'You don't like him, do you?' asked Linda.

'It's not a question of liking or disliking,' replied Alix. 'And what makes you think I don't like him?'

'Common knowledge,' said Linda.

'Common knowledge?'

'Yes.' The other girl shrugged. 'You know how people talk. The word is that you and Gavin don't get on.'

'And why aren't we supposed to get on?' asked Alix.

'Because he's supposed to be so brilliant.' Linda grinned at her.

'For God's sake!'

'So they say,' said Linda.

'He's good, I'll grant him that. But brilliant? Where did the word get around that he's brilliant?'

'I don't know,' said Linda. 'He probably spread it himself. But I've heard the guys in settlements say so.'

'What the fuck would they know?' Alix rubbed her forehead.

'Getting to you?' asked Linda sympathetically.

'A bit.' Alix sighed. 'Sometimes I don't know why I put myself through all this, Linda. Sometimes I just think it would be so nice not to have to worry about the office politics and hanging on to my job and all of the other shit.'

'And what would you do instead?' asked Linda. 'I can't visualise you as the stay-at-home type.'

'Maybe I can become the stay-at-home type,' said Alix.

'At least you don't have to worry about hanging on to your job,' said Linda. 'Your profits were good last month.'

'Not the best,' said Alix.

'They don't have to be the best,' Linda told her. 'They just have to be on target.'

～

She met Des Coyle as she walked along the corridor.

'Hi, Alix.' He smiled at her.

'Hi, Des.'

'Making money?'

'Yes,' she said.

'Great.' He stood in front of her, blocking her.

'Did you want me?' she asked.

'Want you?'

'You look as though you want to ask me something,' she said.

'Oh. Well. Yes. Sort of.'

'Sort of?'

'Come into my office,' said Des.

She followed him into the office, her high heels sinking into the deep pile of the blue carpet. She sat down in the leather visitor's chair.

'So what's the problem?' she asked.

Des fiddled with the cap of his Mont Blanc fountain pen. 'I was talking to Guy Decourcelle the other day,' he told her. 'Guy thinks a lot of you.'

'Does he really?' she asked dryly.

'Well, yes, he does.' Des glanced up at her. 'He's very complimentary about you, Alix.'

'How nice,' she murmured.

'And he was telling me that they're looking for people in Paris.'

She sat upright in the chair. 'Oh?'

'Yes. They're looking for experienced people. Highly rated people.'

'And?'

'Your name was mentioned.'

'Was it?'

'Yes,' said Des. 'Absolutely. Guy asked me if we had any

talented people in the dealing room, and of course I said Alix Callaghan.'

'Really?'

'Yes. And he thought it'd be a great idea if you were in Paris.'

'Did he?'

'So I said to him that I'd ask you about it. After all, it's such a great opportunity.'

'To do what?' asked Alix.

Des stared at her. 'To work there. In the dealing room. In Paris.'

'As what?' asked Alix.

'Well, as a dealer, of course.'

'What title?'

'We didn't discuss titles,' Des told her.

'How senior a position?' asked Alix.

'Very senior,' said Des.

'Guy's job?' asked Alix

'I don't know,' said Des. 'I didn't ask. But he didn't imply—'

'So you don't think he's hiring for his job.'

Des looked at her uncertainly.

'Because it wouldn't make a lot of sense for me to go to Paris unless it was an upward move, would it?' she asked. 'Georges' job could be considered an upward move because he has about twenty people working for him. Guy's job would be an upward move because he's head of European Trading. But any other job would be a backward step for me, wouldn't it?'

'Don't be silly,' said Des. 'Paris is such a big organis-ation! Anywhere in their dealing room would be exciting, wouldn't it?'

'You think so?' asked Alix. 'Would I have staff of my own?'

'I – don't know,' said Des.

'If Guy was talking about it, surely you do know.'

'It was just something he mentioned in passing,' said Des.

'But you thought I'd be suitable for a job that you don't really know the description of? Is that it?' Alix's eyes were glinting dangerously.

'It's not like that,' said Des. 'I just thought that maybe you'd like a change. What with the upset about Paul and everything.'

'The upset about Paul,' said Alix slowly. 'What upset about Paul?'

Des looked uncomfortable. 'I heard that he's left you.'

The phone rang and startled both of them. Des answered it. 'I'll call her back in a couple of minutes, Eileen,' he said in response to his secretary's message. 'Thank you.'

'It's true that Paul and I aren't together any more,' said Alix. 'But that certainly doesn't mean that I want to run away to Paris.'

'It's not running away,' protested Des. 'It's just an opportunity to have a change of scenery.'

'Oh, I see,' said Alix. 'I didn't realise that. For a moment I thought you were trying to shift me out of my job.' She smiled sweetly at him. 'Sorry, Des. I misinterpreted your motives.'

'Of course, if you don't want to go—'

'Do you know, I don't think I do,' said Alix. 'I like it here too much.'

Des screwed his fountain pen back together. 'And how are you getting on with everyone?' he asked.

'With everyone?'

'Generally,' said Des.

'Fine,' Alix told him. 'Absolutely fine. Couldn't be better, in fact.'

'Great,' said Des. 'Great. Good.'

They sat in silence. Alix didn't take her eyes from his face. Finally Des stood up.

'I'd better – I was going to drop something up to John Collins,' he said. 'You probably have to get back to the desk.'

'Yes,' she said. 'But it was nice chatting to you, Des.'

'Good. Yes. You too,' he said.

Alix walked out of the room and up the stairs. Her heart was thumping in her chest. They wanted to get rid of her. They were plotting to get rid of her. She wouldn't let them. She wouldn't let anyone force her out of her job.

∽

'Alix, it's Paul for you.' Jenny raised her eyebrows inquiringly as she looked at her boss.

'Thanks,' said Alix calmly. She clicked into the line. 'Alix speaking.'

'You know, I always feel like you're about to spank me when you say that,' said Paul.

'Really?' asked Alix. 'I didn't realise.'

'It's a very provocative way to answer the phone.'

'You think so?'

'Sure do.'

'Well, not in my book it's not. What's the matter?'

'Nothing,' he said. 'I just wanted to say that the interview will probably be next week. How does that sound to you?'

'Sounds fine,' said Alix.

'Can they do it at the office?' asked Paul.

'Here? Oh, Paul, that's so embarrassing.'

'It won't be,' he said. 'It'll be simple.'

'I'm not convinced,' she told him.

'I'll get Colin Willis to give you a call,' said Paul. 'He'll sort everything out with you.'

'What have I let myself in for?' she asked.

'Nothing,' Paul promised her. 'It'll be a doddle, honestly, Alix.'

Jenny stared at her as she disconnected the call.

'What?' asked Alix. 'Why are you looking at me like that?'

'Well?' Jenny said. 'What did he want? Are you guys back together again?'

'Not exactly,' said Alix. 'But I think I'm in the driving seat right now.'

⌒

The dealing room was quiet. The others had gone home. Gavin had stayed the latest, intent, Alix thought, on being the last to leave. But she'd sat at her dealing desk, called clients and gone through piles of research until finally he got up and left. She smiled to herself as he walked out the door.

Gavin should be the one to go to Paris. That is, if Guy Decourcelle really did want anyone there. Alix was pretty sure that this was a plan dreamed up by Des because he knew that there was friction in the dealing room. She knew that the previous holder of her job – a guy called Tony O'Connell – had left after a bust-up with Des. She didn't know the rights and the wrongs of the situation, but she knew that Des could be tough when he wasn't on your side. She wondered exactly whose side he was on now.

The phone rang. She glanced at her watch. Not many people called the dealers at a quarter to seven in the evening.

'Alix Callaghan,' she said.

'Alix? How are you? It's Matt Connery.'

'Hi, Matt. What has you calling us so late?'

'It's early in New York,' he said.

'It's post-lunch in New York,' Alix told him. 'Did you want to do a dollar trade?'

'No,' said Matt. 'I wasn't sure you'd be still there.'

'Do you make a habit of calling the office when nobody's here?' asked Alix.

He laughed. 'No, I don't. Actually, I'm ringing to invite you to a function we've organised.'

'Another one?'

'I know. It sounds as though we do nothing else. But this was arranged months ago. I didn't think to ask you before – goodness knows why because it's right up your street, Alix.'

'Really? You're intriguing me.'

'It's a clay pigeon shoot,' said Matt triumphantly. 'On Saturday. It should be great fun and I thought you might enjoy it.'

'Clays aren't really my thing,' Alix told him. 'I'm more a paper person myself.'

'Paper?'

'Targets,' she explained. 'Clays are completely different.'

'But you'd still enjoy it?'

'I – I suppose so.'

'You'll join us then?'

Gavin Donnelly would have a breakdown, she thought.

She'd mention it tomorrow. Nonchalantly. Bring it ever so casually into conversation. He'd be fuming. She grinned. 'OK, I'd love to.'

'Great!'

'What time and where?' asked Alix.

'It's near the Glen of the Downs,' said Matt. 'But we've organised transport.'

'Oh, it's OK, I'll drive,' Alix told him.

'Don't do that,' said Matt. 'We're bringing people down by helicopter.'

'What? How many people are going?'

'About twenty,' said Matt. 'We've got choppers departing from the Point Depot and Clonskeagh. The Point is probably nearest to you.'

'You're some flash bastards,' Alix laughed.

'We've made a lot of money from the animated film,' Matt told her. 'This was organised before then but it's turned into a celebration. And we think that it's good for people to feel appreciated.'

'I haven't done much for you,' said Alix.

'You've given us some good advice,' Matt said. 'And you helped on the foreign currency credit facility.'

'Anyone could have done that,' said Alix.

'But you did it.'

'Flattery is nice,' Alix said. 'You can keep going.'

Matt laughed. 'Four o'clock on Saturday. How does that sound to you?'

'Fine,' she said. 'I'll look forward to it. But don't expect me to be any good at shooting.'

'You're the only woman I know who does it,' said Matt. 'You'd better hit at least one of them.'

'I'll do my best.'

'Oh, and there's dinner afterwards,' said Matt. 'You'll stay for that, won't you?'

'We'll be filthy after the shoot! Where on earth are you having dinner?'

'In the Glenview Hotel. You can use the facilities in the leisure centre to shower and change,' Matt told her. 'It's all organised.'

'What can I say? You seem to have it all worked out.'

'That's Anatronics,' said Matt. 'We think of everything.'

'Thanks for asking me,' said Alix.

'I'm looking forward to seeing you,' said Matt.

She thought about him as she drove home. He definitely fancied her. Flowers, business lunch invitations, corporate outing invitations – he must be attracted to her. And he was nice. Uncomplicated. And unmarried.

A chilling thought struck her. Matt Connery was in his thirties. Still unmarried. Maybe he was looking to find someone to marry and have babies with. Maybe he was feeling exactly the same as Paul. Maybe he thought of her as a good bet.

But he thought she was living with Paul, didn't he? Well, maybe that didn't bother him. She pulled into the car parking space beneath her apartment. She wasn't going to get involved with Matt Connery. Especially as she thought that Paul was just ripe to come home.

⌒

She was drinking hot chocolate when Wyn phoned.

'Hi,' said Alix. 'Any news?'

'I'm going to see him,' said Wyn.

'What?'

'I'm going to see him.'

Alix put her cup on the coffee table in front of her. 'Our father, you mean?'

'Who else?'

'Nobody else, I suppose.'

'Carrie has invited him to dinner on Saturday night and asked me if I wanted to come. I said yes.'

'Why on earth do you want to meet him in some social setting with Carrie?' asked Alix. 'If you have to meet him, wouldn't it be better to do it on your own?'

'I don't want to meet him on my own. And you won't come with me,' said Wyn.

'Fair enough,' said Alix.

'Are you going to come along?' asked Wyn.

'No.'

'Oh, Alix, for goodness' sake! It would do you good to meet him.'

'No it wouldn't,' she said.

'Please, Alix.'

'Look, Wyn, I've said no. Anyway, Carrie hasn't invited me. It's her dinner party, after all.'

'She asked me to tell you about it,' said Wyn. 'Of course she wants you there, Alix.'

'I'm not going,' said Alix.

Wyn heaved a sigh. 'Why not?'

'Because I don't want to. Because Carrie should be the one to ask me. And because I'm out on Saturday night anyway.'

'Out where?' asked Wyn.

'Business,' replied Alix.

'Alix, that job isn't worth missing dinner with Dad over,' said Wyn. 'People will understand.'

'Don't be ridiculous,' snapped Alix. 'If I want to see that man I'm sure I'll have plenty of opportunities. I doubt very much that it has to be this Saturday or nothing. But it wouldn't matter what Saturday it was. I'm not going to see him.'

'You're so bloody obstinate!' cried Wyn. 'What harm would it do to meet him?'

'I've made a decision and I'm sticking to it,' said Alix. 'And that's final.'

'Alix, he's our father.' Wyn's tone was persuasive.

'I couldn't care less whose father he is,' said Alix sharply. 'I'm not going, Wyn. And I'm not saying it again.'

She was rinsing her cup when the phone rang again.

'Yes?' she said.

'You're in a bad mood,' said Carrie.

'No I'm not,' said Alix. 'I've had Wyn on the phone trying to persuade me to go to your dinner on Saturday night and I've told her I won't go. She keeps trying to force me.'

'I won't force you,' said Carrie. 'But I'd like you to come.'

'I can't,' said Alix. 'I have a business engagement all day Saturday and we're having dinner afterwards. So it's absolutely impossible.'

'You could skip the business thing,' said Carrie.

'I couldn't,' said Alix.

'Oh, Alix, you can't go around all your life feeling bitter,' Carrie told her. 'Resenting him. Blaming him.'

'Resenting him for what?' asked Alix. 'Blaming him for what? You two have been reading some God-awful self-help books, haven't you? And you're supposed to confront your feelings

378

or something. I don't resent or blame anybody. I just want to get on with my life.'

Carrie was silent for a moment. 'And how is your life?' she asked finally. 'Anyone in it?'

An image of Matt Connery slid into Alix's mind, followed immediately by a picture of Paul.

'Plenty of people,' she told Carrie. 'And it's working out fine.'

'Seven o'clock on Saturday,' said her mother. 'It would be great if you could make it.'

'Have a good time,' Alix said. 'But I won't be there.'

⌣

He was chasing her down the street. She ran as fast as she could. She was almost tripping over her own feet she was running so fast. And her arms were pushed out in front of her, waving people out of her way. She fell as she stepped off the pavement. She felt herself falling and she tried to cry out but she couldn't.

She opened her eyes. It was 4 a.m.

Alix pulled the duvet round her and went back to sleep.

Chapter 27

Alix wasn't sure about the clay pigeon shoot. She stood indecisively in the hallway of her apartment and wondered whether or not she should simply stay at home. People sometimes didn't turn up at corporate events. Any number of things could prevent them. She could phone Matt on Monday, apologise to him and say that something had cropped up. He'd understand. She didn't know exactly why she was uncertain about going. Even though she'd only once shot clays before she knew that she would enjoy it. And yet – she sighed. She wished she understood what was going through her own head.

She couldn't not turn up. All very well on a week day to say that business had prevented you from attending, but on a Saturday there was very little excuse. And Matt Connery knew that she liked shooting. That was why he'd invited her.

She picked up her padded jacket and her keys. She'd go. If she felt really uncomfortable she didn't have to stay for the dinner later on. Although she had a bag with a change of clothes just in case.

Because it was a pleasant afternoon, Alix decided to walk to the Point Depot. It took about half an hour from her apartment but it was an enjoyable stroll. The water of the Liffey glittered and sparkled under the sun and even the distinctive river smell wasn't as unpleasant as usual.

There were about ten people already at the Point when she arrived. She spotted Matt Connery among them – his tall, fair-haired figure stood out among the crowd.

'Alix!' He smiled at her. 'I thought you weren't going to make it.'

'I was a little delayed,' she lied. 'But I wouldn't miss it.'

'Paddy is just about to take the first batch down now.' Matt nodded over to a bearded man with a clipboard in his hand. 'You'll have to wait for the second run.'

'That's OK,' she said.

'I'll be on the second run too,' said Matt. 'Want to make sure that nobody is left behind.'

'Fine,' said Alix.

She stood on the edge of the group while Matt and Paddy exchanged a few words and then led half of them towards the silver and blue helicopter which was waiting for them.

'Nice, isn't it?' one of the remainder of the group said to her.

'Yes,' she said. 'I'm looking forward to the flight.'

'You ever been on one before?' asked the man.

'On a trip,' said Alix. 'Over some Caribbean islands.' With Paul. The thought stabbed at her. The first year they'd been together when she'd received a huge bonus and blown as much of it as she could on a dream holiday with him. They'd cruised around the Bahamas and then taken a helicopter trip to see it all from the air. It had been wonderful.

'I haven't,' said the man. 'I'm not even a good air passenger. I don't like flying.'

'It's different to a plane,' said Alix. 'You'll probably enjoy it.'

'I doubt it,' he said gloomily. 'But it seemed like such a good idea at the time.'

Alix smiled sympathetically.

'My name is Dermot Donoghue,' he said. 'In case you need to identify me.'

'If we go down, we go down together, Dermot,' she said solemnly. 'We'll be on the same flight.'

'That's some comfort,' he said. 'What's your name?'

'Alix Callaghan. I'm a dealer. My bank looks after Anatronics' foreign exchange business.'

'Really?' Dermot looked at her with interest. 'And have you ever gone shooting before.'

'I do some,' she said cautiously. 'But not usually clays.'

'I went on an outing a couple of weeks ago,' he told her. 'Great fun. I only hit about two but I sure as hell terrified the instructor. Mind you, my shoulder was so bruised afterwards I could hardly move my arm.'

'That's why I have the jacket.' Alix nodded at her bag with the padded jacket neatly folded on top. 'There's a lot more kick from those guns than you expect.'

They both looked upwards as the helicopter lifted gracefully into the sky and clattered overhead.

'You'll be fine,' said Alix.

Matt Connery strolled over to them. 'All prepared?' he asked.

'Absolutely.' Dermot beamed at him. 'I can't wait.'

∽

Alix had forgotten how noisy it was inside a helicopter. Although people could talk to each other through small mikes and hear the conversation through their earphones it was almost impossible to make out what anyone was saying.

Beside her, Dermot Donoghue was clutching at his seat and staring straight ahead. She thought she'd heard him praying earlier but she wasn't certain. She leaned her head against the window and gazed down. She loved the sensation of flying in the helicopter. So much more real than being in a plane at thirty thousand feet.

It didn't take long for them to arrive at the Glen of the Downs. Dermot Donoghue bent almost double as he left the helicopter. 'In case it chops my head off,' he told Alix. 'Now that we're here safely, I don't want to be injured by the bloody thing while I'm on the ground.'

She smiled at him. She couldn't help liking him.

'Right, everyone!' called Matt. 'Can you follow me, please?'

He strode through the long grass towards a wooded area. Alix slapped at some midges that instantly surrounded them.

The rest of the group was already in the clearing waiting for them and drinking cans of Coke.

'We wanted beer,' said one of them. 'But Richard here wouldn't let us.' Richard was the instructor, a thick-set man with blue eyes and a weather-beaten face.

'Safety is paramount,' said Richard. 'And alcohol and guns don't mix.'

He began to lecture them about the guns and safety and explain what they'd be doing that afternoon. Alix half listened to him as she looked around at the rest of the group. They were all men. She didn't feel uncomfortable in a group of men, she was used to it, but she couldn't help feeling that a solitary woman among them would cramp their style. Alix was very pragmatic about men and women. In single-sex groups both behaved very differently to mixed groups. Without her presence, she was sure that the clay pigeon shoot would be a much bawdier affair.

'OK, who's first?' asked Richard.

'Me,' said a short, red-haired guy with glasses whom Alix remembered having seen at the film presentation. 'I'll have a go.'

'Fair play to you, Andy!' called one of the others. 'Give 'em hell!'

Alix watched as Andy stepped up and took the gun gingerly. Richard helped him to get comfortable and pulled the clays. Alix stuffed her earplugs into her ears.

The bright orange clays fell back to earth unscathed as Andy fired and missed. Everyone roared with laughter and Andy's face coloured to match his hair.

'It isn't as easy as it looks,' said Richard. 'Wait until the rest of you have a go.'

Andy clipped one of the next targets to much applause but he failed to hit any more.

'You'll do better than that.' Matt stood beside Alix.

She took one of the earplugs out of her ears. 'Pardon?'

'You'll do better than that,' repeated Matt.

'I wouldn't bet on it,' said Alix. 'Stationary targets are fine. But I'm not sure about this.'

'You'll be great,' said Matt confidently.

Alix wished she could be so certain. She was definitely regretting her decision to come now. She felt as though the weight of women everywhere was on her shoulders. She wanted to do well so that the blokes knew that whether you were male or female, you could still do just as good a job. She didn't want them to look on her as a token, included out of a sense of duty. Shooting in the club was different. They were her friends. These people were other business people. And in front of them she desperately wanted to do well.

Three of the others had shot with varying degrees of success before Alix was bundled forward.

'Have you ever shot before, young lady?' asked Richard kindly.

'Yes,' she said firmly. 'But not clays.'

'What do you shoot?' he asked.

'Targets. And silhouettes.'

'OK,' he said. 'Of course this is different. What rifle do you use?'

'An Anschutz .22.'

'Nice gun,' he said. 'You'll be using a Beretta today. It's a double-barrel and we'll be using twelve-gauge cartridges.'

'OK,' said Alix.

'Just take it nice and easy,' said Richard. 'Squeeze the trigger.'

'I know the theory,' said Alix. 'I'm just not sure about the practice!'

She loaded the gun and brought it up to her shoulder. She tried to breathe as evenly as she could.

'Pull!' she called.

She winged the first clay and caught the second cleanly.

'Well done,' said Richard. 'Ready again?'

'Pull!' she called.

She got the next two dead centre.

'Pull!' She called again.

Orange fragments fell into the trees.

'Jesus,' whispered one of the guys in the group. 'You wouldn't want to get on the wrong side of her, would you?'

'Let's make it a little harder,' said Richard.

'Pull!'

Another two targets, another two hits.

'Pull!'

Everyone was quiet as Alix demolished another two clays. And another. And another.

'That was exceptional,' said Richard. 'Well done!'

She broke open the gun and handed it back to him. 'I enjoyed it. Thank you.'

The group applauded her as she turned round. She grinned at them. 'Thanks.'

'When you said you shot I didn't quite realise what you meant,' said Matt as she walked back to her place beneath a tree. 'I thought you might miss something from time to time.'

'I was lucky,' she confided. 'Normally I would miss.'

'You never thought about doing this professionally?' he asked.

'My body wouldn't manage it.' She massaged her shoulder. 'It's hard work.'

'You've put us all to shame,' said Matt. 'You'll have destroyed everyone's confidence.'

She laughed. 'I doubt it.'

But no one else came near Alix's accuracy.

'It's only reasonable that I should have done better than anyone,' she told Matt as he walked back having missed all but three of his targets. 'I do have experience of it, after all.'

'Most of these guys have done clays before,' said Matt. 'That was why I invited them.'

'It's different,' said Alix. 'The occasional event isn't the same as being in a club.'

'Why are you making excuses for us?' he asked. 'You were better.'

She grimaced. 'I was lucky.'

～

She sat in the sauna in the leisure centre and allowed herself to relax. She'd enjoyed the afternoon. She enjoyed being the best at something, at having everyone appreciate her skills. She'd stopped saying that she had some experience as a shooter and allowed them to praise her and it had been very, very satisfying.

Sweat trickled from her forehead and down her nose. She ladled more water over the coals and revelled in the sizzle of heat.

Afterwards she stood in the shower and pepped herself up with one of Carrie's aromatherapy gels. And then she thought of Carrie and John and Wyn sitting down to dinner together that evening. She felt suddenly sick.

She turned off the shower and wrapped a white towel round her. Would they expect her to show up? Would Carrie set a place for her even though she had refused to go? She towelled her hair vigorously. How dare he come back. How dare he try to insinuate himself into their lives again, having had his time with Imogen, having been a father to Kate. How could he even bear to face Carrie and Wyn again? Especially as he was asking for a favour. For divorce and forgiveness. Well, he was asking the wrong person if he was asking her. She'd been so secure in her three-year-old world. Everything had been perfect. Her father, her mother, her elder sister. And he'd ruined it all by leaving them. By walking out to have babies with someone else.

She bit her lip until she tasted the salty tang of blood.

She left the sauna, had a quick swim, followed by a shower, and got dressed. She wore her black Jasper Conran dress with a soft grey cashmere cardigan over it. She unplaited her hair and put it up, secured by a silver clip.

'Alix, you look wonderful!' Matt smiled as she entered the bar.

'Thank you.'

'What will you have to drink?'

'Beer would be nice,' she said.

'You look far too lovely to drink beer,' he said. 'I feel as though you should be sipping a cocktail. Although I'm not going to argue with a girl who can stop a clay at five paces.'

She grinned at him. 'I'm thirsty.'

'Have a seat, Alix.' Brian Dolan, one of the other guests, pushed a bar stool over to her.

'Thanks.'

'So, Alix, how often do you shoot?' asked Peter Morgan.

'I used to do it once a week,' she told him. 'But not so much in the last few weeks, unfortunately.'

'And what do you shoot?'

She went through it all for them again. They stood around and listened to her.

'Just as well my wife doesn't have a gun,' said Pat Riley. 'I'd be dead by now.'

The others laughed.

'What about you, Alix?' asked Dermot. 'Is there a Mr Callaghan?'

She shook her head.

'Young, free, single and with a rifle,' said Pat. 'It's a heady combination.'

'But there is someone,' said Matt casually.

She shot him a glance. 'There is – was – is a Mr Hunter,' she told him.

'Is or was?' he asked.

She sipped her beer. 'I'm not exactly sure at the moment.'

'God, hope he didn't do something awful to you,' said Dermot. 'I mean, Alix, let's face it, who'd want to have you hating them? You'd be walking around in terror for the rest of your life!'

'I'm not that bad!' she laughed.

'All the same.' Dermot winked at her. 'Better be on the safe side.'

It was another hour before they went in to dinner. Alix had drunk three bottles of beer and was feeling light-headed. She looked at her watch. It was half eight.

They'd have started dinner in Carrie's house by now. Alix knew what her mother would have cooked. Roast lamb with garlic and rosemary. Rosemary for remembrance, Carrie used to say. Garlic for remembrance, Alix would laugh.

What was John telling them? That he'd never meant to hurt them. That he'd always cared about them. That he'd meant to come back and see them but that things hadn't worked out that way.

'Excuse me, madam.' A waitress put Alix's starter of smoked salmon in front of her.

'Thank you.'

Carrie would have done cheese soufflés for starters. Carrie had found the recipe in a Delia Smith book and had thought that it was the most wonderful starter ever. Simple but effective, she'd told the girls as she produced it three Sundays in a row. And for dessert? Carrie wasn't a dessert person. Neither were her two daughters. She'd probably just have cheese.

'Alix?' Matt Connery, who was sitting on her left, leaned towards her. 'Don't you want your food?'

'What?' She glanced around. Everyone else had started. 'Of course. I was daydreaming.'

'What about?' he asked.

'Nothing in particular.' She picked up her lemon and squeezed it over the slices of salmon.

'You were miles away,' said Matt.

'Not really.'

'Thinking about Mr Hunter?' he asked.

She smiled faintly. 'No.'

'What's the story about Mr Hunter?'

'Why?'

'I just wondered.'

'I've known him for a long time,' said Alix simply. 'Things don't always go smoothly.'

'It really can't have helped when I sent you the flowers.' Matt looked almost contrite.

'It didn't make any difference.'

'So – what do you think will happen?'

'I don't know,' she said.

'Do you love him?'

'Really and truly, Matt, that's a very personal question for an accountant to ask a banker.'

'I was hoping we weren't just accountant and banker,' he said.

'What were you hoping we were?' she asked.

'Friends?'

'Not a good idea, really. I might not give you the rate you want and you'll feel put out by that because we're supposed to be friends. I might give you the best advice I can but you mightn't want to act on it and I'll get pissed at you because we're supposed to be friends. It doesn't work, Matt.'

'I see.'

She applied herself to her food. He watched her as she cut some salmon and popped it into her mouth. A strand of hair fell across her cheek. He had to fight the urge to brush it away. He had never felt like this before. Not with Emma or Grainne or Helen or – not with any of them. He'd never felt both admiration and a desire to protect at the same time. He'd never seen someone who looked so capable and yet so vulnerable. And so incredibly sexy. He'd hardly been able to take his eyes off her earlier when she was sitting on the bar stool, her long legs crossed demurely at the ankles but encased in shimmering black stockings. And he was pretty sure that she was wearing stockings, not tights. He'd seen a glimpse of lace as she'd got down from the stool.

Maybe they were all laughing together, thought Alix. Maybe Carrie and Wyn had forgiven him for leaving. Maybe they were playing happy families. In Carrie's house. She took a sip from her glass of wine.

'What do you think about the new administration in the White House?' asked Matt.

'What?' She looked startled.

'The new administration. Do you think that their economic policies are better than the last lot?'

She smiled at him. 'Economic policy varies so little from administration to administration these days it's hardly a cause

391

for either elation or depression when a different person is in the White House.'

'Is it likely that the dollar will begin to appreciate against the yen?'

'Possibly,' said Alix. 'Although Japanese policy has been more expansionary of late which is why the yen is stronger than it has been.'

'And interest rates?'

'In the States?' She put her knife and fork neatly on her plate. 'Will continue to have an easing bias.'

'Oh, come on, Alix.' He looked at her in exasperation. 'Why don't you tell me to sod off?'

She laughed. 'Because I enjoy talking about politics and economics.'

'What else?' he asked.

'Oh, anything. I talk a lot whenever people let me.'

'How do you get on with the guys in the dealing room?' asked Matt. 'Don't you find that they resent your authority?'

'Why should they?' A mental image of Gavin Donnelly's sullen face flashed before her eyes. 'I'm the boss.'

'But do they—'

'Matt, I'll talk about anything. But not the internal politics of Europa Bank.'

'Fair enough,' he said. 'I guess I wouldn't want to talk about the internal politics of Anatronics Industries.'

'Hey, Alix!' Pat Riley called across to her. 'What kind of gun do you shoot with?'

'Mine is an Anschutz,' Alix told him. 'But there are lots of different types – Brno, Marlin, Lakefield.'

'How much would one cost?' he asked.

'Second-hand you can pick up something for under five

hundred,' said Alix. 'Mine was more expensive. And I have a lovely little scope, a Tasco dot scope, which helps. My rifle is very different to what you were using today, though, because I shoot targets.'

'What made you take up shooting?' asked Dermot, who was sitting on her right-hand side.

She shrugged. 'I don't know. I was always interested.'

'What else do you do in your spare time?'

'What spare time?' She smiled at him. 'I go to the gym.'

'Definitely not worth getting on the wrong side of you,' said Dermot. 'If you couldn't shoot me, you'd probably knock me out.'

They went back to the bar after dinner. The men told ribald jokes and Alix laughed with them. Then she told some ribald jokes of her own. Matt ordered a round of tequila slammers.

'I can do this, but I'm not going to,' said Alix.

'Oh, come on.' Dermot urged her on. 'You've been one of the lads all day. The least you can do is finish a drink with us now.'

She looked at her watch. 'Actually, I have to get home. I was just about to order a taxi.'

'I'll order a taxi for you,' said Matt. He walked off towards reception.

'Come on,' said Peter. 'Down the hatch, Alix.'

She sighed and drank the tequila in one gulp. The men applauded her.

Matt returned to the bar. 'There's a taxi already outside. He'll take us to town.'

'Us?' Alix looked at him. He was coming in and out of focus. Tequila always did that to her.

'I'll see you home,' he said.

'Way to go, Matt!' called Ronan Hogan, another of the Anatronics people.

'It's the least I can do,' said Matt.

'Fine,' said Alix. 'Do you remember where I left my bag?'

'It's here.' Matt picked it up. 'Are you ready?'

'Yes,' she said. She slid off the stool and stood unsteadily beside him. 'See you, guys!'

''Bye, Alix. See you again.'

'Cheers, Alix!'

'Listen, Alix, if you're ever looking for a spot of drinking company . . .' Dermot handed her his business card.

Suddenly lots of business cards were being thrust at her. She shoved them all into her bag. 'Thanks, guys. I've got to go.'

Matt walked beside her. 'Are you OK?'

'It's the tequila,' she told him. 'I can't drink tequila.'

'Why did you?' he asked.

'I couldn't let you all down,' she said. 'You all so desperately wanted me to drink it.' She got into the car and yawned. 'It was a good day, though. Thanks for asking me.'

'I'm glad you enjoyed it,' said Matt. 'I wasn't sure you'd come.'

She glanced at him in the darkness. 'Neither was I.'

The car moved slowly down the road. She closed her eyes and felt herself drift into sleep. She didn't really want to sleep, she was too aware that Matt was in the car with her and he was a business contact and it wasn't a great idea to fall asleep beside him, but she couldn't keep her eyes open.

He wanted her to fall asleep on his shoulder. He thought it

would be a good sign if she fell asleep on his shoulder. But she was leaning in the opposite direction, her head against the car window. As he watched, she heaved a sigh.

What was she really like? he wondered. When she wasn't dealing or working out or shooting? What went on inside her head? And what was the inside track on that boyfriend of hers? Was it worthwhile making a move, or would it be something he'd regret forever?

The taxi pulled up outside Alix's apartment.

'Will I wait?' asked the driver.

'I'll see her home. It's OK,' said Matt.

'Best of luck, mate!' The driver grinned knowingly at him.

Alix prised her eyes open. 'Oh! We're here.'

Matt got out of the taxi and opened the door for her. 'Come on,' he said. 'I'll see you safely in.'

'I'm quite all right,' she told him. 'I've had a sleep.'

'I know,' he said. 'You snored.'

She stared at him. 'I did not!'

'Just little snores,' he told her. 'Nothing too awful, honestly.'

'I don't snore,' she said firmly. 'I know I don't.'

Matt paid the taxi driver who pulled away.

'He's gone!' exclaimed Alix. 'He should have waited for you.'

'It doesn't matter,' said Matt. 'I'll call another one.'

'Do you want to come in for coffee?' Alix looked at him doubtfully.

'Great,' said Matt. 'I'd love to.'

He followed her up the steps to the apartment building. She fumbled with the key but eventually got the door open.

'This way,' she said as she walked along the corridor. She

stopped in front of her door and turned to him. 'Just coffee,' she said firmly.

'Absolutely,' said Matt.

She was glad that she'd tidied the apartment that morning. They stepped inside.

'Wow, Alix, what a wonderful place!' Matt stood in the living room and looked around.

'I like it,' she said.

'It's great.' He took in the wooden floors, the white walls and the lack of clutter. 'Makes my place look a complete mess.'

'It's not always this neat,' she confessed. 'I cleaned up this morning.'

'I love it,' he told her. 'It's almost Nordic in its neatness.'

She grinned at him. 'I'll make coffee.'

He opened the doors to the balcony and stepped outside while Alix spooned coffee into the percolator. She still felt unsteady from the tequila and from the beer and wine she'd drunk before then. She wasn't sure why she'd asked Matt to her apartment. She hoped he was the sort of guy who knew that no meant no.

'I like it here.' He stepped back inside. 'Did you do all the decorating yourself?'

'More or less,' she said. 'I like to keep things simple.'

'So I see.' He sat down in one of the armchairs. She bristled. That was Paul's armchair. It was wrong of Matt to be sitting in it. She felt ill at ease about having someone new, someone different in a place that had been their place. But Matt didn't notice how uncomfortable she felt. He leaned back in the chair.

'Love the music system,' he told her.

'Bang and Olufsen,' she said.

'I know,' said Matt. 'I work in a hi-tech industry, remember?'

She opened the fridge door and looked inside. 'Is black coffee OK?' she asked. 'I forgot to buy milk this morning.'

'Sure,' said Matt. 'I love black coffee.' He picked up one of the magazines on the coffee table in front of him. 'Is this your reading matter of choice?' he asked as he flicked through *The Securities Review*.

'Not choice,' she said. '*The Economist* is my reading matter of choice.'

'Don't you ever leave it behind?' he asked. 'Don't you ever just read something for fun?'

'Like what?'

'I don't know. Women's magazines. Books.'

'I'm reading Margaret Thatcher's autobiography at the moment,' she said.

'You're joking.'

'No.' She handed him a cup of black coffee. 'It's interesting.'

She watched him as he settled into Paul's chair again. 'What do you read? *Accountant Monthly*?'

He laughed. 'No. Thrillers mainly. Michael Crichton, John le Carré, that sort of thing. You probably think that's hopelessly illiterate of me.'

'No,' she said. 'I like thrillers myself. Although I'm more of a P.D. James than a Michael Crichton.'

'What movies do you like?' he asked.

She shrugged. 'Depends on my mood. I'm not really into arty movies. Or ones with nothing but special effects. I like plot-driven stuff. If Hugh Grant isn't in it, I'm prepared to give it the benefit of the doubt.'

'Where's your boyfriend tonight?'

The change of subject startled Alix. 'What?'

'Your boyfriend,' repeated Matt. 'The on-again, off-again boyfriend.'

'Not here,' said Alix.

'Where?'

'Mind your own business,' she said sharply.

'I'm sorry.' Matt put the cup on the table. 'You're right. It *is* none of my business.'

'That's OK.' Alix looked at him warily.

'I should get home.' He stood up and so did she.

'Thanks for a great day,' she said.

'I'm glad you enjoyed it. We do our best at Anatronics.'

'We do our best at Europa Bank too. Will I phone for a taxi?' she asked.

'I will,' he said. 'I have the number coded.' He took his mobile phone out of his jacket pocket. 'Ten minutes,' he told her. 'But I'll wait outside. No point in both of us sitting around.'

'If you're sure?'

'Absolutely,' he said.

'OK.'

She walked with him to the apartment door. 'Thanks again.'

'You're welcome.'

They looked at each other hesitantly. Then Alix opened the door and Matt walked away.

Chapter 28

Alix woke up on Sunday morning to the sound of rain beating against the window. She pulled on her dressing gown and padded into the kitchen. The cups with the dregs of last night's coffee were still in the sink. She'd forgotten to wash them.

She turned on the tap and rinsed them under running water. She thought that she might have been rude to Matt but she couldn't remember. The time after she'd drunk the tequila slammer was a hazy blur. She remembered him coming to the apartment and sitting in Paul's chair. She remembered making him coffee and feeling uncomfortable. But she couldn't remember what they'd talked about.

Anyway, coffee was what she needed again now. She spooned roasted Java into the percolator. Bugger, she thought. No milk. She wished she could get her head around remembering the milk. Matt Connery certainly wouldn't have been impressed by her catering arrangements.

The buzzer to the apartment went. Alix walked over to the monitor to see who was there. In a corner of her mind she wondered whether or not Matt was sending her flowers again. But it was Wyn who was standing outside waving at her.

Alix pressed the entry button to let her in.

'You're out and about very early,' said Alix as she opened the apartment door. 'Is anything the matter?'

'No.' Wyn slid out of her wet coat. 'Of course not. I just thought you'd want to know how things went last night.'

'Last night?' Alix was still thinking of Matt Connery and how she'd misjudged his interest in her. As far as she could recall from her jumbled memories, he'd been quite happy to get away from her. She wasn't sure exactly how things had gone.

'With Dad. Alix! Surely you haven't forgotten about dinner last night?'

'No, of course not.' She yawned. 'I was out late myself. I've only just woken up. I'm sorry, Wyn, I'm not with it.'

'I don't know how you can be so blasé about it,' said Wyn.

'I'm not blasé,' said Alix. 'Just sleepy.'

'I thought you were at a work thing,' said Wyn suspiciously.

'I was,' Alix told her. 'But it was late when I got home.'

'Oh. OK.' Wyn sat down on the sofa. 'That coffee smells good. Do you have any more?'

Alix winced. 'Yes. But no milk.'

'For goodness' sake, Alix!' Wyn shot her an exasperated glance. 'Don't you do any shopping any more?'

'Do you want it or not?' Alix ignored Wyn's question.

'Fine,' said Wyn.

Alix brought over two cups of coffee and sat down beside her sister.

'He was there when I arrived,' said Wyn. 'Terry dropped me off. He told me to ring any time I wanted to leave.'

Alix studied the design on her cup.

'He – I kind of remembered him, Alix. I know that sounds crazy but I had a picture of him in my head and he wasn't all that different to it.'

'Older,' suggested Alix.

'Yes,' said Wyn. 'And his hair is grey. And he was wearing glasses. But I could still see him as the father I remembered.'

'How nice,' murmured Alix.

'It was nice,' said Wyn defensively. 'It put me in touch with stuff.'

'So did he fall on you and say "I'm back and I've always wanted to see you"?'

'Don't be ridiculous,' said Wyn. 'It was civilised. We said hello and Carrie gave us some drinks and then he told me that he was sorry about everything but that he'd tried to keep in touch with our lives. Of course, he was out of touch for ages because Carrie wouldn't really speak to him. He understood why and he accepted that.'

Alix yawned again. Wyn didn't notice.

'So he said that he knew it would be difficult for us to understand and that it was a pretty shitty thing that he did and that he never meant to hurt us.'

'People never mean to hurt other people,' Alix interrupted, 'but they usually do a pretty good job of it all the same.'

'He said that every year on our birthdays he used to buy cards and sign them but he never sent them. Carrie had told him not to. So he brought them with him. He gave me mine. He has yours for you.'

'Oh, please.' Alix made a face. 'That's so corny I don't know how you fell for it, Wyn.'

'I didn't fall for anything! I have the cards at home.'

'He could have bought them all just before he came over!'

'No,' said Wyn. 'They were old.'

'OK.' Alix began to plait the ends of her hair. 'So what then?'

'He told us about his life in the States. He's done awfully well, Alix. He's the president of a computer company there.'

'Everyone who's anyone is called president in the States,' said Alix dismissively. 'You know the Yanks, they love titles.'

'He has a home in Connecticut and another on the West Coast,' said Wyn.

'Good for him.'

'He showed me pictures of Imogen. And of Kate. I have them with me.'

Alix got up and took the cups into the kitchen.

'Would you like to see them?' asked Wyn when she returned.

'Not especially.'

'Kate is very like you,' said Wyn. She reached into her handbag and took out an envelope. 'Here. Have a look.'

Alix took the envelope and turned it over in her hand. He had touched this. He had put the photographs inside and closed it. She swallowed.

'Have a look,' said Wyn again. 'You're hardly compromising your principles by having a look, are you?'

'It's not a question of principles,' said Alix. 'I just don't see why I'm supposed to be thrilled that this bastard has come back and wants to be a father to us. What a load of crap! He thinks he's in some American afternoon soap.'

'He's not like that,' said Wyn. 'Really he isn't.'

Alix turned the envelope over again. 'So why did he have an affair with Imogen in the first place? Why did he get her pregnant? Why did he piss off to the States at the first available opportunity?'

402

Wyn sighed. 'He wasn't making excuses,' she said. 'He knew it was wrong. He feels very guilty about it. He says that sometimes he doesn't know if it was the right thing to do. But Imogen was very different to Carrie. Imogen couldn't have coped on her own.'

'Of course she could,' said Alix dismissively. 'All that fragile maiden stuff is just an act. Carrie had to cope. She wasn't given the choice, was she?'

'But she coped well,' said Wyn.

'I can't believe you're so prepared to forgive and forget,' said Alix. 'And what about Carrie? How does she feel?'

'She talked about it,' said Wyn. 'She said that she used to be very angry but there's no point in being angry all your life. So she's forgiven him.'

'She thinks she's in a fucking soap opera too! What was last night? An orgy of forgiveness?'

'No,' said Wyn. 'You weren't there, were you?'

'Too right I wasn't.' Alix handed the unopened envelope back to her sister. 'And I won't be part of some kind of love fest between you all.'

'Alix, why be bitter about it? You can't even remember him!'

'No,' said Alix. 'I can't. My own father. And I can't even remember him.' But she did. The flashbacks were coming more often lately. Of them sitting at the table together. Of him buttoning her coat. Of him waving to her as he went to work.

'It was good to see him,' said Wyn. 'It helped, Alix. Truly it did.'

'I don't need any help,' said Alix. 'And I don't need to see him.'

'What about pictures of the house?' asked Wyn. 'There are pictures of his house in this lot.'

'Wyn, can't you get it through your head that I'm just not interested,' said Alix sharply. 'I know you've always felt that you wanted to see him and get some kind of explanation from him. I haven't. So I don't need all this crap.'

Wyn sighed. 'How do you know you don't?'

'I just know.' Alix began to plait her hair again. Why did they all want to fall over John? What was so wonderful about him coming back? What did they expect to gain out of it all? A mention in the will? She laughed to herself. Maybe he was stinking rich and maybe he'd leave them all a fortune. But they'd be waiting a long time. He'd only be in his sixties now. Hardly ready to pop off. Unless he was, like so many captains of industry, overweight and underexercised. She didn't care anyway. They could say all they liked. She wasn't going to be taken in by him.

'Where were you last night?' asked Wyn.

'Out.'

'Out where?'

'One of our clients had organised a clay shoot for the afternoon and a dinner afterwards. It was fun.'

'I don't know how you can do that,' said Wyn distastefully.

'You've never even held a rifle and aimed at a paper target,' said Alix. 'But you've probably played one of Aoife's video games where you laser a whole bunch of people to death!'

Wyn looked shamefaced. 'I like video games,' she said.

'Clays are fun,' Alix told her. 'Although I prefer targets really. But it's nice being out in the open on a bright sunny day.'

'How many people were at the shoot?'

'About twenty,' Alix said. 'We got a helicopter down to the event.'

'You're joking!'

'No, seriously.'

'Do you like your life?' asked Wyn.

'Pardon?'

'Do you like it? Whizzing around in helicopters. Jetting to London and Paris. Shouting at blokes down the phone? Pumping iron at the gym and pumping bullets into a target?'

'You've got a completely distorted idea of how I live,' Alix said. 'I've only been in a bloody helicopter twice – the first time was with Paul. I'd hardly describe the free-for-all to London as "jetting" and Paris isn't a lot better. I don't shout at anyone down the phone. And I don't pump iron. Nor do I pump bullets. My gun isn't pump-action.'

'But what about other things? What about a boyfriend?'

'For heaven's sake!' Alix looked at Wyn in exasperation. 'I've only just split with Paul. Why on earth would you want me to jump into a relationship with someone else?'

'So it's definite with Paul, is it?'

'I don't know,' said Alix. 'I'm not certain.'

'Because I heard that he was living with the French girl. Sabine.'

Alix stared at her. 'Who told you that?'

Wyn shrugged. 'Just heard, that's all.'

'He might be,' said Alix.

'You're not seriously thinking that he'll come back to you after a few weeks with the blonde bombshell, are you?'

'She's not a bombshell,' said Alix. 'She's more modern-looking than that.'

'Seriously, though. He's not going to come back to you, is he? And even if he did, you'd hardly have him back.'

Alix sighed. 'I know.'

'It would be embarrassing to take him back.'

'I know,' said Alix. 'It's just that – well, it's an easier option.'

'Easier than what?'

'Starting all over again with someone else,' said Alix.

Wyn looked at her sympathetically. 'I know,' she said. 'I understand, Alix. Honestly I do.'

'And someone else would probably want exactly the same as Paul,' continued Alix. 'A wife and a family and someone to love him.'

'Maybe if you met the right someone?'

Alix sighed. 'Maybe the right someone for me just doesn't exist.'

◡

Alix was glad when Wyn left. She hated it when her sister tried to manipulate her into feeling how she felt. That had always been Wyn's way. She tried to twist you emotionally to make you do the things she wanted. But Alix had wised up to her a long time ago. Nobody could make her do anything she didn't want to any more.

She went to the gym and worked out for an hour. She always felt invigorated afterwards. Then she went shopping. She drove to the Merrion Centre and loaded up her supermarket trolley with kilos of fresh fruit and vegetables, cartons of juice, milk and fresh soup, meat that she would freeze, bread, biscuits, yoghurts and an array of cleaning stuff. She was going to advertise for someone to do the cleaning. She hated it.

'Have you a club card?' asked the cashier.

Alix sighed. Her shopping bill was astronomical. She should have taken the card from Paul.

When she got home the message light was blinking on the machine. She hit play.

'Alix, is there ever a time when you are available to take a call? This is Carrie. Phone me when you get in.'

She groaned. She didn't want to call her mother. She didn't want Carrie's requests for them all to be a family again to be added to Wyn's desire to forgive and forget.

She spent ages unpacking her shopping. She looked at the pineapple and wondered when on earth she'd get around to eating it.

She didn't phone Carrie for another hour. She had to steel herself to pick up the receiver and dial the number.

'Hello.'

'Hi, Carrie.'

'Well, about time,' said Carrie. 'Where have you been?'

'Out,' said Alix. 'Shopping.'

'Anything nice?'

Alix laughed. 'Grocery shopping. Nothing more exciting than chicken fillets and Domestos. Wyn was around earlier and she was moaning at me because I didn't have any milk in the house.'

'No milk!' Carrie sounded shocked.

'Oh, don't you start. It's not exactly vital for day-to-day living, you know.'

'For tea it is,' said Carrie.

'You should be drinking herbal tea,' Alix chided her.

407

'Actually I hate it,' said Carrie, 'Filthy stuff. I like my tea with—'

'Two sugars and plenty of milk,' Alix interrupted her.

'Yes,' said Carrie. 'You remembered.'

'Of course I do,' said Alix. 'I've made it for you often enough.'

'I suppose so.'

'What did you want?' Alix kept her voice light and cheerful. 'Anything in particular?'

'I thought I'd tell you about last night's dinner,' said Carrie.

'Wyn has already given me the gory details,' said Alix. 'You don't have to.'

'I was disappointed you didn't come.'

'I told you I wasn't coming. I was busy yesterday.'

'Too busy to see your own father?' asked Carrie.

'He's been too busy to see me for the last thirty-odd years,' Alix retorted.

'Look, he was my husband. I had a right to be mad at him. But I've managed to live and let live,' said Carrie. 'There's no reason why we can't be adult about it.'

'I know,' said Alix. 'All the best advice pages would tell us that we can get on with each other and put the past behind us. Not to let bitterness take over. Well, I haven't let bitterness take over. I haven't thought of the man for years. Now, just because he feels it's time to come home, I'm supposed to start remembering. I don't want to, thanks all the same.'

'He never stopped loving you.'

'Carrie! We've been through this a hundred times already. I don't give a shit whether he did or not. I don't want to see him and that's that.'

'You're very like him,' said Carrie.

Alix was silent for a moment. 'That's a horrible thing to say,' she muttered eventually. 'I'm very like me. That's it.'

'OK,' said Carrie. 'Have it your way. He's staying for another couple of weeks. Imogen is with him.'

'Imogen!' Alix almost choked. 'Don't tell me you've met Imogen!'

'No,' said Carrie. 'Although it wouldn't bother me if I did.'

'So what about the pregnant daughter?' asked Alix.

'Kate? Her baby is due in November,' said Carrie. 'She's at home with friends.'

Alix thought of the pregnant Kate for a moment. She wondered what she looked like – the baby that her father preferred.

'Alix? Are you still there?'

'Of course,' said Alix.

'If you change your mind about meeting him, tell me,' said Carrie. 'He'd really love to see you, Alix.'

'I'll tell you,' said Alix. 'But don't hold your breath.'

She curled up on the sofa, a glass of wine in her hand. She opened the book she'd bought on her shopping expedition. It was about a thirtysomething who was too fat, hated her job and kept losing her boyfriends.

Why is it that losers are so much more sympathetic? thought Alix. Why can't someone be a successful, happy, single person who doesn't have a weight problem and doesn't mind sleeping on her own?

Probably because such a person doesn't actually exist, she thought later that night as she pulled the duvet round her shoulders and rolled into the space that used to be Paul's. Just like the person for me doesn't exist either.

Chapter 29

M att Connery didn't ring the dealing room the following week. Alix hadn't really expected him to, yet she couldn't help feeling a frisson of disappointment that he hadn't called. She told herself that she was being particularly silly in wanting a man in whom she had no real interest to phone, simply because she wanted to know that he'd bothered.

On Friday afternoon she went into her office and printed out a list of all the Anatronics deals they'd done. The account was a mid-range account, she decided, as she analysed the profits. But of course the big trade had yet to come. They always wanted the big deal to come from all of their clients.

'Gavin.' She buzzed his desk.

'Yes?'

'Can you come in for a moment?'

'OK.'

He walked into the office and leaned against the glass door.

'I was at a lot of meetings this week,' she said. 'You were busy in my absence.'

He sighed heavily. 'And? Is that a problem?'

'Not at all.' She leaned back in her chair. 'You seem to think I have some agenda as far as you're concerned, Gavin. And, I guess, not a particularly pleasant agenda.'

'You don't encourage me,' he said darkly.

'I try,' said Alix. 'But I also have to keep your trades within our risk limits. I know you haven't been in the market all that long, Gavin. I know that it can be irksome to have somebody tell you that you can't do something when you clearly feel that you can, and that you can make money out of it.'

'That's just the point,' he exploded. 'You spend more time telling me no than yes. Everything I want to do you want to think about first. It's safe, Alix, but is it good dealing?'

'I think so,' she said calmly. 'In all the years I've been doing this I've never presided over some dramatic loss. I've had losses, like everyone, but I've always had limits on them. That's all I'm trying to instil into you. Stick to the limits. Know when to cut your losses. Run with your profits.'

'I do OK,' said Gavin.

'Of course you do,' she said. She sat up straight. 'Anyway, the reason I asked you to drop in was to tell you that I've allocated three new accounts to you. Harris-Gilpin, Constant Images and Anatronics.'

'Oh.'

'I hope you're happy with that,' she said.

'Sure,' he said. 'I get on well with all those people anyway. Jack Harris likes me. So does that dizzy blonde from Images, and Matt Connery had a great time on the golf outing.'

'So he said.' Alix nodded.

'I deserve these accounts,' said Gavin.

'I know you do.'

'Right. Well, I'd better go ring them,' said Gavin. 'Let them know that it's me they should be talking to in future.'

'Sure.'

He shrugged his shoulders. 'Thanks.'

411

'You're welcome,' said Alix but he'd already left the room.

She was reading the *Financial Times* when Jenny knocked at the door.

'Come in.' Alix folded the pink newspaper and put it to one side.

'I want to talk,' said Jenny abruptly. She sat down in the chair opposite Alix and frowned.

'Something bothering you?' asked Alix.

'Of course there is,' she replied. 'You've given that bastard Donnelly three new accounts.'

'I thought you told me that he was entitled to the Anatronics account,' Alix reminded her.

'That was ages ago,' said Jenny dismissively. 'And whether he's entitled to it or not makes no difference. You gave him Harris and Images as well.'

'He's done a lot of research for both of them,' said Alix. 'I thought it would be a good idea for him to talk to them.'

'I get on with Susan Darcy,' said Jenny. 'I should have got Constant Images.'

'I know you do,' Alix told her. 'But so does Gavin. And he has talked to them more than you.'

'It's not fair,' said Jenny mutinously. 'I work bloody hard here, Alix. But I get passed over for some little shithead with his brains in his arse!'

Alix stifled a grin. 'It's not like that, Jen.'

'Oh, but it bloody is,' retorted Jenny. 'He goes around making so much noise – "I'm Gavin Donnelly, shit-hot trader!" – and everyone thinks he must be great. He pisses off playing golf when there's stuff he could do in the office. But it's put down to entertaining clients. Meanwhile, what do

I do? Plod along talking to accounts, getting trades and not getting rewarded for it.'

'You got a good bonus last year,' said Alix.

'But I don't get any respect!' Jenny thumped her hand down on the desk.

'I respect you,' said Alix. 'I always have.'

'But you don't think I'm as good as them, do you? You don't think I'm as committed because I don't spend my whole life talking about dollar/yen or the operations of the Fed or whatever! Just because I have another life you think that I don't care!'

'That's not true,' said Alix sharply.

'It is,' Jenny insisted. 'They only ever talk about work in the office. Work and the number of women they shagged at the weekend. I talk about other things, like movies I've seen or books I've read. But it isn't enough. You don't think that I have enough drive to get to the top, do you?'

Alix sighed. 'I probably don't feel as though you want to put as much into it as they do.'

'But you'd be wrong,' said Jenny. 'I want to do well, Alix. I try my best. I know I sometimes miss trades because I advise customers against doing something. But I'm usually giving them good advice. I don't want them to lose money – it's not good for us in the long run. Gavin Donnelly doesn't give a shit once he gets the trade. He'll sympathise with them afterwards, but that doesn't help their profit and loss.'

'Helps ours, though,' said Alix.

'And that's what it's all about?' Jenny looked at her defiantly. 'You don't care if a customer loses money as long as we make it?'

'That's not true.' Alix shook her head. 'I do care. But I can

413

see Gavin's point of view too.' She got up and walked to the window. 'When I was in London I used to be really helpful to all our clients. I gave them the best advice I could and I know I saved some of them from making complete fools of themselves. And I thought it was better for us in the long run too. In a lot of ways, I still do. But there was one account, Jeffrie Wallace, and the guy there used to trade almost every day. One day he wanted to buy dollars and I told him not to because I thought that the Fed would move on rates and the dollar would go down. From the bank's point of view, if he'd done the trade and I was right, we could have made a lot. But he said, OK, he'd leave it, and sure enough the Fed made the move. The dollar plunged afterwards. So I rang him up and said that he'd been right not to deal with me. And then he told me, very sheepishly, that he'd called one of my rivals and that they'd done the deal for him. He had to do it, you see, and he felt embarrassed dealing with me after I'd told him it would be crazy. So I lost the deal and the bank lost the money and I never really got back on track with that bloke again.'

'So what are you saying?' asked Jenny. 'That we shouldn't give them good advice?'

'No,' Alix sighed. 'Just that sometimes we're looking at things from a different perspective. And that they always have another bank they can deal with.'

'That's not a lot of help to me,' said Jenny flatly.

Alix sat down at her desk again. 'So what do you want?' she asked.

'I want to be treated like Dave and like Gavin,' said Jenny. 'I don't want you to think of me as someone who's just putting in time.'

'I don't think like that,' said Alix.

'I'd like to believe you,' said Jenny. 'But I think that in some ways you're harder on me because I'm a woman.'

'What!' Alix looked at her in amazement.

'I think that because you're a successful woman you don't want me to be successful too. Because that would diminish your achievements. The only woman head of treasury. But if you have another woman snapping at your heels, it puts more pressure on you.'

Alix gazed at Jenny. 'That's not true, Jenny.'

'But you haven't helped me,' Jenny insisted. 'You haven't made it any easier for me even though it's hard doing this job. You're so concerned that I shouldn't get preferential treatment that you sometimes discriminate against me. Because I don't kick up a fuss like the other two, you don't give me new accounts. I'm sure I don't earn as much as Dave did when he was doing my job.'

'You do,' said Alix.

'But you believe in them more,' said Jenny. 'And I don't feel that I can depend on you to look after my interests.'

Alix was silent. 'I'm sorry you think that,' she said eventually. 'I really don't think it's true, Jenny, but maybe you've got a point. I need to think about it a little more.'

Jenny rubbed the bridge of her nose. 'I'm sorry,' she said. 'I didn't mean to lose my temper. I just felt—'

'Don't apologise,' interrupted Alix. 'Do you think either Dave or Gavin has ever apologised for losing their temper with me?'

Jenny bit the corner of her lip. 'I guess not.'

'I have more rows with Gavin Donnelly than with anyone else in the world,' stated Alix. 'And he's never once apologised for losing his temper.' She smiled slightly. 'Besides, you didn't lose it. You just said a few things.'

'Maybe I should have lost it,' said Jenny.

'I'm glad you didn't.'

'But would it have been better if I had?' asked Jenny. 'You see, I hate having rows. Gavin thrives on them. I hate asking for things. Dave demands them.'

'I hate to admit that you might be right,' said Alix dryly.

'I'm as entitled as either of them to do well,' said Jenny. 'Just because I take a slightly different approach doesn't mean that it's wrong.'

'I know,' said Alix.

Jenny stood up. 'That's all I wanted to say.'

'OK,' said Alix. 'I'll keep it all in mind, Jenny. I understand how you feel.'

'I hope you do,' said Jenny.

'I do. Honestly.' Alix smiled at her. 'Any plans for the weekend?'

Jenny blushed. 'I'm going to Galway with Mike.'

'The new boyfriend?'

Jenny nodded.

'Well, well.' Alix grinned. 'And how serious is this relationship?'

'I don't know,' said Jenny. 'I like him a lot, Alix. He's fun to be with and he's really good to me. At the moment,' she added darkly.

'Maybe he'll always be good to you,' said Alix.

'I'm not holding my breath. But right now, we're having a good time together. And I'm glad I met him.'

'I'm glad for you,' said Alix.

'But just because I've met a bloke it doesn't make any

416

difference to our discussion,' said Jenny. 'I'm not likely to run off with him and settle into a life of domestic bliss or anything like that.'

'I didn't for one moment imagine you were,' said Alix.

'I just want my cards on the table,' Jenny said.

'Jenny, you've made your position perfectly clear,' Alix told her. 'Don't worry.'

'But I do worry,' said Jenny. 'I worry all the time.'

When she'd gone, Alix sat back in her chair and thought about what Jenny had said. Was it true? she wondered. Did she discriminate against Jenny because she was female? She didn't think so but maybe she was lying to herself. Maybe deep down she saw Jenny as a more potent threat than Gavin. She sighed. She really didn't seem to know her own mind any more. And it bothered her.

⁓

It was seven o'clock before Alix left the office. After talking to Jenny she'd had a brief meeting with John Collins, in credit, and bumped into Des Coyle again. The managing director had asked her about the week's trading but hadn't mentioned anything about Europa Bank Paris and Alix hadn't said anything either.

'What are you doing for the weekend?' he asked when she told him that she had to get home soon.

'I'm going to a wedding in London,' she told him. 'My friend, Sophia, is getting married tomorrow afternoon.'

'That's the girl who works in Russell Cobham, isn't it?' said Des. 'I met her when she was over last year.'

Alix nodded.

'Cracking-looking girl,' said Des. 'Wasted in financial services.'

'What do you mean?' asked Alix.

'Body like that!' Des looked pityingly at Alix. 'She'd have made a fortune doing modelling.'

'Do you think so?'

'Absolutely,' said Des.

'I'll tell her,' said Alix and went home to pack.

Alix owned one hat. It was a cream-coloured Philip Treacy that she'd bought when she worked in London and it had cost her over £500. The reason she'd bought it was that she'd been invited to the wedding of one of her best clients at the time, a guy named Ossie Livsey, who worked on Wall Street. She hadn't wanted to appear as though she couldn't afford to get dressed up for Ossie's wedding, but it broke her heart to spend so much money on a hat. Particularly as she hated wearing them.

But, even though she hadn't been very keen on wearing it, everyone had told her – in the warm way that Americans have – that her hat was 'truly fabulous'. She half believed them which was why, any time she went to a wedding, she hauled the hat out of its striped box and bought something new to go with it.

For Sophia's wedding, she'd bought a navy and cream Nicole Fahri suit. She also bought new navy shoes and a navy bag. It could have looked like office wear, but the suit was loose and unstructured and was chic without being too formal.

Richard kissed Sophia and the small crowd of people broke into spontaneous applause. Sophia turned and smiled at them.

She looked lovely, thought Alix, in her peach voile dress with flowers in her hair. Lovely and pregnant. The dress did nothing to hide the fact that Sophia's bump had expanded since Alix had last seen her. But Sophia didn't care.

Her mother did. Mrs Redmond had muttered to Alix that she'd never understand why Sophia hadn't waited until after the baby was born. There was no hurry, Mrs Redmond said. It wasn't as though she needed to get married.

Maybe she did. The thought occurred to Alix as they left the registry office and walked the hundred yards to the restaurant where they were having a celebration meal. Maybe she felt that being married was important when she had her baby.

I wish I knew what it was like to want a child, she thought. I wish that feeling would surge through me so that I would look at every man I saw as a potential mate. I wish I knew what all the bloody fuss was about.

There were about thirty people at the meal. Alix liked the low-key approach to the day. She hated big, fussy weddings where the bride wandered around like a meringue and scattered guests every time she passed by.

'You're Sophia's friend, aren't you?' The girl beside her looked at the place name in front of Alix's plate.

'Yes,' she replied. 'Alix Callaghan.'

'I'm Nicola Rowntree. I work with her.'

'Oh, Nicola! She's talked about you a lot.'

Nicola raised an eyebrow. 'Good, I hope.'

'Naturally.'

'She's mad as a hatter, of course.'

'Sorry?'

'Sophia. Mad. I don't know why she wants to marry him at all.'

419

'Because she's crazy about him?' hazarded Alix.

'Come on, Alix.' Nicola pushed her heavy-rimmed glasses higher on her nose. 'You can't possibly believe that. Nobody gets to our age and is "mad" about someone.'

'Our age?' asked Alix.

'Thirtysomething. You are thirtysomething, aren't you?'

'Afraid so,' admitted Alix.

'And you know quite well that you'll never be "mad" about someone again, don't you? Not like you were when you were a teenager, for example. And not like you were when you were in your mid-twenties and you wanted someone for life.'

'I don't think I ever wanted someone for life in my twenties,' said Alix.

'Didn't you?' Nicola looked surprised. 'I thought everyone went through that phase. But – and I think you have to agree with me here – when you've reached your thirties you know that the whole thing is a con. What do you need a bloke for anyway? Sexual fulfilment can be found without a phallus, you know.'

Alix almost choked into her consommé.

'Why commit?' asked Nicola. 'Why decide that this one man has to be it? There are plenty of them around. You can even hire them if you want.'

'For sex?' asked Alix.

'For anything,' replied Nicola. 'You can pay a bloke to wallpaper your house, tile your kitchen, fix your car, mend your roof – why the hell do you need one living with you as well?'

'Good point.' Alix was enjoying the one-sided conversation.

'I was married once,' said Nicola. 'But the bastard left me.

420

For a fucking teenage nymphet with massive breasts. I realised then that you can never own them. They're like cats. They do their own thing when they feel like it and then come back to you looking for food and attention. Take it from me, Alix, she's out of her tiny little mind.'

❧

'You know you're crazy, don't you?' Alix and Sophia stood in the marble and glass ladies' room and reapplied their make-up.

'Crazy?'

'Your friend Nicola thinks so.'

Sophia laughed. 'I didn't think Nicky would come,' she said. 'She has a thing about weddings.'

'She told me that her husband left her and ran off with a big-breasted woman.'

Sophia nodded. 'Nicky was devastated,' she said. 'She used to go on and on about how Dorian loved her for her mind. She said that theirs was a relationship based on intellect.'

'Was it?' asked Alix, 'At first?'

'Who knows?' Sophia blotted her lips with tissue. 'Although Nicky looked a lot better when she was married to him. She wore contacts and her hair was better styled and she took more care about her clothes.'

'And when he left it all went downhill?'

'I think she decided that the looking good thing was all a con. So she went to the other extreme.'

'She is quite attractive even if she doesn't bother with the clothes.' Alix examined a spot on her chin. 'How is it I have

421

a bloody spot, Soph? I'm thirtysomething, as Nicky pointed out. Why haven't my spots disappeared?'

'Mine have,' said Sophia triumphantly. 'Ever since I got pregnant my skin has been flawless.'

'Just as well there are some compensations.' Alix snapped the top back onto her lipstick. 'Ready to face them all again?'

Sophia nodded. 'Come on, let's go.'

∽

'Nice hat.'

Alix turned to look at the speaker. She'd seen him at the registry office earlier, looking bored.

'You were wearing the cream hat earlier,' he said to her. 'I noticed it.'

'I was,' she agreed.

'And I liked it. It wasn't a fussy hat. No feathers or bits of lace or anything. Just plain. And nice.'

'It cost me a fortune,' Alix told him. 'So I'm glad you liked it.'

He was in his thirties, she guessed. Tall, mid-brown hair, grey eyes. He'd been sitting beside Richard's sister during the meal. Tara Comiskey was flame-haired and gorgeous and regularly broke men's hearts. At least, that was what Sophia had said.

'Where's Tara?' asked Alix.

'Tara?'

'Beside you at dinner. Red hair? Tumbling around her face in little curls. Creamy skin?'

'Large chest?'

Alix grinned. 'That's the woman.'

'I think she got tired of me when she realised that I was a lowly teacher and not a hotshot financier.'

'I don't think she's like that,' said Alix.

'Do you know her?'

'Better than I know you.'

'I'm sorry,' he said. 'My name's Marcus Bridgewater.'

'Alix Callaghan.'

'Nice to meet you,' he said.

'What do you teach?' asked Alix.

'Chemistry,' said Marcus. 'At the local grammar. Nice kids.'

'I liked chemistry.' She smiled. 'I enjoyed mixing stuff together and causing explosions.'

'I thought you might,' said Marcus.

They looked at each other for a moment. He was going to ask her if she wanted a drink, thought Alix. And then he'd steer her to a corner of the room. And he'd probably tell her that marriage was overrated. He looked like someone who thought marriage was overrated. And then he might ask her where she was staying. And, after that, who knew—

'There you are!' Tara Comiskey put her arm round Marcus's waist. 'I thought you'd left me.'

'Would I?' He smiled at her.

'You're Sophia's friend, aren't you?' Tara turned to Alix who nodded.

'Glad you could make it,' said Tara. 'Come on, Marcus. I want you to tell me all about being a teacher . . .' She dragged him away from Alix who sat down at the nearest table.

'That girl needs help.' Nicola lit a cigarette and offered one to Alix. 'She'll never keep him if she hangs on to him like that.'

'I thought you disapproved of the whole idea.' Alix took the cigarette and lit it.

423

'I do,' said Nicola. 'But I hate seeing women make fools of themselves.'

'Maybe she's not making a fool of herself.'

'We all make fools of ourselves over men.' Nicola inhaled deeply then blew out the smoke in a steady stream. 'They're bastards. All of them. I just hope poor old Sophia knows what she's letting herself in for.'

Chapter 30

Monday morning was very busy but Alix was still feeling tired from the weekend. They'd stayed in the restaurant until after nine, then she, Nicola and a couple of others had gone to a nearby pub. Nicola hadn't stayed long and then Alix, who had drunk far too much, ended up making a pass at Marcus Bridgewater.

He'd been surprised but charming about it. He told her that he was with Tara and that though she, Alix, was undoubtedly a lovely girl, he was staying with Tara. Alix remembered the feeling of humiliation as he smiled at her and then made his way to the other side of the pub where Tara was chatting to some friends. He'd spoken to her and then the two of them had picked up their jackets and left.

Alix felt sick as she remembered. No doubt he'd told Tara that she had made a move and that they'd better leave. God, she thought, I'm such a bloody idiot!

She hadn't even been all that interested in Marcus. It was just that she was feeling left out of the general feeling of love and contentment that Sophia's wedding had generated. And she was feeling sorry for herself.

I am a sad case, she told herself as she scrolled through a

story about the European Central Bank's economic forecasts. A sad, sad case of a frustrated single woman.

'Alix!'

She turned to Jenny.

'You were miles away. Paul is holding on line three.'

Alix dragged her thoughts back to the present and clicked in to the line. 'Paul?'

'Hi,' he said. 'How are you?'

'Fine.'

'Any news?' he asked.

'What sort of news?'

'Any sort.'

'Sophia got married at the weekend.'

'Your friend? The girl in New York?'

'She's been in London for ages, Paul. You know that. The last time she stayed with us she came over from London.'

'I forget,' said Paul simply. 'Who did she marry?'

'Richard Comiskey.'

'Oh, I remember,' said Paul. 'Dark-haired bloke. Played lots of sports.'

'That's him,' said Alix.

'I hope they'll be very happy,' he said.

'I'm sure they will.' Alix bit her lip.

'Anyway, I called to see if Friday would be good for the interview.'

'I thought someone else was meant to organise it,' said Alix.

'I offered,' said Paul. 'Is Friday OK? Or is it one of those Fridays when there's a slew of figures coming out and you can't possibly be civilised with anyone?'

'I'm always civilised,' said Alix tartly. 'And Friday is fine.'

'Great,' said Paul. 'There'll be three of them. One of the new reporters is doing the interview – Damien O'Riordan. I'm not sure who else will be there. There'll be a sound guy and a camera guy and probably someone else.'

'Why on earth don't they have a female interviewer?' asked Alix. 'You said the programme is about women achievers. Well, why haven't they got a woman fronting the programme?'

'Maybe if it was all women, people would find it too boring,' said Paul. 'Perhaps they want some balance.'

'You only ever talk about balance if all the participants are women,' snapped Alix. 'Nobody thinks about it if they're all men.'

'Get out of the wrong side of bed again?' asked Paul. 'There's no need to bite my head off, Alix.'

'Isn't there?'

'No,' he said. 'Fortunately we're just in a business relationship here. I don't have to think about your feelings.'

'Don't you?' she asked.

He was silent for a moment. 'I'm sorry. Forget I said that.'

'I will,' said Alix.

'Friday is OK, then?'

'Sure,' she said dispiritedly. 'Afternoon rather than morning if you can arrange it.'

'Of course I can,' said Paul. 'I'll give you a call on the day to remind you.'

'I'll remember,' she said. 'I'll write it down.'

'Take care, Alix,' he said.

'Sure.' She clicked out of the line and walked out of the dealing room.

'What's wrong with her?' Dave looked at Jenny inquiringly.

Jenny shrugged.

'She's in rotten form today,' he continued. 'I thought she went to the UK for the weekend. You'd imagine she'd be in better humour after a weekend away.'

'She was at her friend's wedding,' said Jenny. 'I think she's feeling a bit down after it.'

'For God's sake!' Gavin looked disgusted. 'What is that woman's problem?'

'Maybe the fact that her boyfriend dumped her for a younger, leaner model?' suggested Jenny.

'You have to expect that,' Gavin sniggered. 'You girls don't realise what—'

'Gavin!' Jenny's eyes glittered in warning.

'Oh, come on! Alix is getting on a bit. She had to expect that sooner or later she'd get traded in.'

'Thank you for those words of wisdom, Gavin.' Alix's tone was icy. 'I'll certainly keep it in mind for the future.' She walked round to her desk and picked up the phone.

Gavin got up and left the room.

∽

Because Europa Bank was a wholesale bank and dealt only with corporate clients, not personal ones, none of the staff had accounts there. Alix was happy with that, she didn't like the idea of anyone she was working with knowing the state of her bank balance! Which might be a bit dodgy this month, she thought, as she queued at her own bank's automated teller machine at lunchtime. The month had seen lots of payments, including some big ones like the house insurance and her gym membership. She sighed as she thought of her gym membership. The number of times she'd been lately was abysmal, it was becoming a complete waste of money. And she knew that she wasn't as fit as she had been. The tightening waistband on her skirt was evidence of that. It was just that all the things that she'd once enjoyed doing didn't have any appeal right now.

'Hi, Alix!'

She turned round. Eimear Flaherty, who had left the bank the same time as Paul had left Alix, walked up to her. She was pushing a stroller with a sleeping baby inside.

'Eimear! It's nice to see you.' Alix smiled. 'How's life?'

'Oh, not so bad,' said Eimear.

'Do you miss us?' asked Alix.

Eimear laughed. 'Not a bit! I thought I would, but I haven't had time, to be honest with you. I'm looking after the two of them at home now, so there isn't a minute.'

'Does she always sleep like this?' Alix nodded at Eimear's daughter while she frantically tried to remember her name. Kate, she thought and grimaced. No, that was John Callaghan's daughter – her half-sister! How could she possibly think of that name right now?

'She's a little pet,' Eimear said, 'and she's really good about sleeping, Alix. Funny, she wasn't great all the time I was at work, but since I've given up she seems to have settled a lot more.'

'And what about her brother?' Alix couldn't remember his name either.

'Oh, Tom's always been a good sleeper.' Eimear laughed. 'Like his father!'

'Where is he now?' asked Alix.

'Tom is at his grandmother's,' said Eimear. 'She loves him,

loves looking after him. I had to bring missy here to the doctor – nothing wrong, just a check-up, so that's why she's with me. I was in Europa earlier – had to pick up some documents for the tax man. You know how it is.'

'And you didn't feel the urge to do a few quick settlements?'

'Not on your life!' Eimear shook her head. 'Honestly, Alix, I don't miss it at all. I miss the people, but you'd expect that. But I don't miss rushing around every morning trying to organise a husband and kids and myself and then rushing around every evening as well. Besides, the kids are fun. I know not everyone would think so, but I get a great laugh out of them. Tom still goes to the kindergarten in the mornings, of course, and I miss him while he's there.'

Alix slid her card into the ATM and keyed in her personal number. Despite the house insurance and the gym membership, her account was still in credit.

'And how are you keeping?' asked Eimear as Alix took her cash and replaced her card in her wallet. 'Not tripping up the aisle yourself yet?'

Alix laughed. 'Not me.'

'Don't you and Paul want kids?' she asked curiously. 'At some stage?'

'Even if I did, I wouldn't be having them with Paul,' said Alix lightly. 'We split up.'

'Oh, Alix, I'm sorry! I didn't know.'

'Of course you didn't. It's no problem. To be honest, I was upset at first, but I'm over it now.'

'So you'll have to find someone else to have babies with,' joked Eimear.

'It's not me,' Alix said. 'I don't have your patience, Eimear.'

'Of course you do,' said the other girl. 'It's instinctive.'

'That's a myth,' Alix laughed. 'I panic around kids.'

'Doesn't your sister have a few?'

'Two,' confirmed Alix. 'And I look after them from time to time. But it's a different kettle of fish when you can go home every night.'

'I think you'd be a great mother,' said Eimear. 'You're smart, you're fair, you're—'

'Going to be late if I don't get back!' interrupted Alix. 'It was nice to see you, Eimear. I'm glad it's all working out for you.'

'I'm sorry, I tend to gabble a bit these days,' said Eimear. 'It's probably because I do spend so much time with the kids. I've lost the knack of adult conversation.'

'Not at all,' said Alix. 'I'd love to chat for a little longer. But we've had a tense morning in the dealing room and I don't want to leave the bruised egos alone for too long.'

'That's something I certainly don't miss.' Eimear pulled the blanket more firmly round her baby. 'All that testosterone around the place. People trying to shaft other people! I lead a much more peaceful existence now.'

'Maybe you're right.' Alix smiled at her. 'Maybe one day I *will* settle down.'

'It's wonderful,' said Eimear sincerely. 'I'd heartily recommend it.' She waved at Alix again as she walked away.

Cliona, thought Alix, as she made her way back to the bank. Her daughter's name is Cliona.

∽

'Europa Bank, dealers.'

'Hello, Alix. *Ça va?*'

'Guy.' She made a face. 'I'm well. And you?'

'I am well also. I am phoning to say that I will be visiting the Dublin branch on Thursday.'

'Great,' said Alix insincerely. 'What time will you get here?'

'I'm coming from London,' said Guy. 'We expect to arrive in Dublin at around ten.'

'Who's coming with you?'

'Jacques Monet,' said Guy.

Jacques Monet! A high-profile meeting, thought Alix. Jacques was the manager for all of the European branches of the bank.

'I look forward to seeing you,' she said.

'And I look forward to seeing you,' said Guy. 'I know that Jacques will be lunching with Des. But perhaps you and I can have something to eat together?'

'Wonderful,' said Alix. 'I'll book a restaurant.'

'Perfect.'

'See you Thursday,' she said.

'*Au revoir*,' said Guy.

She sat back in her chair and scratched the top of her head with her pen.

'Was that Decourcelle?' asked Dave.

She nodded. 'He's coming over on Thursday. With Monet.'

Dave made a face. 'Wonder what's up.'

'I dunno.' She rubbed her nose. 'Something, for sure. They just don't drop in like that.'

'Maybe they're going to close the branch.' Jenny looked worried. 'Perhaps we're not profitable enough.'

'Don't be ridiculous,' said Gavin, although there was an edge in his voice. 'We're very profitable.'

'The treasury department is profitable,' said Alix. 'But the credit department was down last year.'

'That's because of the syndicated loan,' said Dave. 'Nobody thought that would end up being rescheduled.'

'And Paris was involved with that too,' said Alix. She sighed. 'I don't know, Dave. Maybe they're just visiting all the branches. They're coming from London.'

'Not so bad.' Dave nodded. 'Could be a whistle-stop tour.'

'Could be,' said Alix. 'But let's make sure we're on top form on the day.' Her phone line blinked and she picked it up. 'Europa Bank, dealers.'

'Hi, Alix.'

Her grip tightened on the receiver. 'Matt. Nice to hear from you.'

'I need to buy a tiny amount of dollars. Only fifty thousand.'

She glanced at the screen, then paused. 'I'll pass you on to Gavin, if that's all right, Matt. He's looking after your account and he's the one that should quote you.'

'I know. He rang to tell me. Why did you do that?' asked Matt.

'I don't take responsibility for many individual accounts,' she told him. 'I have overall responsibility for the room. So the accounts are usually allocated among the others.'

'Unless it's a huge account?' guessed Matt.

'I look after one or two,' she agreed.

'So when I have a big, big deal to do I might get to talk to you. Is that it?'

'Don't be silly,' she said.

Gavin looked across the desk at her.

433

'I thought you might ring me,' said Matt.

'Oh?'

'Yes. To tell me why the dollar has cheapened up so much against the yen.'

'Because people think they'll cut rates again,' she said automatically.

'I didn't know that,' said Matt.

'I think you did,' said Alix.

'Did I say or do anything to offend you?' Matt sounded aggrieved.

'When?' asked Alix.

'After the shooting,' said Matt. 'At your apartment. I thought I must have upset you somehow.'

'Of course you didn't.' She was very aware of Gavin following the conversation. The fact that he could only hear her side of it didn't make any difference.

'I thought you might have got a bad impression of me.'

'Matt, I've no idea what you mean.'

'Maybe it was me,' he said. 'Maybe I'm misreading the situation.'

'You're certainly misreading something,' said Alix.

'Well, look, before you pass me over to the young Turk, how about dinner?'

'Pardon?'

'Dinner. You know. You eat it in the evenings.'

'I know what it is,' said Alix.

'I was wondering if you'd like to eat it with me,' said Matt.

'I should ask you,' said Alix. 'You're the client, after all.'

'I was asking you as a friend. We can talk business, of course, but I wanted to be the one to ask,' said Matt.

Alix bit her lip. 'Remember what I said about that before? The next time you ask for a better rate or don't take advice or anything like that, both of us will get pissed at each other because—'

'I remember exactly what you said,' Matt said. 'But if you're handing over the account to Gavin, it doesn't matter, does it? Because I'll be getting all my advice and all my rates from him. So neither of us will get pissed at each other, as you so elegantly put it.'

She couldn't help smiling. 'When did you have in mind?'

'Thursday,' said Matt.

'I'm sorry,' said Alix. 'That's a really bad day. The European manager and the French head of European trading are both coming over. I'm meeting Guy at lunchtime and I'm pretty sure I'll need to be around later too.'

'Is this an excuse?' asked Matt suspiciously.

'Absolutely not,' she said.

'That's a pity,' said Matt. 'Because I'll be away myself the following week.'

'Oh.'

'Never mind,' he said cheerfully. 'Another time, maybe. You'd better put Gavin on the line, Alix. The dollar could have soared in the time we've wasted.'

'It hasn't,' she said.

'Just as well,' said Matt. 'Or I could sue you for keeping me chatting so that you could give me a rotten rate.'

❧

She never minded being alone. When Paul had lived with her she'd enjoyed the evenings he was away, savoured curling up on the sofa with a bottle of beer and a book. Because she spent so much time talking during the day, she loved not having to speak in the evenings.

But tonight was different. Of all the nights she'd spent since he'd left, tonight was the first night that she felt truly lonely. She wished things had been different. That he'd talked to her about babies. She might have taken more heed of him if he'd insisted on talking about it. She looked around at her white apartment and visualised sticky fingerprints on the walls. She sighed. She couldn't bear to think of sticky fingerprints on the walls.

∽

She wore her purple suit on Thursday and pulled her hair into a neat chignon. She took time over her make-up, ensuring that she looked perfect when she stepped out of the apartment. Her perfume was Chanel. She remembered that Guy Decourcelle liked Chanel.

Guy and Jacques arrived at a quarter past ten. Eileen Walsh phoned the dealing room and told Alix that they were meeting in Des's office. Pat Enright, the chief accountant, would be there too.

'Here goes,' she told the others as she left the room. 'Let's hope it's good news.'

'Ah, Alix! Good to see you.' Guy kissed her on both cheeks.

'And you, Guy.'

'Alix.' Jacques Monet kissed her too. 'You are looking well this morning.'

'Thank you, Jacques. I hope your flight was enjoyable.'

The older man made a face. 'We were late,' he said. 'Airlines do not seem to understand what "on time" actually means.'

Alix smiled at him as they sat down.

Eileen came in, carrying a tray loaded with cups and a large pot of coffee. She poured for all of them and then left.

'OK,' said Des. 'What brings you to Dublin?'

'Europa Bank in Paris will be making an announcement on a euro loss of fifty million due to unauthorised trading,' said Jacques.

Des, Alix and Pat looked at each other.

'Oh, shit,' said Alix.

'We have discovered the trader took positions in derivative products and was valuing them at a price significantly different to the actual market value.' This was always a nightmare scenario for trading houses. Because there were so many different products that a dealer could get involved in, and because so many of the risk managers and accountants found them difficult to value, there was always the possibility that a trader with a loss-making position could hide the potential loss.

'How did that happen?' asked Pat.

'We have an excellent futures trader,' said Guy. 'Unfortunately he managed to get himself into a position that depended entirely on interest rates going up. As you know, they haven't.'

Alix thought back to the Fed rate cut in July. The problems had probably started then.

'We have visited our European branches so that we can keep people informed ourselves,' said Jacques. 'There will, no doubt, be adverse press reaction and ridiculous stories about rogue traders and high-flying dealers and all the usual stuff

437

that comes out around this time. Obviously this will impact on the share price.'

'Obviously,' said Des.

'So we are also thinking of ways to increase our control on trading,' said Guy. 'Our systems let us down in this instance. We thought that they were foolproof but nothing ever is.'

'No,' said Pat. 'If someone has a shit position they'll find a way to hide it.'

'We hope not in the future,' said Jacques.

'So what does that mean for us in Dublin?' asked Des.

'Increased reporting to Paris,' Jacques told him. 'Also, we are thinking very much of bringing more of the trading function under the Paris umbrella.'

'The Paris umbrella wasn't very effective in the instance you're talking about,' said Alix. 'We haven't had that problem here.'

'I appreciate that,' Jacques said. 'But we are having to make radical changes in the way we operate. We haven't yet decided what way things will go but obviously since Dublin is such a tax-efficient operation for us, it might be worthwhile to take less risk here and channel more business through.'

'Which would make us a booking office and not a trading centre,' said Alix.

'It's only a possibility,' Guy reassured her. 'We haven't made any decisions yet. And nothing will happen before next year.'

'Next year will be here soon enough,' Alix said.

'We will be in constant contact with you,' said Jacques. 'But we will be conducting an audit of all the branches who trade. So that we can be sure there is nothing to hide.'

'That's fine by me,' said Alix. 'I know what's going on.'

'I agree with Alix.' Pat nodded. 'Our operation is relatively small and that means we have a good chance of finding anything untoward.'

'The auditors will come here next week,' said Jacques. 'So I hope you are right in what you say. We cannot afford any unpleasant surprises. As it is, the market will jump on this story.'

'It's tough,' said Des.

'You have to expect it from time to time,' Guy sighed. 'But you always hope that it won't happen to you.'

They discussed the situation for another fifteen minutes then Jacques looked at his watch. 'We have a meeting with ABN-Amro in ten minutes,' he told them. 'I think we had better leave. Des, I am meeting you at lunchtime, yes?'

'That's right.' Des nodded.

'And I am meeting you, Alix?' Guy smiled at her.

'Yes,' she said. 'I've booked Wrights for us. I'll meet you there.'

'Excellent.' Both men stood up and shook hands with their Dublin colleagues.

Des accompanied Jacques and Guy to the main door while Alix and Pat remained in his office.

'This is not good,' said Pat gloomily. 'It's been ages since any shock-horror huge trading loss story hit the market. The share price will take a battering.'

'I hope that fifty million is the whole size of it,' said Alix. 'You know these bloody things. They end up finding all sorts of horrible trades under the carpet.'

'Alix, there isn't anything like this in the dealing room here, is there?' Pat looked at her in concern. 'If there's anything I should know about, I'd appreciate finding out now, before the sharks from Paris descend on us.'

'I promise you there's nothing,' said Alix, grateful that because the room was so small she was able to keep abreast of everything that went on.

'We don't know enough,' said Pat, 'us accountants and risk managers. We take so much on faith, particularly on those structured products.'

'That's why I don't deal them,' said Alix kindly. 'Just to keep you happy, Pat. Anyway,' she smiled at him, 'since the hedge fund debacle in nineteen ninety-eight, a fifty million loss isn't the great disaster it once was. If you haven't lost four billion dollars, like John Meriwether and his friends, you're nobody.'

'I'm quite glad to be nobody, thanks,' said Pat sourly. 'I just hope you're right, Alix.'

The office door opened and Des walked back in. His face was grim. 'Right, you two,' he said. 'Let's get to grips with this. Starting now, Alix. I want to go through all your outstanding positions.'

Chapter 31

Guy Decourcelle was already sitting at the table in the bistro when Alix arrived. She walked through the restaurant to join him.

'I already ordered wine, I hope you don't mind,' he said.

Alix glanced at the bottle. Chablis. Guy only ever ordered French wine although he knew she preferred Italian.

'Not at all.' She sat down opposite him.

'You are concerned,' said Guy.

'Not for Dublin,' said Alix. 'I know everything that's going on here. It's just not good for the bank overall.'

'It's shit for the bank overall.' Guy poured the wine into her glass. 'And, Alix, it is not good for me. I should have known about this trade.'

'I know,' said Alix. 'Do they expect you to fall on your sword?'

Guy laughed. 'Not this time, I hope! The trader and his immediate superior have gone, but I've managed to stay put.'

'You were always good at getting out of a tight spot, Guy. Remember the Thai trade?'

He made a face. Guy had been long Thai government debt, a trade which had been spectacularly profitable for him. He had added to the position until he was close to his limits. And he had cut it in September 1997, a month before the Asian crisis hit the markets and caused spectacular losses. Guy and Alix had been talking about Asia during September of that year. Alix had seen a report on riots in Indonesia and had speculated that there would be unrest in the region. Guy had agreed with her. But not in Thailand, he'd said. He liked the Thai position. So it wasn't any great trading insight that had suddenly made him sell the debt, but a need for capital to fund a different project in the US. Guy had liquidated the entire position and, a month later, he was a hero.

'Better to be lucky than smart.' He chanted Europa Bank's mantra.

'You were always lucky.'

'So are you, Alix.'

'So far,' she admitted.

A waiter approached them and they gave their order.

'We will be looking for replacements in Paris,' said Guy.

'Oh?'

'We will not stop trading derivatives. Sure, they can be very risky but they are also very, very profitable. We will be making some changes in the room after this.'

'Recruiting from outside?'

'Yes,' said Guy. 'We want to shake up some of the teams. Change things around. Bring in new blood.'

'It's a good idea.'

'We would like you to join us, Alix.'

She stopped buttering her tomato bread and looked at him.

'Me?'

'Yes, you. You have experience. You are trustworthy. You're

not some hotshot trying to make a name for himself – or herself.'

'I might not want to move to Paris,' she told him.

'Why not?'

'I like my job in Dublin.' She resumed buttering the bread.

'Oh, come on!' Guy looked at her in disgust. 'It is a small operation, Alix. Surely you must find it very restrictive! I remember when you were in London. You were dealing in big size, running big positions. Lots of potential to make large sums of money and even larger bonuses. You can't get that in Europa Dublin.'

'I know. But it's interesting. I get to do a whole range of different things, not just specialise in one product. We have a diverse client base. I talk a lot to the credit people, the accounts people, the banking people. I get involved in a whole lot more than just trading.'

'And you find this more interesting than running the swaps desk in Paris?'

She sat very still. The swaps desk in Paris, where they dealt in fixed and floating rate borrowings, was a very big and very profitable area. If Guy was offering her the senior position on the swaps desk, it was a very good job.

'Swaps?'

'We're moving Michel Petit to the derivatives desk. That will leave an opening in swaps.'

'It's an interesting thought,' she said slowly.

'And you will accept?'

'I don't know,' she said. 'You've sprung this on me, Guy. I haven't had time to think.'

'You're a trader.' He smiled at her. 'You shouldn't need time to think!'

'About this, I do,' she said seriously. 'It would be a big change for me.'

'You will not have too much time to decide,' said Guy. 'I can only keep this offer open for you for two or three weeks. After that, we will approach someone else.'

'I see.'

'You should accept this,' said Guy. 'It is a good opportunity, Alix. Probably one of the best you'll ever get.'

He was right, she thought, as she listened to him talking about the Paris operation. It probably was one of the best offers that she'd ever get.

~

Dave, Gavin and Jenny were eating sandwiches at the desk.

'There's definitely something up,' said Jenny. 'They were at meetings all morning and Alix is late back from lunch.'

'You know Guy Decourcelle, he takes ages over lunch,' said Dave.

'But there was an atmosphere this morning,' Gavin said. 'Didn't you sense it?'

'We were creating it,' said Dave. 'Because we're worried.'

'Do you think we're right to be worried?' asked Jenny. 'Do you think they're going to close us down?'

'I can't see why.' Dave cracked his knuckles and made the other two wince. 'It's not as though we're losing money! Last year was phenomenal.'

'But they might be going to rationalise,' said Gavin.

'We wouldn't be the only place,' Jenny pointed out. 'There've been a number of cutbacks over the last eighteen months.'

'Maybe it's time to dust down the CV,' said Gavin. 'Get out there early before anyone realises something is up.'

'You were offered a job in Banco Andalucia, weren't you?' asked Jenny. 'Why don't you give them a call?'

'It was a crappy position,' admitted Gavin. 'They were looking for a junior.'

'I thought—'

'I know I made it out to be great,' said Gavin, 'but it wasn't what I wanted. Otherwise I'd have gone.'

They sat in silence.

'Maybe it's good news,' said Dave eventually. 'Maybe Europa has taken over another bank.'

'Maybe.' Jenny's face brightened.

A phone line began to ring. They all rushed to answer it.

∽

When Alix walked back into the room after lunch everyone looked anxiously at her.

'Well?' Dave asked.

She sat down at her desk and looked at the screens. The dollar was lower. The bonds they were holding had fallen in value but only slightly. Things were reasonably all right.

'They've made a monumental cock-up in Paris,' she told them.

'What?' asked Dave.

'Some junior managed to lose fifty million on an options trade.'

'Stupid fucker,' said Dave. 'Didn't anyone catch it?'

'Oh, Dave, you know how it is. He was marking it to market

at some totally unrealistic price. The head of derivatives didn't even notice.'

'You'd notice,' said Jenny.

'I hope so,' Alix grinned. 'But the upshot is that they're sending a team of auditors over in a week or so to look at the books. So, please, guys, no mad trades, no unauthorised positions.'

Although there were always strict limits on positions in place, sometimes an urgent customer trade might cause a dealer to breach that limit and ask for a retrospective authorisation. It was what had happened to Alix when she'd been trading Kiwis in London, and when she was almost fired by Logan McDonald as a result.

'They might want to take more control from Paris,' she added.

'Why?' asked Gavin. 'What can they do there that we're not doing here already?'

'They think that they might book more trades through us, but decrease our overall independent limits.'

'That's crap,' said Gavin. 'They'll be handcuffing us if they do that.'

'I know,' said Alix. She thought again of Guy's offer. If Paris did try to take control over Dublin then her job would be a lot less interesting than it was now. It made the offer look even more attractive.

'They just want pen-pushers!' Gavin was disgusted. 'They don't want dealers.'

'It's a reaction to the loss,' said Alix. 'They haven't decided what they want to do yet.'

'What about in Paris?' asked Gavin. 'Will there be more jobs there?'

'What do you mean?'

'I presume they're going to fire a whole bunch of them. They have to fire a bunch of them, Alix, you know how it works. So maybe there'll be jobs in Paris. That'd be more exciting.'

'There could well be,' she said carefully.

'Have they offered you something?' Jenny caught the tone in her voice.

'They might,' said Alix.

Dave, Gavin and Jenny stared at her.

'Guy is talking about a position on the swaps desk. It might not come to anything, of course.'

'What about us?' asked Dave. 'Where would that leave us?'

'They're not talking about losing jobs in Dublin,' said Alix. 'You guys will be fine.'

'But maybe not as busy,' said Jenny.

'Busier, if they start dealing more through Dublin,' said Alix. 'But maybe without as much autonomy.'

'And that's why you'd go, isn't it?' asked Dave shrewdly. 'You don't like people telling you what to do.'

Alix shrugged. 'It might be that they just don't want to keep me here. But I'd prefer to be my own boss, yes.'

'And you don't give a fuck about us,' said Gavin.

'That's not true,' she said sharply. 'Des and I will be having a number of meetings to discuss the future direction of the bank. We are concerned about everyone. Not just the dealing room either.'

'So if you go, there'll be another job here?' Dave looked at her with interest.

'I have no idea whether I'm going or not,' she said. 'I don't

447

even know whether I have a choice in the matter. But if I do then I suppose one of you will become head of treasury. I doubt very much that they'd recruit externally.' She looked at her watch. 'I have to go and talk to Pat Enright. I'll be in his office if you need me.'

'Well,' said Jenny when she'd left the room. 'Food for thought, don't you think?'

'I wonder will she go?' Dave frowned.

'Or will she be sent?' Jenny mused.

'Of course she will,' said Gavin. 'And it's a good opportunity for us if she does. You know how bloody conservative she is. It'd give us the chance to take some meaningful positions.'

'Not if we have Paris breathing down our necks,' said Jenny.

'You can get around that sort of thing,' Gavin said. 'It's easy enough. We could get bigger intraday limits, maybe. Make the trading easier.'

'From all accounts, Paris wants to make trading harder,' said Dave.

'Oh, you're cast in the same bloody mould!' cried Gavin. 'You just don't want to put your balls on the line.'

'I don't mind putting them on the line,' said Dave. 'It's the chopping block I have an aversion to.'

'Either way,' said Jenny hastily, 'we have to consider our own futures. Alix is going to be all over us like a rash making sure we don't do anything crazy.'

'We won't,' said Dave. 'Anyway, the Paris guys will be over soon so we don't want anything out of the ordinary on the books while they're here.'

'So we play it cool,' said Jenny.

'Absolutely,' said Dave.

'OK.' But Gavin looked dissatisfied.

〜

Alix arrived home at six o'clock to find Wyn's car parked outside the apartment. There was no sign of her sister.

She let herself in and changed from her suit into a pair of Levi's and a jumper. She brushed her hair and pulled it into a loose ponytail. Almost immediately, she looked about five years younger.

The doorbell buzzed and Alix looked at the monitor.

'It's me,' said Wyn unnecessarily. 'Let mc in.'

Alix let her sister in the main door and opened the door to the apartment. A minute later Wyn appeared.

'I called earlier,' she said, 'but you weren't home.'

'What's up?' asked Alix.

'I dropped over because if I phoned you'd make some excuse not to come,' said Wyn.

'Come where?'

'Dad is going home on Saturday,' Wyn told her. 'We're going out tonight. Carrie has booked a table in Milano. She's booked for four, Alix. You must come.'

'Wyn, does nothing I say penetrate your thick skull?' demanded Alix. 'I've already told you a thousand times that I've no intention of being a sop to John Callaghan's conscience. I'm not going out to dinner with him and that's absolutely final. Besides,' she added, 'I'm meeting Guy Decourcelle from the Paris office for dinner this evening.'

'Oh, Alix, just for once can't you forget about the job and think about your family?'

'He's not my family,' she hissed. 'He never was and he never will be.'

'We really want you to be with us,' said Wyn miserably. 'It doesn't feel right without you, Alix.'

'It doesn't feel right because it isn't right,' snapped Alix. 'He can't just come back and pretend that everything's OK. So I won't be there and I don't care, Wyn, I'm not going to be pressurised by you or by Carrie.'

'So what's the business dinner about?' asked Wyn.

'Guy Decourcelle is head of European trading in Paris,' said Alix. 'They've had a serious loss in the Paris office which has caused them to fire a number of people.'

'How does that affect you?' asked Wyn.

'Guy has suggested a job in Paris.'

'Paris!' exclaimed Wyn. 'Would you go?'

'Why not?' asked Alix. 'It might be fun.'

'I'd miss you,' said Wyn simply.

'What?'

'If you went to Paris. I'd miss you and so would the children.'

'That's nice to know,' said Alix. 'But they wouldn't miss me for long, I'll bet.'

'Why do you always have to pretend that nobody cares about you?' asked Wyn. 'Why don't you feel upset that you might miss us?'

'Of course I'd miss you,' said Alix. 'But it's no big deal. Lots of people work abroad. Anyway, I mightn't have a choice if I want to stay with Europa.'

'What about Paul?'

'What about him?'

'How would you ever get him back if you were in Paris?'

'I don't know if I will ever get him back,' said Alix.

'What about your aversion to finding someone new?'

450

'That doesn't matter at the moment.' Alix rubbed the back of her neck. 'Right now I'm more concerned about Paris. Of course,' she looked at Wyn thoughtfully, 'I could always just change jobs in Dublin. Or go back to London, maybe. Or even New York.'

'Would you?'

'Would I what?'

'Go to New York?'

'Why not?'

'It's so far away.'

'God almighty, Wyn, you're so parochial!' Alix glared at her. 'I've nothing to tie me down here and I don't want to have. Doesn't that make sense to you?'

'I know what you're saying,' Wyn responded. 'I just don't think it's very worthwhile, that's all.'

'So what would make you happy?' asked Alix.

'Seeing you happy,' said Wyn.

'I am happy!' snapped Alix. 'How can I prove that to you?'

'I don't know.'

The sisters were silent.

'Would you like some coffee?' asked Alix. 'I was just about to make some.'

'Yes, please.'

Alix filled the kettle and spooned coffee into the mugs.

'I brought some photographs,' said Wyn.

'Not again!' Alix stared at her. 'What is this, Wyn? Some kind of war of attrition?'

'I just thought that—'

'Don't think,' said Alix. 'Just forget it.'

'But if Carrie can forgive and forget—'

'I doubt very much if Carrie can do either.'

451

'I think she has,' said Wyn. 'She says there's no point in nursing a grudge for thirty years.'

'If that means you think I'm nursing a grudge, you're mistaken,' said Alix. 'I'm not nursing anything. But what you both seem to forget is that I can hardly remember the man. I was only three when he left. So he wasn't all that much a part of my life. I just don't see the need to fawn all over him now. That's all.'

'But don't you want to know what he's like?' asked Wyn. 'That's what I don't understand, Alix. You're usually so curious about people.'

'Not about him.' Alix opened the fridge. There was just enough milk for one cup of coffee. She poured it into Wyn's cup. 'Here.' She handed Wyn the coffee.

'Thanks.'

'I hope you have a good time at Milano,' said Alix after a few moment's silence.

'I'm sure we will,' said Wyn.

'Tell Carrie I'll call her tomorrow or Sunday,' said Alix.

'OK.'

'Tell me one thing.'

'What?'

'How does Imogen feel about all this togetherness?'

Wyn shrugged. 'I don't know.'

'Because if I was her I'd sure be pissed off about it.'

'Why?'

'She's been his main woman for the past thirty years. Now he's gone all gooey about his wife and kids. If I was her I'd be feeling worried.'

'I don't think she is,' said Wyn. 'I think she accepts it. She's a strong woman.'

452

'I thought she was weak,' said Alix. 'I thought that's why he left us.'

'Oh, Alix.' Wyn drained her cup. 'You just won't accept that people grow up, will you?'

'Don't talk rubbish.' Alix took the cup and put it on the counter.

◡

She really wasn't in the mood to meet Guy Decourcelle for dinner. But she had to talk to him so that she could assess the potential job in Paris. And find out more about their plans for Dublin. So she'd booked Les Frères Jacques in Dame Street for nine o'clock. She knew that Guy liked the French restaurant.

Really, she thought, as she applied her make-up, it would be so much nicer to just flop in front of the TV and chill out for the night. It would be much more agreeable to send out for Chinese than eat haute cuisine. Alix's favourite meal was beans on toast but she'd never admitted that to anyone.

Her taxi arrived at a quarter to nine, just as she was beginning to think it wasn't going to come at all.

'Ready for a nice night out?' asked the taxi driver.

Alix muttered noncommittally. She wanted to think about what she needed to say to Guy. What was important for her and for the others in the dealing room.

She arrived at the restaurant exactly on time and was shown directly to her table. The waiter brought her a glass of Perrier and then Guy arrived.

'You look lovely, *ma chérie*,' he said as he took in her simple

453

black dress, the strand of pearls round her neck and her pearl earrings.

'Thank you,' she said.

'I like the way you do your hair,' he told her. '*Très chic.*'

'You think so?' She'd redone the chignon.

'Absolutely,' he said. 'Although I would like it more if it were around your face.'

'I don't wear my hair down when I go out for dinner,' said Alix.

'You never wear your hair down,' said Guy.

'I wear it down in the office,' she told him. 'Although I tie it back.'

'But never loose,' said Guy.

'No,' she said.

'Because you are not truly relaxed.'

'Because it gets in my eyes,' she told him as she handed him the menu she'd been given earlier.

Guy chose mussels and boeuf bourguignonne. Alix ordered salad and chicken.

'Excellent,' said Guy when the waiter left with their order. 'I like this place, Alix.'

'That's why I chose it,' she said.

'So.' He looked at her. 'Are you going to come and work for me?'

'I don't know,' she said.

'It will be a good job,' he told her. 'A senior position, Alix. You will earn more money than you do now. I think you would enjoy it.'

'What about my family and friends?' she asked.

'Pardon?'

'What about my family and friends here?'

'Well, for sure, they cannot come!' Guy laughed at his own joke.

'I know,' said Alix. 'I might miss them.'

'You are not serious, *ma petite*? A woman like you, you do not miss your family and friends. Besides, Des told me, the boyfriend is history!'

'Des told you that, did he?'

'Yes. We were talking about you some weeks ago.'

When Des had first mentioned the possibility of a job in Paris to her, had he known about the losses already?

'We were talking about Paris generally,' Guy explained, as if he sensed her unspoken question, 'and I said we could always do with fresh talent.'

'And I'm fresh talent?'

'For Paris, yes.'

'And Des wanted me to go?'

Guy shrugged. 'He said that he thought you were under-utilised in the dealing room.'

'I see.' Under-utilised my foot, thought Alix. Des was just trying to make life easier for himself. He thought things would run more smoothly with Dave in her job. So, she thought, if she took the Paris job she'd be playing directly into Des's hands. But if she didn't, she could be cutting off her nose to spite her face. She sighed.

'What's the matter?' asked Guy.

'Nothing,' she said. 'I just have a lot to think about.'

'Why don't you come over to Paris soon,' said Guy. 'Have a look around. Get the feel of the place as somewhere you might work rather than just visit.'

She nodded. 'That would be a good idea.'

'Because we do have to resolve things quickly, Alix. The market will expect it.'

'I understand,' she said. 'And I'll come over as soon as I can.'

～

It was late when she got back to the apartment. Guy had asked her to join him for a drink in his hotel, but she refused.

'I'm tired,' she told him. 'I need to get some sleep.'

'I am also tired,' said Guy, 'but not so tired that I cannot enjoy a brandy with you.'

'I would fall asleep,' she told him. 'It's been a busy week for me.'

'Take the job,' he said as she left him. 'You'll regret it if you don't.'

He was probably right, she thought, as she looked through her wardrobe to select what she'd wear the following day. A good job with a good bank in a beautiful city. Why would she even have to think about it? What was there left for her in Europa Bank Dublin? Where would her career go if she stayed? Would she fade into insignificance?

'Bugger,' she suddenly said aloud, as she took a suit from the wardrobe. It was the bloody TV interview tomorrow! She groaned and selected a different suit. One more appropriate to appearing on TV and telling the world what it was like to be a successful female executive in a male-dominated industry.

She wished she bloody knew what it was like herself!

Chapter 32

Paul rang early to remind her about the interview.

'I hadn't forgotten,' she said testily. 'You don't need to remind me.'

'The crew will be there by half past two.' Paul ignored her tone. 'Be nice to them, Alix.'

'Of course I'll be nice to them!' she exclaimed. 'What d'you take me for?'

'Alix, if you're in a bad mood you can strike a man down at five paces,' said Paul. 'And Damien O'Riordan is new to the job. I don't want him terrorised.'

She laughed. 'I won't terrorise him. It's not in my interests to terrorise him, is it? I'm supposed to be a showcase for the successful woman. You know, caring, sharing but with an edge of steel.'

'It'll take about an hour,' said Paul. 'You can spare him that much?'

'Sure.' She could spare him as much time as he liked. 'Are you still expecting to broadcast it before the end of the year?'

'I think so,' said Paul.

Alix hoped it would be before she moved to Paris. If she moved to Paris.

'Good luck,' Paul said. 'I'll phone you later, see how it went.'

'Thanks.' She noticed Jenny gesticulating at her. 'Got to go. Talk to you later.'

'Charlie Mulholland for you,' said Jenny. 'Line two.'

Alix picked up the line. 'Hi, Charlie. What can I do for you this morning?'

They were busy all morning. Alix tried to imagine what it would be like without her. She glanced at the other three dealers. Dave was chatting to one of his favourite clients about the weekend's football matches, Jenny was talking to another about the potential for world recession and Gavin was trying to explain the theory of Elliott Wave technical analysis to a guy who could hardly add two and two together.

Dave would get the job, even though Gavin probably harboured a secret hope that he'd be promoted. But Dave would run things efficiently. Alix wondered whether or not he'd have the same measure of control that she had. If Paris was going to become more involved, it probably wouldn't matter.

The phone rang again. 'Europa Bank, dealers,' she said.

∿

The TV crew arrived at exactly half past two. Alix had spent ten minutes in the ladies' reapplying her make-up before they arrived. She knew that she looked good in her olive-green Louise Kennedy suit, her understated jewellery and her hair slicked back into a French plait. She just hoped that she wouldn't make a complete fool of herself.

Rita McDonough, the receptionist, was chatting to Damien

O'Riordan when Alix stepped out of the lift on the ground floor. Damien was promising to interview Rita for a piece called *Unsung Heroes*.

'Alix Callaghan.' Alix extended her hand.

'Damien O'Riordan, nice to meet you.'

He was younger than she'd expected, in his early twenties, with gelled hair and silver glasses. He wore a navy suit, white shirt and red tie.

'I didn't know where you wanted to do this, Damien,' said Alix. 'We have a meeting room on the first floor or we could use my office which is attached to the dealing room. But there isn't a lot of space in my office.'

'I think we should do the interview in the meeting room,' said Damien. 'Then Phil can take a few shots of you at work.' He turned to the cameraman. 'What do you think, Phil?'

Phil nodded. 'Sounds OK to me.'

Alix led them to the meeting room where Phil and his sound technician set up the equipment.

'You're younger than I expected.' Damien smiled at Alix.

'You're younger than I expected too,' said Alix.

'I just look young,' said Damien. 'It's been a terrible curse. People think I should be doing children's TV because I have this youthful face.'

'How old are you?' she asked.

'Twenty-nine.'

She looked surprised.

'You see,' he said. 'Everyone reacts like that. I want to do serious stuff but they see my face and they think I'd do best telling four-year-olds how to make things out of old washing-up bottles.'

Alix laughed. 'Your shelf life will be longer. You can progress as you age gracefully.'

'I want to get on to the meaty stuff now,' said Damien. 'I've done lots of puffball pieces. I think this series will help.'

'So why have they got a male interviewer doing it?' asked Alix. 'Why not a woman if the piece is about women?'

'Because it was my idea,' replied Damien. 'And I wasn't going to hand it over to one of the female sharks, thanks very much!'

'Female sharks?'

'Barracudas,' said Damien. 'Once you get your teeth into something you don't let go.'

'Maybe because it's so difficult for us to get our teeth in in the first place,' suggested Alix.

He laughed. 'This is going to be a good interview. I can feel it.'

'How old did you think I was?' asked Alix.

'Pardon?'

'You said that I was younger than you thought. How old did you think I was?'

'I expected someone in their forties,' said Damien. 'But you're a lot younger than that. I've done a couple of these already and most of the women were older than you.'

'This is a young person's game,' said Alix. 'A few more years and I'll be too old.'

Damien smiled at her as he excused himself to check something with the cameraman. Alix stood at the window and gazed over the Liffey. She suddenly realised that the words she said were true. A few more years and maybe she would be too old for dealing. Everyone said that you burnt out in your thirties. That you had to move on before then. She

460

shivered. This was all she had ever done. All she ever wanted to do. She couldn't accept the idea that one day she wouldn't be able to do it any more. That younger people, snapping at her heels, would push her out of the way.

But they still wanted her in Paris. There was a role for her there. And perhaps, there, she could move higher in the corporate structure. Become part of a management group. Perhaps she could take over from Guy or even Jacques eventually. There was no reason why not. She spoke fluent French and both her Spanish and German were passable. She could easily be a manager for Europe. It might be an interesting job, shuttling between capital cities, devising strategic plans for Europa's branch network.

'Alix, we're ready.' Damien cut into her thoughts.

'OK,' she said. 'Where do you want me to sit?'

The TV camera didn't bother her. Although she'd only ever done one TV interview before, camera crews were part of the lives of people in financial markets. Anytime there was a sudden surge in prices or a sudden fall, camera crews popped up in dealing rooms zooming in on already harassed people trying to salvage something from the mess. During her time in London, when markets went through a particularly volatile phase, Alix was used to seeing herself on TV almost every evening as part of a run-in to that day's news item.

Damien O'Riordan cleared his throat and smiled at her.

'Alix Callaghan, head of treasury at the prestigious Europa Bank in Dublin, successful career woman, welcome.'

She smiled slightly at him, conscious that the camera was focused on her.

'Where do you get your drive?' asked Damien.

I don't know, she thought. I don't know why I get up every

461

morning to battle with everyone else in the market. I don't know why I want to pit my wits against people I've never even met.

'I've always been interested in financial markets,' she replied.

'But it's essentially a man's game, isn't it?' asked Damien.

Yes, she thought, it is. Maybe that's why I like it. Maybe I enjoy fighting with people like Gavin Donnelly. At the time I don't think I do, but it must be part of me.

'That's changing, Damien. There are more and more women in financial services these days.'

'So is it harder to be taken seriously as a woman in this industry?'

She remembered an argument with Dave Bryant one day when she'd insisted that he cut a position and he'd yelled at her that it was making money and that he was going to run it. And she'd screamed at him, literally screamed, that he was to cut the fucking position now! There'd been a moment's silence and then he'd muttered 'time of month'.

'I think many men still find it difficult to accept women in positions of authority,' she said.

'But not you,' said Damien. 'You have a reputation for being strong.'

Afterwards, she'd gone into the loo and stayed there until she'd managed to get herself under control again. It hadn't been the time of the month. Not even close.

'Everyone has to be strong if they want to do well.'

Damien continued to ask questions and she continued to answer them. What would he say, she wondered, if I told him that I'd spent the last couple of months in a power struggle with one of my junior dealers and that, at the end of it all, it mightn't make any difference?

'So what about your personal life?' asked Damien.

'Pardon?'

'Personal life. When do you get time?' He glanced at his notes. 'You're in the office for ten or twelve hours a day. Is there someone special in your life and, if so, how do you cope with that?'

Had he been talking to Paul? He must have spoken to him, he must know already that her personal life was, currently, nothing to write home about.

'I go to the gym and I'm a member of a shooting club,' she said. 'So that gives me outside interests.'

'But what about a family?' asked Damien. 'Don't you ever feel that the time is approaching when you'd like to settle down?'

She smiled even though she was gritting her teeth. I'll kill Paul, she thought. I'll fucking kill him.

'Sometimes,' she said easily. 'But not yet.'

'But this is a problem for career women, isn't it?' Damien persisted. 'Because you commit so much to your career you have to put the family side of things on hold. And then, suddenly, it's too late. So how do you cope with that?'

'It's not too late for me yet.' She smiled at him. 'So I don't know how women for whom it has become too late actually cope.'

'It's something that must concern you, all the same.'

'I think about it,' she said. 'But it doesn't occupy my waking thoughts.'

'And if the right man came along, would you abandon everything?' asked Damien. 'Would you say, yes, I've had a great career but things have changed now?'

'Would you ask a man that question?' Alix regarded him

463

stonily. 'Why should I give up my career? If you were interviewing a man you wouldn't ever consider asking him that question.'

'But it's an important issue for women, not for men.'

'I beg your pardon!' She stared at him. 'Are you saying that only women should care about family and children? That the choice is ours alone?'

'No.' Damien looked uncomfortable. 'I'm just saying that most women eventually give up their jobs and I wondered what the catalyst was.'

'Maybe the fact that, at present, so much of business is played by rules that have been set by men,' suggested Alix. 'The workplace is not overly friendly towards women although certain companies have tried. But as long as the route to the top is by confrontation rather than compromise, women will always struggle.'

'Is that because women are hopeless at confrontation?' asked Damien.

'It's because we prefer compromise,' said Alix. 'Because we don't think you have to stamp a rival into the ground. Because we don't feel you have to constantly score points off each other. But men seem to enjoy that.'

'So, at present, you have no plans to give up work and have a family?' Damien returned to his original question.

'I don't think the two are mutually exclusive,' said Alix.

'Alix Callaghan, thank you very much.' Damien grinned at her as the camera was turned off. 'Great interview, thanks.'

'I didn't realise you were going to get so personal,' said Alix.

'Oh, we always have to on the woman-in-work front,' Damien told her. 'It's the great dilemma thing, isn't it? Home and family versus the corporate struggle.'

'I suppose so,' said Alix.

'Anyway, that was great. Can we take a couple of shots of the dealing room now? You know, a few of you answering the phone, jumping up and down, that sort of thing?'

'Of course you can,' said Alix, 'but I can assure you nobody will be jumping up and down.'

In the dealing room Dave, Gavin and Jenny were discussing their futures.

'I bet she'll take that job in Paris and not give a shit about the rest of us,' said Gavin.

'What would you do?' asked Jenny.

'I'd take the job and not give a shit about the rest of you,' Gavin laughed.

'So why are you blaming her?'

'I'm not,' said Gavin. 'I'm just pointing out what she'll do.'

'And what are you going to do?' asked Jenny.

'I'm going to continue to be a valued member of the team.' Gavin grinned at her and Dave.

'If she goes you'll probably get promoted, Dave,' said Jenny.

'And so will I,' said Gavin.

Jenny looked at him. 'Promoted to what?'

'Senior dealer.'

'But you're still only learning,' said Jenny. 'If anyone becomes senior dealer, Gavin Donnelly, it'll be me.'

'Guys, guys!' Dave interrupted them. 'It's all pretty irrelevant at the moment. Let's just wait and see, shall we?'

'Sure,' said Jenny. 'But I don't want you giving any favours to him over me, Dave. Just keep that thought with you.'

'And remember,' said Gavin, 'that I might be the most recent member of the team, but it was me who made ten grand last week out of Harris. So I'm valuable.'

'I'll keep it all in mind,' said Dave, who was beginning to feel very pressurised.

'Here she is.' Gavin gestured to the other two as Alix walked in, followed by Damien O'Riordan and the cameraman.

'Alix! You never said that we were going to be on TV.' Jenny looked anguished. 'I would have done my face again.'

'It's OK,' said Alix, 'it's only a few general shots.'

'All the same,' moaned Jenny, 'if my mother is watching I don't want her to think I look a wreck.'

'We'll only take you from your good side,' said the cameraman. 'Is this unusual – half of the people in here are women?'

'Put like that I suppose it is,' said Alix. 'But maybe it's because we're a relatively small unit. Certainly you wouldn't get half of a thirty-strong room being women.'

'And how do you like it?' Damien turned to Gavin. 'Working for a woman?'

Alix held her breath.

'I'd prefer to work for a man,' said Gavin. 'But I suppose that Alix isn't too bad.'

'I'm not sure whether I'm being damned with faint praise or not,' said Alix.

'It's an interesting idea for a follow-on,' mused Damien. 'Men under women – what do you think?'

'Don't ask me,' she said. 'I always believe in being on top.'

Damien laughed but Gavin's smile barely reached his eyes.

⌐

It was almost time to go home by the time the camera crew had left. Alix poured herself some coffee and sat down.

'We're having a management meeting on Monday,' she told the others. 'We'll be going through the accounts and positions and all that sort of thing ahead of the audit. I thought we should have a meeting ourselves at five o'clock on Monday to talk it through. Does that suit everyone?'

'It'll have to, won't it?' said Gavin.

'Yes, it will.'

It would be nice, thought Alix, not to have to worry about Gavin any more. Of course there would still be someone. There was always someone ready to rip your face off when it came to trading.

'Five o'clock Monday,' she repeated.

Her phone rang and she answered.

'Hi, Alix, this is Rita at reception. There's someone here to see you.'

'Who?' asked Alix in surprise. She never scheduled meetings for Friday evenings.

'It's a gentleman,' she said. 'His name is John. He didn't give his surname. He said you'd know what it was about.'

Alix held the receiver in her hand and said nothing.

'Alix? You still there? Are you coming down or do you want me to send him up?'

'No!' she said sharply. 'Don't send him up. I'll be down. Tell him it might be a while.'

'OK,' said Rita.

Alix sat at her desk and stared unseeingly at the computer

screen in front of her. How *dare* he come here! How dare he try to confront her at work. In the place where she felt safe. She'd made her position perfectly clear. She wasn't going to see him.

'Alix, are you all right?' Dave looked at her curiously.

'Yes, sure,' she said.

'I think I'll head off,' said Dave. 'It's nearly five.'

'Fine.' She didn't look up. 'Actually, anyone who wants to go, just go.'

Gavin and Jenny exchanged glances.

'OK,' said Gavin and pulled on his jacket.

'See you Monday.' Jenny smiled at Alix.

'Yes. See you Monday,' said Alix.

She sat in the silence of the room and watched the numbers on the screen change in front of her. The dollar was down again. She'd known it would go down.

She wasn't going down to reception. She wasn't going to see John. Her father. The deserting bastard.

She picked up the phone and dialled Wyn's number but there was no reply. Then she dialled her mother's beauty salon.

'Carrie is with a client at the moment,' said Samantha. 'Do you want me to interrupt her, Alix?'

'No,' said Alix. 'It's OK. It's not important.' She hung up.

He needn't think he could browbeat her like this. He needn't think that she'd come running just because that was what he wanted. How dare he, she thought again. How dare he mess with her life.

She got up from the desk and looked out of the window. Tomorrow he'd be gone back to the States, back to Imogen and Kate and the life he'd made with them. And, if she met him, he'd go back congratulating himself on having smoothed over the cracks of his previous life. He'd feel exonerated. Forgiven. Well, she wasn't going to help him feel good.

She picked up her handbag and her car keys and walked out of the dealing room to the lifts. She got inside and pressed the button for the car park. Let him wait. She didn't care.

❧

Rita glanced at her watch and at the man sitting on the uncomfortable seat in the reception area. He was reading the paper, oblivious of the amount of time that had passed. He hadn't hassled her to phone Alix again and find out why she was keeping him waiting for so long.

Rita wondered who he was. She felt as though she should know him, as though she'd met him before. He'd only given his first name and when she pressed him for his surname he'd shaken his head and said that his first name was enough. That was very unusual. And, although he was smartly dressed in suit and tie, he didn't look like the usual businessman that came to Europa Bank. Although, Rita had to admit, sometimes the strangest looking people had business with the bank.

'Excuse me,' she said brightly and he put down the paper to look at her. 'Alix has obviously been delayed. I'll call her to remind her.'

'Fine,' he said.

There was a trace of an American accent, thought Rita. And there was something about the cut of the suit and the shining grey of his hair that reminded her of America too. She dialled Alix's extension. Phones in the dealing room rarely rang for more than a couple of seconds before someone picked them up. But there was no reply from extension 2421.

469

'Excuse me,' she said again and this time he folded the paper and walked over to her. 'I'm really sorry but it looks like Alix has gone home. She must have forgotten you were here. It's so unlike her.'

'I see,' he said.

'Can I give her a message on Monday?' asked Rita. 'Or will you be able to contact her before then?'

'I'm not sure,' he said. He stood hesitantly at the reception desk.

'If you like I can try her number again. She might have just popped out for a couple of minutes.'

He shook his head. 'It's OK. Tell her I waited for her, will you?'

'Of course,' said Rita. 'Can I give her your full name?'

He thought for a moment then smiled at Rita. 'No, it's OK. Just tell her I waited.'

Chapter 33

Wyn opened the bottle of Californian Chardonnay which John had given her and poured two glasses of wine. She handed one to Carrie who was sitting in the armchair, her legs curled up beneath her.

'Thanks.' Carrie smiled at her elder daughter and they clinked the glasses together before Wyn sat down opposite Carrie.

'I wish Alix had met him,' said Wyn. 'I think it would have put a lot of things in perspective for her.'

'Oh, I don't know.' Carrie ran her finger round the rim of her glass. 'She was only a toddler when John left. I guess she doesn't feel any attachment to him.'

'You always feel an attachment towards your parents,' said Wyn. 'Even a parent who has deserted you.'

Carrie sighed. 'Alix isn't like you. She's more detached. More self-contained. Maybe she doesn't feel the same emotional pull.' She took a sip of wine. 'I know she certainly doesn't feel it towards me.'

'That's not true!' Wyn stared at her mother. 'Alix is devoted to you.'

'Wyn, come on, it's me you're talking to! Alix isn't devoted to me.'

'Of course she is,' said Wyn.

'She cares about me,' said Carrie. 'I'm sure, in her way, she loves me. But she's always been difficult to know.'

'Is that because he left?' wondered Wyn. 'Would it have been different if he'd stayed?'

'You don't know how many times I've asked myself that question.' Carrie sighed. 'I don't know. Perhaps it's just the sort of person she is. She can compartmentalise her life so easily.'

'But she's cut up over Paul,' Wyn reminded her.

'Not in the way you'd imagine, though,' said Carrie. 'I called to see her when she was sick, remember? And she was cool as a cucumber about it. Said she might get him back and might not.'

Wyn shook her head. 'I think she was more upset than she let on. When I told her to go out and meet new people she said that she didn't want to. That it was too difficult.'

'She's the hard part of it,' said Carrie. 'She's so unyielding. I always felt sorry for her boyfriends, having to live up to whatever ideal she'd decided. Anyway, she hasn't let it interfere with her work, has she?'

'God, that bloody job!' Wyn put her glass on the coffee table beside them. 'It's a substitute for her. A substitute for everything.'

'Oh, Wyn, that's not fair.'

'It is,' said Wyn fiercely. 'She throws herself into it, wanting to be one of the lads all the time, pretending that it matters. It's a load of rubbish, Carrie! All this shifting money around the place. What does it achieve in the end? Makes a few rich people even richer, that's all.'

'It's made Alix fairly well off,' said Carrie in amusement.

'But she doesn't have a life,' complained Wyn. 'She spends so much of her time in there. Seven in the morning until six in the evening! Why? Surely there's more to life than that. It's no wonder Paul decided to dump her. She was never there for him. And as for kids,' she snorted, 'what chance would any kid of Alix's have? She'd never be there.'

'I worked long hours,' said Carrie. 'When you two were younger and I was setting up the salon I was there morning, noon and night. I remember you giving me grief about it, Wyn. You told me that Daddy spent all his time at work and so did I and it wasn't fair.'

Wyn blushed. 'I remember that too.'

'So you can't blame Alix if she's inherited the work ethic.'

'I don't mind her working so hard,' said Wyn. 'I just don't think it's worth sacrificing everything for.'

~

Alix switched off the computer monitor and rubbed her eyes. They were always sore after a day's trading which was why she rarely watched TV. After staring at a monitor for ten hours the last thing she wanted to do was to look at a TV screen.

She collected the sheets of paper from the printer. This month's profits were excellent. Two really good trades which accounted for over half the profit and a steady stream of income from the smaller accounts. Although it was always exciting to make a killing from a couple of big trades, it was satisfying to know that the income stream was diverse. You couldn't expect big ones every month and sometimes the big deals ended up losing you money. But not this month. This month was good.

'Still here?' Des Coyle put his head round the door.

'Just going,' said Alix. 'I was doing up the month-end figures.'

'How does it look?'

'Great.' She grinned at him. 'Paris will be pleased.'

'We've always shown them good profits,' said Des. 'And I'll be sorry if you decide to go, Alix.'

'Come on!' She laughed at him. 'You were trying to get me to go before all this blew up.'

Des looked embarrassed. 'Not really.'

'Oh, absolutely.' She looked him in the eye. 'You think that life will be easier with Dave in charge, don't you? You think that he'll get on better with Gavin and there'll be less tension.'

'It's no secret that you and Gavin—'

'That I rein in some of his worst impulses,' interrupted Alix. 'And if I do go, Des, you'd better look after Jenny Smith. She's worth ten of Gavin Donnelly.'

'I might have guessed you'd play the female card,' said Des.

'I'm not playing any card,' said Alix. 'I'm just telling you that Jenny is a smart girl and you'd be mad to lose her.'

'I'll keep it in mind,' said Des. 'Have you decided to go then?'

Alix shook her head. 'No. Not yet. I'm going to Paris to look things over. I won't decide until then.'

'I meant what I said,' Des told her. 'I would be sorry to lose you. But the opportunities are better there and I guess you've always wanted the opportunities, haven't you?'

'Maybe I'll get the opportunity to come back and grab your job.' She grinned at him and he smiled.

'I'll watch out for that.' He opened the dealing-room door. 'By the way,' he said, 'don't forget the Institute dinner next weekend.'

'Oh, God!' Alix stared at him. 'I *had* forgotten.'

'That's the sort of thing you can't forget if you want my job,' said Des and closed the door gently behind him.

Alix opened her desk drawer and rummaged around for her invitation to the dinner. She'd responded to the RSVP and then completely forgotten about it. Or, she admitted to herself, she'd pushed it to the back of her mind because she hated these kind of events. She found the invitation at the back of the drawer, a little the worse for wear. 'The Directors have much pleasure in inviting Alix Callaghan & Partner' it said coyly. She grimaced. They'd have to do with Alix Callaghan on her own. She'd told them she'd be coming on her own. She could do a bit of networking that way. God, she thought, I hate that too!

The phone rang.

'Alix Callaghan,' she said.

'Still there?' Paul's voice was teasing.

'Still here,' she said.

'I meant to ring you sooner,' said Paul. 'Damien says that you did a great interview. He's really pleased with it.'

'They'll probably edit it down to nothing,' said Alix.

'They'll edit it,' admitted Paul, 'but not to nothing. They think you were great, Alix. And you looked wonderful! But you always looked good in that suit.'

'You've seen the interview?' she asked.

'Yes.'

'I was very hassled that day,' she told him. 'Guy Decourcelle and Jacques Monet were over the day before. They were talking about restructuring the bank worldwide. Guy offered me a job.'

'You have a job,' said Paul.

'In Paris,' Alix told him.

'And will you take it?'

'I don't know,' she said. 'Part of me wants to and part of me doesn't.'

'What part doesn't?' asked Paul. 'I always thought you enjoyed the times you've worked abroad.'

'I do,' said Alix. 'It's just . . .' She sighed. 'I like my apartment. I like the way Dublin has developed over the past few years. I enjoy living here now.'

'You always waxed lyrical about Paris,' said Paul. 'I can't imagine your not wanting to live there.'

'I know,' she said. 'It's just something I need to think about, that's all.'

'Sabine is homesick,' Paul told her.

She said nothing.

'She likes Dublin,' he continued, 'but she misses her family.'

'I can understand that,' murmured Alix.

'So I'm sending her back to Paris next weekend,' he said. 'As a treat. For her to see how she really feels.'

'And will you miss her?' asked Alix.

'Of course I will,' said Paul. 'But she'll come back.'

'You're full of confidence.'

'Not really,' he said, 'but I think it'll do her good.'

Alix fingered the crumpled invitation in front of her. 'If you're at a loose end,' she said cautiously, 'you could always help me out.'

'Help you out with what?' asked Paul.

'The Institute dinner?'

'Oh, Alix! Not that stuffed shirt affair! I thought you weren't supposed to bring partners to it. I distinctly remember you telling me the last time you dragged me to one of those events that they never usually invited the spouse.'

'This year they have,' said Alix.

'I don't believe you haven't got someone else you can bring,' said Paul.

'I probably have,' she said, 'but I thought that, if you were doing nothing, you might like to come. It's purely business.'

'Great,' he said, 'you're dragging me to a boring business function.'

'It'll be your way of repaying me for doing that sodding interview,' she told him.

'Oh, well, if that's the case . . .'

'You'll come?'

'I suppose so,' he said. 'You could always wrap me round your little finger. But, Alix, it's just a friendship thing.'

'Of course it is,' she said. 'I'm not interested in you in any other way, Paul. I promise you.'

'I don't know whether I should be pleased about that or not,' he said.

'I'll phone you next week to arrange everything,' she said.

That worked out well, she thought, as she clicked out of the line. Des and Dave would be surprised to see her with Paul again. Dave had made a few pointed remarks about ageing dealers being left on the shelf in the last few weeks. It would be nice to show that she wasn't entirely without male company – even if it was Paul Hunter.

She was feeling full of energy when she got home. She threw her sports gear into her bag and drove to the gym. The changing rooms were full of women in various states of undress.

'Hi, Alix!' One of the aerobics instructors smiled at her. 'Haven't seen you in a while.'

'I've been busy,' she said. 'But I thought I needed the workout.'

'Are you coming to one of my classes?' she asked.

Alix shook her head. 'I'm just going to do some weights and have a run.'

'Good luck.' The instructor smiled at Alix and went off to take her class.

Alix changed into her Reebok top and shorts and pulled her hair back into a ponytail. She stretched a couple of times then walked out into the gym area.

'Don't forget to warm up properly!' called the instructor and Alix made a face at her.

But she stretched again, then warmed up for ten minutes on the bike before beginning a circuit of weights. She liked being at the gym. The only thoughts that came into her head when she was working out were of the number of repetitions she was doing. Even on the treadmill she simply watched the people swimming in the pool below and didn't think of anything at all. But this time, as she ran, she couldn't help wondering about John Callaghan. Had he waited long when he'd come to see her? she wondered. Or had he realised quickly that she wasn't going to waste her time coming down to see him? She gritted her teeth as the incline grew steeper and she had to run harder. It was his own fault, he shouldn't have called in like that. If he wanted to see her, he could have rung her first. And she wouldn't have answered his call.

~

'Alix, Matt Connery wants to talk to you.' Gavin glared at her. He'd done a trade with Connery, another small purchase of dollars by the client, and he'd thought that Connery was happy enough with the price. But he'd asked to speak with Alix. Gavin didn't want him to speak with Alix.

'Hello,' she said.

'Hi there.'

'How are you?' she asked. 'How was your trip?'

'Oh, fine.' He sounded tired, she thought.

'When did you get back?'

'Yesterday,' said Matt.

'Profitable?'

'I sure hope so.' He laughed. 'I like the Japanese but I really haven't managed to get to grips with their culture. I feel as though they're all looking at me as a stupid foreigner even though they're smiling at me.'

'I suppose they've finally got something to smile about.' Alix glanced at the dollar/yen exchange rate. 'The economy is beginning to turn around a little.'

'You bring it back to basics so quickly,' complained Matt. 'I was talking about the people and their culture and you've reduced it to economic performance!'

'Sorry,' said Alix. She was conscious of Gavin watching her. Why should he be worried? She'd given him the account, hadn't she? She could chat to a client if she wanted to.

'Have you ever read *Tai-Pan*?' asked Matt.

'By James Clavell?' Alix smiled. 'Actually, I have. And the follow-ons right up until *Noble House*. They were very interesting.'

'They explain a lot,' agreed Matt.

'I had a number of Japanese clients when I worked in London,' said Alix. 'You learn to work differently with them.'

'"He who smiles rather than rages is always the stronger",' said Matt.

'I beg your pardon?'

'It's a Japanese proverb,' he told her. 'And it's one that I try to follow.'

She laughed. 'It wouldn't work in the dealing room, I'm afraid. A little healthy rage goes a long, long way.'

Matt laughed too. 'I don't want you to rage at me,' he said, 'but I did want to ask you something.'

'Sure.'

'Before I went away I asked you to dinner but you couldn't come. You were meeting people from your Paris office.'

'That's right,' interjected Alix, 'Guy Decourcelle. He's the head of European trading over there.'

'So I thought I'd renew the invitation,' continued Matt. 'How about Friday night?'

'This Friday?' asked Alix.

'Yes,' said Matt. 'Actually, I've got tickets to *Phantom of the Opera* at the Point Depot. I know it mightn't be your thing, but I thought it could be fun. Then dinner afterwards? It's just a thank-you for all the help you've given us.'

'Oh, Matt, I'm really sorry,' she said, 'but on Friday night we've got a Bankers' Institute dinner. I can't miss it. I'd be murdered if I did. Besides, I haven't been that

480

helpful. If anything, I should be asking you to dinner as my client.'

'My timing is all off,' he said ruefully. 'Never mind, another night perhaps.'

'Yes, sure,' she said. 'Another night.'

'Do I have to book it in your diary months ahead?' he asked.

'Don't be silly.' She laughed but it was forced laughter.

'How about the following Thursday?'

She looked at her electronic diary. 'Please don't get insulted, but I'll probably be in Paris on Thursday. I'm not sure whether I'll be back at the weekend or not.'

Matt sighed. 'I'm away around then myself. I might have to go back to Tokyo. Maybe I'll give you a call when I get back.'

'That's a good idea,' she said.

'OK,' said Matt. 'Sorry we couldn't have sorted out something first. Next time we should try and synchronise our diaries better. In the meantime have a good night at the Institute dinner and enjoy Paris.'

'If you want to talk about anything urgently we could do lunch,' suggested Alix.

'No. I wanted something more leisurely,' said Matt. 'I'll call you.'

'Fine,' said Alix. 'Talk to you then.' She ignored Gavin's black look as she hung up.

◡

Matt replaced the receiver and leaned back in his chair. He really didn't know why he was pursuing Alix Callaghan.

She was attractive and intelligent, certainly, but she was too damned independent for him. And she hadn't apologised half enough for not being able to go to the theatre with him.

He looked at the tickets on the desk in front of him and sighed. He picked up the phone again and punched in a number.

'Hello,' said a female voice.

'Kats?'

'Hello, Matt.'

'How are you?'

'I'm fine. Haven't heard from you in a while.'

'No. I've been busy. Listen, I was wondering if you're doing anything on Friday night?'

'No,' said Kats. 'I'm not.'

'Great. Would you like to come to *Phantom of the Opera* with me?'

'Who's let you down now, Matt?'

'Why should someone have let me down?'

'Why are you phoning me if it's not a case of someone letting you down?'

'OK,' he admitted, 'it's a woman I met. I thought she might like to come but she's busy that night.'

'Too busy for you?'

'Kats, please!'

'Oh, all right,' Kats laughed. 'But couldn't you find someone else?'

'I don't want to find someone else,' he told her.

'Oh!' She sounded surprised. 'Is this serious, then?'

'How can it be?' he asked. 'I haven't managed to get her out yet!'

'She'll fall for your charms eventually,' said Kats. 'They always do.'

I wish I could be so sure, thought Matt as he hung up on his younger sister. I really wish I could be so sure.

Chapter 34

Alix was torn between the pearl-grey knee-length Jasper Conran dress and the charcoal-grey Kaliko trousers. She stood in front of the mirror wearing the Conran and holding the trousers in front of her. They'd both look equally good for the Institute dinner, she thought, but which would make her look that little bit special?

She wanted to look special. She wanted Paul to look at her and wonder why on earth he had left her for Sabine Brassaert, painter and decorator, homesick Parisienne. She kept asking herself why she wanted to impress Paul, whether she really wanted him back in her life, what exactly her game plan was, but she didn't know the answers.

She slid out of the silk dress and into the trousers. The cut of the trousers was very flattering and she couldn't help wanting them. But the dress was more feminine. She toyed with the idea of buying both. She tried on the dress again.

It would have to be the dress, she decided. And she might buy the trousers but not today. If she bought the trousers she'd need to buy a top as well and she didn't have time to look for the right sort of top. She glanced at her watch. She was already late back from lunch as it was.

She took the dress to the cash desk and handed over her credit card.

'It's beautiful, isn't it?' The sales girl smiled at Alix. 'I want one myself. They've only just come in.'

'It's lovely,' said Alix. 'But I must be supporting that man by now. The amount of money I spend on his clothes is ridiculous.'

'They're classic pieces,' said the sales girl, 'and you get great wear out of them.'

Alix nodded. Actually, she got very little wear out of any of the clothes she bought for evening functions. She attended a few each year but she always felt as though she should be wearing something different each time. On the one occasion when she'd worn the same dress to two events in a row Des Coyle had asked her why.

'Because I like it,' she'd told him, wondering at the same time whether he was wearing a new suit.

She rarely dressed up for events other than work-related ones. At the weekends she wore jeans and sweatshirts, and she always changed into a comfortable pair of trousers and a sloppy jumper when she came home in the evenings.

Maybe that was another reason Paul had deserted her for Sabine, she thought as she walked along Abbey Street to the office. Perhaps he was tired of always seeing her encased in denim. But he was a casual dresser himself, surely he wouldn't have expected her to be wandering around the apartment in slinky dresses.

Or maybe he would. She wondered what Sabine wore. When she'd seen her in the airport, the girl had looked chic and elegant in designer jeans and a well-cut jacket. And at the reception in Europa Bank Paris she'd worn the stunning red

485

dress. And yet – that was such a contradiction. If Paul had really wanted the earth-mother type, why had he ended up with French chic like Sabine?

Alix gritted her teeth then sprinted across the road against the traffic lights.

〜

'I can do those for you at fifty-five,' said Gavin.

Dave Bryant glanced at his colleague.

'Yes,' Gavin confirmed, 'fifty-five.'

'Who are you dealing with?' mouthed Dave.

Gavin ignored him. 'Fine,' he said. 'Settlement Monday.'

'Who was that?' asked Dave when Gavin had concluded the call. 'And what exactly have you done?'

'Bought dollars,' said Gavin, 'from Harris.'

'At fifty-five?' Dave stared at him. 'How many?'

'We're short, aren't we?' asked Gavin.

'Yes, but Jenny already bought some from Ronan McMahon,' said Dave. 'And it's on the way down, Gavin.'

'I bought a bar,' said Gavin, using the slang for a million.

'Oh, fuck it!' Dave glared at his colleague. 'Jenny bought a bar too. We were only short half a bar. You knew that.'

'Sure, but Matt Connery was a buyer this morning and he hasn't dealt yet. I'll give him a call, try and lose some at a better level. You can sell the rest in the market.'

'At a loss,' said Dave. 'It's moving against us.'

'I'll ring Connery now.' Gavin pressed the speed dial on his phone.

'Matt Connery.'

'Hi, Matt, Gavin Donnelly here.'

'How are you, Gavin?'

'Fine, thanks. Look, remember you wanted to buy dollars this morning? The market's moved your way and I can show you some now.'

'I said I might be a buyer,' Matt told him, 'I didn't ask you for a firm price this morning. I'm not ready to deal yet.'

'But you'll need to, won't you?' asked Gavin. 'You were pretty definite about it earlier.'

'I know,' said Matt. 'But our US people didn't confirm so I won't know that I need them for sure until tomorrow.'

'That doesn't matter,' said Gavin confidently, 'I can sell them for you forward settlement.'

'It's OK,' said Matt. 'I'll wait until we get confirmations. I don't know what date I might need to settle.'

'But the dollar is moving your way now.' There was an edge to Gavin's voice. 'If you deal now you'll get a much better rate.'

'I'll have to risk it,' Matt told him. 'Anyway, it's been sliding all week. Maybe another day will move it even more in my direction.'

'I thought you were meant to cover risk not run it,' said Gavin.

There was a silence at the other end of the phone.

'Matt?' he said.

'Look, I appreciate the call,' said Matt eventually. 'I just don't need you telling me how to run my business. OK?'

'Of course,' said Gavin hastily. 'I'm sorry, Matt. I didn't mean to imply that you didn't know what you were doing.'

'That's OK,' said Matt. 'Hey, is Alix around?'

'No,' said Gavin shortly. 'She's shopping.'

'No, I'm not.' Alix stood behind him. 'I'm back. Anything the matter?'

He closed his eyes. He hadn't heard her come in.

'Matt Connery wants to talk to you,' said Gavin.

Alix walked round to her desk, dumped her shopping on the floor and picked up the phone. 'Hi.'

'Hi, how are you?'

'Fine,' said Alix. 'And you? Are you dealing with us?'

'Not today,' said Matt. 'Though Gavin was showing me some dollars.'

'Was there something wrong with the price?' asked Alex.

'Not at all,' said Matt. 'He wanted to sell dollars and he thought I was a buyer because I told him I might need some soon. But I don't have the goods yet and I don't want to buy until I do. I know I could do an option trade but I might actually just shift funds between a couple of Anatronics accounts. I think Gavin must really want to sell them – he was very determined!'

'Was he indeed?' Alix glanced at Gavin who was having a muttered conversation with Dave. 'I'm sure he has it all under control.'

'So am I,' said Matt. 'And I'm glad he put you on to me. How's your diary?'

'Still a little frantic,' said Alix.

'So's mine,' said Matt. 'But I'm determined to make a dinner date with you before the end of the year.'

'I'm sure we'll find time eventually,' she said.

'With a bit of luck,' said Matt. 'Enjoy the Institute dinner.'

She hung up and looked over at Gavin. 'What's going on in the dollar?'

'We're long,' said Dave. 'Gavin and Jenny bought some at the same time.'

'No we didn't,' said Jenny. 'I bought them from Coburn's before Gavin took them.'

Both Dave and Gavin glared at her.

'So are we very long?' asked Alix.

'A bar and a half altogether,' said Dave. 'We'd been holding a half.'

'And what are we long at?' asked Alix.

'Fifty-five,' said Gavin.

'An average of fifty-three,' said Dave, 'when you take Jenny's into account.' Alix looked at the screen. If they cut the position now they'd take a thousand-dollar loss.

'How has the dollar been trading?' she asked. 'It looks like it's still on a down trend.'

'It is,' said Gavin, 'but technically it's oversold.'

'What do you think, Dave?'

'It's a small enough loss,' he said. 'We can afford to run it a little, see if the dollar moves up a bit.'

'And why do you think it's going to move up?' asked Alix.

Dave shrugged. 'Gut.'

'Technicals,' said Gavin.

'I'll leave it up to you,' Alix told them. 'But don't run it past a five-grand loss.' She sat down and began to eat the sandwich she'd brought back for her lunch.

~

By five o'clock the dollar had hit the stop-loss limit that Alix had imposed and Gavin sold them to the market.

'It shouldn't have gone past ninety-five,' he told her as he wrote the ticket. 'Technically, ninety-five should have stopped it.'

'Technically it doesn't always do what you think,' said Alix.

'Oh, things could be worse,' Dave said. 'At least we made a few grand this morning out of the swap position.'

'And we made a grand out of the sterling position,' Jenny reminded her.

'Hallelujah.' Alix looked at the three of them. 'We've broken even on the day. I'm sure Guy Decourcelle will be very pleased about that.'

'It wasn't my fault,' said Gavin.

'I never said it was.'

'You're implying it.'

'Gavin, stop behaving like a bloody four-year-old.' Alix stretched her arms over her head. 'Go home, have a good weekend.'

Gavin got up and slung his jacket over his shoulder. 'I will,' he said and left the room.

'Why didn't you just cut it, Dave?' asked Alix when Gavin had gone.

Dave shrugged. 'I don't know. I wanted him to make the decision.'

'He won't,' said Alix. 'He's hopeless at cutting losses. He always thinks there's some magic way to turn them into profits again. He needs to learn.'

'You're right,' said Dave. 'And I suppose I should have done something.'

'It was a cheap lesson,' said Alix. 'Maybe it'll rub off this time.' She stood up. 'I'm heading home now, Dave. Got to soak in the bath and all that before the dinner tonight. I'll see you there, shall I?'

'I'll be in the Horseshoe Bar,' said Dave.

'OK.' Alix picked up her shopping. 'See you later.'

⁓

She mixed the hair colour carefully. She was getting quite good at this, she thought as she checked her roots for grey. The sprinkling was there, mocking her. She covered it with the purple gel hoping, as she always did, that it would definitely come out the shade of auburn that was on the packet.

Her heart was beating more rapidly than usual. She could feel it pumping away inside her chest and she could feel, too, a frisson of nervous excitement. It was like the first time she'd gone out with Paul – a feeling of mingled anticipation and hope.

'Idiot,' she told herself as she sat on the sofa and painted her nails with fast-drying varnish. 'When you're with him you might decide that you've gone off him completely. Shit!' She swore softly as she painted the side of her thumb with carmine red.

When the time was up she rinsed the colour out of her hair and dried it. Perfect, she thought, as she surveyed it in the mirror. Much glossier than it ever was before she started colouring it in the first place!

She took time over her make-up, not rushing it like she usually did but blending the foundation carefully into her face and blotting her lipstick with a tissue before reapplying it for a more professional finish.

She wore the necklace and earrings that Paul had given her

and they glittered under the bedroom light. The grey silk dress was perfect, she decided. Simple and plain but with a low neck which she knew would draw eyes to her cleavage. And tonight she had a cleavage because she was wearing her Wonderbra. She knew that Paul had always liked the Wonderbra effect!

The doorbell buzzed. She went into the living room and checked the monitor.

'It's me.' Paul was looking directly into the camera. 'Will I come up or do you want to meet me down here?'

'I'll come down,' she said. She didn't want Paul in the apartment. Not yet.

She took her grey coat from the stand beside the door, picked up her bag and keys and went downstairs to meet him.

Paul was standing by his car, his hands in his pockets, when he saw Alix walk down the steps of the apartment. He drew in his breath sharply as she stood for a moment in the light of the doorway. She looked fantastic, he thought. So tall and elegant, her hair swept up into the sophisticated style that he so loved to undo at the end of the night, her coat open, revealing the knee-high dress and her shapely legs. Sabine was very pretty, he told himself, in her young, gamine way, but Alix was truly elegant.

'Your chariot,' he said as he opened the car door.

'We can take mine if you like,' she said. 'I'll leave it in town overnight and get a taxi home.'

'Don't be silly,' he said. 'I'll drive you home. It's the one advantage of being a non-drinker.'

'Sure?' she asked.

'Of course.'

She got into the car without further protest.

'You look lovely,' he said as he turned the key in the ignition.

'Thanks.' She smiled at him. 'So do you.'

'I hate this suit,' he told her, 'as well you know.'

She smiled again. 'So I'm especially grateful to you for wearing it.'

'You're exacting a tough payment for that bloody interview.'

'You know they'll give me such a hard time in the office.' She sighed.

'Don't pretend not to enjoy the attention,' he said. 'You love it really.'

She laughed and he turned on the car radio to listen to live football on Radio 5.

It was nice to sit beside him again, thought Alix, even if it was strange to be in his car. She leaned back and closed her eyes.

'Tired?' he asked.

'Not really. Just chilling out.'

'Hard day?'

She opened her eyes again. 'That Donnelly dickhead lost money. Not much but enough. Trying to be a hero.'

'*You* try to be a hero,' said Paul.

'Maybe,' Alix agreed, 'but I also know when discretion is the better part of valour.'

'And how are things in the dealing room these days?'

'*Comme çi comme ça*,' she replied. 'A bit of trouble in Paris which might have a knock-on effect.'

'Is that why they offered you a job over there?' asked Paul as he drove into the carpark.

'I think it's either go to Paris or leave Europa,' she told him.

'And what have you decided?'

'I haven't.'

'It's not like you to take a while to decide anything,' said Paul.

'I'm trying to be more mature,' Alix told him. 'I'm not going to rush into anything. Maybe I'll go. But maybe someone will offer me a wonderful job in Dublin tonight. Stranger things have happened.'

'It just seems so weird,' he said. 'That you might end up in Paris while I—'

'It does, doesn't it?' she interrupted him.

Paul parked the car and she opened the door and got out. 'Come on, I'd better not be late.' She strode purposefully towards the carpark exit and he had to hurry to catch up with her.

'Would you like to go?' he asked.

'I'm not certain.'

'How long would it be for?'

She turned to him. 'It's a permanent job.'

They stepped out into the side-street and Alix shivered. 'It's suddenly turned very cold.'

'Come on, then.' Paul put his arm round her shoulders. 'Let's walk quickly and you'll warm up.'

But she still felt cold even with the warmth of his arm round her.

Chapter 35

The foyer of the Shelbourne Hotel was crowded. Alix pushed her way through the Friday night throng towards the famous Horseshoe Bar. If anything, it was even more crowded. She stood on tiptoe to see if she could spot Dave but it was futile.

'Would you like a drink?' asked Paul.

'If you can manage to order one,' she replied doubtfully.

'Of course I can,' said Paul. 'Do you want a beer or a vodka?'

'Vodka and tonic, please,' said Alix. 'One cube of ice—'

'And no lemon. I know,' Paul interrupted her. 'Wait here.'

She leaned against the wall as he disappeared into the mêleé and wondered how long it would be before he emerged again. She eavesdropped on snatches of conversations between the other people near the bar. The row between the slim brunette and the overweight businessman was particularly interesting. But Alix missed the remainder of their argument when Paul squeezed by and handed her her vodka and tonic.

'Dave's in there,' he told her. 'With some girl.'

'Do we know her?' Alix swirled the drink in the glass.

'I didn't recognise her.' Paul shrugged.

'Great.' Alix beamed at him. 'Someone for me to annoy him

about. It doesn't happen often enough. Cheers!' She raised her glass to him.

'Cheers,' said Paul as he clinked his glass of 7-Up against it.

'What time did Sabine leave?' asked Alix casually.

'Lunchtime,' said Paul.

'Did you drop her to the airport?'

He nodded.

'When will she be back?'

'Next week, I hope,' he said.

Alix looked at him quizzically. 'Is it OK between you?'

'I don't really want to talk about it right now,' said Paul. 'Dave is about to join us.'

Alix turned as Dave Bryant and his companion stopped beside them. 'Hi, Dave,' she said unenthusiastically.

'Hello,' he said. 'This is Marilyn. Marilyn, this is Alix Callaghan.'

'Hi, Marilyn.' Alix extended her hand which the other girl shook briefly.

'You're his boss,' said Marilyn.

'I prefer to say colleague,' Alix told her.

'But you are his boss.'

'Yes,' said Alix.

'He loves being dominated.' There was a sudden twinkle in the other girl's eye. 'I should know.'

'Marilyn!' Dave looked aghast.

'It's true.' She shrugged and leaned her head on his shoulder.

'Don't you think we should be moving into the function room?' suggested Alix. 'It's after eight.'

'Suits me.' Paul drained his glass.

'You go ahead,' said Dave. 'We'll follow you.'

'See you later,' said Alix.

Paul walked beside her but he didn't take her arm or try to steer her by keeping his hand on the small of her back. She stopped to greet some of the other bankers who all smiled at her and nodded in recognition at Paul.

'I've missed this,' said Paul as she led him to their table.

'What?' she asked.

'These kind of stupid evenings.' He sat down. 'We don't have them in work.'

'I'm sure you do,' she replied spiritedly, 'and not only that but you have much more lovey-dovey arty kinds of things. Think of the Oscars for starters.'

'The Oscars are for movies,' said Paul calmly. 'The Emmys are for TV.'

'Oscar, Emmy, who cares what you call them,' said Alix impatiently. 'They're all the same.'

'Not if you're a winner,' Paul told her.

'Maybe you'll win something for the series,' she said.

'I don't think so,' Paul responded, 'but yours was the best by a mile, Alix. The others were so pushy but you were just yourself.'

'That's because you know what I'm like,' she said. 'The others were probably more interesting than me.'

'Not at all—' He broke off as Dave and Marilyn arrived at the table. 'Hi, there. Sit down.'

They glanced at the name cards then sat down opposite Alix and Paul.

'Paul is just telling me about the Oscars and Emmys,' said Alix.

'Actually we were talking about your TV interview,' he reminded her.

'That bloody thing!' Dave snorted. 'Why did they have to come in and film the place when we were so busy?'

'I thought it was a good time.' Paul glanced at Alix. 'You said it'd be OK.'

'And so it was,' she told him. 'As well you know, Dave Bryant. You guys were in the middle of a heated debate when I walked in. And I bet it had nothing to do with the dollar/yen rate!'

Dave grimaced. He hoped she hadn't overheard any of their discussion on the future of Europa Bank's dealing room without her.

❧

The dinner was like every other dinner that Alix had ever attended. Generally stilted or careful conversations but occasionally too much drink leading to the revelation of true feelings. There'd been a bust-up already between Shane Morgan, the very young chief executive of one of the German banks, and Piet Beumer, the much older chief executive of a Dutch bank. Alix had watched with interest as the younger man grew more and more red-faced while Piet Beumer chomped on a huge cigar and looked self-satisfied.

The speeches were particularly boring, with references to recent financial market turmoil and the credit crunch that borrowers were currently experiencing. But, she noticed, the banks were more concerned with eliminating risk than they were about lending to potentially viable customers. Alix knew that banks went with fashionable trends just like everyone else. When it was fashionable (and profitable) to lend money to emerging markets such as Brazil and Korea, the banks rushed around handing out money as fast as they could, although it all went horribly wrong for them later. Renowned figures like Rupert Murdoch found it easy to obtain credit simply by telling one bank that he could get the money cheaper somewhere else. Banks hated to think that their rivals were lending to the tycoons more cheaply.

Alix fiddled with her napkin while she listened to the same stuff she'd heard the year before and the year before that too. She glanced at Marilyn who was staring into the distance, a glazed look on her face. No wonder she looks like that, thought Alix. I understand what they're talking about and I'm bored too!

But eventually the speeches were over and people began to circulate around the room.

'Hi, Alix!' Chris Curtis of State Bank of Boston waved at her. 'How are you?'

'I'm great.'

'I've been meaning to call you,' said Chris. 'I haven't seen you in ages.'

'Busy lives,' Alix said.

'Don't talk to me about busy,' Chris sighed. 'We're up to our necks at the moment. How are things in Europa?'

'OK,' said Alix.

'Any fallout from that Paris loss?' he asked casually.

She smiled. Competitors always loved to hear about losses. 'Nope,' she said. 'Except that the Paris guys are frantically running around making sure that it can't happen again.'

'It always can,' said Chris gloomily. 'I remember when I was at – well, it doesn't matter. You're not in the market, are you?'

She looked at him in surprise. 'Me personally?'

499

'We're looking for people,' he explained.

'For what?'

'Couple of new jobs.'

'Reporting to?'

'Me,' said Chris.

She smiled at him. 'I'm happy where I am,' she said. 'But if I hear of anyone, I'll let you know.'

Paul walked over to them, carrying a couple of drinks.

'Do you know Paul Hunter?' she asked Chris.

'Of course.' Chris held out his hand. 'We met at some Christmas do. Last year or the year before. How are you, Paul?'

'Fine, thanks.'

'You worked in, um . . .'

'Journalism,' supplied Paul helpfully.

'Yes, that's it!' Chris grinned. 'Better not say too much in front of you. Don't want it all spread across page one.'

'Oh, I don't think there's anything you could tell me to fill page one,' said Paul.

'You'd be surprised.' Chris tapped the side of his nose with his finger. 'But say nothing, that's my motto.' He smiled at Paul and Alix and then returned to his table.

'What a shithead,' remarked Paul.

'Oh, he's OK,' said Alix defensively.

'He's a tosser,' Paul said.

'You're so charming,' she told him.

'That's your job,' said Paul, 'Aren't you supposed to be mingling?'

It was easier when he wasn't beside her. She could chat more freely with her colleagues and rivals, secure in the knowledge that he wasn't listening and wasn't about to make some smart remark about how mercenary they all were. And yet, she thought, it's so nice to know that he is here. She sighed, then smiled as Laurence Coleman walked over to say hello.

Paul had gone to the gents when Dave Bryant collared her.

'What on earth is he doing here with you?' he demanded. 'I thought you two had split up.'

'We had,' said Alix. 'We're good friends. It can be like that, Dave.'

He regarded her sceptically. 'No it can't.'

'Of course it can. When you're mature about it.'

'Bollocks,' he said rudely. 'Are you taking him back? Has he finished shagging the French piece?'

'Dave Bryant, don't be so utterly disgusting!' She was annoyed with him.

'Oh, come on, Alix. You can't go back. You know that.'

'I'm not going back,' she said. 'I don't know what gave you that idea.'

'Seeing you with him,' said Dave. 'I mean, Alix, he's living with somebody else!'

'Not right now,' she told him. 'Right now he's on his own.'

'And you think?'

She shrugged. 'I don't think anything. I wanted to bring someone along tonight – Des was so bloody insistent about it – so I brought Paul. It's perfectly simple.'

'There isn't a hope in hell that I'd bring one of my ex-girlfriends to a boring old fart evening like this evening,' said Dave.

'But you drag your new one along?' asked Alix.

'I don't know her too well,' admitted Dave. 'But we get on. And she was a sport about coming along tonight.'

'So was Paul,' said Alix sweetly.

'So was I what?' asked Paul.

'A sport about coming along tonight,' Alix told him.

'That's me.' Paul grinned. 'Sporty till the end.'

Alix went to talk about swap rates with Dermot Power of Citibank.

'I can't see them tightening,' said Dermot. 'Not in the current environment, Alix.'

'Neither can I,' she sighed. 'But it's been so one-way lately. Makes it very difficult to trade.'

'Or easy,' said Dermot, 'depending on your point of view.'

'Difficult,' she disagreed. 'There's no liquidity in the market. People just get caught up in positions they can't unwind.'

'Any position you get caught up in, Alix, I'll be only too pleased to unwind for you.' He smiled knowingly at her.

'I'll let you know,' she said and got up from the table.

She rejoined Paul. 'Sorry about that.' She sat down beside him. 'I got stuck talking to him. Couldn't get away.'

'That's OK,' said Paul.

She glanced at her watch. It was almost midnight. 'We can go soon if you like.'

'Whatever,' he said, 'it's up to you.'

'I'll just say a quick hello to Joan Farrell from Nedbank.' Alix got up again. 'I haven't had a chance to talk to her yet.'

Joan yawned then smiled at Alix. 'Sometimes I just want to pack it all in. Nights like tonight for example.'

'I know,' said Alix. 'I'd much rather be at home with a book.'

'Well, I was thinking of something more exciting myself,' said Joan. 'But this crowd wasn't it.'

'It's not the worst of them,' said Alix.

'Close,' Joan told her. 'All this crap about bringing partners along too. Ridiculous. They don't care about what we do and you spend the whole night feeling guilty because you're talking to people.'

'Where's Bill?' Alix looked around for Joan's husband.

'At the bar. With John, Peter, Trevor and Garrett. They're talking golf. At least that's a topic they can all share. What about Paul?'

'Oh, you know Paul!' Alix laughed shortly. 'He's sitting at the table making notes about us all.'

'At least he's never said anything.'

'He's with RTÉ now,' said Alix. 'He forced me – sort of – to do this interview with them.'

'Really!' cried Joan. 'How exciting.'

Alix made a face. 'Not really. I'm just terrified I've said the wrong thing and will make a complete fool of myself.'

'Oh, you'd never do that,' said Joan. 'You're competent, Alix.'

'You say the nicest things.' Alix smiled at her.

'It's true.'

∽

'I'm ready to go now.' Alix stood beside Paul. 'If that's OK with you.'

'Sure,' he said easily.

'I hope you didn't find it too boring,' she said.

'As boring as all the others,' said Paul.

'Oh, really?' She looked at him anxiously. 'I'm sorry.'

'It's not your fault,' he said. 'Even you couldn't make an evening like this exciting.'

'We need a few film stars,' said Alix. 'Make it more like the Oscars or the Emmys or whatever you want to call them.'

'Michael Douglas giving the keynote speech?' Paul smiled. 'I could think of worse.'

'You'd have to write the speech for him,' Paul laughed.

'No problem,' said Alix decisively. 'I could do it.'

'I bet you could.'

They stood at the top of the steps. It was raining. Not very heavy rain but enough to make sure that they'd be wet by the time they got back to the car.

'I'll run down and get it,' said Paul. 'Save you getting soaked.'

'Are you sure?' asked Alix. 'I don't mind, really.'

'Why should both of us get wet?' asked Paul. 'And it's no problem.'

'All right,' she said gratefully. 'Off you go.'

He was being really, really nice tonight, she thought. In this Paul she could capture the feelings she had with the old Paul. With the Paul who left you for Sabine, she reminded herself. But he had a reason for that. The reason was a house and a garden and children and a wife who was happy to stay at home all day. That was why he had gone. She had to force herself to remember why she hadn't stopped him.

The Rover pulled up outside the hotel. She ran down the steps and got in quickly.

'It's getting heavier,' she said as she wiped the rain from her face. 'I hope you didn't get too wet.'

Paul shook his head. 'I ran.'

He indicated and moved into the traffic.

'I stepped in a puddle.' Alix slid off her high-heeled shoes and wriggled her toes.

'Will I give them a blast of warm air?' asked Paul.

'That'd be nice.'

He switched on the fan and Alix held her feet under the vents. But they weren't dry by the time they arrived at her apartment five minutes later.

'Want to come in?' she asked casually.

'Why not?'

She was surprised. She'd been expecting him to say that he couldn't come in, that he had things to do. She'd expected an excuse from him.

'Hasn't changed a bit,' he said as he followed her in the door.

'Did you think it would?' she asked.

He considered the question for a moment. 'I suppose I did, although I don't know why. After all, you picked the décor, didn't you?'

'You never liked the white walls,' she said.

'It just seemed sterile to me,' Paul told her. 'I still think terracotta would be warmer.'

'I like white,' she said firmly. 'Would you like some coffee?'

'Sure,' he said.

He sat down in the armchair near the TV. Alix watched him covertly as she spooned Java into the percolator. He was sitting in his old chair, legs spread out in front of him, as he always had.

'I'm just going to take off my wet stockings,' she told him.

She closed the bedroom door behind her and peeled off the stockings. It was difficult having him in the apartment. She'd thought that seeing him here might convince her that

505

he meant nothing to her any more, but it hadn't. It had made her feel more confused than ever. She slipped out of the grey dress and pulled on a sweatshirt and jogging pants. She didn't want to appear as though she was trying to seduce him now that he was back in the apartment.

She walked into the living room.

'Was the interview really OK?' she asked as she sat down on the sofa opposite him.

'Of course it was,' he said. 'I told you that.'

She shrugged. 'I wasn't sure.'

'That's not like you,' he said.

'What?'

'Uncertainty.'

'I've been less certain about things lately,' she told him wryly.

'About what?' he asked.

'Things.'

'Alix, if there was ever a word needed to describe you, uncertain is not that word. You've never been uncertain. You've always known exactly what you want and exactly how you intend to get it. Uncertainty was for other people, not Alix Callaghan.'

'You have a warped view of me.' She tucked her legs underneath her.

'No,' he said. 'I know you so well.'

'What am I thinking, then?' she asked.

'You're wondering if I still find you attractive,' said Paul.

Alix flushed.

'That's not difficult,' Paul said. 'After all, I'm wondering if you still find me attractive.'

'Are you?'

'Of course,' he said. 'Look, Alix, I know it's over between us but that doesn't mean I stopped caring about you. You still matter to me.'

'And Sabine?'

'She's different,' said Paul. 'She'll give me all the things I want.'

'A wife and family,' said Alix.

'Yes,' said Paul simply.

'Why does it matter so much?' asked Alix. 'Why couldn't you have been happy with me, Paul?'

'I was happy with you,' he said. 'But you wanted different things from me, Alix. You wanted support for your career and someone who agreed with you all the time. And that wasn't what I wanted.'

'What did you want?'

'Someone to support *my* career,' he said. 'And someone who believed my opinion was as good as theirs.'

'I believed that!' Alix stared at him. 'I believed in your opinion. And I did my best for your career. I got you that interview with the managing director of Carlow China when that scandal broke and he wouldn't talk to anyone! How can you say I didn't support your career?'

'I'm sorry.' Paul got up and sat beside her on the sofa. 'I know you did your best for me. It was just that I felt you did it because you felt obliged to, not because you wanted to.'

'That's so wrong,' whispered Alix. 'So wrong.'

They sat in silence for a moment.

'But you're not sure about Sabine,' Alix said finally. 'She's gone home for a while.'

'We want to be absolutely sure,' said Paul. 'I love her, Alix. She's everything I wanted in a woman.'

'She's very pretty,' said Alix.

'How do you know?' asked Paul. 'You hardly remember her, do you?'

'There was a picture,' said Alix hastily, 'of us at the Europa Bank reception. She was in it. She's blonde and small, isn't she?'

Paul smiled. 'Yes.'

'Complete opposite of me, in fact.'

He made a face. 'Yes.'

'And ready to have lots and lots of babies.'

'Yes,' he said again.

'But what about her career as a decorator?'

'Interior design,' said Paul.

'Whatever.'

'It's not the same as being a dealer. She can be home when she chooses.'

'But she'll still be the one painting the house in whatever colour she wants.' Alix forced a smile. 'You won't be able to voice your opinion on that one with her either.'

He laughed. 'I suppose not.'

Alix yawned. 'Sorry.'

'Tired now?' asked Paul sympathetically.

'You know how it is.' She closed her eyes and leaned back. 'With the possible changes in Europa, I'm trying to keep on top of everything and it isn't always easy.'

'Why do you do it?' asked Paul. 'Why do you push yourself all the time?'

Alix opened her eyes again. 'I don't.'

'You do,' Paul insisted. 'Over and over again, Alix. Why don't you just do something easier with your life?'

'Why should I?' she demanded. 'I like what I do, Paul. That's what you've never really understood, isn't it? I enjoy it. Yes, it makes me tired. Yes, it can be stressful. But I like it.'

'It won't always be there,' said Paul.

'What do you mean?'

'You know, Alix. When you get older and burnt out. It won't be there for you then. And you won't have anything else.'

'That's bullshit,' she told him. 'I won't be in dealing all my life, but I'll move on. There are other aspects to financial services, you know.'

'I love your passion,' he told her. 'I just wish you could have been like that about us. And about a family.'

Alix said nothing.

'You're so – so – exhilarating to be with,' said Paul.

'Not exhilarating enough,' said Alix. 'You left me.'

He leaned towards her and touched her cheek. She didn't move.

'I had to leave you,' he said. 'You know that.'

She held his hand against her cheek. 'Do I?'

'Alix—'

'*Do* you still find me attractive?' She smiled at him.

'Oh, Alix.'

'I still find *you* attractive,' she told him. She turned her head and kissed him on the hand.

'Alix, I –'

'But it's so hard to know what's just physical and what's more than that.'

'Physically, Alix, you're very, very attractive.'

'So are you.' She moved closer to him, still keeping his hand in hers.

'Thanks,' he said.

She leaned her head on his shoulder. 'I meant to thank

you more,' she said conversationally, 'for coming to the dinner.'

'I didn't mind.'

She stretched out on the sofa until her head was lying in his lap. She let go of his hand, put both of hers beneath her head and closed her eyes again.

'Alix, I should—'

'I get lonely,' she said. 'I know it's stupid but I get lonely at night.' She opened her eyes and looked at him.

'I can understand that,' he said.

She moved her head very slightly and felt him move beneath her. 'Paul!'

'Well, Alix, it's not easy when you—'

She giggled and sat up facing him. Her eyes glinted green as she looked at him. She reached into her hair and undid the diamanté clip that had held it in place. It fell around her shoulders in a cloud of newly coloured auburn.

'God, Alix, you're so lovely when you do that!'

'Paul, I deliberately changed into my ancient sweatshirt and pants so that you wouldn't think I was trying to come on to you or anything.'

'Alix, you'd look lovely in a sack!'

'No, Paul.' She grinned at him. 'I look lovely in the sack!'

He laughed and so did she. She put her arms round his neck and drew him closer to her. He smelled of Dune for men. She smiled. She'd introduced him to Dune for men.

'Alix, this probably isn't a very good idea.'

'I know.' She kissed him gently on the lips.

'It's probably a very bad idea.'

'I know.' She kissed him on his forehead.

'But it's a very pleasurable idea.'

'I know.' She lifted her sweatshirt over her head and dropped it on the floor. She wasn't wearing anything underneath.

'Oh, God, Alix.' He buried his head between her breasts and she held him fiercely to her as he moaned her name over and over again.

~

They lay side by side on the sofa. Alix could hear the thud of the rain against the window and the gentle gurgle of the percolator. The aroma of Java was enticing.

'Would you like some coffee?' she asked.

'What?' He opened his eyes.

'Coffee? Remember, I was making coffee.'

'Oh, yes. Coffee.'

'Would you like some?'

'Yes.' He struggled into a seated position.

'I'll get some for you in a moment,' she said. 'I just need to use the bathroom first.'

She slid away from him and picked up her sweatshirt and pants. She carried them into the bathroom with her. She stood naked in front of the full-length mirror. It was a good body, she thought. Firm in the right places. Round in the right places. She smiled at herself through her half-open eyes. She felt warm and languid and good about herself.

She stepped under the shower for a moment, then dried off briskly and pulled on her clothes.

Paul was still sitting on the sofa, although he'd fastened his shirt and trousers.

She poured out some coffee and carried it over to him.

'It'll have to be black,' she told him. 'I forgot to get milk earlier.'

Chapter 36

Paul sat behind the steering wheel and waited for the lights to change. It was 3 a.m. He'd wanted to leave after the coffee but Alix had talked to him about Europa Bank and her job and the possible move to Paris and he hadn't been able to shut her up. He felt sick every time he thought about making love to Alix. In his heart he hadn't wanted to, in his mind he'd wanted to be stronger but his body had let him down. Or not, he thought with a wry smile, as he remembered the pleasure of being with her. The very physical pleasure. She was a more inventive lover than Sabine. She was more exuberant, more joyful and certainly more acrobatic. Sabine liked him to lie side by side with her, before flipping her onto her back and entering her. Alix had twisted and turned on him, kissing every inch of his body, allowing her long hair to drift over him, sometimes beneath him, sometimes beside him and then, finally, on top of him. And it had been bloody wonderful. But with Sabine – with Sabine it was more meaningful.

The lights changed and he moved forward. Would Alix be able to see it as a one-night stand? He felt himself break into a sweat as he remembered her telling him, very soon after they first met, that she didn't go in for one-night stands. But this was different, wasn't it? She couldn't really believe that he would go back to her, could she? Because no matter how truly fantastic she was in bed, Alix Callaghan wasn't the woman he wanted to spend the rest of his life with. He loved Sabine Brassaert and he wanted to marry her. He only hoped that tonight hadn't ruined everything.

❧

Alix rinsed the coffee cups and left them on the drainer. She was trying to decide whether she'd always meant to make love to Paul tonight. Whether the idea had been there in the back of her mind from the moment she'd asked him to accompany her to the dinner. Probably, she admitted to herself. She'd wanted to see if she could do it. Prove to herself that he was still attracted to her despite the so-called charms of the Parisienne. She wondered exactly how guilty Paul was feeling right now. She'd phone him tomorrow, she thought, as she climbed into bed and, almost immediately, fell asleep.

She didn't wake up until almost noon. It was the longest she'd slept in ages and she felt full of energy as soon as she got up. She thought about ringing Paul but decided against. If she called now, she'd appear needy.

She dressed in her sports clothes and drove to the gym where she ran on the treadmill for half an hour before doing a circuit of weights.

'You look very chirpy today,' remarked Patty McCullogh as she encountered a perspiring Alix on the way to the changing rooms.

'I'm in a good mood.' Alix grinned at her. 'I've had a good night's sleep for the first time in ages.'

'Looks more like you've had a good night's sex,' said Patty.

'Patty!' Alix blushed.

Patty laughed. 'It's a much better workout than this will ever be!' She waved at Alix and ran upstairs to the aerobics class.

She's probably right, thought Alix, as she stood under the shower. Sex certainly gets your heartbeat up. And in a much nicer way than a workout in the gym.

That evening, she dropped in to see Carrie.

'I wasn't expecting you,' said her mother as she opened the door. 'You didn't phone.'

'Do I have to?' asked Alix, although normally she rang before visiting her mother.

'Of course not.'

Alix followed her into the living room and sat down in the armchair near the bay window.

'Would you like a drink?' asked Carrie.

'A glass of wine would be nice,' said Alix.

Carrie went to the kitchen to get the wine and Alix sat back in the armchair. *He* might have sat here, she thought. Talking to Carrie, looking around the room critically, thinking that Imogen would have done it differently. She clenched her fist.

'To what do I owe the pleasure?' Carrie returned with a bottle of Pinot Grigio and a couple of glasses.

'I hadn't seen you in a while,' said Alix. 'I thought I should call in.'

'I'm sorry it's such a chore.' Carrie handed her a glass.

'It's not a chore, you know it's not.'

Carrie settled into the chair opposite. She looked tired, thought Alix, and older. She was wearing a loose jumper and a pair of trousers, both of which had seen better days. Alix was suddenly aware that she hardly ever saw Carrie looking anything but elegant. But that was because Carrie always had a warning of her impending arrival.

'What?' asked Carrie.

'Sorry?'

'You're staring at me. What's the matter?'

'I'm not staring,' lied Alix. 'I was just thinking.'

'And?'

'You look tired.'

'I've had a busy day.' Carrie sipped the wine. 'Lots of people came in without appointments and we were on the go until six.'

'You shouldn't work so hard,' said Alix.

Carrie laughed. 'That's rich, coming from you.'

'I'm younger,' said Alix.

Carrie lifted her eyebrow. 'Thank you. That makes me feel good.'

'What I mean is,' Alix struggled to find the words, 'I'm still at an age where I need to work. Surely you could sell the salon now and retire?'

'And do what?' asked Carrie.

Alix shrugged. 'I don't know. Gardening, reading, travelling?'

'Really, Alix.' Carrie made a face at her. 'Can you see me gardening?'

The house in Ranelagh had a tiny front garden with a small lawn and a couple of bushes. At the back of the house was a paved patio area with a few tubs.

'Maybe not,' admitted Alix. 'But I sometimes think you work too hard.'

'I like it,' said Carrie. 'I need to have something to do.'

They sat in silence for a moment.

'I was disappointed you didn't come to dinner with Wyn and John,' said Carrie eventually.

'I told you,' Alix said, 'I had a work commitment that night.'

'And if you hadn't?' asked Carrie. 'Would you have come then?'

'Probably not,' admitted Alix.

'It's not such a big deal,' Carrie said.

'Yes it is,' said Alix. 'To come back after all this time and then lay on all this stuff about his daughter and a baby – it's a big deal. It wouldn't have been a big deal if he'd stayed away.'

'Alix, life is too short to bear grudges,' said Carrie. 'I hated him for ten years. But I got tired of hating him.'

'I don't hate him,' said Alix. 'I don't care about him one way or the other.'

'Most people like to know their parents,' said Carrie. 'They like to know their roots. I think it would have done you good to meet him.'

'I don't want to be forced,' Alix told her. 'I don't want someone coming into my life and making me like them.'

'Who says you'd like him?' Carrie grinned. 'You might hate him. But at least it'd be a choice.'

'Well, right now I choose to have nothing to do with him,' said Alix dismissively. 'Anyway, he's gone back to the States, hasn't he?'

Carrie nodded. 'Kate's baby is due very soon. He wanted to be back with her.'

'Have you met her?' asked Alix.

'No.' Carrie shook her head.

'But you've seen a photograph?'

'Yes.'

'And does she look like us?'

'A little.' Carrie stood up and opened a drawer in the little desk in the corner. 'Here.' She held out a photograph.

Alix took it from her but didn't look.

'It was a long time ago, Alix,' said Carrie gently. 'Things change.'

Alix glanced at the photograph. The girl in it was sitting on the bonnet of a car, smiling at the photographer. Her long, dark hair was being blown by the wind and she squinted in the light of the sun. But Alix could see the resemblance straightaway. Kate, her half-sister, looked like her. And like Wyn, too.

She glanced up at Carrie. 'Family resemblance,' she said.

Carrie smiled. 'Your father's genes, all right.'

'I don't have to like him.' Alix handed the photograph back to Carrie. 'I don't have to like her either.'

'Nobody says that you do. But Alix, even though he walked out and even though I wanted nothing more to do with him, he didn't forget you completely. He bought you birthday cards.'

'I know,' said Alix. 'Wyn told me.'

'Would you like them?'

Alix shook her head. 'No.'

'Fine,' said Carrie.

'Wyn says that he's president of some corporation,' said Alix.

Carrie nodded. 'He's worth a lot of money.'

'I don't care about that.'

'Of course not. But it's nice to know all the same, isn't it?' Her eyes twinkled.

'He can't come back and buy us with money.'

'He's not trying to,' said Carrie. 'He hasn't actually offered you any money!'

Alix laughed then bit her lip. 'It's just hard,' she said. 'I've always hated him for leaving us. And now I think I hate him more for choosing them over us.'

'I understand,' Carrie said. 'I really do.'

Alix drained her glass. 'Actually, the reason I stopped by was to tell you about Paris,' she said in a firm voice.

'Paris?'

'I've been offered a job there.'

'Really? And do you want to take it?'

'I don't know yet.' Alix outlined the changes in Europa Bank. 'It'd be an interesting opportunity,' she told Carrie.

'I'll miss you if you go,' said Carrie.

Alix smiled at her. 'Thanks.'

'You don't think you could get another job here?'

'I probably could,' Alix told her. 'In fact, at the Institute dinner last night I was chatting to a guy from State Bank of Boston who sounded like he might be interested in offering me something. But I don't think it would be as interesting as the job I have now. I might be better off in Paris.'

'Financially or socially?' asked Carrie.

'Both,' said Alix.

'Do you have friends in Paris?'

Alix shrugged. 'Not close friends.'

'Alix, don't you think it would be really hard to go somewhere new, without anyone?'

'No,' said Alix. 'People do it all the time.'

'Maybe they do,' said Carrie. 'But are they happy?'

'Well, I'm not exactly rolling around in social activity here right now,' said Alix.

'What about Paul?' asked Carrie.

Alix drained her glass. 'Paul wants to get married and have children, but not with me.'

'Have you seen him lately?'

Alix blushed as she remembered last night. 'Yes,' she said. 'I met him yesterday.' She looked at Carrie. 'I've been stupid about Paul.'

'Why?'

'I kept thinking of him as someone who got away from me. And I wanted him back because my pride was hurt. But he loves someone else. I know he does.'

'So you've put him behind you now?'

Alix sighed. 'I still can't help feeling resentful. That he wanted something I couldn't give him.'

'Life is like that,' Carrie told her. 'It'd be boring if it worked out the way you wanted all the time.'

'I guess so.'

Carrie smiled at Alix. 'You don't like it when things don't go according to your plans, do you?'

'No,' said Alix. 'But Paul left for a reason. And that reason is still the same. So, although there's a part of me that would like to have him back, it wouldn't work.'

'He wants kids and you don't.'

Alix nodded. 'Maybe one day I'll meet the person I want to have them with. Maybe one day someone will make me change my mind about marriage and families. But I don't think so. I would have lived with Paul forever. Or for a long time anyway. But the whole settling down thing? That's not me, Carrie.'

'Why?'

Alix shrugged. 'I don't know. It just doesn't appeal to me.'

'It didn't especially appeal to me either,' said Carrie. 'But when I look at all the things I've done, what I'm most proud of is you and Wyn.'

'Gushy sentimentality doesn't suit you,' Alix told her.

'It might be sentimental, but it's true.'

'The bottom line is that I'm not ready for it,' said Alix. 'And I don't know if I ever will be.'

'You've got to let people matter to you,' said Carrie. 'You can't spend your whole life only letting them know a part of you.'

'Don't talk rubbish,' said Alix.

'Alix, you know that saying, don't you? That on your deathbed you'll never say you wish you'd spent more time at the office.'

Alix laughed. 'I doubt very much that people say they wished they'd spent more time slaving over a hot cooker either.'

'You're impossible,' said Carrie. 'But I do love you. And if you want to go to Paris, that's fine by me. Just be happy, Alix, that's all.'

'I will.' Alix smiled at her. 'I promise.'

⌐≈

It was dark and it was raining. She got into the car and drove towards the apartment. But she didn't stop. She drove across the toll bridge and out along the Malahide Road. She wished she didn't feel so uncertain. She wished she knew what was

521

right for her. She wished she knew what sort of person she really was.

Paul's house was in darkness. She sat outside and thought about ringing the bell and waking him up. But she didn't. She drove home instead. She told herself that she'd made the right decision.

Chapter 37

It was a busy day in Europa Bank, Paris. Alix walked around the dealing room with Guy, stopping every so often to check a news headline or an exchange rate. The dollar had started the day looking strong but had begun to slide and was now at its lowest level in weeks. The markets were jittery, the dealers losing money.

'I need to phone Dublin,' she told Guy. 'See how they're getting on.'

'Sure.'

She picked up a phone.

'Europa Bank, dealers.' Jenny sounded under pressure.

'Hi, Jen. It's me.'

'Oh, hi, Alix.'

'How are things?'

'Busy,' said Jenny. 'We've had a lot of customers on asking about the dollar. It's very jumpy.'

'I know. I think there's something going on, Jenny, but I don't know what. I get the feeling it's a Latin American problem. How are our positions?'

'OK,' said Jenny tersely.

'Don't get stuck with anything,' warned Alix. 'We don't need any hassle right now. Can I have a word with Dave?'

'Yes. Hang on.'

'Hi, Alix.'

'Dave, is everything OK?'

'More or less,' said Dave.

'Which?'

'Well, I sold some of our bonds earlier which was a bit of a mistake. But we'd got a really good bid for them at the time and I thought – well, you know.'

'It doesn't matter about the bonds,' said Alix although she was annoyed at the sale. 'Just keep things pretty flat, will you? There's a lot of business going on here and the volume is high. People are very nervous and there are too many different attempts at explaining it. Nothing substantive yet, Dave, but I'll let you know if I hear anything. Keep it safe. It's so near the end of the year now we don't need to take any shit.'

'OK,' he said.

'Dave?' A sudden tremor of nervousness went through her. 'Everything is all right, isn't it?'

'We've got it under control,' he told her. 'Don't worry.'

'Fine,' she said.

'Everything is all right, yes?' asked Guy.

'Yes,' she said, although she felt uneasy for a reason she couldn't fathom.

'Come into my office,' said Guy.

She sat opposite him.

'We are making you a very fair offer to come here,' he said. 'And it is easy for you. You don't have to worry about a family.'

'I know,' she said.

'So, what will your answer be?'

She glanced out of the glass wall at the frantic, busy dealing room. It would be fun, she thought. And she could do well here.

'I'll be happy to join you,' she said.

'Excellent!' Guy leaned forward and kissed her on each cheek. 'I am very, very happy. We want you to start as soon as possible. Two or three weeks.'

'I need to sort out some things in Dublin first,' said Alix. 'I'll let you know the earliest date I can come.'

'That's fine,' said Guy. 'Perhaps we should go to dinner tonight, Alix? Have a celebration?'

'Perhaps,' she said.

'You are staying at the Georges V?'

She nodded.

'We can eat there. Eight o'clock?'

'OK, Guy. Eight o'clock.' She glanced at her watch. It was nearly four o'clock now. 'I'll see you then, Guy. I'll get back to the hotel now.'

'How boring,' said Guy.

'Well,' she confessed, 'I thought about taking a little detour through the Galleries Lafayette on the way.'

She was standing in the lingerie department of the store when her mobile phone rang.

'Hello?'

'Alix?'

'Yes, who's that?'

'Alix, it's me, Richard. Richard Comiskey.'

Sophia's husband. Alix hadn't quite got used to thinking of him like that.

'Alix, Sophia wanted me to call you. She's in hospital. She had a fall.'

525

'What!' Alix grasped the phone more tightly.

'She's OK, Alix. But we don't know about the baby. She was knocked out and – Alix, she wants a female friend.'

'Of course, Richard. I'll be there.'

'I'm sorry to spring this on you, Alix. I rang your office but they said you were at a meeting. So I called your mobile because Sophia is so upset. I thought she'd want me with her. But she keeps asking for you.'

'It's no problem, Richard. I'll get to her. I'll be there this evening. Which hospital?'

He gave her the name and the phone number and rang off. Alix stood amid the thongs and the bustiers and the camisoles and prayed that her friend would be OK. And that the baby would be OK. It didn't seem possible that she might lose the baby. Sophia had been so happy about this pregnancy. It meant so much to her. Life's a bitch, thought Alix despairingly. A real bitch.

She hurried back to the hotel, rang the airport and reserved a seat on the next flight to London. Then she rang Guy Decourcelle to tell him that she had to go back and couldn't meet him after all.

Guy sounded peeved rather than concerned, but Alix didn't care.

The airport was crowded and she almost missed the flight. She didn't have time to check in her luggage and was looked at disapprovingly by the stewardess who took her case – slightly too big to be cabin luggage – at the aircraft door.

Alix was hot, worried and bad-tempered when she sat down. Her mood wasn't improved by the fact that the man beside her was so big he almost took up half her seat too. She'd asked if there were any business class seats available, but the flight was full.

'Excuse me.' The voice came from behind her. She looked round. 'I thought it was you,' said Matt Connery.

'What on earth are you doing here?' She turned in her seat.

'Same as you,' he grinned at her. 'Flying to London.'

'I'm sorry, that was a ridiculous question. But I thought you were away. You said that you were away until next week.'

'I am.' He laughed. 'We're in Paris, in case you hadn't noticed! I've been in Japan and had to do a stop-off here. I didn't expect to bump into you, though.'

'I told you I'd be in Paris.'

'Well, I promise you, I didn't detour especially to accost you.'

'I'm sure you didn't,' she said dryly.

'Why don't you sit beside me?' he asked.

'Because the flight is full,' she said softly, 'and I don't think anyone would want to swap seats.'

'Ah, but there's a spare seat here,' said Matt. 'I booked two. I was going to do some work on the way and business class was booked up. So this was my solution.'

'But you can't work if I'm sitting beside you,' objected Alix.

'I could,' he said, 'although maybe I wouldn't want to.' He grinned again. 'It'd be more comfortable.'

Alix shot a glance at her travelling companion again. Matt was right. It would be a damn sight more comfortable. She excused herself and changed seats.

'Better?' asked Matt as she fastened her seat belt.

'Much,' she agreed. 'But don't let me stop you doing whatever you want to do.'

'I've a meeting in the City tomorrow,' said Matt. 'I'm putting the final touches to our presentation. But it can wait.'

'Honestly, Matt, I don't want to—'

'You're not,' he said. 'Were you at Europa Bank in Paris today?'

She nodded.

'And what's in store for you in London?'

For a moment she'd forgotten about Sophia but now she remembered. 'I'm visiting a friend,' she said. 'She's in hospital.'

'Oh, I'm sorry,' said Matt.

'She's pregnant,' said Alix.

'And is everything OK?'

Alix shook her head. 'I don't know. She had a fall. I don't know how serious.'

'I'm sorry,' said Matt again.

'She wants to see me.' Alix looked at him. 'Though goodness knows why. I can't be of any practical use to her. I think her husband's a bit put out about it.'

'Maybe it's just a woman thing,' said Matt.

'Maybe,' said Alix. She bit her lip as she visualised Sophia lying in a hospital bed, frightened and ill.

The engines of the plane roared as it sped down the runway and lifted into the air.

'I never like that bit,' said Matt.

'Don't you?' Alix looked at him in surprise. 'I do.'

'Don't you ever think that it might not manage to make it?'

'No,' she said. 'Do you?'

'All the time,' he confessed. 'I fly a lot but I absolutely hate it. That's why I'm more than happy to have someone to talk to.'

528

'OK,' said Alix. 'What would you like to talk about?'

'Anything,' said Matt.

'Currency markets were very volatile today,' she said.

'Were they?'

'Yes. And it was very exciting being in a big room where there was a lot of tension, but I was worried about things in Dublin.'

'Don't you trust them?'

'I do,' she said. 'It's just – oh, I feel better being in control of it myself.'

He looked at her thoughtfully. 'Do you feel like that about everything?'

'Like what?'

'Being in control?'

'Don't be stupid,' she said shortly.

'Sorry,' said Matt.

The silence was uncomfortable. Alix stared straight ahead of her and thought about Sophia.

'I was talking to someone who knows you yesterday,' said Matt.

'Oh?' She turned towards him again.

'A guy named Ossie Livsey. I met him in Tokyo. He said that he knew you when you worked in London.'

She smiled slightly. 'Yes. He was a good client. What's he doing now?'

'Working for Sony,' said Matt. 'We're hoping to link up with Sony for one of our products.'

'Hope it works out for you.'

'Thanks.'

Alix turned away again and took her notebook out of her briefcase. There was no reason for her to look in her notebook but she made a show of turning the pages and stopping from time to time as though she was absorbing important information.

Matt was trying desperately to think of something to say to her. He sensed that she was upset and he wanted to be able to comfort her. But he didn't think that being nice would work. The kinder he was, he decided, the more Alix would retreat into herself.

Was it really worth the effort? he wondered. There were a number of women in his life and he'd always had easy relationships with them. Mostly, he knew, because he travelled around so much. So he didn't have to form any deep commitment to any of them. And it was good for his ego that they all hugged him when he was going away and phoned him and wanted him to come back.

But Alix didn't care. It was, he thought, stupid to think of her in terms of someone he could have a relationship with, when so far he'd only managed to suggest a dinner that might or might not actually happen. Yet the more he talked to her and the more he saw of her, the more drawn to her he became.

'Is it true that Europa Bank is interested in merging with Credit Agricole?' asked Matt. There was absolutely no truth in it, he'd just made it up to have something to say.

'Pardon?' She looked at him in surprise.

'Maybe it wasn't Europa Bank, maybe it was someone else,' he said.

'You never know.' Alix closed her notebook. 'Banks are always merging. Economies of scale and all that. But I don't think Europa Bank is thinking on those lines at the moment.'

'I know they're not.' Matt had no idea why he was going to tell her the truth. 'I made it up.'

'What?' She looked at him in astonishment.

'I wanted to talk to you and I thought that mentioning Europa was the best way of getting your attention.'

She laughed and he was pleased to see that it was a genuine laugh. 'You don't have to talk about the bank to get my attention.'

'But you like talking about it.'

'I must be very boring,' she said wryly.

'No.'

'So what do you and the boyfriend talk about?' asked Matt.

'Sorry?'

'Mr Hunter. You said that there is – sometimes – a Mr Hunter.'

'Sometimes,' she told him. She thought of Paul who had loved her and left her and gone to bed with her again anyway.

'Alix?'

'You want to know about Paul?' she asked. 'I'll tell you. I was crazy about him. I lived with him for three years. We split up during the summer but we still see each other from time to time. I did an interview with RTÉ for him a while ago and, in return, he came to the Institute dinner with me last week.'

'So it's one of those adult, civilised kind of things,' said Matt.

'Absolutely.' Except, thought Alix, for the slight matter of him living with Sabine. Which I'm not going to tell Matt Connery about. And for the slightly more serious matter of making love to him after the dinner. Which I'm definitely not going to tell Matt Connery about!

'And you see other people?'

'Yes,' said Alix.

'So my dinner invitation isn't a problem?'

531

'I presumed it was a thank-you dinner for the advice we've given you,' said Alix. 'I know you said you wanted it to be a friendly kind of dinner but you're hardly likely to make a grab for me, are you?'

'Of course not,' said Matt, although he wasn't so certain.

'You see.' She smiled.

'It's just that . . .'

'Yes?'

'I kind of thought of this dinner in a different sort of way.'

'What kind of way?'

'Well – as a – a date.'

'A date?' She stared at him.

'Yes,' he said. 'A date.'

'Oh.' Alix was flattered he'd asked her but uncertain of how she felt. Or how he felt. What he really wanted from this – date.

'Look, it doesn't matter,' said Matt. 'I'm sorry. I've obviously overstepped some mark or other. Forget it!' He opened his laptop computer and started to work.

'*I'm* sorry,' said Alix. 'I didn't handle that very well.'

He looked up from the computer. 'Look, I like you and I wanted to take you to dinner. You don't want to. It's not a big deal. I'm sorry. I thought, perhaps, there might be something between us. But I was wrong. Forget it.'

'What did you think was between us?' asked Alix.

'I don't know,' said Matt. 'I simply felt as though we clicked.'

'On a business level,' she told him. 'But personally – how can you know?' And yet, she thought, as a shiver ran through her, he was right. There was something else. Only she didn't have time for it now. Not since she was going to Paris. And Paris was important to her.

'I can't,' he said. 'You're right, of course.' He turned back to his computer and began working again.

He didn't stop until the stewardess announced that they had begun their approach to Heathrow and asked passengers to switch off all electronic equipment.

The cabin lights were dimmed. The plane circled the airport. Alix looked at her watch. It was nearly seven. It would take an hour to get to the hospital. She hoped they'd let her in to see Sophia.

The plane continued to circle the airport. Alix hated the amount of time wasted in circling over Heathrow. She glanced at her watch again.

'We seem to be doing this for a long time,' said Matt suddenly.

She nodded. 'Probably in some huge stack,' she said.

'I hate this part too,' he told her. 'I'm always afraid that a plane taking off will fly straight into us.'

'You won't know anything about it if it does,' she said prosaically.

'Thanks for the words of comfort!'

An air of concern was building up inside the cabin. They'd been circling for nearly twenty-five minutes. According to the stewardess, they'd been due to land at seven.

'Do you think there's something really wrong?' asked Matt. 'Are we flying around dumping fuel?'

'I wouldn't say we've much to dump,' replied Alix. 'It's a short flight, after all.'

Quite suddenly the tone of the engines changed and the plane made a rapid descent, bumping its way through the low cloud cover and thudding onto the runway.

'Good God,' said Alix. 'That was a bit rough.'

They came to an abrupt halt.

'Welcome to London,' said the stewardess.

They didn't move for another five minutes, then the captain announced that there'd been a slight problem with the undercarriage but it had just been a faulty light. 'We wanted to be sure the wheels were down properly!' he joked.

Alix shot a look at Matt who was pale in the cabin lights.

'There you are,' she said. 'You've lived to tell the tale.'

'I was scared,' he told her.

'Oh, come on, I bet you weren't really.'

'I was really,' he said. 'I told you, I don't like flying.'

'You're the second man I know that doesn't like it. Remember the clay pigeon shoot? One of the other guys was shitting himself in the helicopter. Although you didn't look worried then.'

'I had to put a brave face on it then,' said Matt. 'Weren't you a bit worried?'

'Not in the helicopter,' she said.

'Just now, I meant.'

She shrugged. 'I was concerned. More because I guessed there was something wrong and didn't know what it was.'

'Alix?'

'Yes?'

'Have you ever cried?'

She laughed. 'Big girls don't cry.'

They shared a taxi to the city. Matt let her out at the hospital.

'I hope your friend is OK,' he said.

'So do I.' She held out her hand. 'Thanks for the lift. And thanks for giving me the seat on the plane too.'

'Any time.' He took her hand. His grasp was firm. They

looked at each other for a moment, then Alix pulled her hand away and scrambled out of the cab.

❧

Sophia was terribly pale. Alix tiptoed into the room where Richard sat beside his wife. Sophia's eyes were closed.

'Hi,' Alix whispered.

'Hi,' said Richard. 'She's been asleep for the last couple of hours. They think everything is going to be OK.'

'Oh, Richard!' Alix pulled up a chair. 'I'm so glad.'

'So am I,' he said. 'I was so worried about her. And she was really agitated. She kept asking if I was OK and then asking for you, Alix.'

'Why me?'

Richard shook his head. 'I don't know. But she was so insistent. They gave her something to calm her down, I think, but she still kept asking for you.'

'I'll stay with her for a while,' said Alix. 'Do you want to grab yourself a coffee or something?'

'That'd be great,' said Richard. 'I'll be back in ten minutes.'

He left the room. Alix sat in the dim light and looked at her friend. Suddenly, Sophia opened her eyes.

'Alix,' she said.

'I'm here, Soph.'

'Thanks. Thanks for coming.'

'Of course I came. Richard phoned me.'

'Oh, Alix, it was all my own fault!' Sophia looked at her in anguish. 'I did it. If we lose the baby it'll be my fault.'

'You're not going to lose the baby,' said Alix.

'They don't know that.'

'Richard says they think everything is OK,' Alix told her. 'Don't worry, Sophia.'

Sophia sighed. 'I hope you're right.'

'They wouldn't lie to him, Sophia. Really they wouldn't.'

Sophia bit her lip.

'What happened?' asked Alix.

'I was going to a meeting,' said Sophia. 'The doctor told me to take it easy because my blood pressure was a bit high, and I've been trying, honestly I have. But we're bringing a new issue next month and I needed to get a few things tied up. Ramon had left a bundle of the legal stuff with me. I'd been reading it and I got really tired.' She rubbed her eyes. 'I nodded off, Alix. Imagine that! In my office. The meeting was on the floor below and the phone rang five minutes after I should've been there. I got an awful fright. So I picked up the legal papers – and you know how much it can be sometimes, there was a big bundle and it was heavy – and I waddled as fast as I could to the lift. But it was stuck on the ground floor so I decided to go down the stairs. Between carrying the papers and trying to hurry, I lost my balance and I fell.'

'Oh, Sophia!'

'I blacked out. I don't remember anything! Obviously someone came looking for me and they found me. But I'd been there for a while, Alix. You know how it is in those buildings, nobody ever uses the stairs.'

'You poor thing.'

'So it was my fault,' said Sophia again. 'Alix, you know I want this baby. I told you how important it was to me. Ramon could have done everything to do with this issue, but no, I had to be in charge, I had to do everything. Despite the doctor's advice. And because of that, I nearly lost my child, Alix.' Tears formed in her eyes. 'And I would have lost it because I'm selfish and shallow and stupid.'

'You certainly are not,' said Alix. 'You're kind and caring and you've worked very hard to get where you are. So you wanted to prove you could still do it. So what? You made a mistake, that's all.'

'But it was nearly a fatal mistake,' said Sophia miserably. 'I didn't want people to think that I was giving less than a hundred per cent just because I was pregnant. But that *was* stupid and selfish. Because you can't do everything, you really can't.'

'Hundreds of people before you and after you will probably want the same,' said Alix. 'And it's not fair, Sophia. I know how hard you've worked. I know that you don't want to give it all up. I know how you feel.'

'But not about the baby,' said Sophia. 'You don't know about that, Alix, because you don't feel this way.'

'Maybe not,' admitted Alix. 'But maybe one day I will. And then I'll be asking you for advice, Sophia. You've given me lots of good advice in your day!'

Sophia smiled wanly. 'And have you been taking any of it?'

'Well,' Alix said. 'If you want to hear about a real humdinger of a mistake, let me tell you about the night of the Institute dinner.'

Chapter 38

She'd intended to catch the early morning flight back to Dublin but it was booked out. And then she decided to spend more time in London. There really wasn't any great rush to go back. She was going to leave at the end of the year. Dave could cope on his own. Richard suggested she spend the night in their house in Chelsea and she agreed. But she called the office from Richard's on Friday morning to check on how things were and to let Dave know that she wouldn't be back until Monday.

'Everything OK?' she asked.

'Sure, fine.' Dave sounded casual.

'How about the dollar?'

'It's still strong but it'll probably start to drift down again.'

'All the same, Dave, keep it simple.'

'Sure.'

'No trades about to blow up in our faces?'

'No,' he said cautiously. 'How was Paris?'

'Fine,' she said. She thought Dave sounded tense. She was tempted to hop on the next flight back, just to be sure everything was OK. But she knew that she was being paranoid.

'Have you decided to desert us?' Dave broke in on her thoughts.

She laughed. 'I'll talk about it when I get back. In the meantime, please don't rock the boat, Dave.'

'So you will desert us,' he said flatly.

'I'll see you Monday,' she told him.

'OK, Alix. Have fun.'

It was nice to have an unexpected day off. She had a leisurely breakfast and then went to the hospital to see Sophia. She looked much better this morning, Alix thought. The colour had come back into her cheeks and she'd lost the terrified look of the previous night.

'The baby's OK,' she said when Alix sat down beside her. 'Oh, Alix, it's been a nightmare!'

'I know.' Alix took Sophia's hand and squeezed it. 'But now you can stop blaming yourself and get better.'

'It *was* my fault,' said Sophia. 'I should have known better, Alix. Really I should.'

'Lots of us do things when we should know better!' Alix smiled at her.

'Like the night of the Institute dinner?' asked Sophia.

Alix sighed. 'That was incredibly stupid of me,' she said. 'I had some wild idea that I could get him back because he'd find sex with me so irresistible. I even told myself he might phone although, to be honest, Soph, I knew he wouldn't.'

'So it's definitely over?'

'Sophia, he left me because he didn't think I was the woman he wanted to spend the rest of his life with. I've spent ages thinking about that. If I told him I'd change, would it really make a difference?' She made a face. 'I don't think so. I know he felt guilty about having sex with me. He loves Sabine. And she doesn't even have to think about the baby thing!'

'And do you think you'll start to think about the baby thing?' asked Sophia.

'I wish I knew.' Alix grimaced. 'I don't have any maternal urge, Soph. But what if I suddenly do? What if my hormones kick in and I'm too late to do anything about it? What then?'

'I don't know,' said Sophia. 'I wish I could advise you.'

'I like my job.' Alix stared into the distance. 'I really don't feel ready to chuck it all in yet. I thought I'd spend a few more years in Europa Dublin. I wasn't bored with it or anything. But there *will* be changes because they've had a huge trading loss in Paris. Derivatives.'

'You serious?'

Alix nodded. 'So they've fired two people and, according to Guy, they'll be letting more go. They'll also be taking greater control over some of the branches, which would limit my autonomy in Dublin. But they've offered me a job in Paris. A good job, Sophia.'

'And do you want to take it?'

'I've already said yes.' Alix bit her lip. 'It's a great career move and I'd be mad not to.'

'But?'

'But I'm questioning whether or not I really want to. I'm scared, Sophia.'

'Of what?'

'Of this bloody biological clock thing. It's a ticking bomb and I'm scared that one day it'll go off and I won't know what to do about it! Or, even worse, it never goes off and one day I'm full of regrets.'

'You'll know if it goes off,' said Sophia.

'You didn't. You had to wait until someone primed it.'

Sophia sighed. 'Alix, I don't have the answers for you.'

'I know. I didn't expect you to have.'

'So what now?'

'I go home. And I tell them that I'm taking the job in Paris.'

'Maybe you'll meet someone there,' said Sophia.

'I wouldn't count on it,' said Alix.

༄

There was a woman with a baby sitting beside her on the plane. The woman wasn't much younger than she was. She held the baby on her lap and spoke to the child all through the flight. From time to time she smiled at Alix and Alix smiled tentatively back. At Dublin airport they were met by a man who gathered them into his arms and kissed them. Alix watched them for a moment, then walked away.

༄

She watched CNN that night. The dollar had soared during the day. There was a rumour of a potential Latin American debt default. Alix shuddered. She was glad that she'd told Dave to keep things tight.

There was no point in taking undue risks so close to the year end. And, she mused selfishly, she wanted to leave Europa Bank Dublin in the knowledge that her last couple of months had been profitable. She logged on to the computer and tried to connect to the bank. But there was a problem with the modem and she couldn't gain access.

It doesn't matter, she thought as she climbed into bed. She didn't need to know. Dave would have told her if there were any problems.

∽

She went shooting on Saturday and racked up a very respectable score. Niall asked her if she'd like to go on a trip they were arranging for the following March. 'To Italy,' he told her. 'We'll be guests of a club there and then we'll go on a tour of the Perazzi factory. It'll be great fun, Alix.'

'I'm sorry, Niall.' She put her gun into its case. 'I won't be here next March. I've been offered a job in Paris and I've decided to take it.'

'You lucky thing!' Niall looked at her with envy. 'I'd love to work in Paris.'

'Would you?'

'You bet! All those gorgeous women!'

She laughed. 'It's as good a reason as any. I'll try and come here as often as I can before I go.'

'Sure,' said Niall. 'We'll miss you, Alix.'

'Thanks.'

She got into her car and drove home. Halfway there, she detoured and called to see Wyn. She handed the obligatory earplugs to Aoife and Nessa and followed her sister into the kitchen. Wyn filled the kettle and switched it on.

'I have news for you,' said Wyn.

'Oh.' Alix took a shortbread biscuit from the tin her sister had placed in front of her.

'Kate had a baby boy yesterday.'

Alix broke the biscuit in half. 'Really.'

'Yes. They're calling him Aaron.'

'Stupid name,' said Alix.

'He weighed nine pounds.'

'Bit of a hip cracker.'

'She's fine. John and Imogen are delighted. So's Jack. Kate's husband's name is Jack, I don't think I told you that before.'

'And Carrie?'

'Carrie is delighted too.'

'I'm glad everyone is so delighted.'

'Alix—'

'I've taken the job in Paris,' said Alix. 'I'll probably start in January.'

Wyn stared at her. 'I wish you hadn't.'

'Why?'

'I'd prefer if you were here.'

'You won't notice I'm not. You'll have lots of other things to occupy you. Like John and Imogen and Kate and Jack and the nine-pound baby.'

'Aaron,' said Wyn.

'Whatever.'

'Alix, maybe you should see Paul. Talk to him. Get back with him.'

'As you so kindly reminded me once before, Wyn, he's living with someone else. He has no interest in getting back with me.'

'How do you know?' asked Wyn. 'Maybe it's all gone wrong with the French tart.'

Alix smiled at her. 'He sent Sabine back to Paris last weekend. She was homesick. He came with me to the Institute dinner.'

'Alix! You never told me.'

'I slept with him.'

'Alix!' Wyn was stunned.

'If he was going to come back to me I think I would have heard from him before now.'

543

'Oh, Alix.'

'Wyn, could you stop saying my name like that?'

'But, Al—, but why did you sleep with him?'

'To see if he wanted me.'

'And he obviously did.'

'He wanted sex with me, Wyn. It wasn't quite the same thing.'

'And he didn't even call you?' asked Wyn. 'He slept with you and he didn't even call?'

Alix smiled wanly. 'I think he was embarrassed.'

'I think he's a shit.'

Quite suddenly, Alix wanted to cry.

'You're better off without him,' said Wyn.

'And I'll be even better in Paris,' said Alix as she broke the biscuit again.

~

When she got home she tried to log on to the bank's computer again. But there was still a problem with the modem.

On Sunday she went to the gym. She felt as though her life was getting back into some kind of order. The shooting club and the gym had always been part of her weekends before Paul had walked out.

She wished he'd called. She understood why he hadn't but she didn't want to be understanding. She wanted him to ring and say that he really loved her and that, even if he did decide to marry Sabine, he'd always love her. She knew that she was being completely stupid but she couldn't help wanting him to say it all the same.

When she got back from the gym the green light was winking

on her machine to tell her that she had a message. He'd called after all, she thought as she pressed playback.

'Hi, Alix, this is Matt Connery.' He cleared his throat. 'I just rang to say that I hope your friend is feeling better and that my invitation to dinner still stands. It's become a matter of principle with me now – it was easier to conclude the Tokyo deal than get you out for something to eat! I'll call again. Take care.'

Take care. It was used so impersonally these days and yet, the way Matt had said it, it sounded like he meant it.

Take care. But what was the point in beginning a relationship with him when she'd be in France in a few weeks' time? And he seemed to spend half his life globetrotting. They'd be a couple trying to schedule a night's sex between important business meetings and working on month-end figures. That wasn't what she wanted.

But sex with Matt Connery. She exhaled slowly as she thought about it. He was an attractive man. She'd found him attractive from the moment she set eyes on him as she sat on the steps of Europa Bank and smoked her last cigarette. Almost her last cigarette anyway! Even though she'd been annoyed at him for baiting her. There was something about him that she liked. But liking wasn't enough. Finding someone sexually attractive wasn't enough. God, she thought, what the hell did anyone get out of a relationship these days?

Work was simpler. At work you knew where you stood, where the boundaries lay, what people expected of you. And you knew what to expect of them too.

∽

She arrived at the bank at five to seven on Monday morning.

She was surprised to find Dave, Gavin and Jenny already at their desks.

'Good morning,' she said as she hung her coat on the coat stand. 'You're all very bright and breezy this morning.'

'Under the circumstances I thought we should be here early,' said Dave.

'I don't think Des is really going to notice how early you get in.' Alix sat down and switched on her monitors. 'And if all three of you arrive at the same time it isn't going to help anyone's chances!'

'Not those circumstances.' Dave looked at her in astonishment. 'The position, Alix. That's why we're early.'

It was her turn to look at him in astonishment. 'What position?'

'Didn't you check?' he asked. 'I thought you'd check. I expected you to call me last night.'

'What are you talking about?' She stared at him. 'What the hell is going on, Dave?'

'Why didn't you log in when you got home?' he asked. 'You always do.'

'My modem was down,' she replied slowly. 'Dave, what the fuck has happened?'

'We're short dollars,' he said.

'How many?'

'Five million.'

'Five million! What the hell are we doing short five bar? I thought I said that we didn't want to run anything. What kind of level, Dave?'

'Thirty-six,' he said.

She glanced at the screen in front of her. 'That's not so bad,' she said, relief in her voice. 'They're offered at forty.'

'They're offered at 1.2140,' said Dave. 'We're short at 1.2346.'

Alix looked at him in horror. What Dave had just told her meant that they were currently showing a loss of over eighty thousand dollars. Europa Bank had a policy of cutting any single position that showed a loss of over fifteen thousand.

'You're joking,' she said finally. 'How could we be? And how come we're still running it? Does Des know about it? Have you told him?'

'Jim Carroll of Harris rang late on Thursday evening,' said Dave. 'He wanted to buy dollars. The rate was fair at the time, we thought we could make a little out of it. The dollar was looking pretty shaky then and there seemed to be a few sellers around. So we decided to run it overnight. We left a stop-loss order with New York in case it spiked up. But it didn't. When we came in on Friday morning everything was fine although it was still around the same level. We were just talking about what we should do when it went ballistic. One minute it was trading at 1.2350, next minute it was 1.2250. The Latin American rumour had hit the market. Apparently there'd been some talk of it in Tokyo overnight but the euro hadn't really weakened off. Then the yen started to go. There were big flows back into the dollar and so when Europe opened everyone was a buyer.'

'And why didn't you cut it at 1.2250?' demanded Alix. 'At least that would have been only forty thousand down the toilet.'

Gavin looked uncomfortable. 'The charts looked so over-bought,' he said. 'After all, Alix, it moved on a rumour. The dollar has been getting weaker for ages. There isn't any fundamental reason for it to be stronger now. The Fed will almost certainly cut rates again and . . .' He broke off as her eyes glinted green at him.

'What about our loss limits?' she asked.

'But it was wobbling at that level,' Gavin said. 'It really and truly looked as though sellers would come in again. You know how that can happen, Alix. So we waited. It began to move in our direction so we reckoned we could get the loss down to about twenty thousand. And then there was some talk about debt rescheduling in Latin America. Well, you know that can sometimes have a negative effect for the dollar. But it didn't this time. Everyone started buying it again.'

'And were you running this position when I called you on Friday?' She looked at Dave whose expression was anxious.

'Yes,' he said.

'And you didn't tell me about it?'

'What would have been the point?' he asked. 'There was nothing you could do, Alix. You could debate whether to run it or not. But you weren't going to be able to conjure a new rate out of nothing.'

'Dave, I am still responsible for everything that happens in this room. How dare you decide not to tell me about this! And how on earth do you expect me to explain away the fact that you've busted through our limits on a commercial trade? I'm surprised that Des and Pat haven't been stuck to the dealing room door like glue!'

'Des was away on Friday,' said Dave uncomfortably. 'And Pat left early. So they haven't seen the loss yet.'

She shook her head. 'I don't believe it,' she said. 'Look, guys, if this is some kind of wind-up tell me now. I can't hack the idea of this sort of loss. It's so fucking senseless.'

'It's not a wind-up,' said Gavin. 'Alix, I'll take responsibility. It was my fault. Dave wanted to cut it but I said no.'

'You said no!' She froze him with her glare. 'You! Who are you to tell him whether or not to cut a position? What kind of fantasy world do you think you're inhabiting? What books have you been reading, Gavin? *Rogue Trader*? *Bonfire of the Vanities*? You fucking idiot! And as for you,' she turned to Dave, 'what were you at? You're supposed to keep people within limits, not let them trash through them. You're supposed to monitor the risk we're running. I can't believe this, Dave. I really can't.'

'It's true all right,' said Jenny miserably. 'But it was one of those things that just happened, Alix. Even if you'd been here it would have happened.'

She switched her glare to Jenny. 'I don't think so.'

The three dealers exchanged uncomfortable glances while Alix stared at the monitor. At the European opening, the dollar was doing them some favours, drifting slightly against the euro. But would it continue to move that way? Alix bit her lip as she looked at the screen. If the Latin American story was nothing more than a rumour then it probably would. The market had a habit of getting into a frenzy about something for a couple of days and then forgetting all about it. Yet Alix was uncertain. She'd picked up a very strong vibe in Paris that there were some large buyers of dollars in the market. Maybe they had more information by now. She picked up the phone.

'Jean-Louis. *Bonjour*,' she said as the French dealer answered her.

'Hi, Alix. How are you this morning?'

'I'm OK,' she said. 'I wanted to ask you a question, Jean-Louis.'

'Sure.'

'Remember I talked to you on Thursday about the Latin American stories? About a possible default?'

'Of course.'

'What do you think of those rumours now?'

'I am not certain,' said Jean-Louis. 'I think there is something to them, Alix, because I was talking to our correspondent in Brazil and he said that a number of banks were quite worried. But there is nothing concrete and it could simply be that the country concerned will make a late interest payment.'

'Even that would have a knock-on effect on the markets,' said Alix.

'Oh, yes. But I do not think it is something on which I wish to wager the family jewels.' Jean-Louis laughed.

'I understand,' said Alix. 'Why do you think the dollar is weaker this morning? Is it because of American exposure to the region?'

'Just profit-taking,' he said. 'I think it will pick up again later. For sure, long term it will come down though.'

'OK, Jean-Louis. Thanks.' She hung up.

'What do you want to do?' asked Dave.

She sat back and stared at the ceiling. She could cut the position and book the biggest loss she'd ever made in her life. Des Coyle and Pat Enright would have seizures and would probably fire everyone in the dealing room. But she could argue that the loss was quantifiable and, set against the profits of the department over the whole year, not as bad as it first looked. She could run the position and hope that the dollar collapsed. It had already pulled back this morning and it could do more. If the rumours of a default were completely scotched, then it could get back to the level it was on Thursday. They might not have to book the loss at all – although it was already showing on their Friday night profit and loss account. Every currency position showed the rate at which the position had been taken and the rate at which the position could be immediately cut. When Des and Pat saw the P&L, they'd have hysterics.

She could add to the short position by selling even more dollars. That would alter the average rate at which they were short and, if the dollar did maintain its downward momentum, they could hit break-even more quickly. But would it continue to weaken? Would people want to buy euros instead of dollars? How comfortable would she feel about being even shorter and compounding the break in their limits? She would have to cut the position by the end of the day anyway. If not sooner.

She looked at the monitors again.

'Technically, it's really overbought,' said Gavin.

'You thought that on Thursday,' she said.

'I know. But it is.'

'Maybe the trend has changed.'

'Why?' asked Gavin. 'Things are exactly the same in the US as they were last week.'

But if there was a default there could be a so-called 'flight to quality'. Traders, especially in the US, would buy dollars and dollar assets instead of overseas assets. How worried would the New York guys be when they came in to work this week? She stared at the screens while she considered her options.

'Dave, I want you to buy back the fiver,' she said finally. 'And I want you to buy another five.'

'What?'

'You heard me.'

'You're going long?' he asked.

'Yes,' said Alix. 'And Jenny, buy five million of the US thirty-year bond too.'

Dave stared at her. 'You're taking the complete opposite view.'

'Yes,' she said.

'Alix, that's fucking ridiculous. Just because you think we were stupid doesn't mean you should be even more stupid!'

'I know,' she said.

'Don't you think we're putting all our eggs into one basket?' asked Jenny. 'After all, this could go horribly wrong.'

'I'll cut it if it's going horribly wrong,' said Alix. 'I won't let our losses go above a hundred and forty.'

Gavin winced. The amount of the loss, for a small bank like Europa, was horrendous.

'Do it,' said Alix.

They bought the dollars at 1.2150. Now, instead of wanting the dollar to weaken further, they needed it to go up in value. Because the rate was quoted in dollars per euro, they needed to see the price go down.

This meant that – when they eventually sold the dollars – they would get more euros in return. Jenny bought the bonds at a price of 106.25. They needed the bonds to go up in value too, though in this case they wanted to see the price go up. Alix was betting that the gains she would make on the bonds, plus the profit she hoped to make on the new dollar position would wipe out Friday's loss. It was a dangerous bet.

Alix glanced at her watch although there were clocks all around the dealing room. It was eight o'clock.

At a quarter past eight, Pat Enright phoned.

'What the hell is wrong with the P&L?' he asked. 'It's showing a loss of nearly a hundred and thirty thousand on the foreign exchange book, Alix.'

'I know,' she said.

'It's not a real loss, is it?' asked Pat disbelievingly.

'Not for long,' she said.

'But what happened?'

'Can I get back to you?'

'Alix, I need to know.'

'I'll call you back. I promise.'

Dave looked at her. 'Pat or Des?'

'Pat,' she said. 'Des would be in here by now.'

'Alix, I'm sorry,' he said.

She watched the numbers. The rate hovered between 1.2130 and 1.2160. The price on the bond was unchanged.

She rang Eileen Walsh. 'What time is Des due in?'

'Not until twelve,' said Eileen. 'He's at meetings until then. Do you need to contact him, Alix?'

'No. I'll catch him at twelve,' she said.

That was her cut-off, she decided. It had to come right by then otherwise she'd have to sell the extra five million dollars she'd just bought, sell the bonds and take the loss.

They'd pull the offer of the Paris job, she thought bleakly. Even if she made money out of this trade they'd decide that she couldn't keep control of people. It'd be like the head of derivatives in Paris who'd had to go because of the actions of his junior trader. She felt sick. Losses always made her feel sick. And this gamble that she was taking made her feel even sicker. Because it was a gamble. She was betting money on the fact that the tension she'd felt in the Paris dealing room when they'd been talking about Latin America was real, that the rumours were based on fact, that people would, as she hoped, flock to the dollar as a safe haven. And she could be completely and utterly wrong. It was different when she took a position because she really and truly believed in it. Those times, she felt in control of the situation, she felt that she'd covered all the bases. This was more like a smash-and-grab raid, hoping that she'd get lucky.

Better to be born lucky than smart, she reminded herself.

The phones were ringing now as their customers called to do trades. No new positions, she told the others, cut everything. We have to keep our eye on the ball.

The rate still hadn't moved very much by the time Matt Connery phoned.

'Europa Bank dealers,' said Gavin.

'Hi, Gavin, it's Matt.'

'How are things, Matt?'

Alix glanced up but Gavin wasn't looking at her mockingly as he usually did when Matt called.

'Sure, I can buy some dollars from you,' said Gavin. 'How many? Hold on a second.'

'Connery wants to sell us a million dollars,' he said.

'Quote him and if he deals cut it straightaway,' said Alix.

'I can do that for you at 1.2155,' said Gavin.

'Fine,' said Matt.

'OK.' Gavin gestured to the others that the trade had been completed. Jenny immediately got on the phone and sold the dollars at a profit of two hundred dollars.

'Another four hundred trades like that and we're out of the woods,' said Alix dryly.

'Alix, he wants a word with you,' said Gavin.

She clicked into the line. 'Hi.'

'I phoned at the weekend,' said Matt.

'I know,' she said. 'I got your message. And Sophia is fine, thank you.'

'I'm glad.'

'So am I. She's a good friend.'

'I was wondering about that dinner,' said Matt. 'I know we never seem to manage it but—'

'Any day this week,' said Alix.

'What?'

'Any day this week.'

'You've completely thrown me.' Matt laughed. 'I expected any day next month.'

'I'll be busy next month,' she said.

'Are you OK?' asked Matt. 'Only you sound odd today.'

'I'm fine,' she said, 'just a bit busy, that's all.'

'How about Friday?' suggested Matt.

'OK,' said Alix. 'Where?'

'I hadn't really thought about it. Anywhere you like.'

'The Tea Rooms at the Clarence,' she said. 'Eight o'clock.'

'When you decide to do something you don't hang around,' he said admiringly. 'The Tea Rooms at eight it is.'

'I'll see you then.'

'OK, Alix. Are you certain everything's all right?'

'Absolutely,' she said. 'Goodbye, Matt.' And she clicked out of the line.

'What's the story between you and him?' asked Gavin.

'Pardon?' Her tone was chilly.

'It's just that when he asks for you it's more of a personal thing.'

'It's not a personal thing,' said Alix.

'I thought . . .' But Gavin didn't finish the sentence.

Pat Enright came into the dealing room at ten o'clock.

'Alix, what the fuck is the story about this loss?' he demanded.

'It's a loss,' she said. 'We're doing our best to turn it into a profit. If we haven't done it by today, we can't.'

'For Christ's sake, Alix! Why didn't you tell me about it? What happened? Do you know that you closed the positions over limit at the weekend? I'll have to report it to Des.'

'I know,' she said.

'What the hell was going on?' he asked.

'A misjudgement,' said Alix.

'Well, I don't think Des will be misjudging much when he sees this,' said Pat furiously. 'What are you trying to do, Alix? Close the place down?'

'Pat, if that's the most constructive thing you have to add to the day can you kindly fuck off out of here? We're busy.'

He stared at her for a moment then left the room, banging the door behind him.

She had a stitch in her side. Every time she took a breath it hurt.

At a quarter to twelve the exchange rate slithered in their direction. The dealers exchanged glances as they saw it move from 1.2135 to 1.2100. Alix flicked through the news screens to see if there was anything new about Latin America. There was nothing.

'Maybe we should just book the profit on this morning's fiver,' said Jenny.

'No point.' Alix wished she could breathe properly.

It edged their way a fraction more.

'Cut it,' said Gavin. 'At least this way we're getting the loss down.'

'Didn't I tell you before to run with your profits and cut

your losses?' said Alix. 'Something that you could have borne in mind last week.'

'I know,' he said.

'We'll wait,' said Alix.

She was doodling on the edge of the *Financial Times* when the headline flashed up. The only word she saw was default.

'Alix!' Dave's voice held suppressed excitement. 'It's happened. They've missed a payment. It's been confirmed.'

She looked at the clock. It was five to twelve. She looked at the screens. The dollar was now trading at 1.2050. Someone from the States was bound to come out with a comment about selling dollars to help the Latin Americans. But not yet, thought Alix. Not yet.

'Cut it now,' pleaded Gavin. 'We've clawed back half of it.'

'Where's the bond trading?' she asked Jenny.

'It's up,' Jenny replied. 'Screens are showing 106.75.'

Between the strength of the dollar and the profit on the bond they were now making over sixty-five thousand dollars. Not enough to wipe out Friday's losses, but they were back inside their limits. She could explain it away as some kind of a strategic bond/foreign exchange position. She could make them believe her. It would be the sensible thing to do.

The phone rang.

'Alix, get down here right away,' said Des Coyle.

'Shortly,' she said.

'Now,' said Des.

'I'm trying very hard to cut something here, Des. I can't.'

'Yes you can,' said Des.

'If you want to talk to me, come up here. But leave it for another fifteen minutes,' Alix told him. 'We're busy.'

'You could have gone down,' said Dave. 'We would have looked after it for you.'

She laughed shortly. 'Oh, yeah?'

'Alix, you know Des. He doesn't like that kind of treatment.'

'Tough,' said Alix.

The dollar was now trading at 1.2000.

She phoned Jean-Louis in Paris.

'It's crazy here,' he yelled. 'I can't talk to you, Alix.'

'Are there still buyers of dollars?' she asked.

'Yes,' cried Jean-Louis. 'It will stop. It will turn around. But I don't know when.'

She rubbed her forehead. Neither did she. And she knew it would stop. But not yet, she thought. Not yet.

Des pushed open the dealing-room door and stalked in. 'I want to talk to you, and I want to talk to you now,' he said.

'Des, I'll happily talk to you,' said Alix. 'But not now. I know there was an unauthorised breach of our limits. I know there is over a hundred-thousand-dollar loss sitting on the P&L account. I'm trying to get that back, and right now, I'm succeeding. So don't bug me, Des. Not now.'

He stared at her. Her jaw was set and determined, her eyes were flashing green and she had an intense look on her face that brooked no argument.

'When you've cut it,' said Des. 'In my office. As soon as.'

'Fine,' she said.

She cut the dollar position at 1.1890. At the current rate it left them with a foreign exchange profit of almost one hundred and seven thousand dollars on that day's deal, which she could offset against the previous loss. She cut the bond position at 106.90. Her gamble had paid off. They had made thirty-five thousand dollars on the bond. They had wiped out their losses and booked a net profit of over sixty thousand dollars. It was one of the best trades she'd ever done.

When the trades were booked she got up and walked out of the room. She went into the ladies' where she threw up. Then she went down to Des's office to explain.

Chapter 39

H er TV interview was shown that night. She'd completely forgotten about it until she picked up the paper and saw the programme listings. She sat in the apartment and watched herself talking about what it was like to be a successful woman and wondered if anybody watching would ever guess that Alix Callaghan had been sick that afternoon because a trade had gone right.

She'd gone down to Des and given him a highly edited version of events.

'They couldn't cut it,' she told him. 'The market moved so quickly they were just left completely exposed. It happens sometimes, Des, but not very often.'

'It never happens when you're there,' he said.

'One day it probably will.'

He'd ranted and raved at her. He was going to fire Dave. Fire Gavin. Probably fire Jenny. He wasn't letting her go to Paris, she was far too valuable where she was. He was cutting all their limits. There was to be no trading in future.

'Des, take some time out and think about it all,' said Alix. 'We'll sit down with Pat and talk about it later in the week.'

'I'll never understand dealers,' Des said. 'Never.'

They'd looked anxiously at her when she came back into the room.

'It's OK,' she told them. 'It's sorted.'

It wasn't completely sorted, of course. She knew that there'd be more questions, that procedures would change, that limits probably would be cut back. But Des wasn't going to fire anybody. Des still wasn't exactly sure who was to blame.

'Doesn't he want to talk to me?' asked Dave.

'Or me?' asked Gavin.

'Don't flatter yourselves.' Her smile was tired. 'He barely managed to talk to me!'

'Who does he blame?' asked Jenny.

'Nobody is being blamed,' said Alix. 'It was a dealing-room position. That's the end of it.'

'Alix, thanks.' Dave had looked at her in disbelief. 'Why didn't you just shaft us?'

'Why would I do that?' she'd asked dryly. 'I'm sure you'd never shaft me.'

They had looked at each other in silence and then the phones had begun to ring again.

⌁

Wyn phoned her after the interview. 'Hey, Alix, you were great on TV. You looked fantastic. Very ballsy.'

'Wyn! I looked sophisticated,' she said.

'That too. Has Paul phoned?'

'No,' said Alix. 'He's not going to phone. Don't be silly.'

'He's a bastard not to call you,' said Wyn. 'The least he could do would be to ring on the pretext of saying you looked good tonight.'

'He's seen the interview already,' said Alix. 'And he already told me I looked good.'

'Do you know, I hardly recognised you as my sister,' Wyn mused. 'I look at this person and I think, I knew her when she had runny egg on her face.'

Alix laughed.

'Or, I knew her the day she was so scared about the school test that she wet her knickers!'

'Wyn!'

'Well, you did.'

'I had a kidney infection,' said Alix.

'Right,' said Wyn. 'I believe you.'

'I'm going now,' Alix told her. 'I can only take so many compliments in one night.'

'It was great,' said Wyn again. 'Oh, by the way, are you free to baby-sit on Friday night?'

'I'm sorry,' said Alix, 'but I can't, Wyn. I'll be out.'

'Some other work function,' said Wyn in disgust. 'Another Bankers' dinner?'

'No.' Alix smiled. 'Although I suppose it's kind of work. I'm going out with a client. But he wants to be my friend.'

'What?'

'That's what he's been telling me.'

'Alix, are you going out on a date?'

'I'm not sure,' said Alix. 'I'll tell you afterwards.'

'Oh, Alix.' Wyn sounded delighted. 'Can I ring Carrie and tell her?'

❦

Alix left the office at half four on Friday. She went to the hairdresser's where she had her hair coloured and cut.

'Will you put it up for me?' she asked Tina.

'Oh, Alix, why don't you leave it down?' said the stylist. 'It's so nice that way.'

'I prefer it up,' said Alix.

'You're the customer.' Tina sighed and complied with Alix's request. 'But it makes you look so bloody severe!'

When Alix went home she took the Lancôme nail varnish from the bathroom shelf and painted her nails. She was surprised to find that her hand was shaking a little. She couldn't be nervous, could she? Not about dinner with a client. Even if he did want to be her friend.

She inspected the contents of her wardrobe and chose Jasper Conran again, but this time a bright fuschia-coloured dress that made her skin look darker and her eyes greener. She wore her plain gold earrings and gold chain. She sprayed herself with Dune.

She was ready almost an hour before she was due to meet him.

She arrived at the fashionable Clarence Hotel at exactly eight o'clock. Alix was incapable of being unpunctual even though she'd told herself that Matt would expect her to be at least five minutes late. But the taxi had arrived on time and even heavy traffic on Pearse Street hadn't delayed her.

He was already at the table. He was looking straight ahead of him, across the room. He didn't see her.

She walked over to the table. 'Hi,' she said.

He stood up. 'Hello, Alix.'

She shook his extended hand. It might be a date, she thought, but we're observing the niceties of our business relationship.

'You're on time,' said Matt.

She smiled. 'Of course.'

'I thought you would be,' he said. 'You look like the kind of person who'd be on time.'

They sat down opposite each other.

'I hope you haven't been waiting long,' said Alix.

'No.' Matt shook his head. 'I had a drink in the bar before I came in here. Regretfully there were no beautiful people or celebrities lounging around.'

'I wouldn't have taken you for a celebrity kind of guy.'

'Oh, I don't know.' He grinned at her. 'The last time I was here I almost bumped into Eva Herzogova. Or Helena Christiansen. One of them anyway.'

'You didn't get her number?'

'Nope.' He grinned again. 'But I told myself I'd have better luck next time.' He opened the menu in front of him. 'Do you want to get the ordering out of the way? Then we can chat.'

'Sure,' she said. Chat about what? The way he said it made it sound like an interview.

She skimmed through the menu. 'Goat's cheese and risotto,' she said.

'Wine?' he asked.

'Whatever you like.'

He ordered a Soave. 'Since you're having risotto,' he said. 'Besides, I like Italian white.'

'So do I,' said Alix.

'You know, I can't believe we're actually here having dinner. It seems like months since I asked you.'

'I'm so much in demand!' She laughed.

'I'm not surprised,' said Matt.

She smiled slightly and fiddled with her napkin.

'How was business this week?' he asked.

She groaned. 'Hectic.'

'The Latin America debt problem certainly gave the dollar a boost. Great for me because we were long from a Californian deal we'd just completed. Although I did sell some to you guys a bit too early. I hope you made money out of it!'

She wasn't going to tell him about Europa Bank's dollar trade. Or about getting sick afterwards. 'It was a crazy day,' she said. 'We made money overall. But it wasn't easy.' She felt her stomach churn at the memory of sitting in Des Coyle's office and trying to explain it to him without giving him too much information.

'I'd expect nothing less than that you made money,' said Matt.

'It's my job.'

'You love it, don't you?'

She shrugged. 'I suppose I do. It's all I ever wanted.'

He looked at her thoughtfully. 'I watched you on TV,' he said. 'That was the impression you gave.'

'It must be right.'

'What about your boyfriend?' asked Matt. 'What did he think?'

The waiter appeared with their starters before she could answer. Matt cursed the other man for his sense of timing. Now Alix could change the subject. And he really wanted to know about her occasional boyfriend.

But, to his surprise, she answered him.

'Paul set up the interview,' she said. 'He works in RTÉ. I don't see him any more.'

'I'm sorry,' said Matt.

'Are you?' She looked at him questioningly. 'Given that you're taking me out to a "let's be friends" dinner, I thought you'd be pissed at me if you thought I was still seeing someone else.'

He laughed. 'I was trying to appear caring and thoughtful.'

'Don't,' said Alix. 'It's not necessary.'

'But I am caring and thoughtful,' protested Matt. 'I like to think so anyway!'

'What about you?' asked Alix. 'What about the women in your life?'

'Oh, not that many,' he said dismissively. 'I don't have time, to tell you the truth. I have a lot of female friends, but that's all.'

She felt a frisson of disappointment. She was obviously to be another in a line of women friends that he could take out whenever he needed someone. Sitting here opposite him she'd wondered if there could be something more. He was attractive, there was no doubt about that. She liked the way his blue eyes twinkled at her. She liked his broad shoulders, his apparently well-built body and the way he seemed to glow with health and vitality. She'd let her mind imagine later in the evening, when he'd try to kiss her, and it hadn't been an altogether unpleasant thought. But now he was implying that he wanted a platonic kind of relationship. She sighed. She didn't even have time for a platonic relationship with him. Soon she'd be in Paris with a whole new circle of people to get to know. Despite Des's misgivings about letting her go in the wake of the dollar debacle, he'd managed to get over things enough to agree that she should go to Paris as planned and that Dave would take over her job.

'You OK?' he asked.

'Sure. Why?'

'You were thinking of something and it didn't seem to be very pleasant.'

'Work,' she said.

He sighed. 'I was hoping that, after our initial obligatory conversation about the markets, we could forget about work!'

'OK.' She smiled. 'No work talk.'

They looked at each other in silence for almost a minute and then both of them began to laugh.

'Are we that boring that we don't have anything else to talk about?' she asked.

'Tell me about that interview,' said Matt. 'What was it like? You seemed so self-confident but it must have been quite nerve-wracking.'

She shrugged. 'Not really. You just talk to the person in front of you. You don't think about anything else.'

'You gave him a run for his money.' Matt laughed. 'I could hear the fear in his voice when he was asking some of those questions.'

'That wasn't fear.' Alix made a face. 'He was trying to taunt me. You didn't see his face! He wanted something controversial about working women and kids and all that sort of thing.'

'But you must think about it,' said Matt. 'Having a family.'

Alix smoothed her hair. 'Sometimes.'

'And?'

'And what?'

'Do you think there'll come a time when you want to chuck it all in and stay at home?'

'Perhaps,' she said, 'but it hasn't happened yet.'

'You obviously didn't want to do that with the RTÉ man.'

'No.'

'Was that what went wrong?'

'It was more than that,' said Alix slowly. 'I cared about him a lot, but not enough, it seemed.'

Their main courses arrived and Alix busied herself with black pepper and Parmesan cheese.

'So what's your favourite city?' Matt watched her as she laced her dinner with pepper. He could see that she didn't want to talk about Paul Hunter. 'After all, you must have travelled a lot.'

'Not as much as you,' she told him. 'I don't have a favourite.'

'What about Paris?' he asked. 'You must spend a lot of time there.'

'I never get to see much of it,' she said ruefully. 'I always seem to be rushing from hotel to bank and back again. Do you know,' she looked at him guiltily, 'I've never even been in the Louvre?'

'Oh dear,' he said. 'What about the Arc de Triomphe?'

'Can you get inside that?' she asked in surprise.

'What cultural things have you done there?' he asked.

'Bought lots of clothes,' she said positively. 'Very, very essential when you're in Paris!'

They laughed and this time the laughter was easier, more natural. Matt topped up her glass with wine.

'I like the way you dress,' he said. 'You always look very chic.'

'Thank you. But you haven't seen me outside working hours.'

'This is outside working hours.'

'You know what I mean. Flopping around in jeans and a T-shirt.'

'They're probably designer jeans,' he said.

568

She grinned. 'You might be right.'

She was enjoying herself. He was easy to talk to. Whenever he sensed that she was uncomfortable with a topic he immediately began to talk about something else. He told her about Malaysia and California and his trips to Tokyo. He related stories about long-distance flights where he was terrified to get out of the seat in case something awful happened while he wasn't strapped in. He told her how he'd been poached from another company by Anatronics and how it had been the best move of his career.

'But I don't like the travelling,' he said. 'I'd prefer to stay in one place for more than a couple of weeks. And that's not only because of the flying paranoia.'

'I like travelling,' said Alix. She finished her coffee and glanced at her watch. It was almost eleven. She couldn't believe that they'd been here for three hours! The time had raced by.

'Shall we go?' Matt signalled for the bill.

'That was really nice,' said Alix. 'Thank you.'

'My pleasure,' said Matt.

They walked outside. A cold wind blew along the street and Alix shivered. The jacket she was wearing was far too light for the time of year.

'Would you like a nightcap?' asked Matt.

She meant to say no but she said yes.

They pushed their way through the throng in Thomas Read's.

'This is crazy!' Matt had to shout above the music and the buzz of conversation.

'But lively,' she mouthed back at him.

He nodded. They were squashed against the wall, almost unable to move because the pub was so full.

'Do you come here often?' cried Matt.

'What?'

'Is this one of your haunts?'

'Are you mad?' she asked. 'This is far too trendy for me.'

'Would you like to go?'

She shrugged.

'Come on.' He drained his glass. 'It's impossible to talk here.'

She followed him outside again.

'I guess I'd better head home,' she said.

'OK,' said Matt. 'Do you want me to come with you? See you safely inside? Or would you prefer if I left you now?'

'You don't have to come back with me,' she said. She looked at him carefully. 'But you're welcome to come. Perhaps have coffee. Or a drink.'

'OK,' said Matt.

They sat in the taxi in silence. She wanted him to come to the apartment with her but she didn't know what she wanted when they got there. She still only had vague memories of the night he'd brought her home before. She knew that he'd left almost as soon as he'd drunk his coffee. She wondered if he'd do the same this time. If she wanted him to do the same this time.

'Come in,' she said as she unlocked the door.

He followed her inside and took off his leather jacket which he hung over the back of a chair.

'There's a coat stand over there,' said Alix.

He said nothing but hung the jacket up.

'I'm sorry,' she said.

'Sorry?'

'It's just that living on my own now I've got fussy. I don't hang things over chairs and I put things away – it's stupid.'

'It's OK,' said Matt. 'I'm a tidy person myself. I didn't see the coat stand.'

'Thank you,' she said.

'I'm telling you the truth,' said Matt. 'Not just trying to make you feel good.'

She smiled. 'Would you like coffee? Or a drink?'

'Whatever.'

'I'm going to have a drink,' she said. 'I try not to drink coffee too late because I don't sleep.' She walked over to one of the pale units and took out a bottle of Bacardi Spice. 'What will you have?'

'Beer?' he asked.

'In the fridge,' she said. 'I'll get it in a second. Or you can help yourself if you like.'

'I'll do it.' He went into the tiny kitchen and opened the fridge. She liked yoghurt and cheese and tomatoes, he decided, as he looked at the contents. And lots of juices. And chocolate – there was a huge bar of Cadbury's on the top shelf. But she seemed to like beer more than anything else – there were a dozen bottles of Miller in the fridge. And a mixture of Californian Chardonnay and Italian white wines.

'Expecting to be snowed in?' he asked as he walked back to the living room.

'Pardon?' She was sitting on the sofa, her legs tucked beneath her.

'Lots of beer. And wine.' He sat down beside her.

She laughed. 'I know. My sister goes mad when she comes to see me. I'm a terrible shopper. I buy all the wrong things but I always seem to have loads of beer and wine. And I don't drink all that much. Honestly.'

'Is she your younger or your older sister?' asked Matt.

'Wyn's nearly five years older than me,' said Alix. 'She tries to mother me sometimes. That's why she lectures me about the contents of my fridge.'

'Do you have any other brothers or sisters?'

Alix paused with the glass halfway to her lips. She could see the picture of Kate, hair blowing in the wind, sitting on the car. She felt as though someone had hit her in the stomach. She shivered.

'Alix?' He looked at her in surprise. The expression on her face was unreadable. 'Are you all right?' She looked frozen, he thought. Terrified.

'Excuse me!' She put the glass on the table and almost ran into the bathroom.

Matt stared after her in amazement. What had he said to upset her? Asking about her family? Surely not. Unless there'd been some terrible tragedy. Oh shit, he thought helplessly, I've ruined it now. Maybe she had a brother or a sister who got killed or something and I've reminded her about it. You idiot, Connery. It was going so well!

Alix sat on the edge of the bath and tried to breathe evenly. She'd been about to say no, only one sister, when she'd thought of Kate. And suddenly she hadn't been able to say it. She hadn't been able to ignore the fact that Kate was a real, living person. With a baby. And a husband. And a father who was her father too.

This is crazy, she thought, as her eyes filled with tears. I'm sitting here crying! What's there to cry over?

'Alix?' Matt tapped at the bathroom door. 'Are you OK?'

'Yes,' she said shakily. 'I'm fine.'

'Are you sure?'

'I'll be out in a second.' She checked her face in the mirror and thanked God for waterproof mascara.

'Sorry about that.' She smiled wanly at him as she sat down again.

'Did I say something?' he asked.

Oh God, she thought, I want to cry again. I'm fine. She pressed her fingers against the bridge of her nose.

'Alix, if there's something wrong, please tell me.' Matt moved closer to her. 'I know I'm almost a complete stranger but if I can help at all . . .' His voice trailed off.

She shook her head wordlessly. Why was she behaving like this? She never behaved like this in front of other people. Never. She was a strong person. She didn't need blokes offering to be helpful. She didn't need to talk things through with anybody. Least of all someone she hardly even knew.

'I have a sister,' said Matt. 'Her name is Kathryn. We call her Kats.'

'I thought I had only one sister,' said Alix. 'I thought there was only Wyn. But – I have another sister. A half-sister. I didn't know about her until recently.'

'Alix.' He reached out and took her hands. 'How did you find out?'

'She's my father's child,' said Alix. 'Well, not a child now, she's twenty-nine.'

'And you never knew? You'd no idea?'

She shook her head.

'Your father kept it a secret?'

'He left us,' said Alix tightly. 'When I was three.'

Matt kept her hands enclosed in his. Don't say anything, he told himself. Keep quiet. Let her talk if she wants to.

'He went to the States,' Alix continued. 'He had a girlfriend and she got pregnant and he left Carrie and Wyn and me and he went to the States with her.'

Matt put his arm round her.

'I only found out a couple of months ago. We didn't hear from him. Apparently he'd tried to keep in touch but Carrie – that's my mother – she didn't want him to. And so he stopped trying.'

He held her closely.

'Then he came back.' She was silent.

'And what was it like,' asked Matt finally, 'when you met him?'

'I didn't meet him,' she said fiercely. 'I couldn't meet him. He'd left us. For her. And now he wants Carrie to divorce him so that he can marry her. Because Kate has had a baby.'

'Did he want to meet you?'

'He said so. He came to the office one day. But I couldn't see him. I really couldn't.' She pushed her fingers through her hair and it sprang loose from its clip and tumbled around her face.

'And do you wish you had?' asked Matt.

She looked up at him and smiled slightly. 'I don't know. Part of me. And another part of me doesn't care.'

He pushed her hair out of her eyes. He knew that it wasn't a great time to feel incredibly turned on but he couldn't help it. She was so beautiful and so strong and now, suddenly, so vulnerable. And he desperately wanted to take her to bed.

'I'm sorry.' She pulled away from him. 'I don't know why all this just came spilling out. I don't usually behave like this. I'm an idiot.'

'It's OK,' he said.

'Just forget about it. It's probably the wine and the Bacardi.'

'I don't want to forget about it,' said Matt. 'I'm glad you felt you could tell me.'

Why had she told him? She wished she knew. She'd had no intention of telling anyone about John or Kate or Imogen. She hardly believed in them herself! But now, by spilling out her guts to Matt Connery, she'd made them real. She could imagine Kate sliding off the bonnet of the car and kissing the man who'd taken the photograph. John Callaghan. And maybe linking her arm with his and walking into the house where Imogen was making tea. The pictures flooded into her mind. They were real people. With real lives. And now they were part of her life.

'You were so nice to me tonight,' she told Matt. 'It was a lovely evening. I'm sorry for messing it up.'

'You didn't,' he said.

'You'll never want to deal with us again,' said Alix. 'Knowing that there's a complete flake in the dealing room.'

'Don't be ridiculous,' said Matt.

She sighed and began to twist her hair into a knot at the back of her head.

'Do you want me to go?' asked Matt as he watched her.

'Do you want to go?'

'Alix, I know you're upset and maybe not thinking straight right now. It's not a fair question to ask.'

She looked at him questioningly.

'Of course I don't want to go,' he told her. 'I want to stay. I want to put my arms round you and hold on to you and comfort you and I really, really want to stay.'

'Do you?'

'Don't make me say it again.'

She reached out for him. 'Is this a needy, take-advantage-of kind of situation?'

'Well, yes,' he said. 'That's why I probably should go.'

'I want you to stay,' she told him. 'I want you to take advantage of me.'

'Which is worse?' She was in his arms now, her head on his shoulders, her hair falling loose again. 'Doing something I'd regret or not doing something I'd regret?'

'Matt.' She looked at him. 'No regrets. Just something we both want to do.'

'Oh, God,' he said as she undid the buttons of his shirt. 'OK, Alix. No regrets.'

Chapter 40

S he sat and stared across the room. The words painted on the wall were directly opposite her desk. *'De l'audace, encore de l'audace, et toujours de l'audace!'* During the day, when she was busy, she never noticed them. But now, when almost everyone had gone home, she couldn't help but be aware of them. And be reminded of Sabine. If it hadn't been for Sabine, thought Alix, she might be in Dublin tonight, curled up beside Paul as she had been last Christmas when everything had seemed so settled and so secure.

She had finally rung Paul. It had taken three phone calls before he eventually spoke to her.

'I've been busy,' he said defensively. 'I meant to call you, Alix. Really I did.'

'No you didn't,' she said. 'What would you say if I told you that I was pregnant?'

'What!'

'That's what you'd say?'

'Alix, you can't be,' he said urgently. 'I mean, I thought, I assumed—'

'Keep your cool,' she said. 'I'm not. I just wondered what your reaction would have been.'

'If that was a joke it wasn't very funny,' snapped Paul.

'It wasn't meant to be,' said Alix. 'You could've rung me. Let me know that our night of passion was a horrible mistake.'

'It was a mistake,' admitted Paul. 'It wasn't horrible, though, Alix. It was great. But it was wrong. And I'm sorry.'

'So am I,' said Alix. 'I could have stopped you and I didn't. And the reason I'm ringing, Paul, is to wish you luck with Sabine and tell you that I'll be starting my job in Paris next week.'

'I hope it works out for you,' he told her. 'I really do, Alix. I care about you a lot.'

'Thanks,' she said. 'And I care about you too, Paul. I hope you have lots of lovely babies.'

It had been easier than she thought to finally get him out of her head, out of her heart and out of her life. Even though the quotations still got to her.

Matt Connery had been a different story. Making love to Matt Connery had been almost perfect. He'd been a considerate lover, finding out what she liked and what she didn't, kissing her gently and then more urgently, being both aggressive and tender and making her body tingle with desire. And then, the next morning, he'd brought her a cup of coffee while she lay between waking and sleeping, still languid with satisfaction.

'There wasn't much milk,' he told her as he handed her the cup.

'There never is.' She sipped it cautiously.

'You did say you were a terrible shopper.'

'Especially milk.' She smiled at him.

'Alix?'

'Yes?'

'Last night.'

She looked at him warily.

'It was wonderful.'

She nodded. He was right. It had been fantastic.

'We seemed to – it worked, didn't it?'

'I'm glad you thought so.'

'You didn't?' He looked at her anxiously.

'It's not that.' She placed the cup on the bedside locker and sat up properly.

'What then?'

'It's simply – I was offered a job in Europa Bank, Paris. I accepted. I start in a few weeks' time.'

He stared at her. 'So what was last night all about?'

'No regrets,' she told him. 'That's what we agreed, wasn't it?'

'Yes,' he said. 'Of course. No regrets.' He walked over to the bedroom window and looked out.

'It was great,' said Alix. 'Really it was, Matt. And I like you a lot. It's just that – what would be the point? You're committed to your career. So am I. When you do meet someone that you're interested in you'll want a woman that supports you and looks after you and has babies for you. And I don't think I'll ever be that sort of person.'

'How do you know what sort of person I want?' he asked.

'Because, in the end, that's what you all want,' she told him. 'It's what Paul wanted despite the fact that he used to say kids were messy little beggars and he couldn't stand them. Despite the fact that he used to tell me he'd always be there for me. It's even what my father wanted. He walked out on a family, but he walked right back into another one! It wouldn't be any different with you, Matt. I know it wouldn't. I thought about it last night while you were asleep.' She'd thought about it as she'd looked at him and wished that she was a different kind of person or he was a different kind of person and she knew that it would never work.

'You made all these decisions without talking to me,' said Matt.

'We could go out some more and then it'd be harder because I'd care about you more,' said Alix. 'But I've got to take this job and you've got to get on with traipsing between Tokyo and the States and Ireland.' She shrugged. 'We'd tell ourselves everything would be fine but it wouldn't be.'

'I see.' Matt turned towards her and she'd never seen his eyes look so hard. 'I'm glad we had last night. I don't have any regrets.' He smiled slightly then kissed her on the forehead. 'Thanks, Alix. I'm sure I'll be talking to you before you go to Paris.'

And he left.

But he didn't talk to her before she went. Gavin had talked to him. Gavin had done three profitable trades with Anatronics and had made money out of a five-year swap for them too.

'I really feel as though I'm getting to grips with that account,' he told Alix on her last day. 'It took a while – I thought that you were going to mess me up with it, Alix. Sorry.'

'I told you, I wouldn't knowingly mess any of you up.'

'You got us out of a few in our time,' said Dave. 'Especially the dollar trade. I only wish I could tell people about it.'

'For God's sake don't!' she exclaimed. 'You'd have us in all sorts of trouble.'

'I think Des has forgiven us,' Dave said.

'He might have got over it,' warned Alix, 'but he'll never forget, Dave. So take it easy.'

'I will,' said Dave. 'I promise.'

'I'll miss you,' said Jenny as they had a drink in O'Reilly's together. 'You were great to work for.'

'I'm sorry I didn't do more for you,' said Alix. 'I've often wondered how right you were when you accused me of not giving you enough respect, Jenny. Maybe it was more true than I wanted to believe.'

'I don't care,' Jenny told her. 'You came through for us when you had to and that's good enough for me. Besides,' she grinned, 'Dave told me that I'll be the senior dealer, not Donnelly.'

'I'm glad,' Alix said. 'It's the right decision.'

It had seemed strange to walk down the steps for the last time. Not the last time, she'd told herself as she clamped down on the sentimentality. She'd be back. She'd be back when she was head of European trading. Which was Guy's job. She was pretty sure that one day she'd get Guy's job.

'Alix!' Guy's voice broke through her memories. 'I thought you were going home today? For Christmas?'

'Yes.' She stood up. 'I was daydreaming.'

He grinned. 'Thinking of how good it's been since you came?'

She grimaced. There had been a number of good days and one truly awful one when swaps had traded in the complete opposite direction to her expectations. She'd booked a loss and had been annoyed with herself.

'I think it's working out well,' said Guy. 'You get on with everyone. You're cut out for this job, Alix.'

'*Merci beaucoup*,' she said.

'Have a good time in Dublin,' he told her. 'We'll see you on the thirtieth. But Alix, if you want to take an extra day off, it's OK. For you we can wait until the New Year if you prefer.'

'Not at all,' she said briskly. 'I'll be back, Guy. I hate the end of the year anyway. I'd much prefer to be working.'

She picked up her bag and her case and took the lift to the ground floor. It seemed slightly crazy to be going home so soon after she'd arrived but Carrie had been insistent that she come back for Christmas and she had agreed. Besides, she thought, Christmas on her own in Paris was taking self-sufficiency a little too far.

∽

The apartment was warm. Wyn had been in earlier in the day and had turned on the central heating. She'd also left some milk in the fridge and bread in the bread bin. Alix smiled as she read her sister's note: 'Make yourself some coffee with milk! See you on Christmas Day. Hope you have lots of paracetamol – the kids go manic at this time of year. Give Carrie a ring when you get in. Love, Wyn.'

She looked at her watch. It was nearly eight o'clock. She'd call Carrie soon but now she wanted to sit in the silence of her own apartment and appreciate her own things around her.

The apartment in Paris was fine. Small, but with everything she needed, and in a nice location near Montmartre. It wasn't home yet though, and she had missed this place. She'd rent it out next year, she thought as she poured herself a drink. Make it pay its way.

She woke up early the next morning, wide-awake and with a feeling of anticipation. As a child she'd always loved Christmas Eve. She'd loved the thrill of the preparations, the hope of getting the things she'd asked for and the pervading smell of Carrie's attempts at home cooking that wafted around

the house. It was the same every year and Alix had liked the sameness of it all.

Carrie had booked the Peacock Alley for dinner. Since they'd all be at Wyn and Terry's for Christmas Day, Carrie had yearned for some quiet sophistication on Christmas Eve and Alix had been only too pleased to fall in with her mother's plans. Last year she'd gone to the pub with the other dealers and had been collected by Paul at nine o'clock. He'd been out with friends too and it hadn't bothered him that she'd been drunk. They'd bought Chinese takeaway and had spent the evening at home eating prawn crackers and (in Alix's case) drinking the bottle of port that one of her clients had given her.

She met her mother at the restaurant. Carrie looked wonderful, thought Alix. She was dressed in a green velvet dress and wore emerald jewellery and looked anything but a mother of two grown-up girls.

'Hi, Carrie!' She kissed her mother and sat at the table. 'Sorry I'm late. Traffic was terrible.'

'You're on time.' Carrie looked at her watch.

'It's twenty-five to nine,' Alix objected. 'You said half eight.'

Carrie laughed. 'Five minutes give or take is on time.' She looked at her daughter critically. 'You're looking well, Alix. How's the job?'

'It's fine.' Alix unfolded her napkin. 'It takes a bit of getting used to, of course. And the dealing room is so big compared with Europa Dublin. But I think I'm settling in OK.'

'Homesick?' asked Carrie.

'A little,' Alix admitted. 'But I'll get out a bit more in the New Year and organise a social life for myself. Until now it's all been settling in, that sort of thing.'

'And your new boss – Guy. Is he OK to work for?'

'Actually, that's the best part,' said Alix. 'When I was in Dublin he was always needling me. But he's a lot more professional in Paris. I'm getting on much better with him than I expected.'

'Is he married?' asked Carrie.

'Really, Carrie!' Alix looked at her in annoyance. 'Why do you want to know that?'

'I wondered if there would be a new man for you,' said Carrie. 'It's a romantic city, after all, isn't it?'

'It might be,' said Alix, 'but Guy Decourcelle *is* married with a couple of kids and although he tried to haul me off to bed with him a few times in the past, I have no intention of getting involved with him.'

'I see,' said Carrie.

There was an awkward silence and they were rescued by the waiter taking their order.

'Are you looking forward to tomorrow?' asked Carrie.

Alix made a face at her. 'Christmas *chez* Terry and Wyn and two hyperactive children? Only if they have a large bottle of vodka stored somewhere.'

Carrie laughed. 'It's only once a year.'

'Thank God,' said Alix. 'But those kids are a handful all year round. I don't know how she copes.'

'You do,' said Carrie. 'When you have children, you just do.'

'Not something that'll ever bother me.'

'Alix, there's something we have to discuss,' said Carrie.

Alix looked at her mother warily. 'Not more skeletons tumbling out of the family closet?'

'Don't be ridiculous,' said Carrie.

Alix shrugged. 'How am I to know? You kept enough stuff from us before.'

'I thought I was doing things for the best.' Carrie bit her lip. 'It's not easy to get it right, Alix. You think you've made the right decision and then, years later, you question it.'

'No point,' said Alix. 'What's done is done.'

'Alix, John and Imogen are in Dublin again.'

'Oh, for heaven's sake!' Alix stared at her. 'What's wrong with their bright, exciting, full-of-richness life in the States? What the hell are they doing here?'

'Kate and Jack wanted to come over for Christmas. John managed to fire them with enthusiasm and, of course, Imogen has kept in touch with her own family. So they're here.'

'Where?' Alix looked around as though they would walk by at any moment.

'They're staying here, in the Fitzwilliam Hotel. Kate and Jack and Imogen are having dinner with Imogen's brother tonight.'

'How nice,' said Alix.

'John didn't go.'

'Why? Don't they approve of him?'

'He knew that we were having dinner together, Alix. He wanted to meet you.'

Alix stared out of the window at the hustle and bustle of Christmas Eve in the city. She was angry with Carrie for telling her this, for meeting her under false pretences.

The waiter put bowls of pumpkin soup in front of them.

'Alix, I really think you should meet him. Bury the past.'

'I suppose you're going to say that it's Christmas and I should be in a loving and family-oriented mood,' said Alix sourly.

'I just think that you're carrying a heap of bitterness inside,' said Carrie. 'And meeting him would help.'

'I have nothing inside,' said Alix. 'I don't give a fuck about him one way or the other, Carrie. I know you think that I should, but I don't. I don't feel bitter. I don't feel anything.'

'What makes you feel, Alix? What gets through to you?'

Alix stared at Carrie. 'Lots of things.'

'But John doesn't make you feel anything?'

'Only pissed off,' said Alix. 'Who does he think that he is, coming over here, trying to worm his way back into our lives?'

'He loves you,' said Carrie.

'Oh, don't be absolutely ridiculous.' Alix stirred her soup angrily. 'He loves himself. He just wants to make everything OK for himself.'

'It's not like that,' said Carrie.

'Yes it is,' snapped Alix.

Carrie sighed. She was hopeless at this kind of thing, she thought. Wyn had encouraged her to meet Alix and try and persuade her once again to see John. Wyn had suggested that in the more impersonal atmosphere of the restaurant in the same building where John was staying, Alix might be more inclined to meet him and less defensive about it. But, Carrie realised, they'd underestimated Alix.

Alix stared at the bowl of soup and raged inside. She was fed up with this war of attrition, of all of them trying to make her do things she didn't want to do. They kept going on about forgiveness as though it would make any difference to her life. They watched too much Oprah and read too many self-help books.

Carrie couldn't think of anything to say. She should have waited until after the meal, she realised. Now, Alix would sit in quiet fury and push her food around her plate without eating it.

Alix felt a little sorry for her mother. It hadn't been easy for Carrie, she knew that. And tonight had probably been the product of some ridiculous conversation with Wyn who had probably decided that she might feel differently simply because it was Christmas.

She put down her spoon. She wasn't hungry.

'All right,' she said.

'All right what?' Carrie looked up at her.

'If it'll make you feel better, Carrie, I'll meet him.'

'You will?' Carrie pushed her bowl away. 'When?'

'Now,' said Alix. She stood up. 'I'm not hungry. He's here, isn't he? Let's get the whole thing over and done with.'

'Are you sure?' Carrie stared at her in amazement.

'Look, I don't want to spend every time I meet you skirting around this subject,' said Alix. 'I'll meet him, say hello and goodbye and that'll be the end of it. OK?'

'Yes,' said Carrie. 'OK.' She signalled for the waiter who nearly had a fit when he realised that they were leaving. Carrie signed a Visa chit for the uneaten meal and they walked down to the hotel foyer.

I'm out of my mind, thought Alix as she stood by the wall. I've let them manipulate me.

'He'll be here soon,' said Carrie. 'I'll wait for you in the bar.'

'Fine.'

Alix hoped that she looked OK. She was wearing a red woollen dress by Joseph and black shoes with a low heel because she hadn't wanted to tower over her mother. She wished that she was wearing a suit. She always felt confident in a suit.

'Hello, Alix.'

They stared at each other for a moment. He was taller than she'd expected and looked younger. His grey hair was brushed back from his forehead and his eyes, grey-green, looked anxiously at her. He reminded her of Wyn whenever her sister wanted to tell her something that she might not want to hear.

'Hello,' she said.

'I'm glad you decided to meet me.' He smiled at her.

'It's for Carrie's sake, not mine,' said Alix.

'I don't care whose sake it's for,' said John Callaghan. 'I've missed you. I'm sorry.'

She wasn't going to give in, she thought. She wasn't going to feel emotional about this. She wasn't going to let him think that she cared one way or the other.

But when he held out his hand to her, she grasped it and, quite suddenly, his arms were round her, hugging her fiercely while he said 'I'm sorry' over and over again. And she was whispering 'It's OK, it's OK' while the tears slid down her cheeks.

Chapter 41

'When will you be back again?' asked Wyn as she sat in Alix's apartment and watched her pack.

'I'm not sure.' Alix tugged at the zip of her case. 'Depends on how busy we are. You never know, though. I might get a business trip back soon.' She hauled the case off her bed. 'You should come over and visit me, Wyn. I'm sure you'd love it. Only the apartment is so tiny there wouldn't be room for all your shopping!'

Wyn laughed. 'Will you move?'

'Oh, yes,' said Alix. 'It's just temporary. But Wyn, please get me some nice tenants for this place. I don't like to think that it'll fall into the wrong hands.'

'Don't worry,' said Wyn. 'I'll look after things for you.'

The buzzer sounded.

'That's my cab,' said Alix. She kissed her sister on the cheek. 'Thanks for everything.'

'Alix?'

'Yes?'

'Are you glad you met him?'

Alix was silent for a moment. She wasn't sure that glad was the right word. When John had hugged her it had been the strangest feeling of her life. She'd often heard people talking about a weight being lifted from them, and that was exactly how she had felt. Of course, afterwards, their conversation had been stilted and awkward, with neither of them sure of what they wanted to say; yet Alix had felt more at ease with herself than she ever had before. She still hadn't got used to the feeling.

'I suppose I am,' she said. 'But I don't think I'll ever feel close to him.'

'That doesn't matter.' Wyn picked up the case. 'You've taken the first step. I'll lock up afterwards. You go ahead.'

'OK,' said Alix. 'I'll give you a call on New Year's Eve. I'm sorry I can't be here, but I promised to be back in Paris. Guy has invited me to a party so I won't be sitting at home moping. You don't have to worry, Wyn.'

'I'm your older sister. It's my job to worry,' said Wyn.

Alix hugged her and they went out to the cab.

Wyn waved to her until the taxi was out of sight then she went back up to the apartment. It was a lovely apartment, she thought. She could understand why Alix liked it so much. She tried to imagine Nessa and Aoife running around in it but failed miserably. It was very peaceful, she thought. She made herself a cup of coffee and sat down. Ten minutes, she told herself, and then she'd go back to the madhouse. But she didn't get as far as drinking the coffee. In the silence and the peace of the apartment she closed her eyes and fell asleep.

✎

The phone rang and Wyn jumped into wakefulness.

'Hello?'

'Alix?'

'No, this is Wyn.'

'Oh, Wyn. Her sister.'

'Yes. Can I help?'

'I was looking for Alix.'

'You've missed her,' said Wyn. 'Sorry.'

'Oh. Will she be back soon?'

'No,' Wyn said. 'She's gone back to Paris.'

'Bloody hell! Already?'

'Can I take a message or anything? Who's calling?'

'I'm a – friend, I suppose.'

'Which friend?'

'My name is Matt.'

'Are you the date?' asked Wyn.

'Pardon?'

'The date? Alix told me that she was meeting a client a while ago and it was a date.'

'Did she?'

'Well, I'm not sure how certain she was about it being a date. She said you wanted to be friends. Was that you?'

Matt sighed. 'Yes. That was me.'

'But it didn't work out?'

'Not the way I'd hoped,' said Matt. 'But I want to change all that. I tried to meet her in Paris.'

'Oh.' Wyn clutched the phone more tightly. 'Where are you now?'

'I'm in Dublin,' said Matt. 'They told me she was in Dublin for Christmas. I rang a few times but she was never at home and she didn't leave her damn machine on.'

'I don't suppose she was expecting people to phone,' said Wyn.

'I called round on Christmas Eve but she wasn't there.'

'She was with our parents,' said Wyn.

'Parents?' said Matt. 'Both of them?'

'Yes.'

'You mean, she's met her father?'

'What do you know about it?' asked Wyn. She couldn't believe that Alix had told anyone about Carrie and John. Even if they'd been on a date! It wasn't her sister's style. Besides, she'd been in denial about John until a couple of days ago.

'Everything,' said Matt.

'You're joking!'

'She told me about him before she went to Paris.'

'Alix *told* you?'

'Shouldn't she have?'

Wyn was amazed. 'I just wouldn't have expected her to. She's not the sort of person who—'

'She probably didn't mean to. But – she did.'

'Are you and Alix – is she . . . ?'

'Good question,' said Matt. 'We've been out together once. Only once! But it was wonderful. Then she dumped me to go to Paris! She has some weird notions, your sister.'

Wyn exhaled slowly. 'That's Alix.'

'She's so practical,' said Matt. 'She told me that it wouldn't work because I'd only want her to settle down and have babies and I'd be hopelessly unsupportive of her work.'

'That sounds like my sister,' said Wyn grimly.

'And I let her say all those things and I let her go. But I made a mistake. I want to talk to her again. I've thought of nothing else but her since she went.'

'Oh, my God.' Wyn was enthralled. She was in the middle of Alix's relationship – a relationship that she hadn't even known existed. So typical of Alix not to tell her. To pretend that her life was caught up in Paris and in her job. While all the time she was part of a real-life romance. The things that Matt Connery was saying certainly sounded romantic enough to her.

'She didn't tell me much about you,' she said to Matt.

'She doesn't seem to tell people much about anything.'

'So what do you want to do?' asked Wyn.

'What time is her flight?' asked Matt.

'Two o'clock,' replied Wyn.

'I'm going to the airport.' And Matt hung up.

Wyn stood in her sister's living room in complete shock. Then she picked up the phone and dialled Carrie's number.

꒰ꂧ꒱

Dublin airport was crowded. Alix checked in her luggage and went straight through to the departure area where the crowds were a little thinner. She bought a coffee and sat down at one of the tables. She took a copy of *Marie-Claire* out of her bag and skimmed through it. But she kept thinking of the last few days, of Carrie and of John and of meeting her half-sister Kate and Kate's adorable baby son. She hadn't expected to meet Kate, but when John suggested it she'd agreed. And Alix had liked her. She wasn't a dreamy, fragile person at all, but a strong-willed woman who worked in a call centre and had fifty staff working for her. Alix had been very wrong about Kate. They'd agreed to keep in touch. And Alix felt that they probably would.

Her flight was called and she joined the queue to board. As the plane hurtled down the runway, Alix turned over a page in the magazine. Then she stopped reading and looked out of the window. This time, it seemed more real. This time it actually hurt to go away.

Matt watched the plane take off. He thrust his hands in his pockets and cursed under his breath. He'd imagined calling to her as she walked through the gates. He'd imagined her turning round and seeing him and running towards him. He'd imagined her falling into his arms and telling him how much she loved him. He hadn't imagined spending twenty minutes trying to find a parking space. He hadn't imagined pushing his way through the crowded terminal only to discover that the flight had already closed. He hadn't imagined going home without her.

She wasn't looking forward to work the next day. There still seemed to be too much stuff going on in her head to care about work. For the first time in her life it seemed unimportant in relation to everything else. But she'd be OK when she got in, she decided. When she sat down in front of the screens and looked at the numbers, a different part of her brain seemed to take over and she slotted back into the rhythm as though she'd never been away. That was the way it always worked.

She unpacked her bags and curled up on the sofa. She switched on CNN and watched the market news from the States.

She was restless. She couldn't stay sitting in front of the TV. She pulled on her heavy quilted jacket and her fur-lined boots and crossed the Place du Tetre towards the Sacré Coeur. She walked up the steps to the cathedral and stopped to look over the lights of the city. It was beautiful here, she thought. People were right when they called Paris romantic. It seemed such a shame to be here on her own. She thought of Paul but without the anger that she'd felt before. She thought of Matt Connery and she bit her lip. She remembered the way he'd kissed her. The way he'd held her. She remembered how very secure she'd felt with him beside her.

She hadn't expected to see many people around tonight but there were. A young couple sat on the steps near her. They huddled together for warmth and kissed each other. Alix watched them for a moment, then, embarrassed with herself, she turned away. She stopped at the little shop at the bottom of the steps and bought herself a paper-thin crêpe dredged in lemon and sugar. She ate it as she walked back towards her apartment, shivering slightly in the cool easterly breeze.

'Alix!'

She was so surprised that she stopped with the crêpe between her teeth. She turned round.

'Alix!'

She blinked in astonishment. It couldn't really be Matt Connery walking along the street towards her. She had to be imagining it. But it wasn't her imagination, it was definitely him – she recognised his voice and his build and even the way he walked. Her heart began to beat faster. She bit into the crêpe and swallowed the chunk without chewing it. She wiped the lemon and sugar from her lips.

'Matt! What on earth are you doing here?' she asked as he caught up with her.

He looked at her in silence. He'd never seen her looking like this. Casual and relaxed, her long hair flowing loose and blowing across her face. She looked younger, less commanding and very, very shocked to see him.

'Look,' he said, searching for the right words, 'I know this seems crazy to you. I'm sorry if I surprised you.'

'You've surprised me but it's OK.' She looked around for a bin to dispose of the remains of her pancake. 'Are you here on business?'

'No,' said Matt.

She looked at him inquiringly. She wanted to reach out and touch him, to make sure that he was real.

'I think I've made a horrible mistake,' he said.

'Do you want to walk back to my apartment with me?' she asked. 'It's not far – about five minutes. You can tell me about your horrible mistake if you like. Or not.'

He fell into step beside her. It had seemed such a great gesture to make, to follow her here. He'd phoned Wyn when he missed the flight and she'd given him Alix's address and encouraged him to come. But, he realised, it was a crazy, stupid thing to have done and Alix – even this different Alix – would treat him with cool politeness while hiding her embarrassment at his actions. Maybe he would be better off pretending that he was here on business. That it hadn't been some kind of mad desire on his part to pull her into his arms and tell her over and over again that she was the only woman in the world for him.

'Here we are.' Alix stopped in front of an old, green-painted door. 'It looks worse than it is.'

He followed her up a narrow, dimly lit stairway and into the tiny apartment.

'Coffee?' she asked. 'Or something stronger?'

'Stronger,' said Matt. 'Cognac if you have it.'

'*Bien sûr.*' She smiled at him. 'When in France . . .' She

poured a generous measure of the amber liquid and handed it to him.

'I heard you met your father,' said Matt. 'I'm glad.'

She stared at him. 'Who told you that?'

'Your sister. Wyn. I was talking to her today.'

'Today!' Her tone echoed her astonishment. 'You were talking to Wyn today?'

He nodded.

'Why?'

'Because I rang your apartment and she was there.'

Alix blinked. 'You rang my apartment? But you knew that I was in Paris.'

He shrugged. 'I knew that you were in Paris last week,' he said. 'But the day that I was in Paris, you'd left for Dublin.'

'What were you doing here?' she asked.

'I was visiting another company,' he said. 'I rang to see if you'd meet me. But you'd left to go home.'

'That was a pity,' said Alix carefully.

'I was coming to Dublin the next day myself,' said Matt. 'So I thought I'd manage to catch up with you. But whenever I rang you didn't answer and the day I called to your apartment, you were out.'

'I'm sorry,' she said. 'You seem to have gone to a lot of trouble to see me.'

'Of course I did,' he said. 'You don't think I was simply going to leave things the way they were?'

'What do you mean?' she asked.

'Oh, Alix, don't make me humiliate myself by telling you how much you mean to me,' said Matt. 'I already feel like a complete idiot for coming here in the first place.'

She stared at him. 'I thought you agreed with me,' she said.

597

'I thought that you knew that our careers were really important and that I wouldn't be able to support you the way you'd probably want . . .' Her voice trailed off.

'You said all those things,' Matt reminded her. 'I didn't agree or disagree on anything.'

She got up and hugged her arms across her chest. 'I didn't want to get involved,' she told him. 'I care about you, Matt. But it'll be like Paul and me. One day you'll want more than I can give you and it'll be me that ends up feeling hurt.'

'Alix, I'll never want more than you can give me.'

She wanted to believe him. Since she'd come to Paris she'd thought about him more than anyone else. More than Carrie or Wyn or Paul. A day hadn't gone by when she hadn't thought about him. And how wonderful it had been with him. And how much she missed him. But she didn't want to admit to herself that she missed him. She wanted to know that she could cope without him. She didn't need anyone to help her live her life.

'My career is important to me,' she told him. 'I've worked so hard to get where I am.'

'I'm not trying to take it away,' said Matt. 'I'm just suggesting that there might be room for something else too.'

'I don't want to get it all wrong,' she said slowly. 'I seem to get it wrong quite a lot when it comes to relationships and I'm getting too old to keep making the same mistakes over and over again.'

'Alix, you're only thirty-three!'

'I've got grey hairs,' she told him.

He laughed. 'So have I. They're a mark of experience!'

'I'm sorry about the things I said to you that morning,' said Alix. 'But I was afraid that if I went out with you again I'd suddenly decide I didn't want to take this job and I'd be turning down a great opportunity. Matt, let's face it, you're working in Dublin, I'm here. It doesn't make a lot of sense.'

'Who says it has to make sense?' asked Matt. 'We can commute until I get a job here.'

She laughed. 'You – work here?'

'Why not?' he asked. 'You said yourself that I spend a lot of time travelling. I do. It doesn't much matter to me whether I work in Ireland or on the Continent. I speak French. I also speak Italian, German and a little Spanish.'

'Matt, I can't ask you to throw away *your* career for me,' she said. 'You'd always resent it and I'd always feel guilty.'

'Alix, I wouldn't be throwing away anything. I love what I do but there are more important things in life. Anatronics is about to be bought out by a US animation company. I'll make a good sum from my shareholding. I have time to choose what I want to do.' He got up and stood beside her. 'If you want me to go, I will, Alix. But I had to talk to you. The last time you were the one who did all the talking.'

She looked into his eyes. His deep blue eyes which returned her gaze with concern and affection.

'How much money?' she asked.

'Sorry?'

'From the shareholding?'

He pulled her towards him. 'Alix, you're not the only one who can make money. Are you afraid you'll have to support me?'

'It was a big problem with Paul.' She leaned her head on his chest. 'He resented the fact that I earned more than him. I think that was partly why he left me.'

'You won't earn more than me,' said Matt.

'Really?' She lifted her head to look at him. 'The deal is that good?'

'Alix, my shareholding is worth a lot. Money is not the immediate problem. Whether you think you can bear to go out to dinner with me ever again is of more concern.'

'Oh!' She leaned her head on his chest again. 'What about the baby thing?'

He smiled. 'What about it?'

'It's just that I don't know if I'll ever want children. Maybe I will. But maybe I won't, Matt, and then you might want—'

'Alix, I love you. You. Not what you can give me. Not money. Not children. Not anything. Just you.'

They stood immobile in the centre of the room. She could feel the beat of his heart beneath his cotton shirt.

'I can't say that,' she whispered. 'I'm not good on words.'

'You don't have to,' he told her. 'Just give it a chance.'

She pulled his face towards her. He kissed her on the lips. She held him more tightly. She could feel his arms round her, drawing her closer and closer to him, and it felt good.

'The bedroom is over there,' she mumbled.

He lifted her up and carried her across the room.

'That was brave,' she said as he dropped her onto the bed. 'Not many people can carry a five-feet-eight-inch woman into her bedroom and live to tell the tale.'

'Shut up, Alix,' said Matt and kissed her again.

She took her extra day off work the following morning. Markets were volatile ahead of the year end. Swaps were dealing frantically as traders tried to close out their books. But there was nothing that she could do about it. There'd be other deals, other trades. But for today, she was far too preoccupied to care.